The JUDAS POOL

The JUDAS POOL

GEORGE OWENS

G. P. PUTNAM'S SONS / NEW YORK

G. P. Putnam's Sons
Publishers Since 1838
200 Madison Avenue
New York, NY 10016

This is a work of fiction. The events described herein are imaginary, and the characters are fictitious and not intended to represent specific living persons.

Published simultaneously in Canada

Library of Congress Cataloging-in-Publication Data
Owens, George, date.
The Judas pool/George Owens.
p. cm.
ISBN 0-399-13925-7
1. Teacher-student relationships—United States—Fiction. 2. High school teachers—United States—Fiction. 3. Murder—United States—Fiction. I. Title.
PS3565.W566J8 1994 93-31260 CIP
813'.54—dc20

Printed in the United States of America
1 2 3 4 5 6 7 8 9 10

Many thanks for the encouragement of my teachers, including Elizabeth Cullinan, Jay Neugeboren, George Cuomo, and the late Tom Molyneux; thanks also to Neil Olson and Eric Ashworth for their patience and steadfast confidence, and to Stacy Creamer for her enthusiastic support.

For Debra

Drowning is not so pitiful
As the attempt to rise.
Three times, 'tis said, a sinking man
Comes up to face the skies,
And then declines forever
To that abhorred abode,
Where hope and he part company—
For he is grasped of God.
The Maker's cordial visage,
However good to see,
Is shunned, we must admit it,
Like an adversity.

EMILY DICKINSON

1

The summer Steven Blake was ten, an infestation of Japanese beetles swarmed the fields and lawns of Delaware. The leaves of every rosebush and vegetable patch were thick with them as they piled three high, clambering over each other. He was paid, a penny for two, to pluck the coppery beetles from his grandfather's garden. Duck-walking through the bush beans, always a Nescafe jar clutched in his left hand because its odd shape—tapering in below the rim, then flaring out—gave him a steady grip on the soap-slick glass, he pulled each single beetle from its lacy leaf in mid-meal. And then he steeled himself against the helpless, doomed skitter of its tiny legs against his fingers, and dropped it into the jar. Detergent broke the surface tension, so the beetles slid easily from air to water—no hesitation, no hope of water-walking to safety, no pause when wings might seize air. Each fell, tumbling, onto the heap at the bottom of the jar, and twitched its legs, feebly, for longer than he would have thought or cared to think possible.

Almost thirty years later, after all the lies and betrayals and the bigger drownings that led one to another, the lessons so easily learned and forgotten when he was ten would haunt him again: ground gave way when he thought it most solid, air could be stolen between two heartbeats, any life could be quenched with breathtaking speed.

The story begins on a sultry August evening much like those he'd spent in his grandfather's garden, the air heavy with the lush stench of rotting vegetation, the sun a sullen red disk hovering above the horizon. Steven stood halfway up a peeling rank of bleachers. His shirt was drenched, and a steady stream of sweat coursed down his spine and soaked into the waistband of his shorts.

Next to him a boom box as big as a five-year-old child blasted a tape of last year's marching band playing the *Star Wars* battle theme, and before him sixty-five kids, minus instruments, milled around the DeVries High football field as if each were searching for one special friend on a crowded beach. Steven knew he should send them all back down to the end zone to begin again, but rebellion simmered in the slow heat. It was the second practice of the new school year, though classes wouldn't start for another three weeks. Few of the kids were ready for summer's end; neither was Steven.

Suddenly the boy standing next to him leaned down and punched Stop.

"What's up?" Steven was more curious than annoyed at this sudden display of energy.

"This sucks." The kid was this year's band president, a skinny blond trombonist named Jeffrey Bird and, naturally, nicknamed Jay. "They look like hell."

"Same routine we used first game last year," Steven said, though he agreed.

"It sucked *then.* I don't know why we can't do something new."

"Because it's too hot for me to think up anything new," Steven replied calmly. He offered the bullhorn to Jay. "Here. Run them through it once more, and we'll all go home."

Jay's eyes narrowed; he was inordinately suspicious for a seventeen-year-old. "Already?"

"Take it, for God's sake, before I change my mind."

Jay snatched the hailer so eagerly that Steven nearly held on to it at the last moment—the kids were already stumbling in the heat. "Go easy," he cautioned. "It's not worth a heatstroke."

Jay leaned down and pushed Rewind. The band straggled back to the end zone, groaning and complaining, and Steven climbed to the top of the bleachers to get above the noise of the boom box.

He leaned back against the pipe railing, arms outstretched on either side. The metal held the day's heat. This perch was one of the highest points in the seaside town, and he closed his eyes and tried to imagine a breeze, but the air was steam-thick.

Jay barked instructions with the uncertain eagerness of new command, and Steven straightened up and turned his back on the field before the boy could glance up and catch him smiling.

Elbows resting on the railing, he waited patiently for the kids to wrap up. He felt lazy in the summer heat, too relaxed to go home yet. Gail would either be gone—late at the office, dinner with a client, networking, whatever—or home, with her questions: Had he made the calls today? Any leads? Any hints of a job coming up? Her eagerness to move north, away from the resorts and closer to Philadelphia, had been building all summer. Steven was more than content to settle into Lewes for another school year; once the tourists cleared out after Labor Day, the town would become habitable again. He contemplated the brown grass fifty feet below, and had a sudden image of himself swan-diving into the sun-baked earth behind the stands. Uneasily he shook this plunging vision aside, and watched a white Oldsmobile pull in amongst the band's clunkers and parental loaners.

A portly figure stepped out and waved Steven down from the bleachers.

He waved reluctantly in return, too late to pretend he hadn't spotted or recognized Bill Thompson, the high school's principal. He made his way carefully down the bleachers. Thompson and he shared a truce grown increasingly strained the last few years, and the odds were long that the principal brought good news. Steven passed Jay and the boom box, both still blasting at full amplification, then strolled down the red all-weather track, around the corner of the bleachers, and across the scorched turf to the parking lot.

The principal leaned against the fender of his Oldsmobile, pale arms folded across his flabby chest, dark patches of sweat spreading across his light blue shirt. He'd left his engine idling, windows up, air conditioner no doubt blasting full tilt.

"Bill," Steven said, "rare privilege. Never knew you had a taste for marching band music."

"I'm always interested in seeing what my kids are doing," Thompson said.

It was an open secret in town that Bill Thompson spent most of each summer at Atlantic City's casinos, and normally nothing short of a major losing streak brought the nominally straitlaced principal back before Labor Day. All Steven said, though, was, "I just meant it's unusual to see you at a summer band practice."

"Sometimes problems come up that require my personal attention," Thompson said, and his voice was so quietly conversational that Steven became instantly wary.

Thompson seemed almost uncertain how to continue, and shifted his gaze over Steven's shoulder and out to the field, where Jay Bird was marshaling the band once more. After a moment he met Steven's eyes, then glanced away again. "How long have you been teaching here?"

"Fourteen years."

"Remember Tony Stanfield?"

Steven shook his head.

"Math teacher. I don't think he'd been fired yet when you started."

Thompson paused again, clearly savoring the moment.

"Bill, I've got to send the kids home," Steven said. "Why'd you fire him?"

"We had no choice. The man was lucky to stay out of jail."

"Sex or drugs?"

"I'd be interested in hearing which one you'd guess."

"How would I know? I've never even heard of him."

Thompson smiled, seeming to warm to the conversation now. "Fifty-fifty chance. Aren't you a gambler, Mr. Blake?"

"Not when I don't know the game."

"You might improve your own odds if you thought of anything you wanted to tell me now. Before I go any further."

Steven considered the principal's pale bald head and wished he weren't too smart to smack it. Knowing he should calmly ask Thompson exactly what he meant and why he, Steven, should be facing any odds at all, he said instead, "Have you got a real reason for coming out here tonight, or did the Taj Mahal run out of chips?"

"Stories," Thompson said immediately, and for the first time Steven detected a note of satisfaction in the principal's voice. Thompson backed it up with a small, smug smile. "One of your female students has got the most interesting stories about you and her."

Despite the blanketing heat and his steadfast refusal ever to take Thompson seriously, Steven felt a sudden clammy chill grip the back of his neck. "That's ridiculous," he said. "Who is it?"

"Why don't *you* tell *me?*"

"Because I don't have the foggiest idea what you're talking about."

Thompson pursed his lips and shook his head. "Bad choice. Two other kids back her up. So does her father."

"Who is it?" Steven repeated. "What does she claim I did?"

"I suggest you spend the rest of the evening trying to remember the answers to those questions," Thompson said. He grunted and pushed himself up from his car fender; the Oldsmobile rose six inches. "We'll discuss it tomorrow. My office. Ten-thirty."

Steven's palms were sweating, just as they always did when he was called to solo or otherwise account for himself, ready or not. "Come on." His voice sounded thin to his musician's ear, missing its lower harmonics as his throat constricted, and he hoped Thompson couldn't hear this sign of fear. He coughed and began again. "I've taught here for fourteen years. Why would I risk that to screw around with a teenager?"

"Good question," Thompson said immediately. "Why did you?"

"You know how often kids make these things up."

"I know how often they really happen, too." Thompson waddled to his car door, then stopped and turned back and grinned toothily at Steven. "Whatever you did, thank you," he said. "I've been waiting years for this."

"You've got a lot more waiting ahead of you," Steven said. "I haven't done a damned thing."

Thompson snorted skeptically, maneuvered his belly behind his steering wheel, and shifted the Olds into drive before he'd even closed his door. Steven watched the principal cruise out of the parking lot, and knew that Thompson was speeding away with the last of his, Steven's, comfortable life. The accusation alone could be a career-stopper. And if Gail by any stretch needed a last excuse to walk, this was guaranteed to do it.

Panic rose around him like the surge of a storm tide at full moon, and in quick order he considered and discarded the urge to run Thompson down now to get the truth and face his accusers; to run home either to prepare Gail, or to hole up and hope this passed; and, most attractive, to stop home only long enough to pick up his saxophone and clothes and finally head back to New York—to move on before the whole sordid, unpredictable business began.

Behind him Jay Bird counted cadence in a high, tense shout, and a loud third of the band echoed the count back at him, half a beat late. Steven turned back to the field. Rebellion had boiled over to full revolt—kids randomly marched and stopped and turned so the ranks humped and jerked and ran into each other like sheet metal buckling in a bad head-on. Jay Bird screeched, then spun away from the band and hurled the light green hailer as far up the football field as he could. Steven followed its arc, winced as it bounced, then vaulted the waist-high chainlink fence that circled the playing field.

"All right," he bellowed, and the effect was nearly miraculous. Few of the kids had noticed him returning, and the silence was immediate. Jay Bird, red as a bad sunburn, stalked past him without a glance, heading for the parking lot.

"What the hell do you think this is?" Steven shouted at them. "Go on, go home."

He stood next to the gate, and as the band filed past he searched for guilty glances or averted faces, particularly among the girls. They all looked so sheepish from the way they'd treated Jay, though, that any one of them could have been the accuser that had set Thompson gunning for him.

Their chatter welled up again once they got ten feet past his watchful eye. Steven watched the stragglers past the bleachers and out to the parking lot, then walked slowly up the football field to retrieve the school's bullhorn. Behind him engines roared and tires squealed as the kids all headed out, and then the evening fell silent. Dusk descended to darkness, and fireflies were thick in the hazy evening, and still he lingered. The air seemed heavier in the darkness; each breath hurt.

EVERY WINDOW IN the house was thrown wide open, and in the dead-quiet night even the light click of Gail's computer keyboard ticked out across the lawn. Steven came quietly in through the kitchen doorway and waited a moment to see whether she'd come out; then he went on through the living room and to the edge of the smaller front room she'd taken over as an office. A desk lamp threw a bright cone of light across a fan of yellow legal pads and left deep shadows in every other corner of the room. Gail's dark hair was piled on top of her head to free her neck in the sticky heat, and she wore an extra-large T-shirt over shorts. Her left leg was folded beneath her, so she sat on her foot. Staring intently at her screen, perfect right profile to him, she seemed oblivious to his presence until he cleared his throat and she held out her right hand, forefinger up. "I'm sorry," she said without looking at him. "I have to be in court first thing in the morning."

Both her hands returned to the keyboard, and she tapped one key twice and her screen changed. Steven remained in the doorway, still silent, watching her and wondering how she'd take his news, knowing she'd be delighted if it meant they could leave town.

She turned to look at him. "What?"

"Nothing," he said. "How late will you be?"

"Half an hour. What's up?"

"It can wait." He withdrew without another word. It was a bit before ten, and he considered going out to the Lamplighter for a drink, where someone might at least talk to him. But that would let Gail retreat into sleep before he returned, and he had this story to tell, so he splashed a generous amount of bourbon over a couple of ice cubes and retreated to the darkened living room. He switched on the tiny spot above the stereo rack long enough to find a Miles Davis tape—"Kind of Blue" on the A side and "In A Silent Way" on the B—then slouched back on the couch with the headphones on to wait her out. Eyes closed, he drank the first half of his bourbon all at once. The heat exploded in his stomach, then spread slowly outward, and he let music and memory bear him up.

The first time they'd made love had been on this couch, sweat-slick after weeks of delicious pursuit, with this same tense and mysterious music rippling through their sex. He'd played it loud then, so the speakers shook the room and they felt the music through their skin and into the rhythm of their bones. More than once he'd wondered whether that had been the pinnacle of their relationship; it had been good off and on since then, but never quite as intense as the first few months on this couch.

The second side of the tape was nearly over before Gail's bare foot tapped at his ankle. He'd already refilled his drink once and felt loose and drifty, but not especially drunk. He slid the headphones down around his neck, and the music, faint and tinny, drifted into the room. Gail's printer screeched like an unoiled seesaw.

"Hi." She was sprawled in the easy chair perpendicular to the couch, long legs stretched out toward him, big toe just brushing his anklebone. "What's up? Any news?"

Steven still hadn't worked out what to tell her about Thompson, so he stuck to the normal routine. "Nothing."

"Did you call?"

"All four districts."

"Did they say anything at all? Any possibilities?"

He shook his head, wishing he really had called the school districts up north.

"I wish you'd let me help."

He sipped his drink, thinking of the probable outcome of tomorrow's meeting, and for the first time said, "Maybe I will."

Never shy to press a concession, Gail said immediately, "I'll make some calls tomorrow."

Steven hesitated, then said, "Let me sleep on it, okay? I'll call you at work."

Disappointed, she settled back into the easy chair and contemplated him for a moment. "I got some news today you should probably factor in," she said.

"What?" he said, wondering if she'd already heard about the accusation Thompson had brought him.

She watched him closely as she spoke. "I've got an offer." She stopped, waiting to see how he'd react.

Steven let her sit as he considered how he wanted to react. Relief was the first option—she could give him a reason to leave gracefully and duck this oncoming business with Thompson. *If* she intended for him to accompany her. "Where is it?" he said.

"Philadelphia. It's a small firm that does a lot of criminal law."

She'd interviewed with them over a month ago; Steven had assumed the lead was cold. "How's the money?"

"The money's fine," she said, then went on: "Will you say what you think, Steven? You're acting like this is someone else's life."

"Are you going to take it?"

"I don't know. I wanted to talk it over with you first."

"Do you want to take it?"

"You know I do. You know I've got to get out of this town."

"I know, you keep saying that."

"We need a fresh place," she said. The phrase had become a litany this summer, and he still couldn't understand why.

"I don't," he said. "This is where I live."

"That doesn't necessarily mean it's going to be where I live," she said calmly.

They'd never carried the discussion all the way to this impasse, and now Gail seemed as surprised as he felt. For several minutes they sat, Miles Davis still buzzing from the headphones, Steven imagining life without her. He thought it might not be so bad; then he thought again of Thompson and his attitude and threats, and reconsidered. "I'm sorry," he said. "It's just sudden news."

"How sudden can it be?" she said. "I've been sending out résumés since March."

Though her words were sharp, he could hear a note of relief in her voice, and despite himself he said, "Maybe we should take a drive up next Sunday and look around."

"At what? I grew up there."

"I don't know," Steven said. He'd only been trying to placate her. "We could check out some housing, whatever."

"We could stay at my mother's temporarily. The place is practically empty."

Clearly there was some planning behind this, and Steven expected that Gail's mother already had the help clearing one wing of her Main Line home. "Could we sleep on it?" he said. "I'm not saying no. I just want to get used to the idea."

"You can sleep on it," she said. "I've got more work to do tonight."

"I'll wait up."

She didn't bother answering, and he couldn't think of anything else to say to her that he hadn't already said in the past few months, so he simply sat and drank her in, knowing Thompson was too crafty to have called him in before he had all the accusers, charges, and decisions already lined up. This would likely be the last time for a while that they'd sit together this calmly, and while he might not be certain of love anymore, at least tonight he could still convince himself that the possibilities remained open. After tomorrow morning, who knew? It could be nothing or it could be everything—he might even find Gail suspicious of him, given the tenuous nature of their last few months. He couldn't let himself put it off anymore, and said, "Thompson showed up at band practice tonight."

"For what? Layoffs would be perfect now."

He shook his head, took a bracing breath, and then somewhere between his mind and his mouth his words changed, and he heard his own voice say casually, "One of the kids has got a problem. I've got to go over in the morning and straighten it out."

"What kind of problem?" Gail's voice was tired and distracted, and Steven stretched up and snapped on the table lamp in the corner between them, flicking its three-way bulb up to high. She shaded her eyes, but couldn't hide the dark half-moons beneath them.

"You look beat," he said. "What's the case?"

"Boundary dispute. Nothing." Her gaze flicked back toward her desk, visible through the open doorway. "I should get back to it, though."

"Yeah." Steven paused for two heartbeats, then said, "Why don't you try to come up early?" He lifted the headphones from around his neck and laid them on the cushion next to him. The tape had automatically reversed, and Miles Davis and the rest of his electronic brew simmered on, ignored or not. "Where's Patches?" he said.

"I don't know. I thought she came in with you."

"She wasn't there."

"She'll show up."

Steven wished he could be so certain of even the small things. "I'd better go look for her."

Clearly relieved, Gail gathered her legs in toward the chair, stood, and stretched so languidly Steven had to look away. Some twinge of obligation made her ask, "So what did Thompson want?"

"Nothing important," he lied smoothly. "I'll tell you about it tomorrow."

THE HIGH SCHOOL was a two-story, brick, glass, and aluminum sprawl built in the late sixties. Steven's shoes squeaked so loudly down the gleaming, abandoned hallway that he imagined Thompson tracking his approach. Showered, clean-shaven, suited and tied for the first time all summer, he carried in front of him a soggy brown paper sack containing two large and leaking coffees. He'd slept only long enough to launch a rare and monumental hangover.

He entered the outer office, stepped around the end of the chest-high counter. The door to Thompson's inner office stood six inches ajar, and Steven pushed it open. Three unsmiling faces greeted him: Thompson; Randy Wise, the vice principal; and Melinda Samuels, the school psychologist. Thompson was seated behind his desk, a gleaming walnut hulk he'd personally substituted for the original institutional beige steel found everywhere else in the school. Wise and Samuels sat in armchairs at either side of the desk, bracing the principal like lions at the library doors. A lone student chair, small writing table built on, faced the three administrators, and Steven wondered how much time Thompson had spent thinking that one up.

"Looks like I didn't bring enough coffee," Steven said.

"Sit down, please," Thompson said. "We've had ours."

"Just a minute." Steven set the wet sack on Thompson's walnut desk. To his right, two more full-sized armchairs stood against the wall, and he carried the student chair over and swapped it for one of these, which he set squarely in front of the desk. He smiled at Thompson. "All adults here, right, Bill?"

Retrieving his coffee, Steven sat and gently eased the plastic lid from one cup, all the time straining to still the tremor in his hands. Thompson alone he could have handled; three administrators meant more serious trouble. Steven had always felt provisional at the high school, despite his fourteen-year tenure. When school costs went up and property taxes didn't, his job was usually the first threatened. He wasn't a *real* teacher, after all, who could give the kids any skills they'd be able to use in the real world. Music was more play than work, the thinking went, and he'd made it even worse by being an actual musician who'd played in New York and continued to perform at local bars. To Thompson and all those like him in this small town, Steven's life carried too many hints of late, smoky nights, alcohol, drugs, Negroes, and, compounded by the fact that he'd stayed single long into his thirties, illicit and certainly much too frequent sex. And then when he finally had married, it had been to the recent ex-wife of the town's biggest real estate developer, who'd walked out on her husband and straight into Steven's house. He'd enjoyed the small-town notoriety, but suspected that his reputation was about to get a boost he didn't need.

"So," he said. "I'm pretty curious why you've called me on the carpet, Bill."

Thompson plunged in with rare directness. "Steven, you've been accused of having sexual relations with one of your students. Two of her friends confirm they've seen the two of you in decidedly compromising activities, and her father has seen you drop her off near her house several late evenings this summer."

"As I told you last night, that's ridiculous." Steven said. He knew he hadn't driven any of the kids home this summer, male or female, so there was no way this could even be an honest mistake. "I've done nothing."

Thompson sighed, and Randy Wise stepped in. "Steven, this is serious stuff, buddy. You're gonna find yourself nailed if you're not careful."

Randy was about thirty-five, short, curly-haired, and shifty. Steven had played basketball with him the past couple of winters in an over-thirty league, and he'd learned to trust neither the man's moves nor his words. "Randy, I just haven't done anything to get nailed for. Who's the student? When's all this supposed to have happened?"

Randy and Melinda looked to Thompson to proceed.

Before he could, Steven said reasonably, "How can I defend myself if I don't know who's accusing me? Unless this is just something the administration has dreamed up in order to scare me into resigning."

"Oh, no," Thompson said. He leaned forward. "We've deliberately kept this informal, Steven, without involving the school board or legal counsel at this stage, so that we can discuss some of the alternatives and options available to all of us in this situation . . ."

"It's Lisa Wood," Melinda Samuels said, and the attention of all three men swung to her. She looked defensively at Thompson. "He's right—he should know who's accusing him."

"Thanks," Steven said. Though he did his best to hide his reaction, his cup shook enough to send a splash of hot coffee over his fingers. He braced the cup against the chair arm, and, speaking directly to Melinda, said, "You understand where this is coming from, don't you? Do you know the history here?"

"What on earth makes you think your history operates in your favor?" Thompson said.

Ignoring him, Steven continued to address Melinda. "I'm married to Lisa's former stepmother," he said.

"And?" she said.

"And her father, Jacob, still bears a grudge because of the way his marriage to Gail ended. But Lisa's also the best student I ever had."

"In every way, apparently," Thompson said. "We all know how closely you worked with her, and we all understand that Lisa's been a troubled girl, and she's certainly displayed some behavior traits that would tend to lead me to believe that an incident of this particular type might not be unexpected."

A silent moment passed while they all deciphered this; Steven watched Melinda closely. Near his own age, with chin-length blond hair, she was pleasantly round-featured. She'd started at the school midway through last year, and though he'd never had an extended conversation with her, she seemed to be the only one willing to give him any benefit of the doubt. To her he said, "You're sure it's Lisa? You heard her say this?"

She held his gaze for a moment, unsmiling, then looked at Thompson as though asking permission to speak. Steven sensed the tension of disagreement between them. Thompson shook his head once, and Melinda shrugged. "I can't repeat anything Lisa has told me."

"Do you believe her?" he pressed.

"The question isn't who we believe," Randy Wise cut in. "The question is how we make this problem go away."

"Easy," Steven said. "Make Lisa tell the truth. You know how often kids make these things up."

"I've got no reason to believe she's lying," Thompson said. "Her father wanted to be here this morning to back her story up. But given the nature of the situation and your past relationship with him, I thought it best not to introduce that kind of emotional tension to our discussion."

"Bill, you'd believe it if somebody said I screwed the Cape May ferry all the way across the bay," Steven said. Struggling to stay cool, he peeled the lid off the second coffee and drank half the lukewarm cup. "Don't you understand this is just Jacob stirring up trouble?"

"This school has weathered enough of your scandals," Thompson said. "You won't get away with this one." He was so calm and sure of himself that Steven felt his remaining optimism ebbing fast.

"Someone tell me what this is about, please," Melinda Samuels said. "I don't have the background here."

"Mr. Thompson disapproves of my marriage," Steven replied. "He's got the quaint notion that I somehow stole away another man's wife. Against her will, of course."

"What I personally believe has no real bearing here," Thompson cut in. "The question is what kind of behavior this community will tolerate from people who are supposed to be role models, and you've stepped over that line too far this time, Steven."

"Mr. Thompson," Melinda said. "We do need to allow Mr. Blake to defend himself. If we're not absolutely professional, the school could find itself with a great deal of exposure."

Thompson sat for a moment, sour and tight-lipped but clearly unable to disagree, and Steven wondered if Melinda understood what she'd just done to herself. Finally the principal nodded. "Go ahead, then, Ms. Samuels. Fill in all the boxes."

Melinda's puzzled gaze lingered a moment on Thompson, then swung to Steven. She was all blunt business. "Mr. Blake, you know you're entitled to have a lawyer here with you today, don't you?"

"Do I need a lawyer?"

"You tell us," she said. "Have you had sex with any of your students? Fooled around with any of them in any way?"

"Absolutely not. I spent hours of my own time helping that girl prep for her auditions."

"Can you suggest why Lisa might have made this up? Did you have any disagreements with her?"

Steven shook his head—there had been no outright disagreements—only weeks of bitter anger after she'd quit practicing and blown off the admissions auditions he'd worked so hard to arrange, then refused to explain her decision. "I haven't even seen the girl since she graduated."

"I've looked at her records, so I know you didn't fail her. Did she have a crush on you?"

"If you've been looking at records, you've probably checked mine, too," Steven said. "Is there anything in there that indicates I'd sleep with a student in order to handle a crush?"

Samuels waved her left hand impatiently, brushing his question aside. "Is that your answer?"

"I haven't screwed around with Lisa Wood or any other student. I'm happily married, teenagers don't appeal to me, and I've got far more responsibility to my students than this administration has ever given me credit for."

Unable to cede control any longer, Thompson cleared his throat. "I can't say I understand or agree, but Jacob Wood feels this might not be entirely your fault, given the girl's past behavior."

Steven was thrown by this, unable for a moment to understand why Jacob might be willing to give him the benefit of any doubt. "That sounds pretty unlikely," he said.

"That's probably the first time you and I have agreed on anything in years," Thompson said. "Nevertheless, he's agreed not to pursue this if you'll resign immediately."

"Of course he would," Steven said. "Because he knows there's no way this thing would ever be borne out. It just didn't happen."

"Jacob Wood's a hell of a lot more generous than I'd be," Randy Wise said. "We'll go along with it, though. Take it."

"Think of the school." Thompson said. "Think of the disruption this will cause, how all the other teacher-student relationships will be affected if we have to pursue this publicly."

"Bill, cut it out," Steven said. "You had your mind made up before you even came to see me last night. What's the deal?"

Thompson sprung his trap. "Two options. Resign today, or we'll take this sorry mess to the school board. They'll require a complete investigation, and given the fact that Lisa Wood was a minor at the time these incidents occurred, there's a good chance you'll go to jail. Randy, what're the penalties there?"

"Two to five at Smyrna," Wise said with an alacrity born of recent research.

For a long moment Steven looked from face to face to face; the only one reflecting the least glimmer of sympathy was Melinda Samuels, whom he knew the least. She watched him even more closely than Thompson and Wise, and for a second he held her gaze, trying to guess where she sided. She was unreadable, and he gave it up and turned back to Thompson. "I suppose you've already got a letter typed for me."

"Of course." Thompson's voice was thick with satisfaction. He slid a single sheet of paper across his desk.

Steven skimmed the letter quickly—it was a standard voluntary resignation, with no mention of the conditions under which it was being signed. For a moment he was truly tempted to sign it and move on—he'd never convince the school or the town that he wasn't guilty, even if he kept his job. And the energy he'd spend battling this might be better invested in building a new life elsewhere with Gail. Again he looked slowly around the circle, at Melinda, Randy, Thompson, and all three looked so ready to see him sign that he crumpled the page. Some battles had to be fought. "Go ahead," he said. "Investigate me."

Thompson's exasperated sigh broke the silence. He said, "Steven, I could almost feel sorry for you until now. That's a very stupid decision."

"I've made worse," Steven said, hoping he really had. "You probably haven't, though." He stood, then leaned down until his face was close to Thompson's. "It feels to me like this is something you've cooked up with Jacob, Bill. I know you're an old friend of his, and I know the kind of grudge he holds. And I promise you this will come right back on you."

Thompson stared back at him, eyes as lidless as those of a giant tortoise.

"Remember, Steven, you did this to yourself. We gave you a chance." His voice was deliberately bored. "Stay off the property and away from the students until this is resolved."

"Fine," Steven said. The only person he wanted to talk to was Lisa, and since she'd graduated in June, she was open hunting. "Get me whatever so-called evidence you've got."

"Get a good lawyer," Thompson said.

"I've got the best one around."

Thompson smiled, sure of his hand. "If you mean your wife, don't count on it."

Steven became very still, and waited until Thompson's smile faded. "I'll decide who and what I can count on, Mr. Thompson."

The principal shrugged. "There may be something of a conflict here given Gail's past relationship with Lisa. But I suppose we'll have to let the lawyers sort that out, won't we?"

Steven would have traded years of his life and everything he owned to come forth with the perfect cutting remark, crafted to pierce Thompson's bluster and prove his own impervious innocence. He drew nothing. "You'll hear from me," he said. "Not my lawyer. Or my wife."

He thought he was under control until he flung Thompson's door open with such force that it crashed into the coatrack. Spinning back, he caught the rack before it hit the floor and stood it upright again. Then Steven charged down the empty, gleaming hallways and back out into the white August heat. The sultry air shimmered like water over the asphalt parking lot, and as he swam back to his car, he could almost hear the waves crashing over his head.

2

Sandwiched between matching Winnebagos, Steven inched through the center of town, keeping a careful eye on his temperature gauge—the Jeep was running nearly as hot as he was. Lewes was a tiny old town of narrow streets and salt-weathered houses, nestled just inside the lip of the Delaware Bay. Though protected by Cape Henlopen from the Atlantic, and by the luck of one prescient governor from the blight of high-rise hotels and condos that walled the coast to the south, it was defenseless against the tides of summer people.

Finally he broke left onto Front Street, which became Pilottown Road a few blocks up. Gail's red BMW was parked behind the front house, and he whipped his Jeep in next to it.

She stood in the center of her study, wearing her navy blue court skirt and a white raw silk blouse; her suit jacket was hung meticulously on the back of her desk chair, and her pumps were paired exactly beneath the chair; and this order told him immediately that she knew.

Again most of her curly hair was gathered into a topknot, escaping in small curls around her neck. Boxes surrounded her. Her file drawers and bookshelves stood empty, and her computer monitor and keyboard sat on the floor next to the doorway, cables coiled neatly atop them.

"What are you doing?" he said.

She gave his suit and tie a quick once-over. "What does it look like I'm doing, Steven?"

"Come on, talk to me. Why are you doing this?"

"You knew about this last night, didn't you?"

"Not the details. I would've called you after the meeting."

"So I would have been the last to know about you and your pride and joy."

"Cut it out," he said. "You know me better than that."

She shook her head and sighed. "Yes," she said. "I do."

"And you know this is just Jacob's grudge working."

She paused, then admitted reluctantly, "I suppose it is."

"Then why this?" His hand swept over the disarrayed office. "What are you doing?"

"No, what are *you* doing? Did they give you a chance to quit today?"

"Sure," Steven said. "But you know I couldn't admit doing something I didn't do. You've got to stand with me in this one, Gail."

Her stare drilled him with such intensity that he felt he had her full attention for the first time in months. Her face was nearly a perfect triangle: high brow over widely spaced brown eyes, straight nose, lips full, bottom teeth a little cramped and crooked in her narrow jaw, high cheekbones tapering down to a finely pointed chin. Finally she said, "This is it, Steven. We've been talking and talking about going, and if this doesn't get you out of here, nothing will."

He stared at her for a long minute, stunned at this second betrayal. "So you're out of here just like that?"

"Not yet. I just can't live in the same house with you right now."

This was small relief. "Why not? That's going to make it look like you think I really did this thing."

"Because I'm afraid if I stay here we'll just keep on the way we've been. No one has to know as long as I'm right out back in the cottage. I'll stay there for a week or so while I wrap things up and you make up your mind."

He felt their marriage ebbing even faster than he'd expected, and he couldn't stop the loss any more than he could slow the tide. The indifference he'd feigned for months failed him. "Don't," he said. "Please."

For a moment she seemed about to waver, but then she said, "Why couldn't you talk to me? You knew about this last night."

Stung, aware of how pathetic he appeared, he said, "Maybe I just wanted a last good evening before you did what you're doing now."

"Did you get it?"

Regretting his momentary weakness, Steven shrugged. "I've had better," he said. "How'd you find out about this so fast, anyway?"

Her eyes flicked away for the briefest second, as though she'd caught some motion in the corner of the room. "Jacob was waiting at my office this morning."

"I didn't know you two spoke."

"We don't." It seemed to Steven that she spoke a touch too quickly, and he felt the first queasiness of suspicion.

"Why was he so eager to tell you about it?"

She shrugged, and lifted a stack of paperbacks from her desk, scanned the black and blood red and neon green spines. They were all nonfiction accounts of mass murderers and serial killers. She tossed them into a waiting carton, then said with exaggerated slowness, "You've seen enough to know the accusation is as good as the deed. You're in trouble, Steven."

"Maybe," he said. "But I don't think Jacob can buy off the whole school board."

"He won't have to."

"Will you help me?"

Without looking at him again, she said, "As much as I can."

"Where are you going?"

"To the cottage."

"The cottage is booked starting this weekend."

"Cancel them."

"The people already paid."

"Give their money back."

"We can't afford it."

She opened a desk drawer, then slammed it shut. "You mean *you* can't afford it, Steven. What I can't afford is to stay in this house anymore. You're driving me out of my mind."

Steven watched her as a trickle of sweat rolled down her right temple, down her cheek and neck to stain her silk collar. "Why?" he said. That seemed to be the question of the summer.

He wanted to believe she hesitated before she picked up another book from her desk. She leafed through an entire sequence of grainy black-and-white police photos showing the corpses of a family sprawled where each had been caught in flight, before she finally snapped the book shut and said, "Because you're just not who I thought you were."

He took a short step toward her, then another back, confused in his anger. He didn't know who or what he was supposed to have been, how he'd failed to measure up, or why it seemed to be his fault that he hadn't met her expectations, and he wasn't prepared to raise any of these questions. "Then just move the hell out," he finally said. "Somewhere else, for God's sake, where I don't have to look at you. I'll handle this mess myself."

"The cottage will do for now."

"You want to keep me guessing? Keep yourself in sight but out of reach?" Though she shot him a glance that he'd heard could wither any witness, he couldn't stop himself now. "Maybe you're afraid I'll have a better claim to the real estate if you're the one who takes off?"

Gail took sudden action at this, flinging books, file folders, pictures, boxes of diskettes, and all her other odds and ends ajumble into whatever empty box stood nearest. After a furious minute of motion, she suddenly stopped and glared at him. Her voice was frosty with superiority when she said, "The last thing I'm concerned about is your real estate, Steven. Or what little money you've got."

"Fine," Steven snapped. "I'm clearing out for a while. Walk your talk."

He spun away, stopped. "Where's Patches?"

"In the bedroom. She kept getting in my way."

The comparison was too obvious; he studied her, trying not to show the betrayal he felt, but he said, "You've been waiting a long time for this chance."

"Do you really think I don't love you, Steven? Do you really think I need another failed marriage?"

"I think you decided a long time ago that that's what this was. Only I had to be the one to make it fail."

She paused to consider her words, seemed to try to stop herself, then said quietly, "Maybe that's because that's what you do best."

He took the stairs two at a time, trying to calm himself enough to coax the dog from under the bed. Patches read his true feelings, though, and it was a long minute before she finally wriggled out, covered with a second coat of fluffy dust and lost dog hair, and rolled onto her back. A Border collie/Australian shepherd mix, she was abnormally sensitive to Steven's states of mind.

"It's okay, baby," he said, over and over. His face burned with anger and embarrassment and the fear that Gail might be right. "Come on," he wooed the dog, "let's go for a ride in the boat."

This ultimately brought Patches wagging to her feet, and the two of them went downstairs, Steven more gently this time.

Gail called his name, and he stopped on the porch and waited without turning around. After a moment she said from her office, "I'm sorry I said that."

His pride too deeply wounded to permit an answer, he crossed the screened porch with the dog on his heels and brushed out through the overgrown hydrangeas that arched over the front steps.

Houses stood on the west side of Pilottown Road only. Along the east side ran the Lewes and Rehoboth Canal, separated from the roadway by a strip of land ranging from ten to thirty yards wide, where town zoning allowed each resident only a small boathouse or gazebo and a dock. Midway across the blacktop to his dock, Steven stopped and circled back around to the kitchen door. He owed one call to Jay Bird to cancel band practice.

Gail stopped moving around in her study the moment he came back in, as though expecting him to resume their conversation. He sensed her listening as he dialed, and only because she was listening did he control his reaction when told that Randy Wise had beat him to the telephone tree. According to Jay Bird's mother, practice was set for two o'clock that afternoon, without him. She pressed for further details, but Steven cut her off.

He was stunned by how quickly the school had bypassed him, and realized that Thompson must have plotted this coup for days. Ducking out the back door to avoid passing Gail, he made for his boat again. Patches panted along next to him, and leapt happily down from the dock into his Boston Whaler. He checked the gas, cranked up the outboard, and let it warm up.

The canal was a No Wake zone, and he idled down the mile or so to the turning basin at the center of town. A hot breeze swept across the canal, strong enough to keep the greenflies off. He was exhausted. Still slightly hung over, he felt utterly overmatched and unprepared for the fight he saw brewing. And yet it all still seemed quite unreal—he tried to visualize Lisa making the complaint about him, as if imagining her saying the words might show him why she said them. He pictured himself sweating before the school board, Gail defending him, Lisa dramatically recanting, and Thompson and the entire committee ignoring Gail as they passed judgment on him.

By the time he tied up at the town docks, he'd convinced himself to call Thompson that afternoon and accept the resignation offer. After he ate.

Patches kept pace with him up through the small park with its cast-iron cannons, over the drawbridge, then left into the parking lot of the Lighthouse Restaurant. They circled around to the waterside, where Steven left her guarding one of the awning stanchions at the edge of the restaurant's deck. Inside, he ducked into the bar to see if Jimmy Van Dusen had come in yet, but the stools were still up on the counter and the room was empty.

Outside on the deck, fewer than half the tables were occupied. Shielded from the sun by a dark blue awning with a scalloped red fringe, they overlooked Fisherman's Wharf, now empty, where the deep-sea party fishing boats docked.

The waitress knew them both, and raised no objection when Patches sneaked in and rested on Steven's feet so he couldn't creep away while she slept. Steven ordered aspirin, crabcakes, and iced tea, and settled back to watch the passing boats and contemplate the unexpected shambles of his life.

Back in his early twenties, fresh out of music school and working seven days a week with bar bands, jazz bands, and wedding bands, playing whatever he could get to build his chops and pay the rent, he never would have pictured himself here and now: nearly forty, same day job for fourteen years, his only steady gig playing tenor sax with a quartet at the Lamplighter Lounge, out on Highway One, where they'd rework standards every Friday and Saturday night from Memorial Day through Labor Day.

He'd met Gail there, after she'd showed up on a Friday night with Jacob and a group of investors he was romancing. Steven had noticed her immediately from the stage—tanned, slim, and elegant in a sleeveless white dress, obviously bored with the group. He'd picked her out to play to, the same way he picked out one person or one table each night, to ease his own boredom.

She'd returned the next night, alone, and waited through two sets until he finally approached her table and asked to join her.

She'd smiled up at him. "Only if you'll tell me what you're doing stranded here," she'd said.

Without planning it, he told her then about a documentary he'd recently seen about a huge Russian lake called the Aral Sea, whose source waters had been so heavily tapped for irrigation that the sea was shrinking by many feet daily. The image that had stuck with him most vividly was that of fishing trawlers beached miles from the fading shoreline, rusting away in the midst of a salt desert. He'd long wondered why the captains couldn't at least have moved their boats to follow the vanishing sea. Evidently they had decided to stick to familiar landmarks rather than risk unknown waters.

"But how do you know," she'd asked, "that those captains didn't just shed what they couldn't use and move on to better places?"

Already feeling a little foolish for bringing in this story of real tragedy to try and explain his own inertia, Steven had said, "It'd be nice to believe that, wouldn't it?"

She'd stayed through the last set, and was still waiting when he had packed up his tenor. He'd stopped at her table, intrigued, cautious.

"Well," she'd said, and raised her club soda to him. "Here's to moving on."

"Can I ask you something?" he'd said, and when she'd nodded went on: "You came here with a group last night."

"My husband and his latest crop of investors," she said. "My husband the client. Or my client the husband."

"Ah," Steven had said. "Are you separated?"

"Does it matter?" she'd said.

"It's a small town."

"Then I suppose I am." Her brown-eyed stare was so frank and intelligent and challenging that Steven had feared he was hooked.

But he'd said, "Sounds like it's pretty recent."

She'd shrugged, watching him.

"I'd like to see you when it's not so recent," he'd said.

She'd smiled, more to herself than to him. "You will," she'd said, and she'd soon fulfilled her own prediction.

Now the charter boats began to dock one by one—the *Keena Dale, Pappy's Lady, Thelma Dale II*. He signaled the waitress for a refill on his iced tea, and watched the schools of vacationers scramble ashore, sunburned, woozy from riding the deep swells in forty-foot boats. A fresh bunch waited nearby to board the afternoon cruise out the mouth of Delaware Bay and offshore.

He waited until every boat had returned, disgorged, refueled, loaded, and left, then checked his watch; if Gail was really moving to the cottage, she should be gone by now. He eased his feet out from under Patches. She groaned, but didn't completely wake, and he left her beneath the table while he went inside to the men's room. Before returning to the deck to clear his tab and retrieve his dog, he leaned through the doorway of the Drawbridge Bar and scanned the room again. It was dim and cool after the deck.

As he'd hoped, Jimmy Van Dusen was perched at the bar, facing the doorway. Van Dusen showed up here nearly every afternoon after teaching and playing tennis all morning. From here he'd usually go directly to his boat, a big Grady-White sportfisher docked in Rehoboth Bay. He waved laconically at Steven, drained his beer, and spoke over his shoulder to the bartender. Steven crossed the deserted lounge, and by the time he reached Van Dusen, two cold beers waited. Jimmy was the high school's basketball coach and had been Steven's near neighbor until the year before, when he'd unexpectedly sold the house in which he'd grown up and moved to a raised ranch in a raw new development several miles to the west. He was a couple of inches taller and seven years younger than Steven, and the two were often mistaken for brothers or cousins. They met here intentionally at least once a week in the summer, though today's meeting was unplanned.

"It's my turn," Steven said.

"It's already on my tab," Jimmy replied. "How you doing?"

"Not too well." Steven glanced at the bar clock, and figured that if he got home too early, he might find himself moving boxes from one house to the other just to get Gail out of his face. "My dog's out on the deck," he said. "You mind sitting out there?"

Van Dusen glanced around the room, as though this idea was completely new to him, then shrugged. "What the hell. Fresh air'll keep me sober."

Patches lay beneath the table, tongue lolling and gaze locked on the restaurant doorway. She stood long enough to lick Jimmy's hand in greeting, then curled again at Steven's feet.

"I never think to sit out here," Van Dusen said. "Usually too many bugs." The wharf was empty again, opening the view, and he looked out across the canal. "That's your Whaler, isn't it?"

"Good eye." Steven hoisted his beer, brought the mug down half empty.

"What are you doing sitting out here by yourself, anyway?"

"Thinking. Have you had any news?" This was a standard question, and one Steven hated to ask this late in the summer, though Jimmy'd work it into the conversation if he didn't. Van Dusen still held out hopes of a college coaching job, and pumped out resumés by the dozen every spring.

As usual, he shook his head and answered the question with another completely unrelated query. "How's the knee? Got full motion yet?"

"Eighty percent," Steven said. He'd partially torn a ligament in his knee in the last basketball game of the season, and the doctor had prescribed rest, then light exercise. "I'm still swimming every day."

"You'll be a hundred percent by the time the season starts."

"I'm not going to push it this year," Steven said. "Maybe I'll ref."

"I still say they could have done that arthroscopically, and you could have been up and around a hell of a lot sooner."

Steven shrugged; his knee was the least of his worries. As casually as he could, he said, "Have you been over to the school lately, Jimmy? Talked to anybody?"

Van Dusen looked at Steven as if he'd just suggested grave-robbing or shooting geese out of season or any other activity as pointless and distasteful. "You know I never go near the place in the summer."

"It looks like I could be out of a job," Steven said. He watched Van Dusen closely, but couldn't guess whether he already knew; Jimmy was as calm and self-possessed as any successful coach, accustomed to control.

"What's going on?" he said.

"I guess Lisa Wood has accused me of having sex with her." The name was bitter.

"Did you?" A measuring gleam entered Jimmy's eyes, a look that surprised and disappointed Steven.

"Go to hell," he said, and he started to stand. "I thought I could count on you, Jimmy."

Van Dusen held up both hands, palms out. "Calm down, Steve. It happens, especially with her. I've heard she's pretty wild."

"Not with me."

"Come on, sit down," Van Dusen ordered. Steven slowly complied. "You flunk her, do something to piss her off, or is this about you marrying her stepmother?"

"I wish I knew," Steven said. "I don't have a clue."

"You spent a lot of time with her, didn't you?"

"Best student I ever had. I spent extra hours the last half of her junior year and last summer coaching her for auditions. She would've made Curtis or Eastman for sure, but then she decided she didn't want it, and quit practicing."

"Her brother did the same thing to me. Came in as a senior, one of the best players I ever had, then he quit cold in the middle of the season."

"Ever find out why?"

Van Dusen shook his head. "Pissed me off—you know, you want them to make it, and they just throw it away. Tough."

"I didn't get pissed off," Steven said. "If she didn't want it, there wasn't any point."

"Yeah, well. She's trouble in a tight skirt, that's for sure."

"We're paid to deal with that, right? You know anything about her doing this to anybody else?"

"You know, rumors," Van Dusen said, but he wouldn't meet Steven's eyes. "I don't really see the point in throwing anybody else over there to the sharks, Steven. You'll pull yourself out of this without pulling anybody else down."

They were silent for several minutes, watching as a sailboat that had been waiting in the turning basin powered up, and the drawbridge lifted on schedule. Steven couldn't tell whether Jimmy believed him, or whether Jimmy even cared whether he'd screwed around with the girl, and he realized how alone he was going to be in facing this down.

"So what happened?" Van Dusen said. "How'd you find out?"

"Thompson," Steven said impatiently. "Showed up at band practice last night and ordered me in this morning."

"Bet he loved that."

"He's an old buddy of Jacob's. Been on my case since Gail and I got married."

"Accomplices? Thompson never does these things alone."

"Randy. And Melinda Samuels, the new psychologist."

Jimmy snorted. "I figured Randy'd be in line to stab you in the back. Melinda's a friend of ours, but she hasn't said anything about this."

"She was the best of the three. I guess they're trying to keep it quiet. Jacob's willing to let me quit, they say."

"Sure he is. He'll drum you right out of town."

Steven shrugged.

"How's Gail taking it?"

"She was packing when I headed up here." Steven looked back out at the canal as he said the words, hoping Van Dusen wouldn't see his eyes. "She's going to stay out back in the cottage for a week or so."

"Didn't waste any time, did she?"

"She wants me to take up Thompson's offer to let me resign and move to Philadelphia with her. I guess she's got a job offer up there."

"I have to admit I agree with her," Jimmy said. "For once."

"Come on," Steven said. "If I really did it, it'd be one thing, but I couldn't look in a mirror again if I let this happen to me."

"Win the battle to lose the war," Jimmy said. "Look, even if you're cleared in a week when the girl loses her nerve and everybody figures it was just Jacob out to get back at you, there's always going to be the suspicion. You think the school wouldn't can you the very next chance they got? At least this way you might keep things together with Gail."

"I don't think that's going to happen," Steven grumbled, though he really couldn't guess what would or wouldn't.

"So what can you do?"

Jimmy's voice carried a weary fatalism that Steven certainly didn't feel. "I can fight it," he said. "Talk to Lisa. I haven't even seen her since June."

"Tell me you're not going to show up at her house. Jacob will use you for target practice."

"No, I'm going to call her." He checked his watch. "Soon as I get my house back. Set up a meeting with both of them."

"You're an idiot," Jimmy said.

"Objection registered," Steven said. "I need another Rolling Rock."

Two hours later, they stumbled out into the parking lot and stood next to Van Dusen's blue Ford pickup. Steven hadn't realized how many beers he'd downed until he stood and felt the restaurant deck swaying gently, as if someone had moved it out to float on the canal while he wasn't watching.

"Come on," Van Dusen said. "I'll run you home."

"It's okay. I can't leave my boat down here."

"You're not in any shape to move that Whaler."

"I'll be very careful," Steven said. "Thanks, Jimmy."

He clapped the coach on his shoulder, and turned and headed for the drawbridge, Patches at his heels. Van Dusen caught up with him. "I'll help you get that boat home."

Steven kept walking. "You drank more than I did."

"I'm bigger," Van Dusen said. "And I'm used to it."

Neither of these points seemed arguable, so within minutes they were poking back up the canal at the requisite four miles an hour. Van Dusen coasted the Whaler expertly up to Steven's dock, then moved lightly around the center controls to the open front of the boat, where he secured the bowline. He was surprisingly quick for his recent beer intake.

They stood on the dock.

The coach fastened his gaze on his old house, three lots closer to Lewes's center than Steven's. It was a white colonial bigger than both Steven's cottages combined, and two of Van Dusen's brothers hadn't spoken to him since he'd sold it so suddenly. Whether this was out of family nostalgia or Jimmy's failure to split the profits, he didn't know.

"Let me get my keys, and I'll drive you back down to your truck," Steven said.

"Right," Van Dusen said. "I'm not as dumb as I look, buddy. I want to walk anyway, see what they've done to the old place."

"Miss it?"

"Yeah," Van Dusen said curtly, then: "No. We've got more yard out where we are. Better for the kids, don't have to worry about the traffic."

Steven looked across at his own houses—the white, hip-roofed frame house in front, where he and Gail lived, and the smaller cottage in back and to the right, which they usually rented out by the week from May into October. A small wall of cartons was now stacked on the cottage porch, and Steven realized he hadn't called next week's tenants yet.

"My life's turning to shit, Jimmy."

"So flush it and start over. It's not like you're me, with four kids and a mortgage. Jacob's willing to let you go, you've got no kids, no ties. If you stay here you aren't going to have anything left by the time your wife the queen of real estate, and the school board, and the courts get through with you. Take your chance—quit and clear out of here before they fuck you over."

"I can't run away yet. Gail and I won't be over quite this fast."

Van Dusen eyed him. "Trust me, you let her go up there without you and it's over."

"You know something you're not telling me?" Steven watched Jimmy closely, but the coach wasn't giving anything else away.

"You know it's close to over," he said, and both his tone and his eyes were evasive. "Christ, anybody who's watched the two of you this summer knows how you two have been beating each other up. If you've really got a chance to fix it, go for it."

Steven was sure now that Jimmy knew something more than he was saying, but it wasn't worth extracting at this point. "I'd better go call Lisa and get this other thing worked out."

"Maybe you ought to wait a while on that. Sober up first."

"I'm fine," Steven said. "No time better than the present."

Van Dusen shrugged. "It's your call. Let me know if you need help."

"Thanks," Steven said. "If I can get it cleared up fast, I'll quit. Go with her."

"You know where I am if you need me." The coach waved, then trudged back down Pilottown Road toward the center of town, slowing in front of his old house; he turned back to catch Steven still watching him. He waved again, and shouted, "Good luck."

Steven stumbled across the blacktop, hoping Gail wasn't watching him from the cottage, then forged up the front steps between the looming hydrangeas, vowing for at least the fiftieth time that summer to trim them back when the day cooled off. Immediately inside the front door, the doorway to Gail's study gaped open on the left. Only a couple of bulging green trash bags remained in the middle of the floor.

The living room looked relatively unscathed at first inspection; in the kitchen, the microwave and the Krups espresso maker both appeared to have emigrated.

Patches skittered from room to room, upset as always at any change. Steven checked out the back kitchen window—Gail's BMW was still parked behind the house. He saw no sign of motion inside the cottage, though.

The dog sat in the middle of the kitchen floor, tail wagging, watching him nervously. "What do you think?" he said. "Should I go crawl?"

She wagged.

"I thought not."

He rummaged through the kitchen cabinets until he found an old jar of instant coffee with a couple of teaspoons of flakes crystallized on the bottom. He chipped out enough to make a cup and set a pot of water to boil, then went to piss away a full afternoon of beer. Her bottles and baskets and tubes of face spackle and cleanser had been cleaned out from the open wrought-iron shelves that hung above the toilet tank. He zipped, then stared at his face in the mirror, trying to imagine himself as Thompson and Randy and Melinda had seen him that morning. Gray-eyed, blond hair still thick and worn a bit long, face deeply tanned from a full summer of daily swims, he thought he looked like a man with sufficient resources and appeal to keep his hands off his teenaged students. If a face could look innocent, it was his.

The kettle whistled him back, and in a moment he was seated at his kitchen table rehearsing an opening and hoping he was as sober as he thought he was. The telephone book lay open to Jacob Wood's listing in Rehoboth Beach, and before Steven could think about it any longer, he picked up the phone and dialed.

Lisa answered, voice so carefree that she clearly expected anyone but him on the line.

"Lisa," he said, confident she'd recognize his voice. "We've got a few things we need to talk over."

The low hum of the telephone lines answered him, and he could almost feel her lowering the phone to its cradle, then hesitating, then raising it again. "Mr. Blake," she said, "I didn't want to do this."

His cool opening disappeared beneath a wash of anger, and he said, "Then why the hell did you?"

"I can't tell you right now." Her voice shifted to an urgent whisper. "Can I come talk to you?"

"You're not coming to my house," Steven said immediately. "Is your father there? I want to talk to both of you."

"No! Quick, he's coming upstairs. Where can I talk to you, Mr. Blake? I'm in big trouble."

Steven resisted the girl's panic, but he'd known her and taught her for three years, and Thompson's accusations still seemed suspect, tainted by animosity and his nebulous ties to Jacob. Curiosity won out over self-preservation, and he said, "I swim at the Lewes town beach every day around noon."

"Yes," she said, "tomorrow," then, very quickly, in an entirely new and glassily cheery tone: "Yeah, thanks a lot, Jennie. Bye."

3

Steven swam steadily, a hundred feet offshore, methodically covering the mile and a half between the Lewes town beach and Roosevelt Inlet. The bay was shallow here, and weeks of August heat had simmered the water blood-warm. The sun baked his back, and he imagined himself a mahogany blade slicing through the lazy swells.

Though every muscle in his body burned and his head pounded and bile rose in his throat, though his breath came hot and ragged and salt stung his eyes, he knew he could swim the distance, then turn around and swim all the way back without blunting his anger's edge. Gail had been silently holed up in the cottage for a day, Lisa hadn't shown, and he was feeling sorely manipulated.

He counted his strokes until a scream broke his trance, near enough to pierce the rush of water and the pounding of his own pulse. Steven bobbed upright, neck-deep and treading water, and looked wildly around. Thirty yards away and bearing down on him hard were two windsurfers. Blue and red sails taut in the brisk offshore breeze, they fairly flew at him on a fast beam reach. Both sailors wore wet suits and harnesses, and leaned out hard against the pull of their sails.

Squinting against the sunlight and salt in his eyes, Steven judged they'd pass on either side of him if he stayed where he was. He waved both arms to make sure they saw him, and immediately the inshore sailor jibbed sharply, and the board headed directly toward him. The other sailor screamed again, and Steven had a sudden, incongruous picture of his own head as it must appear from atop the sailboards: a tanned soccer ball, plastered with wet hair and resting on the smooth roll of the Delaware Bay, waiting to be booted east, out past the Cape Henlopen light and into the open Atlantic.

The boards closed on him quickly. Steven looked from one to the other, preparing to dive. The girl screamed again, "Todd, don't do it, you fucker."

Lisa's voice registered this time, as did her brother's name. Stunned, Steven hesitated, and it was this that nearly cost him survival. He struck out for shore, swimming as hard as he could while trying to watch the sailboards at the same time. Lisa veered to head her brother off, but he let the wind slip from his sail for a moment and she overshot him. Todd caught the wind again and his board knifed toward Steven, who dove at the last possible instant. A rushing hiss tore the water above like a bed sheet being ripped full length, and for the briefest second Steven thought he'd made it clear. Then the dagger board caught him a breath-robbing blow across the ribs.

Steven shouted out in surprise and pain, forgetting in his shock that he was underwater. A column of seawater filled his mouth and lungs, and the water that had seemed so warm moments before robbed him instantly of all heat. Coldness penetrated to the very center of his body, and for long seconds he hung stunned in the water.

Eyes wide, oblivious to the salt sting, he gazed at the dim surface light. Slowly it came to him that he should probably struggle upward, but motion didn't seem all that important. He could go either way, rise or fall, float or sink, and couldn't care which direction he took.

This was how you drowned, he understood. Calmly. No struggle.

The anger that had built over the past couple of days was blessedly quenched, as distant now as the sunlight, and he had to wonder if this surrender might not be the best choice after all. Perhaps he'd wasted time thrashing around at the water's surface, when just beneath him had been release.

He settled lethargically, the water cooling as he neared the bottom. The first of the undercurrents that would carry him out to sea tugged gently at his feet, and he relaxed, letting the water take him where it would.

A small hand slid across his shoulder, grasped, missed, pushed him downward. Sharp nails scraped his back, and his feet rested flat on the sandy bottom. Before thought could stop action, his legs coiled reflexively and launched him up from the bay's floor, his body saving itself with no help from his mind.

He broke the surface, choking and sputtering, and arms clad in slick, cold neoprene clutched him. Confused at the sudden light, Steven turned quickly from one face to the other. He seemed to take in everything at once with a vision much sharper than his own: he saw himself cradled between Lisa and Todd Wood; their sailboards floating nearby, brilliant sails awash in the green water; several swimmers splashing frantically toward them from shore; and beyond, a small crowd gathering at water's edge.

"Come on, Blake," Todd said. "Let's get to the board."

From a great distance Steven heard himself wheezing and choking for breath. He let himself be towed through the water, neither helping nor resisting as he tried to find room for air in his chest once again.

"I'm sorry, I'm sorry," Lisa said over and over, half sobbing. "Todd, you jerk, why'd you have to do that?"

They reached the sailboard. Steven flung one arm up over the edge of the board, and sharp pain scored his ribs. A small cry escaped before he could cut it off.

"Oh, Jesus," the girl said. "He's really hurt. Come on, Todd, get him up on the board."

Before Steven could protest, they'd shoved and dragged him up out of the water so he lay on his stomach at an angle across the sailboard. His legs trailed in the water, and he raised himself on his elbows to retch over the far side of the board. Again and again he coughed to clear the harsh bite of saltwater from his throat, and each cough jolted searing pain across his left side.

Half a dozen swimmers churned toward them. Lisa and her brother swam on either side of the board, guiding him to shore. Lisa's hand rested on his back, and Steven recoiled, body tensing with new pain, but couldn't find the voice to protest this touch.

They reached shallow water, the two kids wading the board in until it ran aground. Steven was lifted and jostled ashore, each stumble an agony in his ribs. He bit back his pain until finally he lay in the hot sand. He let go then, and his breath suddenly came as shallow as if he'd just swum two fast miles. He gazed at the faces circled above him: the swimmers who'd helped bring him in, Lisa and her brother, the curious. None of them looked to be more than twenty-five. They were all tanned and fit, and Steven suddenly realized how he must look stretched out on the sand: battered, gasping for breath, as used up as one of the diseased dolphins that had been washing ashore all summer.

"Are you okay?" a voice asked repeatedly. "Are you okay? Can you breathe? Do you feel like anything is broken?"

Foolish questions. His chest was moving, wasn't it? Steven closed his eyes, and shivered, not only at the coldness still deep inside him, but at the recent memory of his passivity beneath the water, the way he'd been so ready to let life drift away. This was a revelation he hadn't needed.

"Cover him," someone said. "Cover him up."

Towels settled on his body, someone touched his cheek, and Steven opened his eyes to find a bearded man of fifty or so kneeling next to him.

"I'm a doctor," he said slowly, as though Steven were an idiot, or still six inches underwater and required to read his lips. "Can you understand me?"

Steven nodded, taking in the man's bathing suit and potbelly, his own reflection in the doctor's Vuarnets.

"There's an ambulance on the way," the doctor said. "Can you tell me where you're hurt?"

"Ribs," Steven said. His throat was raw with salt, but the word was clear enough. "Cracked some ribs, I guess." He reached up to show the doctor where he'd been struck, and winced as the pain seared across again.

"Keep still now. They'll get you out of here in a couple of minutes." He prodded Steven's stomach roughly. "Swallow any water, did you?"

The seawater rose inside him again, and Steven turned his head to the side and puked into the sand. He was humiliated. When he'd caught his breath, he asked, "Can you clear these people out?"

The doctor turned to one of the swimmers. "Good job," he said, then: "Why don't you folks back off now?"

Several of the onlookers turned and left, but most only stepped back a few paces, then immediately edged forward again. Steven settled, grateful now as the heat of the sand soaked into his body and gradually calmed his shakes.

He suddenly roused himself. "Where's Lisa?"

"Right here," she said, and she moved into his line of sight, Todd a step behind. Both kids were pale beneath their tans, scared, the boy blond, lanky, and more than a head taller than his dark-haired sister.

"I'm really sorry, Mr. Blake," Lisa said again. "Todd didn't see you."

"Yes he did," Steven said. Though it was Todd who had hit him, he stared at Lisa. "It wasn't an accident," he said flatly. "Why are you doing all of this to me?"

If she even attempted to answer, her voice was lost as he retched another cup of seawater into the sand.

When he was done, the doctor said, "You're lucky she found you. It's a complete myth that drowning people surface three times, you know. Most go down once, get their lungs filled with water, and don't come up again for days, if they ever show up at all."

Steven closed his eyes again to shut out the man's chatter, reflecting that with a bedside manner like that, he had to be a surgeon. Gradually the coldness ebbed into the sand beneath him, and he focused all his attention on the simple act of breathing. A distant siren wove closer, winding through the narrow lanes of summer cottages that fronted the bay. Embarrassment began to outweigh his sense of physical injury, and he gathered his energy and sat up; the pain was less than he'd expected.

Two EMTs crested the low dunes and surveyed the beach. Several in the group around Steven waved at them, and they began to weave through the beach crowd. Their white uniforms and chrome stretcher were bleak and sharp as death amidst the tanned hides, neon bathing suits, and bright striped umbrellas.

"I don't need that," Steven said before the EMTs could get anywhere close to him; he wanted nothing more than to go home alone and crawl into bed. "I can walk."

"Just relax," the doctor said. "Take the ride."

Steven gathered his feet in under him, and stood slowly, determined that as long as his eyes remained open and he still drew breath, he'd never be carried off the beach, especially not with an audience this large. His legs wobbled a bit, and he hesitated, watching the approaching EMTs.

The doctor stood next to him, close enough to catch him if he fell, Steven realized. "You shift a broken rib around in there, and you could puncture a lung," he warned.

"I'm all right," Steven said. He tried to smile, but it came out a grimace. The doctor shrugged in acknowledgment, and Steven continued up the beach toward the parking lot.

He heard Lisa command her brother to take care of the boards, and after some whispered argument, she trotted up next to him.

"Um," she said, "maybe you should wait, Mr. Blake."

Steven stopped and looked down at the source of all his troubles. Lisa was small, no more than five-two or -three, with dark hair that fell in wet ringlets to her shoulders. This was the first time he'd seen her in several months, and she seemed much older than he remembered her. Her face was darkly tanned, lashes dark and lips deep red with waterproof makeup, and she wore a black and hot pink wet suit, unzipped to her navel. She wore nothing beneath the neoprene. The tan on her chest was unbroken, and the skin between her breasts glistened with seawater or sweat. The August sunlight suddenly seemed several thousand watts brighter. Despite himself, Steven took a cautious step backward.

"Lisa, what is this all about?"

She blinked, licked her lips nervously, and said, "That's what I came to talk to you about. I'm really, really sorry. I didn't think Todd would do anything like that."

"Why the hell couldn't you just walk up the beach to find me?" Steven said shortly. His ribs throbbed, his waterlogged lungs wheezed spongily, and his patience wasn't even a memory. "What's the story?"

She glanced at the approaching EMTs. "I can't tell you right now," she said. "It'll take too long."

Steven sighed and began walking again, suddenly uninterested in any justification she might offer. There could be no good reasons for her actions, and all he really cared about at the moment was dealing with the consequences and defending himself from Thompson. "Get away from me," he said. "Leave me alone."

Wordlessly she walked next to him. Steven walked faster, his irritation rising with each step, and she kept up, pace for pace.

The EMTs, full-uniformed and dripping sweat, stumbled toward them. He knew both by sight. They were natives, not summer people.

"Steve," the nearest called, "where's the accident?"

Steven pointed back over his shoulder, but from behind him the doctor said, "He's the one you want, guys."

The two EMTs eyed Steven as though considering the best way to tackle him. He took a deep breath and raised his hand to warn them off, and the deepest pain yet scored his side. His vision folded in black from the edges, and as he collapsed toward the sand, one small part of his mind still struggled to pull him upright, refusing to believe until the last moment that his body was failing this way, until at last he gave it all up and let himself slip away.

He woke as the ambulance tires shrilled across the metal-grated drawbridge next to the Lighthouse Restaurant, so he couldn't have been out more than five minutes. He was strapped to the stretcher. Next to an EMT, on a fold-out seat, rode Lisa.

"You okay?" she asked.

"What are you doing here?"

She shrugged. "Like I was really going to just go away after you passed out on the beach."

"How'd they let you in?"

"I told them I was your stepdaughter."

Steven closed his eyes. He was surprised and bothered that she'd been worried enough about him to come along. Then he wondered how far news of his suspension from the high school had traveled—Lewes and Rehoboth were basically small towns, despite the crowds of summer, and he was certain that Thompson must have talked, and the kids and their parents must have speculated after Randy took over band practice. He visualized Lisa's brother back at Lewes Beach explaining to the crowd exactly why his sister had accompanied Steven, and then imagined the gossip at the hospital when he showed up there with Lisa, especially dressed as she was. The rocking of the ambulance was making him queasy, and he opened his eyes and glanced around the interior of the ambulance, trying to look anywhere but at the girl. Her brilliant pink and sleek black wet suit seemed to reflect from every inch of stainless steel and white enamel. The August heat overpowered the air-conditioning, and her face was filmed with sweat. Steven reached up and felt his own slick brow.

Lisa met his gaze for a moment, then looked away and licked her lips.

"How much trouble are we in?" she asked.

"Why'd you get into this ambulance with me?"

The girl offered a wan smile and stared out the rear window. "I'm worried about you, Mr. Blake," she said. "This is all my fault."

In moments he'd pass into the bustle of the emergency room, Lisa could go on her way, and he could lose this chance. Steven locked his most intense stare on her. "But why?" he said. "Is this all about me and Gail?"

Lisa shook her head. The ambulance slowed nearly to a stop, and Steven guessed they were making the sharp turn into the hospital entrance. He unbuckled the stretcher straps and sat up. In the last moments before they flung open the doors and led him into the rush of the emergency room, he reached out and clutched Lisa's forearm.

"Tell me," he said. "Why did you do this to me?"

The rear doors swept open. "I'll tell you as soon as I can," she said. She pulled her arm free, and bounded from the ambulance. Over the protests of the crew, Steven climbed out under his own power. He staggered, paused a moment to catch his balance, then navigated himself toward the hospital doors.

Lisa strode four or five quick paces ahead, already inside the swinging double doors. The ridged soles of her wet suit boots chirped and squeaked on the tile.

Steven stalked after her, pain jarring him with every step, determined to find truth, or at least an answer, with his one good chance.

4

Steven and Lisa waited side by side in the emergency room. Across from them, two teenaged girls whispered at each other through cracked lips, faces scarlet and puffy from sun poisoning. To the girls' left sat a guy in his mid-twenties, wearing only denim cutoffs, scuffed workboots, and the deep tan of a roofer or highway worker. He cradled his heavily bandaged right hand in his lap. Knees spread wide and head thrown back to rest against the wall, he focused closed eyes on his pain. Mid-morning on a Thursday, sand-colored walls and pale green tile, the hospital was as calm as an ebbing tide.

Steven watched Lisa without turning his head; she probably wouldn't have noticed if he had, because her nervous gaze was locked on the tinted glass doors of the emergency room entrance. He'd worked with her enough over the past three years to know he couldn't order or intimidate her into telling him anything. Lisa had been one of the prettier girls in the high school, sweet and southern from her early years in South Carolina, but she was far from defenseless. Steven had always seen something crafty and knowing in her, which had come no doubt from fending for herself, negotiating her own breaks as a child. Lisa had lived with her mother, Jacob's first wife, from age five to fifteen, seeing her father three or four times a year at holidays and summer vacation. From what little Gail had learned, the divorce had been savage, the mother bitter and unstable, and Jacob little interested in custody until his first wife had perished in a house fire three years earlier. Then the kids had landed at his house, Lisa in time to start tenth grade, Todd his senior year. Steven had been stunned when Lisa first appeared in his band room—this had been merely a year after Gail and Jacob's divorce—and one of his first questions to the girl had been whether her father knew who her music teacher was. She'd replied that of course he knew, and left it at that. Later, Steven had asked her why she hadn't gone away to school, and she'd said that her father wanted her close by, where he could keep an eye on her.

Lisa noticed him studying her, and made a small gesture of apology with both hands open.

"Lisa," Steven said as reasonably as he could, "please tell me I never touched you."

She glanced at him, then automatically back to the entrance doors, and said softly, "You know you didn't, Mr. Blake."

The past day of accusations, innuendo, and fruitless denials had begun to wear Steven down to the point where he'd been wondering if he wasn't, in fact, guilty in some way he'd never even imagined. Instead of feeling vindication, relief, or triumph now, though, he felt only a deep sadness at the life Lisa must lead—he could see only Jacob behind the accusation. "Will you tell that to Mr. Thompson?"

She shook her head. "I can't."

"Why not?" he said, loudly enough to raise the girls and the carpenter from their own misery. All three stared at him. "Come on, Lisa." Steven's voice was lower, and hard with frustration. "This has gone on long enough."

"Please, Mr. Blake." Clear panic rose in her voice. "I promise I'll explain the whole thing, but I just can't do it now. I'll come to your house."

"How about if I bring Gail over to *your* house and you explain it to her?" Steven said, although he wasn't sure Gail would bother listening at this point.

Lisa bolted up from her chair and quickly paced the length of the waiting room. Steven expected her to keep going, but just short of the doors, she hesitated, head down, then turned and walked slowly back. Wild-eyed, she clenched both arms in front of her.

Her wet suit, still unzipped to her waist, gaped open, exposing the full inner curve of both breasts. Steven glanced away. The carpenter, pain seemingly forgotten, looked him over, checking out the competition, then stared again at Lisa.

"Zip that thing up," Steven said quietly. "You're going to fall out of it."

Lisa sat next to him again. "It's too hot," she said. "I was looking for you this morning."

"You picked a hell of a way to find me," Steven said.

"I swear I didn't know Todd would do that. He said he'd help me."

"So now I have to start ducking your brother, too? Hasn't this whole thing gone far enough?"

"Todd's just mad at you for marrying Gail," she said absently.

"You realize they're trying to fire me, don't you?"

"I can't help it," she said. "That's what I'm trying to explain."

"You haven't explained anything yet," Steven said.

"I can't. Not without showing you something I got from my dad's office."

Curiosity sharp now, Steven pressed. "Something that's going to make all of this go away?"

Lisa shrugged. "Maybe you can use it to make him stop."

Steven was silent for a long moment, considering his next tack. Though he suspected Jacob's hand in this set-up, he needed verification now, while he had the girl in front of him. "Lisa, do you really expect me to believe your father made you tell Thompson I've been screwing around with you?"

"You don't know him." Fear edged her words, and Steven tensed in anger at Jacob. The resulting pain in his side took his breath away. He waited for the wave to pass, then said, "What's the deal, Lisa? This is my life you're screwing up."

"I don't mean to." Lisa sniffled.

Grasping for any lever that might work, Steven said, "How about if we talk to your father about this, then?"

"No," she said, loudly enough to draw the sunburned girls once again from their haze of pain. "Please, please, please, before you say anything to my dad, let me explain to you."

"I'm waiting," Steven said.

Lisa sighed in exasperation, eyed the nurses at their station, checked the entry doors again for any sign of her father or brother. "Is Gail really mad?" she said.

"Not a bit," Steven said. "It's one of her favorite things when I'm accused of sleeping with one of my students. The better-looking they are, the more she likes it. And if it's her former stepdaughter, that adds the best touch."

Lisa bit her bottom lip. Brow furrowed, she stared vacantly at the floor. "I never thought it would make this much of a mess."

"You didn't think about much of anything, did you?" Steven said. "Gail moved out yesterday because of all of this." While this wasn't strictly true, he was angry enough to claim it, and maybe a little guilt would shake the girl's story loose.

She just shook her head. "That's what Gail does when things get bad, Mr. Blake."

Steven filed this to ask the girl about later—Gail had never fully explained what had happened between her and Jacob, though Steven had his own theories. That wasn't today's trauma, however, so he asked again, "Why are you doing this? You were the best musician I ever taught."

Near tears now, Lisa shook her head again. "You were my best teacher," she said.

At this Steven turned half away from her. Off by themselves, in the farthest corner of the waiting room, sat a black couple who looked to be in their early seventies, just emerged from the recesses of the hospital. They were dressed more formally than everyone but the nurses—the woman in a long, pale blue summer dress, the man in dark blue trousers and a long-sleeved white shirt buttoned all the way to the top. The woman stared down at her folded hands while the man spoke to her, softly and continuously. Steven couldn't make out the words, saw only the steady, gleaming roll of tears coursing down the woman's cheeks.

Whatever its roots, real sorrow made his own inconsequential. He shivered in the air-conditioning. The ambulance driver had draped his shirt over Steven's shoulders and added a blanket on top of that, but it suddenly wasn't enough. He closed his eyes, resting with the throbbing pain in his side, and wished for a painkiller and his own bed. None of this mattered. Lisa was clearly too intimidated to help him, and he faced a nasty, probably unwinnable fight for his job, his wife was leaving town, with or without him, and life went on. Even if he could convince Lisa to admit her lies and retract the charges before they went any further, he'd probably never get over the taint of the accusation. He wondered if this weren't in some way the inevitable outcome of his falling in love with Gail while she was still married to Jacob, whether he hadn't earned these hard times. But that implied that life balanced, scales were kept, and Steven had learned long ago that goodness seldom seemed to go unpunished, or wrong unrewarded.

He was weary of all of this, and he said quietly to Lisa, "Go home now. I'm fine."

"I've got to stay," she said. "This is my fault."

"You didn't hit me," Steven said. "Your brother should be here, if anyone should."

"He'll probably be here with my dad any minute." Her voice sounded flat and hopeless. "Promise you won't say anything."

A lanky black orderly, bony wrists jutting from his hospital whites, rolled a wheelchair up the hallway toward Steven.

"Tell me again that I never touched you," Steven said to Lisa.

"Who's going to x-rays?" the orderly asked. "Young lady?"

Steven waited another moment for Lisa, then stood. "I can walk," he said.

The orderly shook his head once. "You ride or you sit here," he said with a finality that precluded any argument. "Hospital rule."

Steven looked down again at Lisa, but she refused to meet his eye. "Well?" he said.

In a low voice, slurring her words, she said, "You never touched me, Mr. Blake."

Steven looked away then, not sure for the moment whether he was relieved or even angrier. He took a couple of deep breaths. "Okay," he said, and sat down in the wheelchair. He was eye-level with her again. "Come tell me about it," he said. "I'll listen."

For the first time she smiled, tentatively. "Tomorrow?"

Caution coursed like current through his nerves, but what did he have left to lose at this point? "Yeah. You got me into this mess. You're probably the only one who can help get me out of it."

The orderly wheeled him away, down the hall and past the chairs the elderly black couple had occupied. They'd disappeared without Steven's noticing, and he wondered whether they'd left the hospital or returned to its depths.

THE ANTICLIMAX OF the final diagnosis—a deep muscle bruise, but no broken or cracked ribs—almost disappointed Steven. He'd nearly drowned, had passed out on a public beach, and been carried to an ambulance. Steven felt his injuries should have reflected the nearness of drowning, his willingness to relinquish breath. The doctor, a balding guy at least five years younger than Steven, wouldn't even tape him up.

"You're in better shape than ninety-nine percent of the people I see," he said. "Including myself. What do you do, work out all day?" He was filling a hypodermic.

"No, I swim. Every day until today." Steven, perched on the edge of a high examining table, looked away as the needle slid into his upper arm.

"Demerol," the doctor said. "How'd the kid hit you, anyway?"

"On purpose." Steven rubbed his shoulder. "How long's this going to take to heal up?"

"Two, three weeks, you'll be fine," the doctor said. "Give your regular doctor a call and have him look at it."

"I don't really have a regular doctor," Steven said. "I had a surgeon work on my knee last winter, but that's it."

"Best time to find a doctor." Stripping off his latex gloves, the doctor washed his hands vigorously, peering all the while over his shoulder at Steven. "Doctors don't want sick patients."

He dried his hands, then scrawled out a prescription slip and handed it to Steven.

"You have any idea why I passed out on the beach?" Steven asked. "That's never happened to me before."

"Probably shock." The doctor was already on the move. "I'll send the orderly back for you," he said as the examining room door closed behind him.

Before another wheelchair or stretcher could arrive, Steven made his own way back to the waiting room. Already he'd been carted around more than he had since he began to walk.

To his surprise, Lisa was still waiting. To his chagrin, next to her now sat Jacob Wood, a tall, hawk-faced man in his mid-fifties. He leaned toward his daughter, speaking intently in a voice too low for Steven to catch. Curious, Steven hesitated. He had met Jacob face to face very few times; except for one brief encounter, in which Steven had come off poorly, and a few sightings in passing, his knowledge of the man was entirely secondhand. He knew him primarily by reputation and comments from Lisa over the three years Steven had taught her, and only slightly from Gail's stories. She'd never been especially forthcoming about her six years as Jacob's wife, but Steven understood Jacob, like Gail, to be determined and aggressive in all things. Jacob owned at least a piece of most of the area's major real estate ventures of the past ten or fifteen years, and was capable of resolutely dazzling charm. He seemed motivated even more by competition than by greed. He'd lived in the same Rehoboth Beach house for many years: a solid and tasteful structure nothing like the nouveau glass and cedar piles in Henlopen Acres. He could be spotted regularly on the front page of the local weeklies, grinning as he bestowed yet another contribution on a local charity. Chances were that the donation was the largest the organization had ever received, and Jacob was never slow to make this clear. His biggest loss in anyone's memory had been Gail's leaving him for Steven, and Steven fully expected Jacob would do his best to even that score.

Still unaware of Steven's observation, Wood grinned, then grasped the large ring on Lisa's wet suit zipper and slowly zipped the wet suit up as far as it would go. The gesture was so unexpected and lingering that Steven's lips tightened and the skin along his spine prickled.

Lisa's expression froze, and she turned her head stiffly away from her father and gazed directly at Steven. So resigned and helpless was her face that Steven stepped quickly forward.

The girl jumped up, her gratitude clear. "Mr. Blake," she said, "are you okay?"

Behind her, Jacob Wood stood. Lean, tanned, six-one or so, Wood was a former air force officer. Though long out of the military, he still wore his iron gray hair closely cropped. Grim-faced, Wood looked ready to finish the deed his son had begun out in the bay.

"Didn't Thompson make it clear you're to stay away from Lisa?" he said without preamble.

Steven stopped, and said calmly, "Maybe you should have made it clear to Todd he should stay away from me."

"You're goddamned lucky it was Todd out there and not me." Wood's voice was tight and clipped with fury, but so low that the nurses at the station fifteen feet away didn't even look up. "If it had been me, you wouldn't have surfaced for days."

"Daddy," Lisa said, "it wasn't Mr. Blake's fault." She stood behind and to the right of her father, worriedly glancing from his profile to Steven's face.

The full strength of the painkiller hit Steven in a warm, rolling rush; the pale sand walls of the waiting room made a few weaving circles, and his legs went rubbery. He stood solidly in place, though, determined not to show any weakness to Wood.

"Don't threaten me," Steven said. His own voice seemed to come from across the room. "You might be able to intimidate your kids, Jacob, and you might have Thompson jumping through hoops for you, but I'm afraid it just doesn't mean a thing to me."

"Lisa, go out and wait in the car," Jacob Wood said.

"No." She refused to look at her father.

"Get out to the goddamned car," he repeated, teeth clenched.

Reluctantly Lisa stood, still watching Steven. "Are you sure you're okay?" she said.

"Yeah," Steven said. "Thanks for hanging around."

"Come on, Dad. We can't just leave Mr. Blake here like this."

Wood glanced at his watch, then said brusquely, "I imagine he can find his own way home. Go wait."

She hesitated, gave Steven a last worried look, then left, taking with her his last chance for a civilized conversation between the three of them. Speaking very slowly in hope the words might penetrate, he said, "Jacob, I've never touched your daughter—you know it, she knows it, and it's not going to take a lot for me to convince even Thompson of it."

"Stow the shit," Wood said. "You're lying and we both know it. What I want to make absolutely clear is that I don't ever want to hear about you even being in the same fucking room as Lisa again. You can believe I'll hurt you worse than this."

Not since he was a teenager marching in an antiwar parade in conservative little Wilmington had Steven faced such open contempt. He studied Wood, perplexed, until he realized that something else glimmered in the man's eyes—an almost gleeful spark of superiority. Triumph. Wood was enjoying this, just as he'd enjoyed zipping Lisa's wet suit for her.

"Whatever you're doing," Steven said, "your daughter deserves better."

"Is that what you call what *you've* been doing with her?"

Steven hadn't hit anyone in anger since the sixth grade; hurt and drugged though he was, it was all he could do to hold back now. He put all the disgust he could muster into his voice. "I can't believe you'd use your own daughter to get back at me," he said. "Just get out of here now." He looked around the waiting room, hoping for witnesses, but their entire conversation had been conducted in such controlled tones that no one paid them any notice.

Jacob's lips moved; his words, delayed by the painkillers, reached Steven a second later. It was like watching someone work on their boat from two hundred yards across Lewes Harbor, motion preceding sound by just a little too much for either to seem convincing. "You're going to leave it at this."

The words were more order than request, and it took Steven a moment to puzzle them together. Then he snapped, "Absolutely not. You're not going to pull this one off, Jacob."

Wood gestured impatiently. "I'm talking about today's accident. Todd said he didn't see you in the waves, and that nobody ever swims out that far from shore."

So this was to be his fault, too. Tiredly he said, "Let Lisa tell you what really happened, Jacob."

"Todd already has," Wood replied, and wearing a small, cold smile of satisfaction, he left.

Steven watched Wood's long strides and wondered what had stirred this fury after four years. He'd heard that Jacob had moved on after Gail, reportedly working his way through half the wives and most of the daughters at the Rehoboth Yacht Club.

He wondered, not for the first time, how Gail and Jacob had stayed together as long as they had. As far as Steven could figure, the root of the attraction between those two had been the fascination of each with the other's single-minded pursuit of any object, accomplishment, or person desired. For them this had led quite naturally from pursuit to marriage to full-blown tests of each's ability to manipulate the other. Initially this had taken the form of financial competitiveness. In the early days of their own marriage, Gail had told Steven a story as evidence of the way she'd once been, before meeting him. She'd first attracted Jacob's attention when she was twenty-eight and working as an associate to the attorney who handled all of Wood's real estate dealings. She'd been working on securing the wetlands permits for a plot edging the state park, where Jacob later built condominiums, and had discovered that a neighboring plot could also be had with only a slight modification of the permits. Knowing full well the illegality of what she was doing, she'd borrowed from Jacob's escrow account to make the deal in her own name, then told him about it. His response had been a dinner invitation.

Their competitiveness inevitably turned to a series of affairs on both sides, until Gail had finally walked in and discovered Jacob entwined with a twenty-year-old lifeguard from Rehoboth. Two weeks later, she'd set after Steven, but he was reasonably certain that her act of simple revenge on Jacob had progressed to a more honest attraction.

Jacob had approached the divorce coldly, leaving all points scornfully uncontested; his attorney handled everything. Gail had her own money going in, kept it coming out, and didn't go after a dime of his, so this was relatively easy. But at the final hearing, Jacob had stopped on his way out of the courtroom, stood in front of Steven, and looked him up and down. Then he shook his head, gave a grin of obvious derision, and said, "You lose."

"Wrong," Steven had said. "I won."

Jacob had grinned even more broadly, and said, "What made you think I was talking to you?"

Steven had laughed out loud and turned his back on Jacob, just quickly enough to catch the flash of uncertainty in Gail's eyes. As Jacob left, Steven told her those had just been the angry words of a bitter loser. And he'd almost believed this himself until two weeks later, when Thompson had come to the music room to tell him that Jacob had just donated $25,000 to the high school for new band uniforms. Of course Steven had refused to appear in the publicity photo, though Thompson was delighted to perform without him.

That had been his last real contact with Jacob. He knew Gail ran across him occasionally—Wood was unavoidable for anyone doing business in southern Delaware—but she rarely spoke of him, even when Steven pressed.

Something was completely wrong about him. Steven's fists clenched again as he recalled Wood's half-dreamy, half-gloating expression as he'd zipped up his daughter's wet suit.

The hospital's sliding doors sucked shut. Steven stood and moved a couple of paces closer to the entry so he could watch Wood climb into his long, gray Mercedes. Lisa was a murky shape behind tinted glass.

So Steven was left with nothing more to clear him than he'd had yesterday, with no reason to trust the girl, only the hope she'd have the nerve to show up, and that whatever she brought with her could give him . . . what? Not his old life back—already that seemed like a discarded pair of shoes that he hadn't realized were too small until he took them off.

What he wanted were reasons, and a way to help Lisa help herself. And the satisfaction of removing that smug smile and gleam of triumph from Jacob Wood's face.

5

For the third time in forty-five minutes, Steven dialed Gail's office number, and for the third time her new secretary either stonewalled or really didn't recognize his voice, and offered to take a message for the unavailable Ms. Moncure.

He stood at the emergency room reception desk, still wearing the ambulance blanket Indian-style over his shoulders. Beneath that he was just as he'd been pulled from the bay—barefoot and wearing only a tiny black racing suit. Slightly disoriented from the painkiller, he felt like he'd wandered into one of those dreams where everyone was clothed except him. He was right on the edge of being relaxed enough to leave a message he'd probably regret later; all he said was, "Tell her that her husband called again."

There was a momentary silence on the other end, followed by a sigh. "Let me see if I can find out where she is, Mr. Blake."

Synthesized strings oozed "Greensleeves," and he drummed his fingers impatiently on the Formica countertop until stopped by a nurse's frosty glance. Turning his back on the counter, he adjusted his blanket again. He'd already endured enough grief here for daring to show up for treatment without his health plan card or any memory whatsoever of his medical record number.

The secretary came back on. "I'm sorry," she said. "She was supposed to be in court this afternoon, but that's been postponed, and there's nothing on her calendar now. You might try her at home."

He'd already left three messages on the machine Gail had moved to the cottage, had even tried the number at the house on the long chance that Gail might have come back to pick up something. "Never mind," he said. "I'll get home another way."

He hung up, stared out at the passing traffic, and wondered where Gail had disappeared to—it was completely unlike her not to leave her whereabouts with her office.

After a moment's thought, he dialed Jimmy Van Dusen's number. The coach lived twenty to thirty minutes away, over near the western shore of Rehoboth Bay. Sharon, his wife, picked it up on the first ring, and recognized Steven's voice immediately. Before Steven could steer her anywhere else, she went straight to Lisa.

"So what is this business?" she said. "Why's the girl doing this?"

"I wish I could tell you," Steven said. "What do you think?"

This was an important test; he wasn't as close to Sharon as he was to Jimmy, and she didn't know Lisa. She might give him his first reading on what he was going to face from others. Uncharacteristically, she hesitated, and Steven's stomach fell a notch.

"I don't know," she finally said. "Jimmy said the girl's not very close to her stepmother, so I suppose it's not got to do with you and Gail."

"That's old news, anyway," Steven said, then went on before Sharon could start up again: "Listen, I'm kind of stuck. Is Jimmy around?"

"He's over working on his boat." In the background, all four Van Dusen children screamed with laughter, and she covered the phone and shouted them quiet. When she came back on, she seemed to have realized that she'd been less than ringingly supportive, and said, "Jimmy and I both believe in you, Steven, you know? Anything we can do, we will."

"I appreciate it," Steven said, though he doubted he'd test her offer. "You think you could give Jimmy a shout and ask him to come pick me up at the Beebe Hospital emergency room?" Van Dusen spent most of his free time working on his big Grady-White, and kept the marine radio on even while puttering around at the marina.

"Oh, God, you should have said that in the first place," she said. "What happened? Are you okay?"

"I'm fine," he said. "I don't have my car here, and I can't get hold of Gail anywhere."

"Hold on, I'll try to raise him," she said. "And if I can't get him, I'll come get you myself."

Her phone clattered on their plastic-topped kitchen table. Steven could hear the television, the kids screaming again, and, blessedly, the static-muffled shouts of Van Dusen coming back to his wife on the radio. In a moment she returned.

"Give him half an hour," she said. "Are you sure you're okay, Steve? What happened?"

"Lisa Wood's brother ran me down with his sailboard," Steven said.

Sharon was silent for a long moment. "This is getting stranger and stranger, Steven. Maybe Jimmy's right, and you should just quit now."

"Not yet," he said, and stretched over the high counter to drop the telephone receiver back into its cradle. Once again he settled in a waiting room chair and watched the procession through the emergency room. A dull ache throbbed in his side, and after a few minutes it came to seem like his own anger gnawing at his chest. He leaned his head back against the hospital wall and closed his eyes. He was angry with Jacob, with Todd, with Lisa, with Thompson, but most of all with Gail because of the way she was trying to force his actions, seizing this chance to work her own agenda and move them out of Lewes. And with the anger mingled a touch of depression, for he knew that whatever happened at the high school, his life had already been unalterably changed, and he was uncertain of his ability to control its next direction. And beneath it all, he had to admit to himself, was more than a little fear, for if he couldn't prevail here, Wood or Thompson seemed capable of sending him to jail.

HE FELT SOMEONE standing over him, and opened his eyes to Jimmy, whose tanned face was creased by a grin. Wearing an Orioles cap, a faded green T-shirt, and cutoffs, he was spattered with dark blue paint from his blond hair to his worn sneakers. Steven stood, ready to leave, and Van Dusen looked him up and down. "Pretty skimpy bathing suit. When did you turn French Canadian?"

"Do me a favor," Steven said, "and save the bullshit for somebody who needs it." He walked to the entrance.

The automatic doors slid open, and they walked briskly out of the air-conditioned hospital into the full blast of the day's heat. Even under the portico where the ambulances stopped, the air had its own pounding pulse. It was another ninety-five/ninety-five afternoon, the temperature an even match for the humidity, and sweat drenched him within ten paces. Steven stopped just inside the shade line, pulled the wool blanket from his shoulders, folded it in half, and wrapped it around his waist sarong-style.

He stepped into the full sun and almost thought he heard the sizzle of raw meat as the soles of his feet met the sidewalk. Whatever shreds of dignity he'd kept fled now as he hopped frantically toward the grass, swearing.

Van Dusen's blue Ford pickup was parked across the lot. Steven winced as he made his way across the blacktop, climbed in, and settled back with a long sigh of relief as Jimmy started the engine. A rush of cold air blasted from the dash; Van Dusen pushed in a Garth Brooks tape, then reflexively lowered the volume in deference to Steven's oft-voiced opinion of country music. Between them on the bench seat sat a blue and white plastic six-pack cooler.

"What a day," Steven said. "What a goddamned day."

"You gonna tell me what's going on?" Jimmy said. "Sharon said Lisa Wood ran you down with her Windsurfer."

"It was Todd, not Lisa," Steven said. "Out off of Lewes Beach. She was with him, though."

"Christ. You okay? That's a hell of a bruise."

"I'm all right. Nothing broken."

"You going to press charges?"

"No," Steven said. "This is about Jacob, not the kids. He showed up while I was being x-rayed. Told me I was lucky it had been Todd and not him, or I'd be at the bottom of the bay."

"Anybody else hear him say that?"

"Only Lisa. She came in the ambulance with me."

They sat in the idling pickup, air-conditioning beginning to get cold now, and Jimmy studied him, suddenly serious. "This was pretty real, wasn't it?"

"Who knows? I probably would have drowned if Lisa hadn't come down to find me."

"So they knock you out, then pull you up. Some deal." Van Dusen shook his head. "Todd say why he did it?"

"Lisa said he's mad at me for marrying Gail."

"Kid holds a long grudge."

When Steven didn't comment, Van Dusen put the truck in gear and backed out. "Let's get you home," he said.

"Just drop me at Lewes Beach," Steven said. "I left my bike and stuff there."

Savannah Road was a solid stream of traffic; Van Dusen spotted a tiny opening, and whipped out with a squeal of the Ford's oversized tires. The truck was a big four-by-four that he used to tow his boat, and they rode high above the other cars.

They coasted up to the traffic light before the Lewes Canal drawbridge.

"There's good news, I guess," Steven said. "Lisa admitted I never touched her."

"What?" Van Dusen was clearly incredulous. "Where was this?"

"At the hospital," Steven said. "I don't know if the orderly heard her or not."

He held off telling Van Dusen about Lisa's promise to come visit and reveal all, both because he wasn't convinced the visit would really happen and because he knew Jimmy would rightly call him the worst kind of fool for letting the girl come anywhere near his house.

"Doesn't do you a whole hell of a lot of good then, does it?"

"It won't save my butt," Steven said, "unless I can get her to say it again."

They hummed over the drawbridge. This was the second-highest point in Lewes, lower only than the highway bridge that crossed the canal a mile or so to the southwest. For a moment the cottages between the canal and the bay spread before them; then they swept down past the Lighthouse Restaurant. Another half-mile brought them to the town beach, where Steven's twelve-speed was locked to a lightpost. They both climbed out, and Van Dusen opened the rear window on the truck cap, then hefted the bicycle over the tailgate in one easy motion.

"You're too woozy to ride that thing home."

Steven offered no argument, but headed for the beach.

"Now where you going?" Van Dusen called.

"Down to get my stuff. If it's still there."

"Stay here," Van Dusen said. "What am I looking for?"

"I'm not dead yet." Steven set out across the hot sand. He'd left his gear a couple of hundred yards up the beach, everything wrapped inside a big red beach towel. Within a few paces he knew he'd made a mistake, and was glad that Jimmy trudged along next to him.

"Thanks," he said.

"For what? I was only painting trim."

"Not just for today." Steven's breath was quick and shallow, and he bit off the ends of his sentences. "For being a friend. I'm glad I ran into you yesterday."

"No big deal," Van Dusen said. "You doing okay? You look pretty shaky."

Steven nodded. He had breath to walk or to talk, but not both, so he put his head down and slogged across the sand. Jimmy matched him step for step.

Van Dusen taught math and coached basketball, though not necessarily in that order of skill or dedication. His teams consistently finished well up in the conference—somehow he'd learned the trick of convincing the sons of resort-town lawyers and developers and inland chicken farmers to put aside their differences for at least the length of a season, and he was immensely popular with the kids. He was a home-grown Lewes boy, whose father and uncles had worked as fishermen supplying the big menhaden processing plant that had been the town's major industry until it shut down in the sixties, then had moved into construction as the condos and second homes sprouted up and down the coast. Basketball had carried him out of town to college, but Larry Bird he wasn't, and he'd landed right back where he'd been born.

Unlike most coaches, Jimmy had kept a rangy athlete's body past his twenties. Despite the slow-witted coach routine he affected at faculty meetings, he was as sharp as anyone else teaching at the high school. Steven could name at least two reasons for their friendship: for one, he was one of the few who actually remembered Van

Dusen as a high school star; for another, they were lumped together by most of the other teachers, who regarded them both as local boys who'd almost made good only to let themselves be pulled back to this small town. Music and sports ranking where they did in the high school hierarchy, Van Dusen and Steven were both extracurricular.

They reached the pickup again, both men dripping sweat now. Van Dusen cranked the air-conditioning all the way up, pulled two beers from the cooler on the seat, popped both, and handed one to Steven without asking.

For a moment they sat in the pickup looking out at the Delaware Bay. The water's surface rolled calmly, laced by powerboats pulling skiers, and Steven wondered how far out he'd be now if Lisa hadn't forced him back to the surface. New Jersey was a hazy smudge on the horizon, and a procession of tankers made their way up to the refineries and tank farms at Delaware City, Claymont, Marcus Hook, Chester, and Philadelphia. Jimmy tapped his fingers on the steering wheel, but didn't reach for his tape player, and after a moment Steven realized the man was thinking.

"As much as you swim out here, you ought to have thirty weight in your veins by now," Van Dusen said.

"There hasn't been an oil spill in a month," Steven said.

"I'm worried about you, buddy."

"Don't be. Doctor didn't even think this was bad enough to tape up."

"Not about the ding in your rib cage," Van Dusen said. He hesitated, then added, "I don't mean to interfere with your business, and you tell me if I'm out of line . . ."

The backs of Steven's bare legs were stuck to the vinyl truck seat, and he peeled them up. "Come on. I'm doing fine."

"Sharon and I both think you should take them up on the chance to quit clean."

Steven stared out the truck window. "You think I screwed the girl, don't you?"

Jimmy gestured impatiently. "Whether you did or not is between you and her and God, but if you said you didn't, I believe you. Point is, you're taking a big risk by even fighting it, because they'll have to press criminal charges if this gets public. It could tie you up for years. How much money have you got?"

Steven smiled and ducked the question. "Enough," he said. "How come?"

"Legal fees. Gail going to represent you?"

Steven had so far avoided even thinking about things getting to the point where he really needed representation. After a moment, he said, "No."

"Didn't think so. Be crazy if you let her, because I'm not too sure she'd work a hundred percent on your behalf, you know? The school still paying you, or did they suspend you without pay?"

"I don't know," Steven said slowly. "I didn't think to ask."

"If they didn't say, they're probably going to keep paying you for the time being, then. Could get too public if they suspended you right now."

Steven watched the bay for another moment, thinking how glassily peaceful the water looked, then said, "Jimmy, I'm tired and depressed and I hurt like hell."

"Well, shit, I'm just trying to help." Van Dusen put the truck into reverse. "You can tell me it's none of my business."

"I just did," Steven said.

Van Dusen backed out of the parking slot and circled the Ford around to the exit. Back past the Lighthouse Restaurant and over the drawbridge they went, then immediately right on Front Street, up past Jimmy's old house.

Across the street from Steven's, on the grass between the road and his dock, Gail played a rainbow of hosewater over the roof of her cherry red BMW.

"And there she is," Van Dusen muttered. "What's up with you guys, anyway?"

"Nothing new since yesterday," Steven said. "I haven't even talked to her."

"I'd hate like hell to lose a friend, but maybe you should work it out with her. At least for a while."

"Have you got something to tell me about her or not?"

"What do you mean?" Jimmy was obviously lying.

"You keep throwing around these hints, like you know something I don't."

Van Dusen shook his head. "You know what I think, buddy. It's your life. Get out of here, with her or without her."

"Where would I go?"

"You'd figure out something," Van Dusen said. "Be the best thing for you. Quit the job, sell your house, split the money with the queen of closings, and take off. Cut bait."

The words made slightly more sense than they had the day before—life was a wave that could break in an instant, and even now the tide could be working him out to sea. But he still didn't feel like letting her walk without him. To keep Van Dusen quiet, he said, "Maybe you're right."

Gail pointedly ignored them. Jimmy turned onto the side street next to Steven's house, then pulled into the crushed-shell driveway and stopped with the Ford's bumper inches from the back of Steven's Jeep. The Jeep was nosed up to the closed doors of a two-car garage, presently so full of storm windows, dead lawn chairs, a dry-rotted rowboat, and other junk that it could hold little else. The building staggered under the weight of rampant wild trumpet vine, now in full August bloom.

"Sure you don't want something cold?" Steven said. "Soda, anything? I can bring it right out."

"I've got a couple more beers in the cooler," Jimmy said. "I gotta get back and finish up with the boat. Promised Sharon we'd go out to dinner tonight, and my ass'll be in a major sling if I don't get a move on."

They climbed out of the pickup, and Jimmy reached over the tailgate and lifted Steven's bicycle out and set it on the driveway.

"Take it easy," he said, "okay?"

"Yeah," Steven said. "Thanks again for bailing me out."

"Glad I could help. But stay out of the water, right?"

"Yeah, yeah." Steven rolled his bike to the back wall of the house, leaned it there, waved as Van Dusen pulled away.

For a quiet moment he leaned back against his house, eyes closed, both gathering energy and assessing his own state of mind. The anger of an hour or so ago had ebbed, and instead he found a desperate, pointless ache for his life the way it had been about three years ago when he and Gail had been together just a year, and the possibilities of *their* life seemed wide open.

Steven unrolled his towel, stepped into his shorts and flip-flops, and trudged around his house to join Gail.

6

Her red BMW 750 was the first thing he saw again when he came around the side of the house, and it annoyed him as much as it had ever since Gail bought it for herself the summer before. She stretched over the bright red roof, her long, narrow back to him, lovingly massaging the car's hide with more attention than she'd given his own in months. She wore a two-piece, black and lime green bathing suit, with the words BODY GLOVE in white block letters circling the waistband. The suit bottom was cut high at the sides, making her legs look even longer than they actually were.

Patches sat alertly nearby, eager to stay close to Gail, but ready to bolt should the hose turn her way. She wagged encouragingly at Steven as he crossed Pilottown Road. He knew by the rigid set of Gail's spine that she sensed his approach, and he stopped ten feet in back of her and waited for her to speak. The last sentence he'd heard from her yesterday had been her apology for words that couldn't be retracted or glossed over, and that he had to believe she hadn't really meant. All he wanted from her now was one sign that her stand had softened, that she was ready to compromise, stay long enough to help him get clear, even if she remained at the cottage.

He couldn't find the patience to outlast her obstinacy, though, and finally said, "Gail, we've got to talk."

She turned slowly to face him, both hands covered with suds. "About what?" she said. "Have you quit?"

"I tried to get you at the office," he said. "They didn't know where you were."

"I've got a lot to wrap up," she said flatly. "They're going to have to get used to not being able to reach me."

Despite his best peacemaking intentions, Steven said, "What, was Jacob waiting for you again this morning? He have any more news about me?"

Gail shrugged, refusing to be baited, and glanced impatiently back at her car, where soapy water was already drying to a dull film.

"Did you want something in particular, or are you just keeping track of me?"

"I needed a ride home from the emergency room," Steven said.

"Looks like you got one," she said, and paused. Steven waited her out this time. "What happened to you?" she asked grudgingly.

Steven considered skipping the accident, as he didn't want her to think he was too obviously playing for sympathy, but she'd hear about it from somebody. "Todd ran me down with his sailboard," he said.

She looked him over, as if checking for injuries, but Steven's arm shielded the bruise on his ribs.

"You're all right now," she told him.

"Just fine," Steven replied. "I got a chance to ask Lisa what the hell's going on."

"And what is?"

"She admitted it. Said I never touched her, that Jacob's behind it all. The girl's terrified of him."

"Of course she is, Steven. We've both known that. The point is, does that satisfy you? Will you call Thompson now?"

"She hasn't cleared me yet."

Gail shifted her weight, stood with one hip cocked. She looked down at the grass between them, and brushed her hair from her brow with the back of one soapy wrist. She looked back up at him, and Steven saw the flicker of impatience in her eyes.

"When does she plan to do that?"

Steven shrugged, unwilling to tell Gail about Lisa's planned visit when he already knew what a bad idea it was. "It's going to take her some help to get up the courage."

"It won't happen," Gail pronounced, and she glanced at her BMW again. "I've got to get back to the office for a meeting."

Steven opened his mouth, prepared to argue, then stopped. Gail had already dismissed any possibility of compromise.

"Go ahead," he said. "Wash your car."

Gail threw him a final curious glance, as if his unexpected acquiescence had thrown her off her stride. Then she scooped up the hose nozzle and began to rinse the dried soap from her car. Determined not to beat a retreat, Steven eased himself down onto a lawn chair at the edge of the dock. Demerol cushioned his anger.

Patches ambled over to join him, circling wide around the spray from the hose, and laid her chin on his knee. He stroked the dog's head gently.

Water drummed against German sheet metal. The August heat, a white, humid weight, pressed him to the nylon webbing of his chair. Steven watched his wife—tan, lean, only a few flecks of gray in her brunet curls. She worked resolutely, focusing every bit of her attention on her car, and he wondered where she'd really been all morning, whether she had in fact been with Jacob. Though she claimed to detest her ex-husband, and had initially been nearly violent in her statements about him and reactions to seeing him, Steven had long suspected she was still linked to the man. There was, perhaps, too much of her own nature in Jacob for her to be able to deny the relationship completely.

Steven had never pushed her for many details. Believing that he was only in Lewes temporarily had required that he never sink roots beyond these two small houses his father had left him, so he had his own history of short-term lovers and never-lasting commitments that he'd preferred not to share with Gail. Without ever really discussing it, the two of them had maintained an unspoken truce of willful ignorance about each other's past that had spared them each from admitting, or at least articulating, any uncertainties about the other. Until this summer.

Gail dragged the hose around to the other side of her car. Steven watched the line of muscle playing up the length of her thigh, the flat of her haunch as she leaned against a front fender, and despite all the bitterness of the past day and because of the distance between them these past months, felt a weakness of longing.

She shut off the hose, and in the sudden silence one cicada rattled frantically in the wild trumpet vine next to the dock, like a tiny, tinny air hammer. The noise drilled through Steven's head. He closed his eyes and tested his pain, and found it lurking alive and well beneath the pills.

"Will you for God's sake stop sitting there with that hangdog expression," Gail said. "What in the hell do you want me to do?"

Steven's eyes blinked open in startlement; unprepared, he answered honestly. "Help me get our life back," he said. "The way we were that first year."

"I wish I could." She paused, and her expression seemed both warm and sad. She shook her head. "But that time is gone, Steven."

"If you're so sure of that, how come you're still around?"

Any warmth in her eyes faded, and her gaze flickered down to his side.

"Are you all right?" she asked quietly. "I just saw that mark."

"There's nothing broken. Just a bruise."

"You're always such a goddamned stoic."

"Maybe," he said, although he didn't think he could have asked her for help any more clearly. "You're really not going to stand by me in this, are you?"

She couldn't look him in the eye, instead glanced distractedly over to the weeds where the cicada shrilled. Another buzzed a reply from the hydrangeas outside Steven's porch, reminding him too much of their own conversation. Gail sighed, brushed back her bangs again with the back of her wrist. "Steven, either way we lose, right? You fight to clear yourself and stay here in that job, or you come with me when you clearly don't want to give up your life here, despite everything you've told me for four years. I don't really care one way or the other anymore."

Steven stared at her until she turned back to her car. She wrung out a chamois and began to dry the roof with impatient circular swipes.

Steven stood. "Do you know what I wish?" he said.

Gail stopped working, waited without turning to face him.

"I wish I'd had the sense to walk away from you that very first night at the Lamplighter."

"You tried," she said. "I wouldn't let you."

"Why'd you do that?"

"Because I thought you could make me change, help me be something I wanted to be." She shrugged again, clearly uninterested in exploring the past. "That's history, Steven. You can still walk away now."

"Not that easily," he said. "I love you."

"Then come with me," she said without pause.

He wished life could be as simple as "okay"; but beyond saving himself, and beyond his determination not to be *forced* from his home, he felt an obligation to Lisa. Though she might be his accuser and the apparent cause of his troubles, she was merely caught in the midst of something he'd started by not walking away from Gail that first night. Jacob was using both Lisa and Todd as conscripted infantry in his campaign against Steven, and this, as much as anything, had solidified Steven's resolution. Knowing the choice he was making, he said, "I can't. Not until I clear this thing up. Can't you wait?"

"No," she said. "Not anymore."

"Why not?"

"You've known ever since you met me that I wanted to get out of here," she said. "You're the only reason I've stayed. And now it's time for me to go, with or without you."

Steven waited a heartbeat for her to go on or back off, waited another, and another, and then exhaled all his anger in a single long sigh. He was left only with the sorrow and loss that had washed over him minutes before, as he'd watched her stretching over her car. He thought that none of their arguments had ever come quite this far, down to the point where a single question could be the end of them, and now, even though she was the one walking away and somehow she'd twisted the decision and the responsibility around so they seemed his, he said, "Yes. It's time."

She said immediately, "I'll start the paperwork tomorrow. You'd better get somebody to represent you."

"Fine." He stared at the long, unyielding bones of her back and wished he'd never seen her, never noticed her that first night she'd come into the Lamplighter with Jacob. "I've got to rest," he said. "I'm tired as hell."

She nodded silently. She still hadn't met his eye.

"So that's it?"

She gave her gleaming BMW a final once-over. "I've got to get back to the office for a closing," she said.

He turned away then, and trudged across the sticky asphalt to the sanctuary of his own house, where Gail used to live. But as he pushed between the blowsy, overgrown hydrangeas that struggled to meet over his front steps, as he stepped into the cool shade of his screened porch, he heard Gail's bare feet slap up the steps.

He stopped cold, and she ran into him, then flung her arms around him from behind. They stood that way, his hands atop hers, Steven wishing he had the strength to lift her hands away from his waist and walk away, until he turned around, held her, kissed her for what felt like the first time in months. She kissed him back, full on the mouth, and pressed full length against him.

Steven stroked the length of her back with one hand, while with the other he reached behind himself, hoping he'd forgotten to lock the front door again. It opened, and he pulled her inside.

They made love on the long sofa in the living room, quickly, Steven ignoring his bruised ribs until he collapsed onto his wife's body, toes to her toes, measuring her length under him. After a moment he rolled to his good side, wedged between the sofa back and Gail's side.

She glistened with a fine sheen of sweat, and he ran the flat of his hand down her slick torso. She traced his chest, squeezed his arms, felt the thickening of muscle at his shoulders, measured the span of his thigh against her hand.

"You've changed," she said. "You feel different."

Compared to whom? Steven wondered, but he said instead, "I swim every day. Two miles, three, four."

"Since when?"

"All summer," he replied drowsily. His ribs throbbed, but for the moment contentment outweighed the pain. We'll never be this close again, he thought, and he asked, "Why can't you wait so I can leave with my name clear?"

She wouldn't answer for a long time; Steven stared at her face, too close really to focus, until he realized that the only logical answer was the worst betrayal of all.

"It's Jacob, isn't it? You don't think I can defend myself against him."

She wouldn't look at him. "Jacob wins whatever he tries," she said. "And I'm tired of competing. He won't let this go. I thought he would."

"You've talked," Steven said.

"He calls."

Steven lay still, not wanting to hear any more about how often Jacob called or when the calls had begun or even what Jacob said, because he understood the two of them had probably never stopped talking. Betrayal begat betrayal, and in his stomach he could almost feel her cold lack of faith quenching whatever last sparks of love he'd held for her.

"You should be glad I'm going," Gail finally offered. "Maybe Jacob will leave you alone now."

This stung even more, this implication that she was somehow sacrificing herself to save him, leaving town to draw Jacob away, much as one of the ground-nesting shorebirds might struggle through the dunes seemingly wounded to draw predators away from her nest. Steven said, "I am glad you're going, but not for that reason. You just said yourself that Jacob won't let go. I won't let him go, either."

"No," she said. "But I will."

Wanting to wound now, or at least leave her with a few words she might carry with her for a while, he said, "I loved you like crazy, you know. More than you've ever deserved and more than you'll ever find again."

"I know you did," she answered softly.

"Was any of this real? Or was all this just some way you had of getting back at Jacob?"

"My problem is getting away from Jacob, not getting back at him. And you and I were more real than anything else I've ever done, Steven."

They were silent after that. Aching, exhausted, spent physically and emotionally, Steven lay with his eyes half closed, watching Gail's profile as she stared at the ceiling. Though he felt himself falling, falling away from her and from this tiny house and this small town, he strained to stay awake, for he knew that as soon as he fell off she'd slip away and be gone, and he wanted at least to watch her go. Finally he let his eyes slip closed, and he hovered on the edge of wakefulness until she stirred and gently moved away.

He watched her walk to the kitchen doorway, where she stopped and leaned against the door frame and stepped into the bottom of her swimsuit. She fastened the top of her suit, then stood for a moment, back to him, head bowed, shoulders slumped, and arms loose at her sides, as though she had somehow been defeated. Steven knew he could call out to her in that moment, unguarded as she was, and he could tell her he'd pack it in and go, and she might even smile at him, and they'd say the words to smooth things over, and they'd make it happen, for a while. But his voice was his own, and he lay quietly.

She took a deep breath, turned and looked over her shoulder, saw he was awake and watching her, and she disappeared without another word.

Steven listened to the pad of her bare feet across the kitchen linoleum and out across the painted boards of the side porch, then, straining, could just follow the sound of her footsteps fading across the lawn.

7

A summer fog, moist and enervating as a blanket of steam, descended on the coast overnight. At dawn it muffled the rumble of the fishing boats on their way up the canal to Roosevelt Inlet, and wet the pavement so the tires of the Lewes Dairy trucks hissed down Pilottown Road as they began their routes.

Stiff and aching, Steven sat in a wicker chair on his front porch and watched the morning gather its light. Droplets condensed on the screen, and the dripping hydrangeas bowed beneath the damp weight of the fog. He peered over them at the dark bulk of another party boat as it burbled past his dock. He'd slept straight through for more than twelve hours, had awoken before first light to find the cottage dark and Gail's red car gone.

He was relieved they didn't have to talk, pretend, prolong.

Already he'd drunk three cups of coffee; his stomach churned and nerves jittered with caffeine and apprehension. Change loomed, as did the chance for more encounters with Jacob or Todd Wood. Steven's first thought when he'd awoken had been that he'd nearly died the day before, and nothing he'd heard from Jacob or Lisa convinced him that Todd wouldn't try again. Or that Jacob himself wouldn't.

Still, his anger was quenched, at least for the moment, and Steven felt oddly eager to get on with his life again, as though Gail had kept him on hold for months, and he'd finally had the sense to hang up.

The fog rolled sluggishly over the canal, stirred by the rush of the tide. Steven drained the last of his coffee, stood stiffly, and went back into the house. It was a simple frame bungalow, built in the twenties, with four rooms downstairs. The attic they'd converted into a large bedroom, adding dormers and a couple of skylights.

The front door opened directly into the living room; to the left was Gail's stripped study. Behind the living room was the kitchen, with a spare room off it to the left where their guests used to stay when anyone could still stand to visit the two of them.

The bathroom stood between Gail's old study and the guest room and opened into both. Gingerly Steven eased off his robe, let it drop, then raised his left arm and studied his side in the mirror. From his armpit nearly to his waist his flesh was an angry purple, with one darker bar in the middle where the daggerboard had struck.

He lowered his arm, studied himself. Gail was right—he had changed, and until now he hadn't really paid much attention to it. He'd turn forty in three months, and looked better than he had at thirty. His daily swims had slimmed his waist, built up his chest and shoulders, and left him deeply tanned. He'd let his hair grow out over the summer, and it was so sun-bleached that his few strands of gray didn't show.

There could have been worse times, he supposed, for his wife to be leaving him. Steven shook out another Demerol. Hoping to blunt his pain's edge without yesterday's muzzy-headedness, he broke the pill in half.

Half an hour later, showered and shaved, he knotted a red-and-blue striped tie, all the while swearing at the stiffness in his side, then buttoned his collar buttons. Sitting at the kitchen table, Steven opened the yellow pages and surveyed the list of lawyers. Some names he recognized from Gail's conversations, but most were strangers to him. He'd never needed much legal advice. Picking an ad at random, he dialed. None of the first five lawyers he reached would see him that morning. The sixth claimed to be a friend of Gail's. Finally he located a guy who agreed to meet him at eleven. While Steven realized he probably didn't want any lawyer who was so slack he could see him at such short notice, time and life were wasting.

Mid-morning, Steven drove down Pilottown Road to the traffic light at Savannah Road. The fog seemed even more dense, and a solid stream of headlight-blazing traffic had congealed in the center of town as carloads of vacationers searched for an alternative to the beach. Edging into a small break, he turned west, then took a series of back roads and shortcuts that circled well wide of the high school and most of the traffic. His efforts were for naught, though, because the traffic light at Highway One was stuck on red. It took Steven ten minutes to work his way up the waiting line and fight across the four solid lanes of cars, trucks, and campers heading north; he spent another couple of minutes waiting in the median strip for a gap in the southbound flow, wishing he had with him the genuises in state government who'd begun a new highway upstate. That one promised to funnel even more traffic around Dover and down the peninsula, robbing these small towns of what little grace and open space was left. He spotted a tiny opening in front of an oncoming Winnebago, and with a quick prayer to the gods of brake maintenance, he pulled out and floored it. The Jeep shuddered, making more noise than speed, and the giant W on the front of the motor home filled his rearview mirror, then receded.

The highway offered a twenty-mile strip of vacation delights: motels, factory outlets, strip malls, fast food joints, water slides, miniature golf kingdoms, mobile home sales lots, roadside crab-shrimp-vegetable stands, and eight-screen cinemas. The few forlorn remnants of farmland still sandwiched in between were weedgrown and subdued by ranks of survey stakes topped with streamers of orange tape.

Once entered, the traffic moved quickly, and Steven pulled into the right strip mall with a few minutes to spare. The lawyer's office was wedged between a health club named The Firm and a linen outlet advertising towels by the pound. Steven was sure there'd been a bakery in this slot not too long ago, but the gold lettering on the plate glass said DEFLAVIS & ROTHSTEIN, ATTORNEYS AT LAW. Before he could reconsider his next step, he eased himself down from the Jeep and entered the office.

White-walled and sea green-carpeted, the space had undergone substantial renovation since its last incarnation. The small reception area was nearly filled by a desk and computer workstation; though the room was empty, the computer screen glowed with text that Steven couldn't quite make out.

"Hello," he called out. The silent air smelled faintly of doughnuts. One low-slung teak and leather armchair squatted between the desk and a dusty rubber tree. Steven eyed the old *People* magazines stacked on the chair and figured that, if nothing else, this guy should at least be in the right price range.

He called out again, and one of the two doors behind the desk opened wide enough for a young woman to squeeze through. She looked vaguely familiar to Steven—probably a student at the high school a few years ago—but all he said was, "Steven Blake. I've got an eleven o'clock with Barry DeFlavis."

She made a show of glancing at her desk calendar, then buzzed DeFlavis on the telephone, and finally ushered Steven into the inner sanctum, back where the ovens had once stood.

The attorney sat behind his desk, both hands palm down on his blotter, and watched Steven walk toward him. Bald as bone and in his early fifties, DeFlavis looked very Italian and very morose. He shook Steven's hand, then waved him to one of the armless low-backed chairs that faced his desk.

"Thanks for seeing me on short notice," Steven said.

DeFlavis shrugged. "I recognized your name," he said. "You're the guy who married Gail Moncure a few years back, aren't you?"

"Yeah," Steven said. "Why'd that make you willing to see me?"

"Just curious. I wanted to meet the guy who made her dump Jacob Wood."

"That's not quite how it worked," Steven said. "Gail pretty well makes up her own mind about what she's going to do."

"I know," DeFlavis said. "She's a tough lady. Good attorney."

"So I hear," Steven said. "How well do you know her?"

"Some. I only brought her up because I'm curious why you need me when you're married to one of the sharpest lawyers in the county."

"Because I've got a whole set of problems, and I can't use Gail on any of them. I've got a fight to keep my job, I'm probably facing a divorce, and I need to keep Jacob Wood and his son away from me."

"You're a busy guy," DeFlavis said, and he opened his desk drawer and removed a microcassette recorder, mumbled the date and Steven's name into it, and set it on his desk top. He leaned far back in his chair and stared at the ceiling for a moment as though to gather his thoughts. Then he lowered his gaze to Steven again, picked up a pen, and said, "Tell me about it."

Steven launched into the sad, surprising tale of Lisa's accusations, the astonishment and sweating panic of the meeting two days earlier at the school, then Gail's decampment, on down to the previous day's literal run-in with the Wood family. DeFlavis asked sharp questions, forcing Steven to back up several times and go over portions of his story, until they finally reached Steven's brief conversations with the girl in the ambulance and the emergency room.

"Lisa said her father forced her to say I screwed around with her. Claimed she had something to show me that would explain it."

"I'll bet she's got something to show you," DeFlavis said. "My advice to you is to run in the opposite direction if you even see that girl looking at you again." He flipped back through his notes, stopping to reread sections several times. "You have any way of proving you didn't fool around with this kid?"

"She admitted it yesterday at the hospital," Steven said.

"Anybody else hear her say it?"

"An orderly. Maybe."

DeFlavis grunted noncommittally and continued to study his notes. The silence stretched on.

"What do you think?" Steven finally asked.

DeFlavis gave him a long, measuring stare. "I think you should have talked to somebody about this before you went into that meeting at the school."

"You think I can keep my job?"

"Even if you could, you really want to teach there after all this? You thought about what that would be like?"

"I guess I have."

"Your wife's right about one thing. The accusation sticks, whether it's true or not. Unless the girl admits she lied, you wouldn't have a chance."

"I think she'll admit it," Steven said.

"Don't hold your breath," DeFlavis said. "Forget the job. They already hired somebody to replace you. I drive past the high school every afternoon, and the marching band's been out there practicing all week. You might have a lawsuit, though."

Caught unprepared by the reminder of Randy Wise out there working the kids in the afternoon sun, Steven took a few seconds to catch up with the lawyer. "He's not permanent. Who am I going to sue?"

"The boy. And his father," DeFlavis said. "Especially if we can prove he hit you on purpose. How bad are you hurt?"

"I don't know about that," Steven said slowly. "Those kids have got enough trouble already, I think."

"So do you." DeFlavis's blunt tone jarred Steven. "Seems to me like you're losing your job and you're getting divorced. Can you afford both?"

Steven studied the carpet between his toes and the desk. He and Gail had kept separate bank accounts the entire time they'd been married; he'd never even known how much money she had, though he knew it was substantial. His means were meager, based totally on his teacher's salary, the rent from the cottage, and what little he made playing weekends at the Lamplighter. All he had beyond his retirement account was several thousand stashed away as an emergency fund. There would be no income from the cottage as long as Gail was living there, and his Lamplighter gig ended Labor Day weekend. "Probably not," he admitted, and looked back up at DeFlavis. "What's it going to cost me?"

"For what?" DeFlavis asked. "A lawsuit, divorce, or the job?"

"The job, first, then divorce, I suppose."

DeFlavis contemplated him. "The job, I'm not sure—I'll need to think about it, and make a few calls, if you don't mind. On the divorce, are you sure that's the route you want to go? No chance of reconciliation?"

"I'm sure," Steven said. "It's over."

"You sound pretty positive of that."

"Gail's leaving town. I won't be going with her."

"She's giving up her practice here?"

"Apparently," Steven said. "You haven't heard anything about it?"

"Not a word, but it doesn't surprise me. She'd been pretty successful here until a lot of her business dried up . . . " He hesitated, then finished lamely, "the last few years."

"After she married me," Steven said.

DeFlavis nodded. "Jacob Wood throws a lot of weight," he said. "And holds a grudge."

"Does that mean you're not willing to represent me against the school? That's his fight, you know."

"Oh no, I look forward to it. Will Gail represent herself?"

Steven nodded.

"Have the two of you talked about property, joint savings, cars, boats, everything?"

"There's not much that's worth anything," Steven said. "The houses belonged to my father."

"They'll be enough. You'll need to fight her," DeFlavis said. "Believe me."

Steven wasn't ready yet to buy into the lawyer's cynicism. He spread his hands. "I doubt she'll be greedy. And I'm not sure what I'll do if she is."

DeFlavis nodded once, curtly, then stood for the first time. He was taller than Steven had thought, probably six-five, and very thin. DeFlavis extended his hand. "I'll make some calls on the school business, try to get a feel for where things stand."

"What about money?" Steven said. "How much do you need up front?"

DeFlavis named a retainer that would account for about half of Steven's savings.

"And what do you think about the Woods?"

"Have you had any previous run-ins with Jacob? I heard he was pretty upset about the divorce."

Steven shook his head. "He didn't fight her on it, and I've never really heard from him until yesterday. I guess Gail has, from what she's telling me now, but I don't know anything about that."

"Hard to believe he'd start stirring up trouble after all this time, then. If you're really worried about him or his son, call the police," DeFlavis said. "Wood will back off at the first hint of trouble like that."

"I doubt it," Steven said. "He doesn't seem like the kind of guy who backs down from much."

"If he doesn't, then we'll slap an injunction on them. And get some kind of suit in the works."

Steven made his exit, carrying away the scent of old doughnuts in his clothes, and rejoined the lunchtime throngs now clogging the highway. The fog had thinned to a high haze, but no one seemed to have returned to the beach.

He took the Lewes cutoff. To his right were six hundred acres of flat fields, lush with soybeans and stretching from the highway to the line of trees that marked the canal and the borders of the state park. These acres had been sold to a housing developer in July.

The high school loomed on his left, and Steven slowed, then pulled onto the right shoulder, and stared across the road. From the practice field behind the school wafted the sharp snap of a snare drum, the boomity-thump of a tenor drum, a few fart-like notes from a sousaphone, and he stepped on the gas.

Those innocent sounds, the endless streams of cars and ranks of survey stakes, DeFlavis's cynicism, Gail's lack of faith and deliberate fade from his life, and the reviving pain in his ribs all converged in an overwhelming sense of loss and dread of the losses yet to come, and once again, as he had after Thompson first visited him at band practice, Steven contemplated cutting and running, just making himself gone. There was nothing here for him now.

But what was there anywhere else? Where could he go? The whole coast was too crowded, all the way down and around to the Gulf Coast of Florida, where his mother lived. Maybe the Northwest. Seattle. He'd never been there.

He sped home, to his dim cave of closed windows and blinds lowered to bar the heat. Muzzy-headedness or not, he needed a full dose of painkiller. For an hour he lay on his couch, buzzed on the drug, until his aching side and mind both eased enough to let him think again.

He couldn't afford to miss the gig that night. Grunting with the effort, he pushed himself up from the couch, stumbled dizzily across the living room, and slid his tenor case out from between the piano and the living room wall. He lay the case across the piano bench, and pulled the horn from the worn plush lining. A 1935 Selmer Balanced Action tenor sax, this had been his main instrument since he was a teenager. The bell was dented, the lacquer worn away to dull brass where his hands rubbed and rested. The key rods had been stretched and swaged so many times they couldn't be done again and rattled loosely with each shake of the horn, and still this sax sounded like no other to him. He'd played it so long its voice was his own.

He assembled reed to mouthpiece, mouthpiece to neck, neck to body, horn to neck strap. His hands fit the keys the way bird wings fit air, and he breathed out a few low, hoarse, smoky notes, testing his ribs.

The pain was workable, and he adjusted his neck strap to take a little more of the horn's weight and eased into a slow version of " 'Round Midnight." The Steinway's strings picked up the horn's song in sympathetic vibration, thickening the notes, stretching the tune to a legato moan. The dark, old Selmer and the gleaming black upright sometimes seemed like living beings to Steven, locked in a conversation for which he provided only breath, not voice. He'd sometimes stand in his living room and play the horn for hours with the piano backing him up on its own, notes piling on notes, until the whole small house hummed along, floorboards and windows and walls all vibrating with song.

The song faded into the piano's hum, and a tapping came at his front door. Carefully Steven lay the tenor in its open case, then opened his door.

Lisa stood on his porch, hand raised to knock again on the curtained glass, and he and she each took a wary step backward. Steven knew he should close the door and lock it, as DeFlavis had directed, but he also knew that his best hope of clearing his name rested in his own efforts. The girl was caught, too, in something Steven and Gail had begun with her father, and deserved at least a hearing.

"I waited until you were done," she said.

Steven glanced beyond her to her car, a black Mustang with a sailboard and mast on a roof rack. "Your brother with you today?"

She shook her head nervously. Clad in jeans and a sleeveless white blouse, she looked younger and less sure of herself than she had yesterday. Her right cheek bore a fresh bruise, and under her right arm she carried a mustard-colored cardboard shipping tube with metal end caps.

Steven stepped back and opened his door wide. "Come in," he said.

Without hesitation, she swept past him, paused for a moment in the center of his living room, and went immediately to his piano. She laid the shipping tube on the floor, then stood and touched the keys lightly, listened to a few soft chords, and turned back with the first smile he'd seen from her in months. "This is it," she said. "I finally got to see it."

"That's it," he said. Steinway hadn't made many upright baby grands. This and the tenor were the only two possessions Steven ever bragged about, and his students had probably heard too much about both over the years. "I had to brace the floor before I moved it in," he said.

Lost for the moment, Lisa stood over the keyboard and played an aimless, wispy scrap of a song Steven didn't know. He moved his tenor and its case from the bench, then nudged the bench up behind her knees, and she sank down, still playing. Steven sat in the armchair off to the side so he could watch her rapt face.

Lisa had been his rarest student—one with a genuine love and feel for music. She'd had piano lessons since the age of five, could play most of the woodwinds well, sang a fine alto. More importantly, she was on her way to her own musical voice already, could immerse herself in a song and come out with an interpretation distinctively her own. She had the talent and looks and appeal to succeed as anything from cabaret singer to concert pianist to star performer in her own heavy metal band. The only thing she lacked was the discipline that could bring her focus, and that showed now in the way she skipped from one fragment of song to another, breaking off one melody and segueing into another within sixteen, eight, even four bars, faster than Steven could follow.

Eyes half closed, she swayed and smiled, so delighted with the sound of the Steinway that Steven didn't have the heart to stop her.

As she played, he tried imagining Lisa as the daughter he and Gail might have had. This was how he pictured her—lively, lovely, sharp. He shook away the image and the sadness that came with it. After another moment, Lisa grew aware of his scrutiny and stopped playing. She turned halfway toward him, long hands in her lap, bashful now.

"I'm sorry," she said. "It's lovely."

"Thanks. It's out of tune right now."

"I know," she said. "Mine never stays in tune in hot weather for long either."

Steven stared at her, trying to decide how to proceed, and settled on an indirect approach. "Are you going to tell me yet why you decided not to try for music school? You going somewhere else this fall?"

"I don't know." This was the only answer she'd given him last winter when he'd pressed the same question with her; his disappointment had been closer to the surface then, though. She added, "My dad says I'm not ready to go away on my own yet. Maybe next year."

"You could have gone anywhere," Steven said. "I could probably even help you get a late admission at the university now."

Lisa shrugged, dispirited, defeated. "It wouldn't do any good. My dad's not going to let me, and I don't have any money."

"You need to go away, Lisa," Steven said gently. "There are ways I could help you."

She shook her head and repeated, "It wouldn't do any good, Mr. Blake."

"What happened to your face?" he asked. "How'd you get that bruise?"

Lisa licked her lips, and glanced involuntarily at the tube she'd left on the floor next to the piano. "I fell off my board this morning and hit my mast on the way down," she said.

"You sail a lot in the fog? There wasn't any wind this morning."

Lisa turned suddenly back to the keyboard. "Play a song with me," she said. "Let's play 'Summertime.'" She launched into the first chords, and Steven strode over and lifted the shipping tube. It was heavier than he'd expected. He held it without opening it until Lisa slowly stopped playing.

"No more games now," Steven said, quietly but firmly. "What's this all about?"

She rested for a moment with both hands in her lap, then took a deep breath, stood, and took the tube from his hands. She pried out one of the end caps, then shook out a tightly furled roll of paper.

Kneeling on the carpet, she unrolled the papers, gesturing for Steven to hold down one end. The top sheet was an artist's rendering on blueprint paper of a long row of buildings—all angles and oddly shaped windows and cedar shingles, they were exactly the kind of condo development Jacob Wood typically built. The title block in the lower right corner said WOOD'S LANDING.

"Let the top sheet go," Lisa said. "Look at the second one."

The second sheet offered an aerial perspective, and as Steven studied it his anger rose. The plans covered four solid blocks of Pilottown Road. None of the familiar landmarks showed, and it took Steven a moment to identify the cross streets. The condos stretched from down below where Van Dusen used to live nearly up to Fisher's Paradise, the largest and oldest house on the road.

"My houses are right in the goddamned middle of this," he said. He let the second sheet go, and like a sprung window shade, it rolled up to join the first.

The third sheet showed the Lewes Canal. The quiet waterway, now dotted with small private docks, was widened and laid out as a full-blown marina, offering dockage for a couple of hundred boats.

"He'll never get this through," Steven said. "They'll never give him the permits, for one thing."

"I guess your property is one of the last ones he hasn't bought," Lisa said, "and it's kind of right in the middle of things."

"I haven't heard a thing about this. He hasn't even asked me if I wanted to sell it."

"He says he knew you wouldn't."

"How could he know that?"

"He just said people told him."

Steven studied her skeptically. "Are you sure about this, Lisa? None of the neighbors have said anything, nobody in town has mentioned anything."

"Daddy's a very sneaky man," Lisa said. "I've heard him talking about this for a long time, and I think he's been buying houses along here ever since him and Gail got divorced. And he can usually do anything he wants to."

Letting the last sheet furl to its mates, Steven reached out and gently touched her bruised cheek with his fingertips. Wide-eyed, Lisa didn't flinch at his touch.

"Did he do this?"

She stared at him, gave a barely perceptible nod, and he lowered his hand and looked at the rolled blueprints.

"How did you get these?"

"From his office at home," Lisa said. "He'll kill me if he finds out I took them, Mr. Blake. He doesn't even know that I know anything about this whole thing."

"I won't tell him. I just can't believe he'd go to this length to get even with me."

"It's a big game for him. My father does things like that."

"How'd he make you lie about me?"

Lisa stood. Arms clasped in front of herself, she paced the length of the room, then back, and sat on the couch. "Did Gail tell you about when my mom was killed? They said she was drunk and passed out with a lit cigarette in her hand."

Steven nodded.

"My mother never had more than one drink, that I ever saw."

Steven took a deep breath. "What are you saying, Lisa?"

She batted away tears. "I know my father made the fire happen, Mr. Blake. I don't know how, but he made it happen."

"What do the police think?" Steven said quietly.

"The police think what he wants them to think—that she was some drunk who passed out and killed herself. I told you, he does whatever he wants to do, and he was probably just tired of paying alimony to her."

Steven felt out of his depth, and wished he'd had the foresight to stop and buy a small tape recorder after his meeting with DeFlavis. "Have you talked to anyone else about this?"

"Todd and I talk about it all the time," she said. "He's such a gutless wonder that he'll never do anything to get himself in trouble with my dad, though."

Unrolling the plans again, Steven studied the aerial view. He counted the units in the first block, then estimated the development included more than two hundred condos. Docking rights would certainly be sold separately. Figuring conservatively, the project was worth tens of millions, maybe even a hundred million. To his knowledge, Wood had never undertaken anything this large, but as revenge it was inspired—Jacob would make a financial killing at the same time he forced Gail from town, Steven from his job, and Gail and Steven from each other.

"Will you tell some other people about this for me?" Steven asked gently. "Will you help me?"

"I can't," she whispered. "I'm afraid of him."

"You weren't too afraid to come tell me. There are people who can help you." Steven wished he could believe that.

Lisa gave a dubious, mirthless laugh. She stood. "You keep the plans, Mr. Blake, and show them to whoever you think can help. Just don't let my dad know you've got them."

Steven stood, too, and touched her shoulder. "Lisa, go to the police with me right now. All they have to do is get one look at that bruise, and they'll talk to your father. We'll find someplace safe for you to stay."

Immediately she shook her head. "I can't leave Todd there. My dad would be so pissed he'd kill him." She stretched up on tiptoe and kissed Steven on the cheek. "Don't be too mad at Todd for yesterday," she said. "He's really afraid of Dad, and he thinks you really slept with me. So does my dad."

Steven blinked in surprise.

"I had to make them think that," she went on, "because that's what my dad told me to do in the first place."

"Your father *told* you to sleep with me?" Steven said.

Lisa nodded. "And you know what? Even if he hadn't told me to, I probably would have if I could have. But I knew you never would."

"You were right," he said. "Has your father forced you to do this with anyone else?"

She stepped back, and her glance was wary. "Who said that?"

"No one," he said. "I'm just guessing this isn't the first time you've been through this."

She shook her head, fear in her eyes, and turned and left before Steven could stop her or even reply. From his porch he watched worriedly as her black Mustang, sporting a Delaware vanity plate reading WNDSRF, rolled out of sight. She'd probably put herself at considerable risk by bringing him the drawings, but short of abducting her, there was no way to get her to the police.

Inside, he glanced at each of the sheets again, still not believing Jacob could let obsession carry him this far. He rolled the plans up, stuffed them back into the shipping tube, and dialed Gail's office. A new temp answered, and told him that Gail was in a meeting and couldn't be interrupted. Immediately he tried Van Dusen's number.

"How you doing?" Jimmy asked. "Ribs still hurt?"

"Yeah, some," Steven said. "Listen, Jimmy, I've got a question for you. Who'd you sell your house to?"

"An Italian family from South Philly," Jimmy said immediately. "The guy owns a couple of delis. How come? Is he making trouble?"

"No, nothing like that," Steven said. "Are you sure he bought it? He wasn't buying it for anybody else?"

"Sure. He and his family used it all this summer," Van Dusen said. "There was a blue Caddie with Pennsylvania tags there every time I drove past. It was there the other day, when you got so shit-faced. What's going on?"

Steven told him about the drawings of Wood's Landing.

Van Dusen was silent for a moment, then asked, "Where'd you get those? Gail?"

"No, somebody left them on my front porch while I was out this morning."

"Sounds pretty fishy to me," Van Dusen said. "Wood didn't have anything at all to do with selling my house. Didn't represent me, didn't bring the buyer."

"Have you heard about him buying any other houses here? Anything at all about this project?"

"Nope," Van Dusen said, "but it sounds like something he'd like to get his mitts into. The queen of real estate say anything about it?"

"I haven't been able to get hold of her yet," Steven said. "She's tied up at work."

Jimmy hesitated, then said, "Even if you two aren't speaking, you better ask her about this one, buddy."

Steven thought quickly. "You think she already knows about it?"

"Maybe," Van Dusen said. "If it's true he's got this project, maybe you should think long and hard about just selling to him. Could be your easiest way out of a lot of things."

"I don't have to think about it. He couldn't afford it."

Jimmy changed the subject, pressing Steven yet again to book a fishing day with him. Steven agreed to the following Tuesday and hung up.

He wished he knew how these plans fit with Gail and her recent urgency to leave town, whether she was anxious to save herself, save them both, or help her ex-husband. None of the choices were particularly appealing, but he suddenly had to know.

He checked the driveway, hoping she might have come in without his hearing her, but his Jeep stood alone. Grabbing the plans, he left and fought his way back through the Lewes traffic again, out to the highway, then south to Rehoboth. Near the center of that town stood a two-story Victorian that housed the offices of Gail and her two partners. The red BMW was parallel-parked in front. Steven pulled in at the curb behind it and marched inside, plans in hand.

The temp glanced up from a paperback romance. Steven hadn't

set foot in Gail's office in at least six months, and had no idea who she was.

"Hi," he said. "Steven Blake, here to see Gail."

"Do you have an appointment?"

"I'm her husband," he said. "At least for a little while longer."

"Have a seat," she said. "She's got somebody with her now, but I'll buzz her and let her know you're here."

The reception area was unchanged—same magazines, same dusty plants, same tired sofa and chairs. Steven sat. Half an hour later he was still waiting. Fuming, he asked the receptionist to buzz Gail again. Just as she lifted the phone, though, several sets of footsteps thumped down the stairs, and a couple in their late twenties appeared, followed by Gail. They were chattering about a closing date.

She didn't see him, and spoke lowly to the temp, who pointed at Steven. Gail turned then, and an expression of such ambivalent hope, frustration, and annoyance flickered across her face that Steven forgot his words.

"Hi," he managed. "How are you?"

"I'm fine," she said guardedly. "Since yesterday."

"I wanted to talk to you."

"Can it wait until tonight? I'm busy this afternoon."

"It won't take long," he said.

Gail waited, as though expecting some further explanation, then turned and led him upstairs to her office. As the junior and, no doubt, lowest contributing partner in this small firm, she rated what had formerly been the smallest of the bedrooms in the house. In the best of times the room was barely large enough for her desk, computer workstation, and bookshelves. Today half the available floor space was filled with cardboard boxes, and few of her law books remained on the shelves. Two wooden sidechairs faced the desk. Steven took one of these, and Gail sat behind her paper-cluttered desk.

"Well," she said. "Is this about yesterday?"

"No, I'd like to talk about that later. What do you know about any big real estate projects planned for Pilottown Road?"

He scrutinized her face, trying to read her reaction, but her words were cool and neutral. "There aren't any. Nobody could get all the permits."

"Not even Jacob?" He stood, and watching her reaction the entire time, unrolled the plans across her desk. It took her a good thirty seconds of scanning the plans and flipping from one page to the next before her eyes widened and her lips tightened, and Steven began to relax. By the time she looked up, he felt they might be on the same side in at least this.

"Where did these come from?" she said.

"Someone left them on the front porch while I was out this morning," Steven said. He'd always lied badly, and knew Gail didn't believe him, but he wasn't prepared to give Lisa up yet.

Gail studied him, decided not to press it, and turned back to the plans. She lifted the first page, then the second. She dropped them both, and gazed for a long minute at the top sheet, which showed the row of condos from the front.

"Have you seen these before?" he asked.

Gail glanced quickly up at him, then back at the drawings. "Where would I have seen them?"

Steven resisted the temptation to voice his suspicions about her and Jacob. "Gail, tell me whether this project is real."

"It looks to me like one of Jacob's pipe dreams." She rolled the plans up and handed them across the desk, then glanced over his shoulder. Steven followed her glance, and found a desk clock at eye level on a bookshelf.

"I've got an appointment," she said. "I'll find out about these plans, though."

"How?"

"Make some calls."

"Would Jacob go to this extent to get back at us?"

"If he could also make another small fortune at the same time? What do you think, Steven?"

"Has he been trying to shut down your practice?"

"Who told you that?"

"Not you," Steven said; he was unwilling to tell her he'd already talked to another attorney because the act seemed to put a period to all their conversations. "Why didn't you tell me about it?"

Gail sighed deeply. "Steven, that question is pointless. We've agreed to go our own ways, and there's no point in rehashing all the ways we've both screwed up over the past four years. I should have talked to you, you should have talked to me, maybe neither of us ever should have talked to the other. I don't know. I'm sorry this is happening to you, and I'll see what I can do to make sure that project isn't real and can't go ahead. It won't be much, but I'll try. Okay?"

"I didn't come here asking you to bail me out of anything, Gail. I just wanted to know if you thought it was real."

"No, you wanted to know if I'd seen those plans before and if I've cooked up some scheme with Jacob to force you out of your property. You're easy to read, Steven. Don't you think my marrying you and living with you for four years would have been pretty extreme measures to go to just to help Jacob make more money he doesn't need?"

"*Have* you seen them?" he pressed, needing a definitive answer whatever the ultimate cost.

"Never," she said.

For a moment they faced each other across the desk, each waiting for the other to make some move. Steven finally stuffed the plans back into their tube, slapped the metal end cap home. "I'm playing at the Lamplighter tonight. Why don't you come over?"

"And do what?" she said. "Watch you play the way I used to and wonder what you could do with all that talent and presence if you really got a chance somewhere big? I've done that, Steven. It doesn't go anywhere."

8

That night's Lamplighter quartet included Steven on tenor, Lester Jones on bass, Marian Jones on organ, and a twenty-one-year-old drummer named Ahmed, one of Lester's Delaware State students who'd joined them the weekend before. He played good, crisp rhythm, but like most young drummers had a tendency to speed up every song. Lester, Marian, and Steven spent all evening digging in their musical heels and dragging the kid back down to a reasonable groove until Lester finally called " 'Cherokee' " midway through the third set, and counted it off at a nearly impossible beat. The three of them had played the tune dozens of times, and by now could spin it out at a speed sure to humble even the cockiest drummer. Tonight Steven had to push to play past the pain in his side, but he refused to be left behind.

Halfway through Steven's first solo chorus, Jacob Wood sauntered into the club, trailed by Lisa and Todd. They sat at a table right center of the small dance floor, and Steven closed his eyes, trying to put them out of mind until he worked his way through the song. He felt a rush of anger far stronger than the jolt of adrenaline he normally rode when a friend or acquaintance walked into his performance. This was his territory, the place where he felt largest and most alive. And he'd only seen Jacob here once before—on the first night he'd also seen Gail.

Steven bumped the tempo up, blew Charlie Parker's original solo note for note, then added three more choruses of his own and handed the tune off to Marian with a final rushing canter of notes ending precisely on the last downbeat.

He stepped back to catch his breath. Lester smiled ever so slightly and nodded, as good as Steven had ever gotten in all his years as the man's student and colleague. Then the bass player's heavy-lidded eyes slid closed again, and he hunched over his string bass, so big the instrument looked almost like a cello in his arms. His long, ebony hands floated, fingertips spatulate from decades of playing, caressing, thumping the heavy strings.

They finished in a joyous sprint, and Steven stepped back by the drum kit to towel the sweat from his face. Ahmed returned his grin, deigning to notice Steven for the first time all evening. The drummer seemed slightly out of breath.

Lester stepped close. "We've had a request for 'Mood Indigo.' You okay on it?"

"Sure," Steven said, although he hadn't played the Ellington tune in three or four years. "Cherokee" had left him cocky. "Who's it for?"

"The man wants it nice and slow." Already counting down, he nodded toward the Woods's table. Steven glanced over. Todd glared back, while Lisa stared down at the table and Jacob lifted his glass in a mocking toast, then turned to speak to his daughter.

Lester, Marian, and Ahmed started up softly, laying down a pensive, flowing intro. Ahmed's brushes pattered like kisses on eyelids, and Lester's bass mused around the soft chords of Marian's organ. Steven watched her, waiting.

Marian was a wiry sprite, bony and nimble, and she swayed on her bench, floating with the rhythm, then looked up and nodded Steven in just when he expected it. He came in sweet and breathy on the melody, his horn as lush and smoky with vibrato as her voice would surely be on the next verse. He turned to play squarely for the small crowd, and saw Jacob Wood standing over his table, Lisa's hand in his. Wood pulled his daughter up toward the dance floor. She resisted, shook her head, tried to pull her hand free. Todd glared fixedly at Steven.

People younger than fifty seldom danced at the Lamplighter, or at least seldom danced sober. Playing along softly behind Marian's voice, filling, embellishing, Steven watched Jacob and Lisa and judged.

The two dancers looked more like gunman and hostage than father and daughter. Lisa moved woodenly, and Jacob held her much too tightly, pushing her around the floor with only the barest accidental acknowledgment of the beat. They spun slowly past the small stage. Lisa's cheeks gleamed with tears.

So angry was Steven that he nearly missed his cue from Marian. He played a short, impatient solo, and handed the song back to her after a single verse, unwilling to prolong Lisa's torment.

The second the song ended, Lisa broke free and walked quickly back to her table, where she grabbed her purse, then bolted for the ladies' room.

Lester announced the break, then turned back and muttered to Steven, "Some weird shit going on there."

"You're right about that," Steven said.

"You know those people? I've never seen 'em before."

"He's Gail's ex. She's his daughter, the kid at the table is her brother. The girl was one of my students. Graduated in June."

"What the hell were they doing out there?"

"I'm about to find out," Steven said. He unhooked his tenor from the neck strap and carefully set it in its stand, working to calm himself.

Lester shook his head, lowered his bass to rest on its side. The constant teacher, he turned to converse quietly with Ahmed, launching into a critique of the drummer's last set.

Steven's anger propelled him from the stage. He was still halfway across the dance floor from Jacob Wood's table when Jacob again lifted his glass in mocking salute.

"Wonderful music, Steven," he said. "I can see now why Gail and my daughter have both been so attracted to you."

Steven stood next to the table. "What do you want?"

"You know, it's funny, but I don't remember you being this good the last time I heard you. Can I buy you a drink?"

"No, you can explain what the hell you're doing here."

Wood's eyebrows arched in mock surprise. "Obviously we came to see how you're feeling. You've made a rapid recovery."

"I'm fine," Steven said. He glanced at Todd, then toward the restrooms to see if Lisa was returning. "Jacob, if you'd like to talk to me, call me at home. Leave the kids out of this—any problems you've got are between the two of us."

"But it's Todd who's got something to say to you." He glanced pointedly at the boy, who turned his surly, blue-eyed gaze on Steven. "Go ahead, son," Wood prompted.

Steven's lipreading skills were weak, so he couldn't tell what the boy said; he could pretty well guess that the boy's thoughts were far from matching his words, though.

"Louder," Wood said. "Nobody could hear that."

"I'm sorry," Todd recited. "I didn't mean to hit you. I'm an idiot for sailing so close to people."

Steven glanced from son to father, and back again. "There's no lawsuit here," he said to both. "Don't worry about it. Just stay away from me."

"Fine," Wood said. His gaze traveled beyond Steven. "Good," he said. "Here's the other one back."

If there had been tears on her face while she was dancing, they didn't show now. Lisa's face was rigid and so pale that the bruise on her cheek seemed livid. She gave Steven a narrow-eyed glare of anger that surprised him with its intensity, then sat between her father and brother.

"Lisa, how are you?" Steven asked. "Are you okay?"

Tight-lipped, she stared down at the chipped tabletop.

"Tell him," Wood said.

Her gaze flickered to her father. She shook her head.

"Tell me what?" Steven asked.

Wood sipped his white wine. He smiled tightly, but his eyes revealed his real fury. "I believe you've got something of ours," he said. "Some property I'd like you to return."

Steven glanced at Lisa in alarm, understanding the cause of her anger—she thought he'd betrayed her by calling her father and confronting him over the plans.

"What are you talking about?" he said.

"Let's not fence, Mr. Blake. You have some drawings of ours, and I want them back."

"I've got nothing that belongs to you," Steven said. He still stood over the table. Neither Lisa nor her brother would look up. Steven realized that people at several of the surrounding tables were watching them, and he suddenly wondered how many of them had already heard about his troubles at the high school, and the reasons behind them. More than a few, he suspected, given the small-town network that still thrived beneath the throngs of summer. He was struck at Wood's gall in coming into this place with the daughter Steven had supposedly been involved with, and wondered exactly what kind of confrontation Jacob was hoping to stage. He leaned over the table and said, too low for the hearing of anyone but Jacob and his children, "Who do you think you are to come in here where I'm working and act like this?"

Wood eyed him, then said quite loudly, "I'm someone who's had something stolen, and I'm requesting that you return it. To my office. Tomorrow morning."

His command was as peremptory as Thompson's had been a few evenings before, when the principal had ordered Steven to his office the next morning, and Steven wondered again at the connection between the two. "I haven't stolen anything from anybody," he said.

"They're numbered, you know. Did you notice that?"

Steven slid the fourth chair out from the table and sat. Leaning forward on his elbows, he studied Wood, wondering how the man had discovered the missing plans so quickly. "If you wanted to buy my house, why didn't you just make an offer?"

"If I'd ever had any interest in buying those little dumps, I would have," Wood replied.

"But you want me out of there, and you want the land they're on."

"Those are concept drawings, Mr. Blake. I had those done several years ago for some feasibility studies. After they were done, we decided it would be too expensive and time-consuming to get the permits we'd need."

"Then why all the pressure to get them back?"

"I like to keep track of what's mine," Wood said. "Those drawings could stir up a lot of pointless aggravation."

"Maybe that's a good reason for me to hang on to them," Steven said. "Pointless aggravation is the least of what you've caused me."

"You've caused all your own problems," Wood said calmly. "Mostly by your inability to keep your hands off other people's wives and teenaged daughters."

Lisa suddenly pushed back her chair. For a moment she glared at her father, then turned to Steven. Tears filled her eyes. "Why can't you all just stop it?" Her voice rose with each word.

Standing quickly, she knocked her chair to the floor, spun away, and wove between the nearby tables. After a moment, Todd rose and followed her out the exit. Steven watched them both go, then turned to their father once again.

"Jacob, you've carried this whole business far enough," he said, voice as low and tight as he could keep it. "Gail's gone. Let it go."

"I haven't even started," Wood said. He grinned, then gestured Steven back toward the stage with a wide, dramatic sweep of his arm. "But for now, I'll defer to your eager public. Play on, please."

On the long walk back to the stage, Steven felt the eyes of half the lounge piercing his back. Lester eyed him quizzically.

"I'll tell you after," Steven said, picking up his tenor. "What's the tune?"

" 'Tunisia,' " Lester said, and after a glance at Ahmed and Marian he snapped his fingers to count it down.

Jacob Wood stayed through most of the last set, alone, cool and unruffled, watching. Steven did his best to ignore him, but his playing was stiff and perfunctory. Midway through " 'Round Midnight," their last song, Wood stood, stretched languidly, dropped a bill on the table, and sauntered out. Steven closed his eyes on the Wood family and let himself ride with the last half of the song.

When the houselights came up, a few people remained in the room, draining their glasses and hanging on to the final strains of the song, and for their benefit and his own Steven tacked on a cadenza, trying to jam an entire evening's frustration and missed notes into one last minute, until he raised the horn in the air and brought the other three players back in for the final chord.

Faint applause pattered through the room. Exhausted, Steven disassembled his tenor, swabbed it out, and laid it to rest, wishing as he did so that someone would tuck him into a padded box as soft and secure as the horn's plush case. He felt tired enough to sleep for a week.

He joined Lester and Marian at their usual table, where they had the usual double Glenlivets waiting. From his trouser pocket he extracted a metal aspirin tin and snapped it open below the table's edge. He palmed a Demerol, planning to wash it down with a stiff swallow of single malt, but stopped himself. He had a feeling he'd better keep his wits as clear as possible for the next few weeks.

"You okay, Stevie?" Marian asked. "You didn't sound like yourself all night."

"Just tired out," he said. "Got a headache. Where's the kid?"

"He doesn't drink," Lester said. "Or smoke, or who knows what else. Just like Wynton."

"There are worse things not to do," Marian said tartly.

"Yeah, well," Lester said. "What was that family business all about, anyway?"

"Good question," Steven sighed. "But the answer's a long story I'd better leave for another time."

Marian shifted in her chair. "That girl's not stirring up some kind of trouble for you, is she?"

Steven stared at her suspiciously. "How'd you hear about that?"

"All somebody had to do was watch all of you."

"What's the scoop?" Lester said.

"She's Gail's former stepdaughter," he said for Marian's benefit. "She was one of my students, too, and now she's claiming she and I were screwing around. Somehow she's got a couple of other kids to back her up. I'm most likely out of a job, even though I didn't do it."

Lester and Marian exchanged a long glance that probably meant something to the two of them, but left Steven feeling even more isolated.

"Anything we can do?" Lester finally asked.

"Nope." Steven leaned back and rubbed his eyes hard with the heels of his palms. The lights glared harshly on the chipped table, and everything in the bar, including him, seemed to be covered with a film of nicotine. "I didn't do it," he said. "No way, no how."

"You didn't have to say that," Lester said.

Steven shook his head. "Tell me something good," he said. "I don't even want to think about anything else tonight."

"Summer's almost over," Lester said. "Only two more weekends here."

"And you'll both start teaching again, and I suppose I'll get fired and find something else to do. I said tell me something good."

"Come on," Marian said. "Tell the man, Lester."

"We've got a leave of absence this year," Lester said. "We're gonna get out on the road and play again. Been a long, long time since we did anything but summer weekends."

Jealousy stirred in Steven. "When? Where are you going to play?"

Lester cleared his throat. "We're talking to a few people about a big band, play some Ellington and so on."

"For Christ's sake," Marian said, "why are you teasing him? He's tired out. Got no time for your nonsense." She turned to Steven. "Have you heard anything about this Smithsonian project they've started, called the Jazz Masterworks Editions?"

Steven shook his head.

"Did you know that out of more than three thousand Duke Ellington songs, there are complete scores for only four? Gunther Schuller and some other people have put together a project to transcribe a lot of that big band stuff. They're doing some Fletcher Henderson and Jimmy Lunceford and Basie and Ellington for the first volume.

"Anyway, Lester and I wrote a grant proposal last year to put together a band to play those transcriptions, go out and perform them, and probably even record them."

"She's the one who did all the work," Lester said. "I never thought we'd get the money."

"Well, we did," Marian said.

Steven looked from Marian to Lester and back, momentarily speechless. Neither of them was given to practical jokes, but this gig seemed too choice to be real. This was, in fact, just the kind of opportunity Gail had been hounding him to seek out for the past four years. They'd have to rehearse for a few months before hitting the road, so he'd have time to clean things up at the high school before quitting. Gail and DeFlavis were right—he wouldn't want to continue working there after all of this, especially not for Thompson. Once the principal was thwarted in this, Steven could expect new attacks on any pretext.

"It's gonna be some serious road time," Lester said. "We just got the official word three days ago, and Marian's already started booking."

"I'm ready. When do rehearsals start? You have the charts with you?"

Lester cleared his throat. "We didn't know you'd be available, actually." He looked awkwardly to Marian for help.

"What Lester means is that we've already talked to some other sax players. We'd rather have you, though."

"My luck," Steven said. "It's sucked all summer. No reason for it to get better, I guess."

"No, no," Lester said. "It doesn't mean you're out. Just means we'll have to come up with some excuses to get you in. Probably have to audition."

"Fine," Steven said. "I'll audition against anybody around. You know that."

"We don't have the charts with us," Marian said. "You sure you want to travel? You need to talk it over with Gail first?"

"That won't be a problem. Practice up at the college?"

"Yeah," Lester said. "It'll be a couple more weeks before we can get in touch with all the people we want to try out, so we'll let you know." Lester unfolded his lanky body from the barroom chair, placed his hands in the small of his back, and stretched up on his toes. His hair nearly brushed the dingy acoustic tiles. "This tired old man better get his ass back to Dover," he said. "You ready, wife?"

"I'm always ready." Marian hugged him round his waist, her head coming only to his breastbone. Steven tried to imagine himself and Gail so settled and natural with each other, but the only image of her he could summon up seemed six feet away and fading fast.

Floating on Scotch, he followed Lester and Marian out into the parking lot, his tenor case so heavy it seemed to stretch his arm. He helped Lester slide the bass into the back of their minivan, and after they'd pulled out he lingered under the buzzing vapor lamps, unwilling to close out the night's music yet.

Clouds of moths and gnats and mosquitoes surrounded the lights, and a steady pulse of traffic drummed past at sixty or better. The night air was a rich, damp haze. A sultry breeze stirred, carrying with it the faint ammoniac scent of the endless chicken farms to the west. Lightning flickered silently behind the strip mall on the other side of Highway One, and though he thought it was probably just heat lightning, he realized he'd left his skylights open, and moved languidly toward his car.

Steven drove home slowly, windows down, Jeep plowing through banks of swirling insects. He pulled into the side street next to his house, swung into his driveway, and stopped with a lurch just inches short of the garage door. The red BMW was conspicuously missing, the cottage dark.

He opened his door, and Patches exploded into the car. She stood in his lap, licking his face, nipping at his earlobes, yelping a long, involved story at him. With some difficulty he pushed her into the passenger seat.

"Who left you out, baby?" She wriggled on the seat, wagging wildly. Gail must have been and gone, Steven thought, and he swore at her carelessness. They'd lost the dog before Patches to a Lewes Dairy truck.

Patches trotted after him as he rounded the back corner of the house, stepped on his heels as he climbed the side porch steps, then rushed past him as soon as he opened the screen door. She streaked through the open kitchen door, and Steven stopped cold. His dark house stood wide open.

He could hear only his own pulse. He called the dog, and she ambled out, licking her chops, and stopped in the middle of the kitchen door. She wagged, and Steven followed her in, flipped on the kitchen light switch, and stepped immediately back out onto the porch. His kitchen looked worse than the high school cafeteria after a major food fight—flour, sugar, ground coffee, milk, orange juice coated everything. The refrigerator lay on its side, door open, empty. The dog trotted around the room, sniffing and sampling. Stunned, Steven could only watch her, until a sudden, stomach-churning thought hit him. He spun and trotted the length of the porch, around the front corner of the house. The front door stood open, and he plunged into the living room. Sheet music and unjacketed records littered the carpet, and he stopped short, clicked on the table lamp near the door.

The Steinway gleamed from the far wall. Steven picked his way across to it, opened the keyboard cover, and tried a quick, rising succession of chords, and sighed with relief at its sweet, untouched voice. Gently he closed the cover and stepped up to the end of the piano. He already knew there'd be nothing between the wall and the piano, in the space where he normally kept his tenor case standing on end, but he peered into the shadowy niche anyway. The drawings in their mustard shipping tube were indeed gone.

For half an hour Steven poked through his small house, sifting the debris, but found nothing else missing. Finally he dialed the Lewes police, and went out and sat on his front steps to wait. A breeze stirred in the hydrangeas that arched over his head, and Steven tried to imagine how he'd ever take this out on Jacob. He was certain this was Wood's doing, either directly, or, more likely, through Todd.

The police station was a scant two miles away, and within seconds a cruiser rolled up and parked, half on his grass and half in the road. A cop climbed out, leaving red and blue lights twirling over the neighborhood, and Steven rose.

"You mind killing the lights?" he called. "You'll have everybody up and over here asking questions."

"Sure, Mr. Blake," the cop said, and the car instantly went dark. The cop strolled up Steven's front walk, into the feeble glow cast by the yellow bug light on the porch. "How ya doin'?" he said.

The voice was familiar, and Steven peered into the shadow beneath the cop's baseball hat. "I've been better," he said cautiously.

"Tommy Langtree," the cop said. "Tenor drums in marching band, timpani in concert band. Graduated six years ago."

"Jesus, I'm sorry," Steven said. "I didn't recognize you in your uniform. Come on in, Tommy."

From room to room they went, the young cop shaking his head in disgust. Steven recognized him in better light—still a skinny kid, blond hair buzz cut, the only different note an incongruously large revolver holstered at his hip.

They halted in the center of the kitchen. Tommy gazed glumly down at his black Corfam oxfords. Their gleam had disappeared beneath layers of mixed food, and a mist of flour surrounded his dark brown trousers up to the knees. Sighing, he pulled a small notebook from his breast pocket.

"Looks like kids to me," he said. "You still teaching at the high school, Mr. Blake?"

"Yeah," Steven said. "I might quit this year, though."

Tommy duly noted this. "Anything missing?"

Steven hesitated, then said, "Nothing. I've checked all over."

Sharp-eyed, Tommy looked at him. "You sure? Most people make something up, just for the insurance."

Steven met the kid's gaze. "I'm sure."

"You have any idea who did this, or why somebody would?"

Steven had plenty of ideas, but none he was ready to share. "None at all," he said.

Tommy glanced around the room, then down at his shoes again. "I'll just take a walk outside the house," he said. Freeing a huge black flashlight from a ring on his belt, he marched out the side door. The screen door slapped behind him. The wall clock, somehow unscathed, showed two-thirty, and Steven went out front to wait for Tommy to complete his circuit. He leaned against the cruiser's front fender.

"Nothing," Tommy said. "*Nada.*"

"Didn't expect there would be," Steven answered.

Tommy leaned through his car's open window and barked something Steven couldn't understand into his radio. The speaker crackled back, and Tommy straightened.

"Well," he said, "we'll keep an eye out." He glanced up at the house. "Mrs. Blake away?"

"Moncure," Steven corrected automatically. "Gail uses her own last name. She didn't do it, Tommy."

The young cop shrugged, unembarrassed. "Gotta ask, you know."

"I guess you do." Steven pushed up from the car. "Anything else?"

"We'll send somebody back tomorrow to talk to the neighbors, see if they heard anything," Tommy said.

"Let me know," Steven replied, and waved him into his car.

The cruiser pulled away and Steven walked halfway back to his house, then turned around and walked away, calling the dog to follow him. Together they crossed Pilottown Road, then walked down the grassy slope to his dock. Steven unfolded a lawn chair that rested against one of the pilings, and sat facing the canal. He breathed in deeply, pulling in the sweet summer air. The breeze had picked up and carried now the smell of salt marsh.

The canal lapped quietly. Fireflies hovered over the phragmites lining the opposite bank. From the west, a thunderstorm rolled in from the Chesapeake Bay, booming its way across the flat Delaware farmland, and he imagined it rattling soybean pods, lashing the broad leaves of the ripening corn, waking the chickens miles inland in their huge commercial coops.

A few fat drops of rain splattered on the dock. In a minute he'd get up and check his boat, make sure the lines and cover were secured for the approaching storm. Tomorrow he'd search out Lisa and try to find out how Wood had known about the plans, and which one of them had done this to him, and try to convince Lisa that he hadn't betrayed her.

The tide was out, the water's surface oily beneath the heavy air. His boat, a nineteen-foot Boston Whaler, bobbed well below the dock, tugging at its lines. He got up, sat on the top of the outermost piling, facing his house, and surveyed Pilottown Road as though he'd never seen it.

This was a quiet road of small houses and cedar-shingled cottages, dead-ending at a wide salt marsh a mile or so north. Most of the places were immaculately kept, and for years they'd been handed down within families. Now, if Lisa could be believed, most of what he saw belonged to Jacob Wood.

His disbelief faded as he looked up and down the row of houses; he realized that most had quietly changed hands over the past four or five years. Taken one at a time, none of the sales had seemed unusual, for prices had escalated to the ridiculous, and many longtime owners in Lewes and Rehoboth had been cashing in.

Sitting where he could see his houses just reminded him of Gail, so he returned to his lawn chair. He tipped his face up, laid his head back on the aluminum crossbar, and looked straight up. Warm rain washed his face, hissed into the canal, water surrounded him, and for a moment he drifted underwater again, weightless, accepting his own drowning, understanding that survival was as accidental as death.

The crashing of the sky surfaced him this time. Monumental thunderheads towered above, piled higher than he could see, lit from within by continuous, overlapping pulses of lightning. The thunder pounded so closely he could feel it on his chest. Beneath his chair the dog cowered, whining and trembling against his leg, and he reached down to comfort her.

And then despite everything, despite the minor mess of his house and the major shambles of his life and the pounding ache in his side, he cast his mind back on the evening just past, when the four of them, Lester, Marian, the young drummer, and he, had plunged into "Cherokee" so much faster than any of them could think, playing strictly on instinct and reflex. It was like a dream, playing like that, where you found you could fly as long as you didn't think about the act but just did it.

The wind pushed against him, his dock creaked as the boat tossed against it, and he smiled up into the rain, grinning like a fool at the unreasonable, unearned, and much too quickly passing beauty of it all.

9

Four days later, on a sunny Tuesday morning, Steven sat in his Boston Whaler and tried to pick out Lisa from the three dozen windsurfers crisscrossing Rehoboth Bay. They all launched from the same reserved beach at the state park, where they could park within twenty feet of the water's edge. He'd anchored upwind, so most crossed his line of vision as they tacked back and forth on fast reaches.

Wearing his long-billed fisherman's cap and a heavy coat of sunscreen, cooler full of sodas and sandwiches, he was set for as long a vigil as necessary. The last four days had been tensely silent—no calls from Thompson, DeFlavis offering no news yet, Gail leaving early and arriving home most nights after Steven had fallen asleep. The only action Steven could think of was to track down Lisa and try to convince her to end all of this. She'd been elusive, though, and three days of driving had failed to produce any sign of her until yesterday, when he'd spotted the black Mustang with its WNDSRF vanity plate parked at the sailing beach. Though he'd waited into evening, when the wind died and the sun became a perfect red circle floating on the glassy bay, she'd never come to shore. He'd hoped she'd been becalmed across the bay and called home for a ride, but today her Mustang occupied exactly the same spot, and he was naggingly worried.

For an hour or so he watched, going over the side twice to cool off in the bay. His VHF crackled on Channel 16, babbling the usual hodgepodge of radio checks and half-clever boat names; he'd gotten so used to the noise that when a loud Mayday cut across the chatter, it took a minute for the words to penetrate. He lowered his binoculars to listen. The boater, nearly hysterical, shouted for help, direction, instructions. CPR wasn't working, he cried, girl was just lying there, and Steven's sense of foreboding mounted. The signal was clear and loud, meaning close. Raising his glasses, he scanned the surrounding waters methodically until he spotted the waving arms of a boater in distress a mile or so to the south.

He jammed the Whaler's throttle wide open and wove between

the sailboards, remembering at the last second to cut wide of the sandbar near the sailors' beach. At least four other boats converged on the reporting boat before Steven got there. Though it took all of his remaining patience, he cut his speed a hundred yards short so he wouldn't jostle them with his bow wave. He edged closer, nudged his way between two other boats, trying desperately to peer over the first boat's gunwales.

Finally he bumped gently into the boat that had summoned help; it was a tan fiberglass Mako, an open fishing boat much like his Whaler. Eight or ten people were on board. Most of them clustered in the bow, looking down. Steven held to the Mako's gunwales, trying to see through the crowd. He saw flashes of movement and heard the rhythmic smack of flesh against flesh.

"Please move," he shouted. With scarcely a glance at him, the two men blocking his view parted.

He recognized her wet suit first, the black and hot pink outfit she'd worn the day Todd ran him down, the one her father had slowly zipped up for her in the emergency room. A knot of anguish clenched deep in Steven's chest, and he clambered from his Whaler into the Mako. Behind him, someone shouted as his boat drifted away, but he wedged his way through the circle of onlookers without looking back.

Two men knelt next to her, one bending his mouth to hers, the other pounding a hopeful cadence on her chest. As Steven watched, one man rocked back on his heels and stared at the other until he also stopped.

She looked as if her tan had been bleached away. Beneath her half-opened eyelids showed crescents of dull white. Dark curls matted her forehead, and her lips were puffy and cyanotic. Silence smothered the boat. Even the lap of water against the fiberglass hull seemed muffled. Steven glanced around; perhaps fifteen people stood on the Mako now, and the boat rode low in the water. At least a dozen boats milled around them, passengers craning to see. From the south came the wail of a siren and the roar of a large boat motor running flat out from the Indian River Inlet Coast Guard station.

The two men still knelt next to the girl.

"Don't stop," Steven said. "Keep trying."

The man who'd tried to force his breath into her lungs looked up at Steven, squinting against the sunlight. He had a short, dark beard flecked with gray and wore a gold chain around his neck. "It's no good," he said. "She's gone."

"But I know her." Steven knew the stupidity of these words even as he spoke them, but he repeated them anyway. "I know her."

The bearded man bowed his head. After a moment he said quietly, "Then you'd better call her family. What's her name?"

"Lisa Wood," Steven said. Lisa's mouth gaped open, and Steven knelt next to her and touched her cheek. It felt like clay, cool to the touch. He tried to close her mouth and eyelids. "Do you have something I can cover her with?"

A couple of beach towels appeared, and Steven draped them over the girl's body. After a moment's hesitation, he pulled one up to shield her cold face from the encircling crowd.

The overloaded Mako wallowed in the wash of the arriving police boat, and Steven stood. The next minutes were a confusion of loud voices and milling boats as the crowd cleared away, back to their own boats. Steven identified Lisa for the Coast Guard and the resort police, and left it to them to call Jacob.

Finally he swam back to his Whaler, fifty yards to where a couple in a small Grumman runabout had latched onto one of his lines. Drifting free, Steven watched while a strapped stretcher holding Lisa's body was passed from the Mako to the Coast Guard launch. Then, trailing a rooster tail of spray, the launch headed north, up toward Dewey Beach.

One by one the other boaters started their engines, and the group dispersed. Each motored away slowly, subdued, until they'd all scattered around the bay and the only one Steven could identify was the speck carrying Lisa's body.

He should have followed, he knew; he owed her the trip after the way she'd stayed by him at the hospital last week. No, even more than that—she'd been the one who'd brought him up for air, and he'd owed her that breath.

Trying to blot his last sight of the girl from his mind, Steven summoned a sudden vision of one of the last times he'd seen her alive, at his house when she'd brought the plans—he pictured the way she'd moved immediately to his piano and bent over the keys, how she'd smiled to herself as she'd laced together all her wandering fragments of melody. Loss slowly sank in. A week before, for reasons he knew he'd have to uncover now, Lisa had lied and torn apart his life. Sharp tears welled and spilled before he knew they were coming; he held back the grief, saving it, and the effort renewed a dull throb in his healing ribs.

Her drowning in this placid, shallow bay made no sense. The water was waveless, rarely even six feet deep, and in most places you could walk half a mile from shore and still not get wet above the knees.

He shook his vision clear and scanned the bay again. Boats towed skiers, windsurfers skittered along, a pontoon boat loaded with partying kids lumbered down from the canal, all as if nothing had happened. Steven started the Whaler's engine and motored slowly up the bay. He'd drifted south on the current, and it was ten minutes before he drew even with the sailing beach again. He circled out toward the center of the bay to avoid the sandbar and the beginning boardsailors floundering near the beach. Shading his eyes, he peered across the dancing glare to shore. A concrete boat ramp led into the water; twenty or thirty minivans, four-by-fours, BMWs, and sports cars were parked within twenty feet of the water's edge. In the midst of them sat Lisa's Mustang.

He turned the Whaler in, wondering if Lisa's car could provide any clues. The bottom of the bay shelved gradually, and he was still a solid hundred yards from shore when he dropped anchor and hopped over the side. He waded ashore, brushing past jellyfish that stung like nettles against his calves.

Lisa's car was parked exactly where it had been the day before. The sailboard rack was empty, and a layer of fine dust coated the car's black finish. Clearly it had not been moved in a couple of days.

Steven circled the Mustang, peering in through the tinted glass. On the floor, between the front buckets and the vestigial rear bench, nearly covered by diet soda cans and hamburger wrappers and cassette tapes, lay a mustard-colored cardboard shipping tube, identical to the one he'd had so briefly at his house.

He couldn't understand why she'd take the plans back, then carry them around in her car, and he tried the driver's door. It was locked, and he cupped his hands by his brow to peer across at the passenger door lock.

A sudden weight crashed into him from behind, smashing his face into the glass, and new pain blossomed in his ribs. His breath rushed out in a grunt. Stunned, he tasted blood. Someone hit him again from behind, bouncing his face off the glass once more, and Steven straightened and spun, arms held high to protect himself. The point of his elbow caught Todd Wood in the teeth as the boy charged him. Todd stumbled back until he leaned against the front fender of the next car, a Chevy Blazer, clutching the lower half of his face with both hands. Steven held up both hands, fists self-consciously ready to protect himself. "Stop it," he ordered. "Now."

Todd slowly lowered his hands and licked the blood from his lips and glared. Two or three inches taller than Steven, he weighed at least thirty pounds less. His curly hair and eyebrows were sun-bleached nearly white, and he was as darkly tanned as his sister. Only around the eyes did he resemble her.

"What are you doing to my sister's car?" he said thickly.

Steven looked toward the beach, where half the kids were watching them; a few guys, twenty, tanned, muscled—Todd's friends, Steven guessed—hovered nearby. He wished he could pull the next blow, but he had to deliver it.

"When's the last time you saw Lisa?" Steven asked quietly.

Something in his eyes or voice alerted Todd, who took a quick step forward. "Where is she? What's wrong?"

"She's had an accident," Steven said. "You want to sit down somewhere?"

"Where is she?" Todd's voice cracked, and he was suddenly a boy again.

"They took her to the hospital," Steven said. "Some people found her in the bay."

For a long moment Todd's blue eyes locked on Steven. Comprehension slowly widened them. "Is she okay?"

Steven held his gaze for a second, then reluctantly shook his head. "They tried," he said. "She'd been in too long."

Spinning away, Todd began to pace frantically back and forth between the two cars, arms folded in front of him. He stared at the ground and shook his head again and again. His lips worked wordlessly. Steven waited, helpless against this grief, and warned away the hovering friends with a glance.

Todd marched back and forth for a couple of minutes, turning back at either end of the cars instead of walking off to be alone, as Steven would have. Finally Steven reached out to stop him.

"Where's your car?" he asked. "We need to let your father know."

Todd stopped and drew himself up. His eyes were hooded and sunken, as if he'd aged twenty years in two minutes. The look he gave Steven was slightly crazed, but his voice sounded rational enough. "Why would we do that?" he said.

"He needs to know," Steven said.

"Why would that be? So he can file the insurance claim?"

"Come on, you're upset." Steven grasped Todd's upper arm, turned him away from the beach, and tried to walk him back into the parking lot. "Let's go call him."

Todd pulled free. "Take your hands off me, Blake. Somebody else can tell my old man."

"It's probably best if he hears it from you," Steven said.

"No," Todd said; he shook his head violently, and a renewed glint of panic showed in his eyes. "I'm not doing it."

Steven studied the boy. Todd had had his share of hellish times in the past few years—the death of his mother, browbeating and abuse by his father, a stepmother who came and went, now Lisa gone. He decided to drop calling Jacob; the cops or the Coast Guard would do it soon enough, and they were welcome to the task. Steven knew it would be thankless.

"What do you want to do?" he asked. "Can I call somebody to help you out?" He was thinking of Melinda Samuels, the school psychologist who'd been on Thompson's team at the school.

"There's nobody to call," Todd said. "Where's Lisa? Where'd they take her?"

"To Beebe Hospital, probably."

Blinking away tears, Todd looked away from him then. A thin line of blood had dried between the right corner of his mouth and his chin, and his lips were puffed and red. Steven rubbed the tip of his elbow, where he'd accidentally caught Todd's teeth, then gingerly probed his own top lip. It felt as swollen as Todd's, but his fingertips came away clean.

"Why couldn't you just leave her alone?" Todd said suddenly. "None of this would have happened."

"I never touched Lisa," Steven said tiredly. He wondered how many times he was doomed to repeat that claim. "I didn't have anything to do with this."

"Bullshit," Todd said. "You couldn't stand it when you found out about my old man and Gail getting back together, so you had to chase after my little sister. You're as sick as Jacob, Blake. You guys both make me sick."

Steven blinked and took a quick breath; the sunlight suddenly cranked up a couple of notches, and its sharp glare bounced from every piece of glass and chrome in the parking lot and straight into his eyes. The heat pressed down, and a knotty ache pounded at the base of his skull. He failed miserably when he tried to keep the edge from his voice. "What are you talking about?"

A tiny gleam of triumph sparked in Todd's eyes, and for a second he looked like his father. "Everybody's known about it for at least a year," he said.

"Well, I don't," Steven said. "And even if it's true, which I don't believe, I never touched your sister."

"Then why have you been following her around now? Why were you messing around her car? Were you out there when she drowned?"

"No," Steven snapped. "The Coast Guard said she'd probably been in the water overnight."

This staggered Todd in a way nothing else had. He blanched and wobbled, then steadied himself against Lisa's car. Steven leaned against the Blazer opposite and watched the boy's bluster and bravado crumble until he couldn't bear to witness it anymore. For a long, silent stretch they both stared out at the bay, and Steven thought about the fact that Todd wouldn't be the only one with questions. Half of Lewes and Rehoboth must know about Lisa's accusations now; dozens of boaters had passed Steven while he'd been anchored in the bay the last few days, and all of Todd's friends had seen him at Lisa's car.

He felt a rush of adrenaline pushing him to action, but he couldn't think where he might do any good—the cops could talk to Jacob, there was nothing he could do at Beebe, he wasn't ready to go back out on the water and face Lisa's new ghost yet, and there was certainly no comfort at home.

Todd wasn't moving, either. Steven wanted to believe the kid's claims about Gail and Jacob were just a wild shot aimed to wound, but he'd recognized the probability of truth immediately. He'd tried to believe Gail would never circle back to Jacob after the vehemence of her parting from him, but the strength of her reaction spoke of too many unresolved emotions. If Todd were truthful, Gail must have known Lisa had lied, knew about Wood's plans for Pilottown Road, knew things about Steven and his future that he didn't even know. For the moment, anger eluded him, though, grasped as he was by the cold, pale, inescapable image of Lisa sprawled gracelessly on the deck of the Mako.

Staring at the wounded kid in front of him, Steven shoved it all aside to think about later, and said, "Let me help you, Todd."

The boy, lost in his own misery, turned a dazed, blank look on him. "What?" he said. "I didn't hear you."

Steven hesitated, decided the act might be less easily refused than the offer, and that he might as well set Todd to figuring this out with him. He asked, "How good a swimmer was your sister?"

"Good," Todd mumbled. "Better than me, and I'm good. Why?"

"I just can't figure out how this could have happened in Rehoboth Bay."

"Maybe a boat hit her. Where's her board?"

"I don't know," Steven said. "I didn't see it."

"We have to find her board." An edge of hysteria rose in Todd's voice; his calmness was fraying as the first comforting numbness of shock passed. "We've got to find her board," he repeated. "I saw you come in from your boat. Take me out there."

Todd grabbed Steven's upper arm and yanked him toward the water, squeezing hard enough that Steven had to grab one of his fingers and lever it back until his grip eased. Steven held Todd by the shoulders for a moment, and looked squarely at him. "Calm down," he said. "They'll find her board."

The boy's eyes slowly cleared, and Steven lowered his hands.

"Do you have a key to her car? Maybe there's something there that'll help us."

Todd automatically dug into his jeans pocket, produced a key ring from the Tropicana casino at Atlantic City, and unlocked the driver's door of the Mustang.

Steven brushed past him. The black car had been closed tight for two August days, and the blast furnace air reeked of old french fries, baked wet suit, and dried seawater. Steven rooted through the trash behind the front seat until he came up with the shipping tube. It was disappointingly light.

"What's that?" Todd held out his hand.

Steven held the tube aloft so Todd could see down its empty length. Both metal end plugs were missing. "Lisa brought me some plans of your father's in a tube just like this one."

"That's why he brought us to that bar to see you last Friday. He's ripshit about them." Todd's voice was flat, and he kept glancing distractedly out at the water. Steven felt nearly guilty for questioning him, but figured the best thing for the kid was to talk, and it might as well be to him first.

"Did you see them? Do you know what he's planning?"

"Jacob's always planning six different things, and they all piss somebody off. You gonna give 'em back?"

"I don't have them anymore," Steven said. "Somebody took them from my house the same night you and Lisa and your father came to the Lamplighter."

Todd looked from Steven's face to the shipping tube to Lisa's car, then back at Steven. "You think Lisa gave them to you and then took them back?"

"No," Steven said. "I don't know who did it. Whoever it was trashed my house pretty bad. Maybe it was you."

Todd shook his head, eyes guileless. "Lisa and I hitched home that night before my dad got out of there."

"How did your father make Lisa lie about me?"

Todd's face stiffened.

"How'd he do it?" Steven pressed. "How could he force her to do something like that?"

Tight-lipped, Todd shook his head. "My dad can be a scary guy. Everybody does what he wants them to sooner or later."

"No," Steven said. "Not everybody."

Todd eyed him speculatively, then said, "They had a huge fight yesterday."

"Lisa and your father?"

He nodded. "She took off in the morning and didn't come home last night."

"What did they fight about?"

"Lisa had a lot to hate my dad for," Todd said slowly. "She told him she wasn't going to live at home anymore."

Steven waited, but nothing more came. "That's it? She said she was going to move out?"

"There was a lot more," Todd said. "Jacob needs to have everybody where he can control them, though, so that's what drove him nuts. That and the fact she stole those plans and gave them to you."

"So what do you think happened? You think she came straight over here to sail? Her car was here in the afternoon."

"She always did that when she was upset," Todd said. "And most of the rest of the time, too. She was here nearly every day since April."

"After school?"

Todd looked at him strangely. "Lisa ditched classes most of her senior year," he said. "She just wouldn't go anymore."

"I didn't know that," Steven said. "She always showed up for music lessons, even if she never practiced. Did she graduate?"

"Jacob made sure of that," Todd said. "No finals, nothing. He just leaned on everybody the way he always does."

"And of course they caved in," Steven said, mostly to himself.

Todd took a deep breath, and let it out slowly. He seemed calmer now, the first wave of hysteria past and the real grief yet to hit him. He dug deep into both front pockets, searching for his keys. "I'd better go to the hospital."

Steven pulled the key ring from the Mustang's doorlock, held it a moment, then tossed it over.

"Good luck," he said. "You need some company?"

Todd shook his head. "I'd better do it by myself. Jacob might be there already." He stared forlornly down at the gravel for a moment, then looked at Lisa's car. "I guess somebody has to move this," he said.

"The police will want to know it's here," Steven said.

Todd locked an intense blue gaze on Steven. "What if Lisa didn't drown by accident? I don't think my mom's fire was an accident."

"There's no reason to think that," Steven said gently. "Lisa could have fallen and hit her head on the mast or on the edge of her board, or anything. We don't know what happened."

"What if I'm next?" Todd said stubbornly. "What if he decides to get rid of me next?"

"You won't be." Steven wished he could believe that. "But if you think you're in real trouble, call me. We can talk to the police together."

"Thanks." Todd hesitated, then said, "I'm sorry I hit you, Mr. Blake. Both times."

It took Steven a moment to understand what Todd meant—

today's events had eclipsed last week's accident at the bay. He shrugged. "I won't tell you it's all right. Don't do it again."

"No," said Todd soberly. "You're not the one I should have hit in the first place."

"You don't need to hit anybody," Steven said. "If you think you're in trouble, call me. Okay?"

"Yeah, sure."

Todd trudged away then to a light blue minivan stacked high with sailboards and masts. Round-shouldered and weary, he didn't look like the kid who'd briefly captained the DeVries basketball team a few years before.

Steven watched him drive away, then locked up Lisa's Mustang, and waded back out to the Whaler. For a moment he sat quietly and watched the windsurfers fly past. The hot breeze had picked up. A girl near Lisa's age waded in, lifting the edge of her sail so the wind could fill it and carry it up from the water. She stepped aboard in a fast and fluid beach-start, then snapped the sail back into position so the board lifted almost immediately onto a plane. Arced out over the water, her body was a taut spring between sail and board, and she flew across the wind and away, out into the bay.

Steven's sorrow welled as he watched her sail off, his sorrow and, he realized, anger that all Lisa's fierce joy in life and music could come down to one fleeting axis of wind and Mylar and fiberglass—nothing more than skimming motion too easily stilled.

He started the boat motor, weighed anchor, and headed up the Lewes and Rehoboth Canal for home.

The speed limit was four miles an hour, to keep boat wakes from eating out the banks, and boaters from bouncing off each other and the numerous docks. Few heeded the limit, but Steven made the trip slowly today, past the marina on the left, through the humid August stench of the sewage treatment plant, past the cheek-to-jowl houses and docks of Rehoboth. He relaxed only when the canal made a sharp bend to the northwest and entered the acres of flat salt marsh along the western border of Cape Henlopen State Park.

From here it was an easy run, under the big highway bridge, past the railroad swing bridge, under the drawbridge in the center of Lewes, through the turning basin where all the deep-sea party fishing boats docked, and on up to his own small dock. From end to end the trip was seven miles. The canal ended another mile north at Roosevelt Inlet, which led out into Delaware Bay.

From the moment Steven left the turning basin, he could see Jimmy's Grady-White tied up at his dock. Van Dusen himself sat in the rear cockpit in a deck chair, feet up on the railing. As Steven drew near, he raised a foam-insulated can of beer and shouted a greeting lost in the burble of Steven's outboard.

Anxious more for solitude than company, Steven waved half-heartedly, then concentrated more than he needed to on edging around Jimmy's towering twenty-five-footer to the other side of his dock. When he could delay no longer, he cut his motor. Jimmy stood on the dock, and took the lines Steven tossed up.

"What's up, captain?" Jimmy said. "Thought we had a fishing date today."

"Sorry," Steven said. "They just pulled Lisa Wood out of Rehoboth Bay."

Jimmy stood with his mouth open for a long minute, then said, "No shit? She alive?"

Steven shook his head, not trusting his voice. He took a quick look around the Whaler, shut off the gas line, and clambered up to the dock. He followed Jimmy onto his boat. "I need a beer."

Van Dusen waved at a green cooler the size of a large footlocker that he kept stowed just inside the cabin door. The two men settled in a pair of deck chairs, both of them with their feet up on Jimmy's railing, sitting so they could look out over the canal rather than at each other.

"What happened?" Jimmy asked quietly.

Steven closed his eyes and drank half his beer before answering. "Boater found her floating about halfway down Rehoboth Bay. Coast Guard guy said it looked like she'd been in the water overnight, but that sounded like a guess to me."

"Boat hit her?"

"I don't know," Steven said. "I hope so." He looked curiously at Van Dusen. "How come? You hear something?"

Van Dusen shook his head. "Weather's been pretty calm, so I doubt she got into anything she couldn't handle on that board."

Steven drained his beer, then went to the cooler for another. Three empties already rested on top of the ice, and he wondered how long Jimmy had been waiting for him. Steven popped a fresh one and stood in the cabin doorway and sipped it, watching the back of Jimmy's head. Straining to keep his tone casual, he asked, "What do you know about Gail getting back together with Jacob?"

Jimmy choked on his beer and leaned forward quickly, coughing. He turned back to look at Steven. Surprise, guilt, and what seemed like a hint of fear played across the basketball coach's face. His gaze slipped all around Steven without actually settling on him, and as soon as he'd stifled his cough he took another long drink.

"What do you mean?" he finally asked.

"Come on," Steven said. "Are you my friend or what?"

Jimmy stared at his deck. After a long pause, he said roughly, "What do you want to know?"

"Anything there is."

"I thought you knew about it," Jimmy said. "It's been going on since last summer, I think."

Steven stared at the tall phragmites waving on the opposite bank, sipped his beer again, and tried to take Jimmy's confirmation as calmly as a boxer refusing to acknowledge a blow straight to the heart.

Two kids in a Starcraft with a 150-horse Yamaha roared up the canal doing at least twenty-five or thirty. Van Dusen stood and hurled his beer at them, foam insulator and all. His arm was good, but he missed by a solid thirty feet and their speed never altered. His boat pitched wildly in the wake for a minute, and Steven's dock creaked and complained like his old house in a hurricane.

"Goddamned assholes," Jimmy shouted. He glanced at Steven as if looking for the reflection of his own uncharacteristic outburst of anger, then bent and fished around in the cooler for another beer.

"Surprised I didn't see you down in Rehoboth Bay when I came through," he said. "You down there all day?"

"Since ten or so. I was anchored over near the sailing beach, down below Dewey. East of the channel."

"Gail and Jacob were out there today, too. You see them? White Cigarette, loud as hell."

"No." Steven stood. "You sure about them, Jimmy?"

Van Dusen nodded.

Steven shoved his hair straight back from his forehead. His face hurt where Todd had bounced him off of Lisa's car, his ribs ached again, and he couldn't recall if he'd ever felt this betrayed and depressed.

"Why the hell couldn't you tell me about them? All this time, I look like a fool."

"You know, you always think a guy knows." Jimmy looked so miserable that Steven almost felt sorry for him. "People can live with a lot of things, and you never know what they've just decided to put up with for whatever good reasons, and it's nobody else's business."

Steven didn't have an answer for this. "I've got to go in," he said. "Make some calls."

"Take care of yourself," Jimmy said. "Another time?"

"Yeah," Steven said. Still he hesitated to go ashore. When he'd first reached the dock, he'd wanted only to be alone; now any company seemed preferable.

"You okay?" Van Dusen asked.

Steven looked down the canal, where another overpowered motorboat roared toward them, bound for Roosevelt Inlet and Delaware Bay. "No," he said. "One of my favorite kids just drowned, and I found out I've been had all over the place."

"I don't mean to sound cold," Jimmy said, "but this could clear up your situation at the school."

"That's the last thing on my mind," Steven replied. "Jimmy, I could be in a hell of a lot more trouble if it turns out there's no good explanation for Lisa's drowning."

"I'd thought of that, too," Jimmy said glumly. "You might be best off to just clear away from here, friend."

Steven flashed his friend a wan smile. "What the hell makes you think I'm going to let anybody off that easy?"

10

Patches boiled up barking from her cushion at the foot of Steven's bed, then scrambled and skidded downstairs in a clatter of unclipped nails. Clasping at a dream that faded as quickly as his vision cleared, Steven sat straight up from a sound sleep. His pulse raced. Through the skylights the morning light was gray, so it was either early or foggy again.

A sharp rapping came at the front door glass, and Patches renewed her tirade. Belting his robe around him, Steven stumbled down into the living room and pulled aside the shade on the front door.

A short, solid man of fifty stared back at him. He had close-cropped sandy hair, a blocky jaw, and looked like a second-string, small-college football player long gone soft. He wore a short-sleeved white shirt and a dull yellow polyester tie.

"Mr. Blake?" he said through the glass.

Steven nodded.

"Detective Gary Hackett, state police. Can I talk to you?"

The first image that came was Gail's red BMW wrapped around a tree at the side of Highway One; he opened the door just wide enough to talk to the cop while keeping Patches inside. "What's wrong?" he said. "What's happened?"

"No emergency," the cop said. "I'm sorry to wake you, but I need to ask you some questions about Lisa Wood."

Steven had spent all night playing his tenor along with everyone from Billie Holiday, Bessie Smith, and Lester Young up through Miles Davis on "Bitches Brew," and had invested the best part of a bottle of bourbon toward working Lisa and Gail and Jacob out of his mind. He'd finally succeeded by falling asleep, or maybe passing out, but now yesterday's sight of Lisa sprawled on the Mako's deck struck back full force. "What about her?" he said.

"Can I come in? This'll take a while."

Reluctantly Steven stepped back and let the cop inside. "Come on, then."

His tenor lay on the couch, fully assembled. Scattered next to it were some of the big band transcriptions Marian had sent down by express mail; the rest of them were stacked on the piano bench. Next to the bench stood a chrome music stand, extended full height and holding an opened chart for "In a Sentimental Mood." Steven had covered the floor and every other flat surface in the room with stacks of albums, cassettes, and CDs, which he was still trying to sort out since his house had been trashed the previous Friday. The power button glowed on his stereo amplifier, on since last night. He snapped it off.

"Come on and sit down," he said. "I need some coffee before I can talk."

The cop followed him into the kitchen, which was at least relatively clean. The only damage still showing was a scrape mark down the front of the refrigerator door. Repairs had cost him money he didn't have, but everything worked.

The cop sat at the kitchen table and opened a small notebook. Steven's hand shook as he scooped coffee into the coffee maker. Like most people, his only real dealings with the police had been a few traffic tickets.

"You mind if I go to the bathroom?" he said. "I just got up."

The cop looked at Steven for a moment, as though gauging whether or not he was going to slip out the bathroom window, then deliberately checked the room over, eyeing the scarred refrigerator door. Patches rested alertly in the middle of the kitchen floor, front legs stretched out in front of her, staring at the cop but staying just out of reach. Steven felt naked.

"Go ahead," the cop said. "Don't take too long, though."

Steven looked himself over in the bathroom mirror. He sported a bruise on his right cheekbone where Todd had bounced him off Lisa's car, his hair stood on end, and he had dark bags under his eyes. He also hadn't shaved in several days.

He did his best to clean up: shaved quickly, dragged a wet comb across his head, and all the while wondered why the police were already out asking questions about Lisa. He didn't know much about how these things worked.

He came back through the kitchen door in time to see Patches sniff at Hackett's pant leg, and the cop shove her away firmly with his foot.

"You want some coffee?" he asked.

"No," the cop replied. "I'm allergic to dogs, so I'll need to make this quick."

Steven settled across the table, coffee mug in hand, and called Patches to sit next to him. "What can I do for you? I've been sick since I saw her."

Hackett locked his gaze on him. His eyes were flat brown and permanently skeptical. "I understand you were at Rehoboth Bay when they found her."

"Sure," Steven replied. "I identified her."

"You have any idea how she got there?"

Steven shook his head. "None. Why?"

"When's the last time you saw her?"

"Last Friday night. She and her father and brother came to the Lamplighter, where I play every weekend."

"That's the last time? Not since then?"

"No," Steven said firmly. "What's going on? You think this wasn't an accident?"

"We're just investigating," Hackett said. His gaze didn't waver. "How well did you know Miss Wood?"

"She was a student of mine at Henlopen," Steven said. "Up through last spring. I guess I knew her pretty well."

"How well is pretty well?"

Steven's face flushed, and he bit back his usual angry response. "As well as a teacher knows his best student," he said.

"It's my understanding there was more to the relationship than that."

"Your understanding is mistaken," Steven snapped.

Hackett flipped back through the early pages of his notebook. "According to what I've heard, you and Lisa were engaged in an affair, and the school administration has recently offered you an opportunity to quit before you're fired. Is that correct?"

"No, it's not correct." Steven stared back at the cop's wide face. "That's rumors and gossip and accusation, but absolutely none of it has any basis."

"Can I ask you why I went by the high school yesterday and found somebody else running band practice? Somebody who told me you were being fired?"

"What does that have to do with Lisa Wood drowning?"

Hackett shrugged. "Maybe nothing. If you didn't screw around with her, how come you're not putting up more of a fight at the school?"

Steven took a deep breath to steady his voice, then said, "Who told you I'm not fighting it? I've got a lawyer working on it now."

"I'm sure you do."

"Thompson and his cronies are ready to convict me without even hearing my side of things. Did they send you here this morning to grill me?"

Hackett held up one hand, as though to stop traffic. "Nobody's grilling you, Mr. Blake, and I'm sorry I woke you up. It's after nine o'clock, though, and I've got a lot of people I need to talk to today. Can you tell me anything about Lisa's boyfriends?"

"I don't know if she had any," Steven said. "I haven't seen her much since June. Didn't see her much at all last year, after she'd decided not to audition for music school."

Hackett noted this. He sneezed, shot Patches a dirty look, then looked back down at his notebook and asked, "What did you remove from Lisa Wood's car yesterday?"

"Nothing." A chill of caution coursed up Steven's spine. "Todd and I looked inside to see if she'd left anything there."

"Like what? What were you looking for?"

Steven shrugged. He was reluctant to mention the plans, unsure whether his knowledge of them would make him appear any more or less guilty in Hackett's eyes. "I don't know. Some reason, I guess. A note, maybe."

Hackett scrutinized him. "So you think she committed suicide?"

"No. I don't think she'd do that."

"Then why were you looking for a note?"

"I don't know," Steven said. "Her brother and I were both upset."

"Will he tell me you were looking for a note?"

"How should I know? You'll have to ask him."

Again Hackett flipped back through his notebook. "I understand you had an argument with Jacob Wood at the Lamplighter last Friday. What was that about?"

Briefly Steven considered how much of a reply to give. "Jacob Wood's holding a considerable grudge against me."

"Since your affair with his daughter?"

"There was no affair with his daughter," Steven said. "I'm married to Jacob's ex-wife. Anything else, now?"

"Just a couple more." Hackett consulted his notes once again. "How'd you happen to be on Rehoboth Bay yesterday when they found Lisa?"

"It was a nice day," Steven said. "I felt like taking my boat out. So did a hundred other people."

The cop grunted skeptically and flipped through his notebook as though looking for one last question. In the same flat, casual tone he'd used throughout the session, he said, "How's that injury to your ribs? Healing up okay?"

"It's fine," Steven said. "How'd you hear about that?"

"It's my job." Hackett scanned the kitchen. "You find out who vandalized your house yet?"

Steven shook his head. His eyes narrowed. Clearly Hackett was demonstrating something—power in knowledge, the impossibility of secrecy in this small town. "That's your job," Steven returned. "Have you come up with anything yet?"

Hackett offered a cold smile. "Local responsibility," he said. "They'll let you know." He stood, and Patches leapt alertly to her feet and quivered next to Steven.

Steven kept his seat. "You don't think she drowned by accident, do you?"

"I didn't say that. How'd you feel about Lisa after you got called on the carpet last week? Pretty pissed off, were you?"

Now Steven stood. "What I thought about Lisa then is what I think now. She was a sweet, talented kid with a lot of problems."

"Like what?"

"Like her father. And I've heard she and her brother both went wild after her mother was killed and they had to move up here."

Hackett nodded curtly. "I've heard about the fire," he said.

"I'd like to know what happened to Lisa."

"So would we."

"Have they found her sailboard yet? Any idea where she drowned or how?"

Hackett shook his head. "None. Mrs. Blake around? I'd like to ask her a couple of questions, if I could."

"Moncure," Steven said. "She uses her own last name. She's not here now."

"You expect her soon?"

He stared back at the cop and did his best not to flinch. "I don't know."

"She still lives here, doesn't she?"

Hackett's casual tone seemed forced now. Steven wondered if even the police knew about Gail and Jacob reconciling, if he'd been absolutely the last person to figure it out.

"My marriage isn't anyone else's business," Steven said.

Hackett extended a business card. "Have her call me if you see her," he said. Finally he turned to go, and Steven followed closely behind, ushering him through the living room. Hackett stopped next to the music stand, peered at the chart, then hummed the opening bars, surprisingly on key.

"Good tune," he said, tapping the music with the back of his fingernails. "This what you play at the Lamplighter? I'll have to come out some night."

"That's for another project," Steven said. "We're almost done for the summer."

"Too bad," Hackett said.

"Maybe next year," Steven said. "Unless you can make it this weekend."

Hackett shrugged, back to business. "Lot of jazz musicians get real good in prison," he said. "All that time to practice, I guess."

"I'm already good," Steven said. "Keep me posted."

Hackett peered at him strangely. "I have a feeling you'll be one of the first to know when we find out something."

Steven stared at the cop for a frozen moment, waiting for a grin, or some other sign that this was Hackett's idea of a joke. "Detective, have you ever been accused of doing something you didn't do?"

Hackett stopped with his hand on the doorknob, and looked over his shoulder at Steven. "Mr. Blake, I don't think I've ever talked to anybody who *did* do what they were accused of. At least not the first time they told the story."

"My story's the truth."

Hackett snorted impatiently. "I don't care if you screwed the girl sixty-three times. Right now we're just trying to find out what the hell happened to her. If you get any bright ideas about that, call me."

He sneezed again and left.

Steven drifted uneasily around the living room after the cop was gone, first cleaning and packing away his tenor, then collecting and organizing sheet music. The speed with which Hackett had sought him out and the amount of information the cop already had about him surprised him. He caught himself reviewing all his answers to see what he might have left out, or what he'd said that he shouldn't have, and within an hour he had himself worked into a near panic.

He needed to talk this one over before he screwed up again, and he dialed Jimmy and listened to the phone ring ten or twelve times. He'd punched in half the number for Gail's office when he caught himself, and he slammed the phone down and paced into the living room, then back into the kitchen.

Lester and Marian would both be unreachable on campus. He looked up DeFlavis's number, hoping the lawyer could see him again at short notice. The secretary announced he'd be in court all day, and Steven took this as one positive sign—at least the guy had another client—and he made an appointment for the next afternoon.

Suddenly everything he saw or touched reminded him of Gail. The house closed in on him, and he led the dog out to the dock, where he gassed up the Whaler, started the engine, and cast off. Patches stood on the bench seat at the bow, nose in the air and plumed tail wagging like a metronome. Steven steered down the canal again, headed for Rehoboth Bay.

The day was hot and overcast, murky with humidity, and absolutely breathless, the kind of weather that bred thunderheads in seconds. Steven's shirt stuck to his back. Even the boat's motion gave no relief from the oppressive feeling of static in the air, like sand in the teeth.

He had barely drawn even with the state park when a streak of lightning lanced down into the Rehoboth Flats, a stretch of salt marsh a mile or two ahead of him.

Thunder bowled Patches right off the bench seat, and she scrambled madly, legs skidding in all directions on the fiberglass deck, back to where Steven stood. She wedged herself between his legs and the seat in back of him, and he cut speed, eased the Whaler around in the tight canal, and sped back to the safety of his own dock.

11

"Figured you'd be back as soon as I heard about the Wood girl." DeFlavis leaned back in his swivel chair, hands behind his head and bald pate gleaming in the fluorescents. A cigar smoldered in an ashtray between them, doing battle with the office's heritage of stale doughnuts and uncleaned deep-fat fryers.

"A state police detective showed up at my house yesterday morning," Steven said. "Guy named Hackett."

"I know," DeFlavis said.

"What else do you know? They think it wasn't an accident?"

DeFlavis shrugged. "Autopsy report's not done yet, but supposedly the girl had some bruises on her shoulders and back, as if she'd been held underwater. How'd you happen to be there when they pulled her out?"

Steven shook away a sudden vision of Lisa's lifeless body stretched on a stainless steel table, abdomen flayed open. "I was looking for her," he said slowly. Much had happened in the six days since he'd first met DeFlavis, and he caught him up now on most of it: Lisa's bringing the plans, Jacob Wood showing up at the Lamplighter, the trashing of his house and the disappearance of the plans, his confrontation with Todd at the sailing beach parking lot. He left out only what he'd discovered about Gail and Jacob, because describing it out loud would make it more real than he was prepared for.

Again DeFlavis taped their conversation and took notes, but he interrupted only twice with questions this time. Steven wound up with yesterday's visit from Hackett. The lawyer reread his notes until Steven could stand the strained silence no longer.

"What do you think?"

"I think you have a problem," DeFlavis said quietly. "Tell me again about Hackett. What else did he say? How did he seem?"

"Like he's already decided I had something to do with Lisa drowning, and he's out to nail me for it."

DeFlavis pinned him with a long, thoughtful glance.

"I didn't," Steven said. "I loved that kid. As a kid and a musician. "That's all."

For another moment the lawyer scrutinized him, then gave a small, satisfied nod. "I believe you," he said. "We just need to make sure the police do, too."

Steven massaged his forehead and temples and eyes, too tired for the lawyer's declaration to matter much; he'd barely slept for two nights in a row. "How do we work this?"

"The main thing is not to do anything that might confirm their suspicions."

"Like what?"

"Like getting in their way. I'd also suggest you get your life back together again. The more normal and adjusted you seem, the better."

Steven stared at him for a moment. "You mean if I get hauled into court, I'd better seem respectable."

DeFlavis nodded. "Got any leads on a job?"

"One." He told him about Lester and Marian's big band project.

The lawyer shook his head dismissively. "Anything a little more reliable?"

Steven shrugged. "Haven't really looked."

"You'd better. How about Gail? Any chance of you two patching it up?"

"Not anymore, if what I've heard is true."

"What's that?" DeFlavis's voice was sharp.

Steven kept his voice as neutral as he could. "I've been told she and Jacob have been seeing each other again for at least a year."

DeFlavis glared down at his notepad, and when he finally glanced up, his eyes danced with anger. "You really interested in having me help you out, Mr. Blake?"

"Absolutely," Steven said. "I need your help."

"Then you've got to tell me everything," DeFlavis said. "We can't work this if you're going to hold out information."

"Sorry," he said. "I don't even want to think about it myself." If he'd had any other choice, Steven might have walked.

"You're going to have to think about a lot of things you don't want to face," DeFlavis said. "Who told you about them?"

"Todd Wood."

"Dubious, then," DeFlavis shot back.

"My friend Jim Van Dusen said it was true."

"Some friend."

"He thought I already knew."

DeFlavis sighed and shook his head. "Well, if we can confirm it, you've got plenty of grounds. Trouble is, filing for a divorce now is the last thing you should do."

"How's it look to you? Where do I stand?"

"Not good. It looks like Lisa was killed, and it looks like Hackett at least thinks you did it. You were on the bay when they found her, you'd seen her recently, you were known to be angry with her for getting you in trouble at your job, and everybody suspects you of sleeping with the girl. You and your wife are on the outs, and she's been seeing Lisa's father again."

"So you're basically telling me I've had it," Steven said.

"Maybe not. We'll need to see what else the police turn up, and wait and see what they'll do. Do you have any idea who might have done this, or any information that might point the police somewhere else?"

"Of course I have an idea who did it," Steven snapped. "Jacob Wood's a maniac—he's held a grudge against me for four years, and he's used his kids to get at me. I'm sure he's used them other ways."

"You have any proof?"

"I would've told the police if I did."

DeFlavis spread his hands. "We just need to wait, then, and see what else they turn up and which way they go."

"And in the meantime I'm just supposed to lie back and take it?"

"That's my advice for the time being," the lawyer said. "Get your personal life straightened out. Get a job."

"How much is this going to cost me?"

"Depends on what happens. I'd prefer to have that retainer we talked about last week, though."

"I'll go to the bank tomorrow," Steven said, then went on: "You know, I figured out why Gail made me cancel our cottage rentals for the rest of the season. She had no intention of working things out—she just wanted to make sure I was broke and couldn't fight her." He stood, shaking his head. "Thanks for your help, but I don't know. I don't think I can sit back and wait anymore for this to clear itself up."

DeFlavis studied him. "Professionally, I do advise you to wait. But I sure as hell wouldn't in your shoes. I'll do what I can to help, but you're gonna have to work pretty hard to save your own tail on this one, I'm afraid."

Steven leaned across the desk and shook his hand.

"Just make sure you don't get yourself in deeper," DeFlavis said.

"At least if I do, I'll have done it to myself this time." Steven turned to leave. "I'll drop off a check tomorrow."

"I've got one more suggestion," DeFlavis said. "When's the last time you slept with Gail?"

"Not long ago," Steven said slowly. "Why?"

"You'd better have yourself tested," DeFlavis said.

"For what?" Steven said.

"HIV."

For a moment Steven stared at the lawyer. "Yeah," he said tightly. "Thanks."

Steven was completely unprepared for this treacherous new world, where lies lurked behind every action and any relationship could lead to death. With this last added worry, the full enormity of Gail's betrayal rolled over him, and his anger rose up until his hands actually shook.

Steven stepped back out into the murky August heat. The relentless sun brought an immediate headache, and he fought his way back into the stream of traffic with rare recklessness.

12

"The drowning of a Rehoboth Beach woman last week has been categorized as suspicious by Delaware State Police," the newscaster led off. Steven froze in the middle of the cottage kitchen, a Limoges teacup in one hand and a sheet of newspaper in the other. "No further details are forthcoming on the death of eighteen-year-old Lisa Wood, whose body was pulled from Rehoboth Bay on Tuesday. Police will not reveal whether they have any suspects in the case. The investigation continues.

"In other news, Sammy Ferro will once again lead the Piping Out ceremony on Labor Day, when we'll kiss another summer goodbye."

Steven turned the radio down and wrapped the cup, then added it to the others he'd already boxed. Violent death in these small beach towns resulted most often from car wrecks, bar fights, and domestic brawls, where the tie between killer and victim was nearly always clear at a glance. Those were uncommon enough, but the mystery around Lisa's drowning had placed her picture on Friday morning's front page and her name at the head of every newscast. Every time the edge faded from his pain, another reminder cropped up.

Today was the first time he'd ventured inside the cottage since Gail had taken it over, and he was cleaning it out primarily to get something settled in his mind; as long as the place was filled with her possessions, spread out as though normal life had been momentarily interrupted, he couldn't feel at home in his own house. He could find no good reason to want her back, nor did she show any sign of returning, or even negotiating. His calls to her office went unanswered, though the new temp admitted she was in, and there'd been no sign of her here in days, and he'd finally decided that if Gail had fallen twice for Jacob Wood, she'd only get what she deserved.

He picked up a saucer. Gail had inherited the tea set from her grandmother, but never used it. Ugly stuff, when you really looked at it, but probably worth a fortune. If he sold it, he wouldn't have to worry about renting the place, but he banked this temptation for the time being. A rental agent was due at three, giving him less than an hour to make the cottage presentable. Gail was no better a housekeeper than he, so the job was daunting.

He packed the last piece of Limoges, then stuffed the remaining space with crumpled newspaper and taped and labeled the carton. He added it to the stack on the right side of the front porch, all of it destined for storage in the garage until Gail picked it up or he sold it or tossed it.

Stepping back into the living room, he looked around at the clutter and wondered how and when she'd accumulated so much stuff. Financial disclosures for a divorce could be interesting, though his own statements would be easy. The real estate belonged to him outright, as did his four-year-old Jeep station wagon. Beyond that he owned his clothing, a piano, a saxophone, a once-prime collection of old jazz, now mostly scratched. Stereo. Dog by default. Teacher's retirement fund. And an eight-year-old, nineteen-foot Boston Whaler, with a four-year-old outboard bought with an insurance check after the first motor was stolen.

Truth to tell, the money didn't matter, and never had; if necessary he'd sell everything and split the proceeds if that would make parting swift and clean.

The cottage was smaller than Steven's house, with the front half one long room, the rear divided into a galley kitchen on the left and a small bedroom on the right. Steven entered the bedroom to see how much more packing awaited.

Standing on the white-painted dresser were two photographs, each in its own rosewood frame. One was of Gail and Steven together on Jimmy's boat, taken the first summer they'd been together, before she was officially divorced from Jacob. Both of them were laughing, tanned, and looking straight into the camera. Gail stood on Steven's left, and had her right hand over his left shoulder, and leaned into him slightly. He stared at this picture for a minute, thinking how impossibly fresh and naive they looked, though the shot was only four years old. They'd really believed in possibilities then, she so high on his music and getting free from Jacob, he high on her and the way she'd stirred him from encroaching lassitude.

The other photograph was of Steven alone, playing his tenor on stage at the Lamplighter. He couldn't recall having seen this picture, and he picked it up and carried it over to the window to get a better look. It was a color shot, taken with high-speed film in available light, so there had been no flash. In the background Steven could make out Lester and Marian and, at the drums, Ahmed, the kid who'd been playing with them the last few weeks. He looked more closely—as far as he'd known until now, Gail hadn't been in the club since the very beginning of the season, and Steven felt uneasy at the idea she'd been observing him so recently without him sensing it. The shot had been taken when he was in the midst of a solo—his eyes were screwed tightly shut, the two veins running up the center of his forehead bulging. He was turned completely inward.

He set the second photo next to the first, and looked at them side by side and realized that she'd bracketed their time together: as they'd begun, and as she apparently wanted to remember him. He wondered if she viewed the last picture sentimentally or as a warning to herself.

Deciding he'd done the best he could for the time, he returned to the porch, where he squatted and hefted up the box of china, ignoring the complaint from his ribs.

The cottage sat at the rear of the lot, and was fronted by a long, narrow lawn. Viewed from the cottage's front steps, this lawn was bounded on the left by a twelve-foot arborvitae hedge, at the front by Pilottown Road, and on the right by the larger house, where Steven lived. The two-car garage, for years too full of junk to shelter their cars, stood behind Steven's house and to the right of the cottage.

He felt his way down the porch steps, peering around the side of the carton. A small, tan imported car pulled up at the front of the yard, and a young guy in khakis and a blazer got out, carrying a leather notebook. Though he couldn't have been more than five-five, he carried himself with the stiff strut of a bodybuilder, and grinned and waved as he approached.

"Hi. Mr. Blake?"

"Yeah." Steven rested the carton on his thigh. "You the rental agent?"

"Tim Dixon." The guy was about twenty-five. "Give you a hand with that?"

"No, that's okay. Let me put it in the garage, and I'll be right with you."

"Okay. Which property we talking about here? You own them both?"

"Yeah. The one at the back. Go ahead and look around."

The rental agent followed Steven around the corner of the garage, trailing fifteen or twenty feet behind. Again Steven braced the carton on his thigh while he struggled with the rusty garage door bolt.

"Let me give you a hand," Dixon said.

"Got it." Steven tugged the big door open; it sagged on its hinges and hung up on the sill for a moment, then rasped free just wide enough for Steven to squeeze through with the box.

His eyes took a second to adjust to the dim light, and as he stepped into the dark garage, he stumbled and nearly went down on top of the carton of china.

"Goddammit." Unable to see around the box, he kicked the object he'd stumbled over, and it gave a hollow, plastic thump unlike anything he remembered owning. Gently he set the china down and stared. A white sailboard dressed with bold green and red graphics in the shape of a lightning bolt rested atop a couple of lawn chairs, presented as if for display across the front of his garage.

"Does garage space go with the rental?" the agent called from outside.

"No," Steven said quickly, and he began to back away from the sailboard.

"You okay in there, Mr. Blake? Need a hand?"

"No," Steven said, more sharply this time. His heart pounded so hard he could hear the rush of blood in his ears. He needed time to think. "Why don't you go ahead and look the place over? I'll be right there."

"Oh, I'll wait." The agent scuffed across the crushed-shell driveway, coming closer. "Sure I can't help?"

Near panic, Steven backed completely out of the garage and briskly shut the door. He turned and forced a smile. "Pretty cluttered in there. Keep meaning to clean it."

"Yeah, mine's the same way. How long you thinking of renting for?"

Sweat streamed from Steven's temples, and he wiped it clear with the back of each hand and struggled to focus his thoughts. "Straight through," he said. "I'd prefer to lease from now through May to one person, then go weekly or monthly after that when the rates go up. I'll settle for weekly for September and October if I have to, then start up again in May. I know it's tough to find a tenant for the winter."

"Let's have a look," the agent said. He gave Steven an amused once-over, then glanced at the closed garage door. "Must've been a heavy box."

"Yeah," Steven said. He tried to stand a little straighter, making the most of his seven-inch height advantage over the kid. "Bunch of china. Come on." He led the agent away from the garage, hardly knowing what he said as the guy chattered on about prevailing rents and the high vacancy rate in Lewes during the off-season, insulation and utility costs, and what pets and habits and living arrangements Steven would and wouldn't allow.

Fortunately the cottage was small, and the tour took only minutes. When they stood once again in the yard, the agent glanced at Steven's house. "How about that one? Want to rent it, too?"

"I live there," Steven replied.

"Well, I got to tell you, we'd stand a better chance of renting the bigger place for the winter," he said. "You interested in selling? I could move both of these places real quick in this market."

Steven had deliberately looked around for a rental outfit unconnected to Jacob, but he felt a twinge of suspicion at the kid's suggestion. "Not yet," he said. "Maybe next year."

The agent shrugged. "Market might be soft by next year."

"Market could be better next spring, too," Steven replied, and extended his hand. "You have anybody you think might be interested?"

"I'll have to check back at the office." He crushed Steven's knuckles with a power shake. "We'll call you," he said.

Steven was back inside his garage even before the agent's car pulled away. The entire rig was there—the sailboard resting across the arms of the lawn chairs, and stacked neatly on the floor in front of it the two-piece mast, booms, sail, everything.

Tentatively Steven circled the board, searching for a nameplate, a note, anything that might tell him how this gear had gotten here. He counted back, trying to remember when he'd last been in the garage, and arrived at Sunday, when he'd mowed the lawn.

Obviously well-used, the board showed dings and scratches. He reached to turn it over, then checked himself and scouted around the garage until he found a pair of gardening gloves. The board was surprisingly light—no more than twenty pounds. About eight and a half feet long, it tapered to a point at both ends and had a trio of hooked plastic fins mounted near the stern. Still he could find nothing to verify the board's owner.

He checked the mast and booms, then unrolled the first eighteen inches of the sail. Stitched to the Mylar at the foot was a name tag reading PROPERTY OF LISA WOOD, followed by her address and phone number. Steven dropped the sail to the floor.

Like a rogue wave catching him from behind as he waded out of the surf, true panic boiled over him now.

Who was doing this to him? No, the who was obvious—Jacob, either through Todd or through someone Steven may not even know. The more pressing question was what else Jacob might have done to go along with this surprise, such as notifying the police. Steven rolled the sail together again to hide the name tag. His best chance probably stood in calling Hackett before anyone else could.

Bolting the garage door behind him, he hustled into his house and tore through the jumble on top of his dresser, searching for the detective's card. By the time he found it in the pocket of a shirt hanging in his closet, his panic had cooled enough for him to reconsider how the cop would take his call—most likely as a confession waiting to be heard, no matter how much Steven protested. The last time he'd been accused of something he hadn't done, when Thompson hauled him in, accusation seemed as good as conviction. Thompson and Randy Wise had cast him as guilty before he could say a word in his own defense, and he had few illusions about things working any differently this time.

Steven checked the refrigerator, found three cans of beer hidden behind half a decaying cantaloupe, took one, and settled at his kitchen table to contemplate his next step.

There was no point in calling trouble down on himself. The stakes were a hell of a lot higher than losing his job, and this time he needed to make his own decision, and make it calmly, without Gail or Jimmy Van Dusen or DeFlavis or anyone else trying to steer the best course for him.

Someone was pushing him, Jacob or not, and it was time for him to push back and see what happened. He took his beer back out to the garage and put on the gardening gloves again. He pulled the garage door closed behind him until only a sliver of light came through; luxuriously untrimmed trumpet vine covered the one small window in the middle of the back wall, casting a dim, greenish light over the clutter. The garage was hot and still, and a cloud of dust billowed whenever he lifted anything.

After an hour of steady work and two trips back to the kitchen for the other beers, Steven had stashed the sailboard and gear in the farthest back corner of the garage, hidden beneath a paint-spattered drop cloth. He rearranged storm windows, old paint cans, a broken wooden porch swing, and other junk into a reasonably random wall, leaving himself a narrow path through.

He bolted the unused set of garage doors from the inside, leaned a sheet of plywood against the back wall to cover the window, then stepped back and inspected his work from the right-hand doorway. Even knowing the board was there, he couldn't make out its shape, and he picked his way closer. Satisfied with the camouflage, he padlocked the garage.

LESTER JONES HUNCHED over his string bass, plucking overtones and checking the strings against each other, then quietly asked Marian for another note. Ahmed warmed up around a big arc, brushes rolling on tom-tom, ride cymbal, snare, high hat, then back again. A couple of early drinkers nursed beers at the table nearest the stage.

"Sorry I'm late." Steven's hair was still wet from the shower.

Lester looked up from his bass and lost no time. "You okay? I hear that girl died."

The drummer pattered on. Marian and Lester both watched Steven closely, and for a moment he wondered if they, too, suspected him of doing away with Lisa.

"I'm fine," he said shortly, and stepped up onto the low stage. "I was there when they found her."

"Somebody think you did this one, too?"

"I guess somebody does," Steven said. He laid the tenor case on the floor at the back of the stage, knelt, and assembled the horn. "Somebody been asking you questions?"

"Somebody has," Lester said. "A detective, I think he said he was."

"Ah-hah." Steven stood, adjusted his neck strap, and jumped straight into Coltrane's "Giant Steps" solo, which he'd once spent the better part of a year transcribing and memorizing. For a minute he played as fast and loose and loud as he'd ever blown, then stopped. Lester and Marian were both staring at him. "What?" he said.

"You want to talk about this mess or not?" Lester said.

"I can never remember whether I became a musician because I couldn't talk," Steven said, "or if I don't have to talk anymore because I became a musician."

In all their years of playing together, Steven had never spoken so curtly to Lester, and now it was as though a veil dropped over the bass player's eyes. He nodded stiffly and turned to confer with Marian on the set list. The drummer never stopped playing, and Steven noticed for the first time that he wore headphones. His lips moved as he played along with his tape.

Steven launched into runs and scales, doing a real warm-up now, and in a minute Lester came back, stuffed a set list into the bell of Steven's sax, and turned away. Steven lowered his horn. "Lester, I'm sorry. Everybody's been on my ass this week."

Lester shrugged, but his eyes thawed a bit. "Cop said he'd be back. You want to sit out tonight somewhere else?"

"Why would I do that? I don't have any reason to hide from Hackett or anybody else."

"Okay, okay, I'm not saying you need to be hiding," Lester said. "Marian just wanted me to make the offer. What's the story?"

"I don't know," Steven said. "Has her old man been in? Guy who was here last Friday?"

Lester shook his head.

"He's the one, I think. And he's trying to put the blame on me."

"How's that?"

"I'm not sure yet. I'll let you know when I can."

Steven felt a sick fear unlike any he could remember; all evening his hands were sweating so badly his fingers kept slipping from the keys, his arms and legs twitched. The air-conditioning gave out before the end of the first set; by ten-thirty, the room was stifling and hazy with cigarette smoke. Sweat drenched Steven's shirt and burned his eyes, but he kept close watch through the murk, expecting both Hackett and Jacob to make an appearance.

He was only half right. Midway through the second set, the cop seated himself alone at a table at the back of the room. Steven's first impulse was to slip out the fire exit at the back of the tiny stage and head directly to his garage to check that the sailboard still rested undisturbed.

He quelled this urge with a couple of deep breaths and marshaled all his concentration to finish out the set. At the break, walking toward Hackett was a hundred times worse than treading a highway stripe under the scrutiny of a state trooper after a couple of drinks. The path across the room was a tightwire, and he could feel the cop cataloging his every movement and reaction. If he stumbled or twitched at the wrong moment, he'd blow it completely, lose control, and tell Hackett to go straight to the garage off Pilottown Road and pick up Lisa's sailboard.

He smiled, and his face felt like it did the day after a terrible sunburn—a tight mask, impossible to control. "Evening, Mr. Hackett," he said. "You're working late."

"Told you I might stop by when I saw you Wednesday. Thought I'd better see you in your native habitat."

"Why?" Steven said.

"Sit down, if you would," said Hackett. His face and voice were neutral, and he gestured, palm up, for Steven to sit across from him. Steven ordered a club soda to match the cop's, and waited.

"I'm no music critic, but you play pretty well," the cop said.

"Thanks." Steven's patience was too thin for chat. "What have you found out about Lisa?"

"This and that. I've been talking to a hell of a lot of people about *you* over the past few days."

"I'm sure that's done wonders for my reputation."

"You might be surprised what people think," Hackett said.

"Like what?"

"Ask them yourself. You thought of anything else you want to tell me about?"

Alarms went off behind Steven's eyes, but he kept his mask intact. "Nothing I can think of."

"You sure?"

Steven's thoughts raced, but he calmly sipped his soda, trying to read the cop. If Hackett already knew about the sailboard and was playing cat and mouse, it didn't matter whether he told him about it or not—no amount of explanation would clear him now. And if Hackett didn't know, telling him would only bring on more trouble, because he had no good excuse for not calling in the police as soon as he found the board. Better to stick with his plan, he decided. He had to throw Hackett something, though, and might even help himself in the bargain, so he said, "Has anyone mentioned a set of plans to you?"

"What kind of plans?" Hackett's flat gaze measured him.

"Blueprint-type plans. Drawings for a real estate development."

Hackett pulled a steno notebook from his inside jacket pocket. "Tell me."

"Lisa brought them last Friday. She took them from her father's office."

"What were they?"

"Drawings of a development he's planning for Pilottown Road."

"Around your house?"

"Right on top of it, plus three or four blocks more."

"And why would she have brought them to you?"

"To show me why her father wanted to pressure me."

"Where are they now?"

"Gone," Steven said. "They were stolen that night, when my house got vandalized."

"Uh-huh." Hackett's eyes were skeptical. "Why'd you tell the Lewes police nothing was missing, then?"

Steven shrugged. "I thought the plans might have been reported as stolen in the first place, and Lisa had enough trouble already. Jacob knew she'd taken them. That's what he was so hot about here last week."

Hackett leaned back in his chair and contemplated Steven for a long moment. "So you're telling me that Lisa Wood came to your house, gave you a set of blueprints she'd stolen from her father's office, then he came here that night and demanded them back from you, and you went home later and found they'd been stolen from you. Right?"

"That's it."

"What's all that supposed to mean, Mr. Blake?"

"I don't know," Steven said. "Jacob was mad as hell, though."

"At the girl?"

"And at me."

"And what you want me to figure from that is that he had something to do with her drowning, Mr. Blake?"

"I'm not suggesting anything," Steven said. "You asked if I remembered anything else."

"How come you didn't remember this when we talked a couple of days ago?"

"I don't know," Steven said. "I was upset. It slipped my mind."

"It slipped your mind." Hackett gazed sadly at the melting ice in his soda glass, as though wishing for something stronger. "Tell me about your wife and Jacob," he said.

"What about them?"

"About why they got divorced and why they've apparently gotten back together," the cop said. "What do you think about that? Makes you pretty mad, doesn't it?"

"At this point I can't think of any two people who deserve each other more," Steven said, and meant it.

A momentary smile crossed Hackett's face, quickly controlled, and Steven knew the cop had talked to Gail. "Where'd you see her? At her office?"

Hackett nodded. "She see these supposed plans, too? She didn't mention them."

"I showed them to her," Steven said. "Before I knew about her and Wood."

"I'll bet she was real sympathetic."

Steven shrugged. "You talked to her. What'd she have to say?"

"She's a pretty mixed-up lady, if you ask me. I can't figure her with Jacob Wood any more than I can figure her with you."

"We used to be . . . ," Steven began, then stopped, wondering what impulse had nearly led him to discussing his marriage with Hackett.

"What happened? Your little thing with her stepdaughter too much for her?"

"There wasn't any 'thing,' " Steven said with what little patience he could still muster. "Why don't you ask her what happened? She's the one who moved out." He leaned back, away from the table. Lester was tuning up again.

Hackett grinned. "You know, I shouldn't tell you this, but this has been an interesting few days. I've been doing kind of a little survey to see who's voted least popular around here—you or your wife or Jacob Wood."

Steven waited, but the cop made him ask. "And?"

"You're not even close." Hackett stood. "Sounds like you've got to get back to work."

"Would you like to tell me just what it is you're looking for from me?" Steven asked.

Hackett studied him. "Are you as smart as you think you are, Mr. Blake?"

"You're wasting time if you're trying to connect me with Lisa's drowning."

"Oh, I wouldn't call tonight a waste," Hackett said. "I'll probably want to talk to you a few more times, Mr. Blake. You have a problem with that?"

Steven shrugged. "I've told you everything I know."

"No telling when your memory might slip again. Could be you'll have something else new for me next time."

"Suit yourself," Steven sighed. "You really think somebody killed her?"

Hackett stared at him. "I *know* somebody did," he said flatly.

"It wasn't me."

"Maybe it wasn't. But I've got to say I admire your choice of Barry DeFlavis. Real sharpy, that guy." The cop could barely contain his snicker as he added, "Your wife's gotta be jumping out of her skin. He's been after her since she kicked his ass in court a couple years ago."

"I hope she is." Steven had no idea what Hackett was talking about, but wouldn't give him the satisfaction of showing it.

"Keep in touch," Hackett said. "And don't plan any long trips. I might need to talk to you."

Steven couldn't trust his legs to support him for several minutes after the cop left. He clasped his hands tightly together beneath the table to still their trembling. Lester and Marian and Ahmed started up without him, playing "Softly, As in A Morning Sunrise," a ballad he hadn't heard in years, and for once he sat and listened, hoping the music would wind him down.

As sweet and contemplative and lingering as it was, it couldn't soothe him. Hackett didn't seem to know about the sailboard yet, but that couldn't last. Whoever had planted it in Steven's garage must have another move in mind, and he had to make his first.

He waited until the song ended, then joined the trio for the remainder of the set. Leaving early would only draw attention he didn't need at this point.

As usual, Marian and Lester were sipping their ritual Scotch by the time he had the tenor packed. Fighting his impatience to get on the road and finish the night's work, he joined them.

Marian raised her glass. "Mr. Steven," she said, "you played as sweetly as ever tonight."

Lester raised his glass. "Better."

Steven clinked them both. "Good times." He drained half his drink.

"You okay?" Marian asked. "Anything we can do?"

Steven shook his head. "Nothing, thanks. Police just need to catch somebody."

"Make sure it's not you," Lester said. "Seems like that cop has his eye on you."

"He does for sure," Steven said. "I don't know why, though."

"You're handy," Lester said. "Sometimes that's all it takes."

"Seems like somebody's trying to make me even more handy, too." Steven finished his drink. "I'm worn out," he said, and made his farewells and headed through the sultry night for home.

He was exhausted, but his night was far from over. Steven drove slowly back to Lewes, eyes on the rearview mirror to make sure Hackett hadn't popped up again. Back in town, he drove all the way up to where Pilottown Road dead-ended in the salt marsh, checking for watchers, then turned around and traced the route back to his house.

The quarter moon was a pale, waxy shadow, too feeble to break through the humid haze. For half an hour Steven sat on his dark front steps, hidden beneath the arch of the hydrangeas, listening and watching. Once certain he was alone and unobserved, he moved cautiously back to his garage. Just inside the door he'd left a flashlight, its lens masked with tape so it emitted only a pinpoint of light. Flashing this on and quickly off, he painstakingly felt his way through the clutter. The sailboard rested untouched.

Each trip between the garage and his boat was a quiet agony of slow steps and long pauses. It took another thirty cautious minutes to load the board, mast, and other gear onto his Whaler and shroud it with the drop cloth. He topped the pile off with a cooler, tackle box, and two fishing rods, then went back into the house to change into his fishing clothes.

Patches leapt all over him, yipping her anguish at being abandoned in the dark house all these hours, and he took her along to keep her from waking the neighbors when he left.

The chanciest part of the trip down the canal was the first mile or so, down through the center of Lewes and under the drawbridge, where anyone could look down into his open boat. Steven propped the fishing rods up so they'd be clearly visible—if anyone wondered, he was meeting up with a friend in Rehoboth Bay, then heading out Indian River Inlet for a little ocean fishing at dawn.

Though it was barely three o'clock, the docks at the turning basin were brightly lit. Crews moved over the charter boats, preparing for the morning run out Roosevelt Inlet. Steven stood behind the center console and held a steady speed down the center of the canal, and in moments had passed under the drawbridge and into concealing darkness. Ahead lay the highway bridge, then the dark run past the state park.

His nerves had never been stretched tighter, but he had no doubts about his action now that he'd actually begun it. Calling Hackett about the board only would have gotten him in more deeply, and he had little faith in his own ability to explain it away, or in the inclination of the police to search out any other explanation than his own guilt.

Sooner or later someone else would tire of waiting and tip them off. And when Steven knew who that was, he'd know where to steer the police. How he'd steer them he hadn't calculated yet, but trusted the answer to come in time.

For now he devoted every bit of attention to making his way down the canal. He rarely ventured out in the boat after dark, and could ill afford to run aground now.

The long stretch of salt marsh between Lewes and Rehoboth was pitch-dark and mysterious. The night air was a bitches' brew, chokingly thick and pungent and rich, whether because no breeze stirred or because he wasn't distracted by sight, he couldn't tell. Silhouetted by his running lights, Patches stood in the bow, her nose straight up in the air, sniffing and snorting loudly. Steven inhaled as deeply as he could, wondering what she made of these smells, whether she could sort them out and set an image to each.

A mile below the mouth of the canal, well out into the middle of Rehoboth Bay, he cut the motor and running lights and anchored in the dark. The pale moon had disappeared completely. A scattering of distant lights ringed the bay, clustered densely to the north. To the south, the reflected lights of Fenwick Island and Ocean City glowed against the clouds.

He could see no other boats, moving or anchored, nor could he hear another motor. Across the flat water wafted a shorebird's faint cry. Tiny wavelets lapped against the hull, and Steven had a sudden, unwelcome vision of Lisa's body floating in these quiet waters overnight, moonlight maybe flashing off her slick wet suit, her arms stretched out to either side and flexing slowly with the water's motion, as though keeping her hovering at the surface, her hair a wild crown of curls. He'd never felt so alone in his life.

Before he could sink any further, he donned his gardening gloves again and unwrapped the drop cloth from Lisa's sailboard and gear. With no ceremony or delay, he tossed the mast, booms, and sail overboard; only the latter floated for a moment, and he pressed it down with a boat hook until it slowly filled and joined the other gear.

He lifted the board cautiously, taking care not to bang or scrape it against his boat, then leaned far over the side and laid it gently on the water. It bobbed next to the Whaler, gathering light to itself until it seemed bright and cheerful and glowing, nearly animate in the darkness. Steven leaned over again and gave the board a push. It floated slowly away, drawing a V of ripples behind it, and Steven stared until he couldn't tell whether he actually saw the board or only its afterimage burned into his vision.

It was long minutes before he could look up and notice anything else again, and when he did he found the sky beginning to lighten out over the Atlantic. He searched his Whaler carefully with the masked flashlight, double-checking for forgotten hardware, then started up and began the run back up the canal, hustling now to beat the dawn.

He felt curiously light; he'd made his countermove, and was eager now to see who moved next.

13

Steven sagged back and rested his elbows atop the cemetery's brick wall and checked his watch again. He'd been waiting more than an hour. Battered and raw from the blows of the last week and a half, sleepless for days, he was running purely on adrenaline left over from last night's trip down the canal. Too much on edge to face the crowd at St. Peter's, he'd skipped the ceremony and walked up to the graveyard from home.

From the weed-grown field behind him, cicadas drilled a direct line into his brain. He squinted through the heat shimmering above the grass. This was the new cemetery, begun in 1952 when the old churchyard in the center of town filled; though four decades in use, it was less than a third filled, and the sparse headstones were as random as a failed crop. More and more, people came to Lewes to vacation or spend time in their second homes; some retired there, but their remains were generally shipped back to their real homes.

Beyond the front brick wall lay Pilottown Road, then the DeVries monument, where the Dutch had built their first stockade, and then beyond that the canal. Roosevelt Inlet was a hundred yards to the left, and the canal buzzed with Saturday morning pleasure boats heading out into Delaware Bay.

Two openings broke the front wall, entrance and exit for the looping, crushed-shell drive. Steven couldn't hear a whisper from the procession when it turned in, and the line of black Cadillacs floated so eerily through the shimmering air that he shivered despite the heat.

One by one they glided past—the hearse, three smoked-glass limos, then the Mercedes and Jaguars and Lincolns of Wood's real estate cronies mixed with the Hondas and minivans and Windsurfer-racked Jeeps of Lisa's friends.

The hearse stopped two-thirds around the loop, near the green-and-white striped canopy that shielded banks of flowers and the moist, sandy soil of an open grave from the sun's blast. Steven pushed away from the wall. Draped next to him was a black linen blazer Gail had bought him two years ago. It was too hot to wear the jacket today, so he slung it over his shoulder and ambled up the cemetery drive, ignoring the whispers and nudges and furtive glances from familiar faces. Forty feet ahead, Todd emerged from the first limo behind the hearse, then Jacob, and then, finally and unexpectedly, Gail. She wore a sleek black silk suit Steven had never seen before, and it was a blow directly to his solar plexus when she reached out and linked her arm with Jacob's.

They didn't see him, and he kept walking. Todd and five other tanned young guys waited behind the hearse. The humid heat muffled all sound, and even seemed to slow all motion to a stately, deliberate pace. A silver and chrome casket glided out on silent rollers, and the bearers hefted it and strode with measured steps toward the canopy. Gail and Jacob followed, then another ten or twelve people in slow procession between them and Steven.

He had the curious sense of being invisible, as neither Gail nor Jacob noticed him. Others did. He scanned the faces around him, the cemetery, the line behind him, the cars still pulling in, doubling up now that the drive was full. Van Dusen's pickup stopped outside the gateway, then made a U-turn onto the grass just above the DeVries monument, and stopped.

Again Steven stared at Gail and Jacob, now twenty feet ahead, their backs stiff and trim, Wood a head taller. They made a patrician couple, acknowledging, no, proclaiming their renewed relationship in front of all Lewes and Rehoboth. Steven's anger and humiliation burned barely within control. His eyes ached. He felt on the edge of danger, even a little afraid of himself, and he dug his fingernails into his palms as hard as he could.

The pallbearers laid Lisa's casket on the lowering straps, now taut above the grave, and retreated. A priest stood at the head of the grave, and though there were folding chairs ringed around, Jacob Wood stood, gazing down, and Gail stood at his side. Jacob looked more haggard than Steven had ever seen him.

Steven positioned himself across the grave from them, behind the innermost circles of friends, and stared over the heads of Jay Bird and a contingent of DeVries High students at his wife. After a moment she looked up from the grave, blinked several times, and fixed Steven with a gaze of surprise and disbelief. Clearly she hadn't expected to meet him here. Face tight, she broke contact first, looking down. She seemed to lean away from Jacob, whose gaze never drifted up.

The service began, but the priest's monotone was lost against the background chorus of rumbling powerboats, and Steven's gaze settled on the silver and chrome casket. He thought he'd already bid his farewells to Lisa on Rehoboth Bay, and wasn't prepared for the black wave of bereavement that swept over him now. He swayed beneath the heat, and the clustered mourners seemed to close in around him. With murmured excuses he pushed his way out of the circle and retreated to the line of limousines, stopping near the Cadillac Jacob and Gail had arrived in. The driver gave Steven a quick glance, but remained safe in his air-conditioning, windows up, engine idling.

The circle of mourners numbered sixty or more; Steven recognized most, either from the high school, the Lamplighter, or the few parties of the resort realty crowd he'd attended with Gail. Directly behind Gail and Jacob stood Bill Thompson, whose cold-eyed gaze slid away the second he saw Steven looking at him.

Near Thompson were Jimmy and Sharon Van Dusen, and with them Melinda Samuels, the school psychologist who'd been part of Thompson's group the morning Steven was called in. As always, Jimmy was ringed by a cluster of kids, students, and team members present and past; normally Steven would have his own group surrounding him, just as they always gravitated to him, and he felt a twinge of envy. He could have used the supporters.

Jimmy mouthed the words "Wait for me" several times until Steven nodded in return.

Standing well outside the circle were several men Steven didn't recognize—cops, he guessed, though Hackett wasn't among them.

Graveside words drifted over, all the stock phrases about time and understanding and life sustained in the memories of others, and Steven scuffed impatiently at the crushed white shells of the drive and tried to compose what he was going to say to Gail. The nearest cop eyed him.

The group under the canopy stirred, seemed to draw in on itself for a moment and lean over Lisa's casket, then subsided like held breath released. People drifted off in twos and threes between the headstones. Only Gail and Jacob remained next to the grave; then they, too, turned away and walked slowly back toward the limousine.

Gail saw him first. She tensed, clutching Jacob's arm and alerting him, and he looked up and spotted Steven for the first time. They continued walking at the same pace, as cool as if Steven were merely an acquaintance come to pay his respects. As they neared him, Steven wondered if these two had worked together all along, if Gail had played a part in Lisa's accusations, in his losing his job, in Lisa's death, in the planting of Lisa's sailboard in the garage.

They halted. Gail stood next to Jacob and perhaps half a foot ahead of him. Her makeup, applied more professionally than she'd ever bothered while with Steven, chiseled ten years from her face. Jacob, on the other hand, seemed to have aged ten or fifteen years since Steven had seen him in the emergency room. His eyes were red-rimmed, and grief made his face more hawk-like than ever.

"What are you doing?" Steven said. "Is this real, Gail?"

"This is a funeral, Steven." Gail's words were clipped. "We can discuss our personal situation later."

He'd given her an opening much too quickly, and in an attempt to recover himself he said to Jacob, "I'm sorry about Lisa. We'll miss her."

"I don't need sympathy from you, Mr. Blake." Jacob's disdain was calculated to make it clear to everyone around them that he needed nothing Steven could possibly offer.

"I didn't come here to get into anything with you," Steven said quietly. "Call a truce, okay?" He started to turn away.

"The police will investigate this until someone is arrested, Blake." Wood's voice carried such a tone of accusation that Steven turned immediately back to him.

"And I hope they get the right person," he replied, and he looked at the two of them, Jacob and Gail, standing nearly thigh to thigh. Tremors of exhaustion and anger shook his legs. "Can you say the same, Jacob?"

Wood lunged forward, face still a mask of iron control. Steven braced, but Gail took a quick sideways step into Jacob's path and blocked him. She took two more quick steps toward Steven, and his surprise turned to shock as she stared directly into his eyes and drove the point of one high heel into the top of his foot. Reflexively he grabbed both her arms above the elbows and shifted her weight away. Around them rose disapproving cries, and Steven could sense others closing in. Walling out the pain and the noise, he clenched her arms for a moment and stared back into her eyes, looking for a hint of affection or any other emotion he could recognize. The gaze she threw back seemed as flat and gray and icy as the Delaware Bay in December, but he held her eyes until he saw the first hints of uncertainty.

"Do you have any shame?" he asked quietly.

"Don't," she said, so lowly that no one else could hear. "Please. I'll explain."

He set her free and stepped back. "No," he said. "You can't."

This stalled her for a moment. Gail blinked, and her glance cut left, then right as she seemed to recall where they were. The circle of faces pressing around them was as greedily curious as those who'd stared down at Steven when he lay on the beach vomiting bay water, and he felt his cheeks beginning to burn as he pictured how they must look.

He looked at Wood, who'd been joined by two younger men in dark business suits, and saw an element of satisfaction in the man's patient stance, and he realized how gratifying this scene must be to

Jacob, the vindication he must feel in having Gail confronting Steven this way while most of the town observed.

Gail seemed to follow his thoughts, and she turned back to Jacob. "I've got to talk to Steven for a minute," she said.

Jacob looked at his watch and nodded. "Don't forget there will be people at the house," he said, and turned and got into the back-seat of the Cadillac. Gail linked her arm through Steven's and led him away from the crowd, out amongst the headstones. After a few paces he pulled his arm free.

"What are you doing?" he asked her again. "How could you do this to me? Why couldn't you tell me about this?"

"I'm sorry," she said, "but this was the only way. I started all of this, and I have to put a stop to it in my own way."

"What exactly are you putting a stop to?"

"Jacob's vendetta."

"By going back to him? You know he's just going to throw you away now, so he can humiliate you the way he thinks you did him."

"He won't get the chance," Gail said, then went on: "I wish I'd never stayed in this town, Steven. I should have left four years ago, and none of this would have happened."

"Are you including Lisa in that?"

Gail didn't answer for several paces, just kept slowly walking, head down. Finally she said, "I'm afraid Lisa would have come to trouble no matter what."

"You don't believe I had anything to do with her drowning, do you?"

She shook her head.

"Did he?"

At this she looked up at him, eyes flashing. She stopped, brushed her hair back tightly from her face with both hands. "I don't think so," she said. "I can't believe he would."

"But you're not sure?"

"I don't know," she said. "I don't know anything about anything anymore. Why didn't we leave here that first summer?"

"Because we thought we had our own world," Steven said. "Why are you with him?"

She gazed back toward the waiting limo; the crowd had thinned slightly, though most still stood and talked and cast surreptitious glances in their direction. As she and Steven watched, the limo's rear passenger window slid down, revealing Jacob. He sat in the dim interior, smoking a cigarette and watching them; he was too far away for Steven to read his expression.

"It's like being in orbit," Gail said. "I've discovered that I could never get completely free from him as long as I stayed this close."

Her candor jarred Steven more than hurt him, like a dive into water colder than he'd expected, and he was suddenly clearheaded. "Then it was never real."

"There's more to it than you know," she said. "Someday when all this has calmed down, we'll talk about it."

He studied this woman, and figured that day would never come. He looked back at Jacob's silhouette in the limo, and said, "Go. Now."

She covered the fifty feet to the car without looking back; the door thudded crisply shut and they disappeared behind smoked glass, and in another moment the Cadillac glided away. Steven walked back toward the ring of spectators; their faces were uniformly hostile, and Steven realized for the first time the real depth of suspicion that surrounded him. Someone had been talking about him, and he picked Bill Thompson's round face from the crowd.

"Kind of makes you think, seeing the two of them together."

Thompson blinked in surprise, but recovered quickly. "What does it make you think, Mr. Blake?"

"It makes me wonder if anyone ever tells the truth about anything. Tell me, did you ever hear directly from Lisa on those accusations you were throwing around?"

"We were scheduling a meeting with Lisa, yes," Thompson began.

"But you only heard from Jacob," Steven said.

Thompson hesitated, then said, "That's correct."

"So now we'll never know what she would have told you, will we?" Steven said.

"The police will continue the investigation from this point." Thompson seemed very stiff and nervous, as though he might even be a little afraid of Steven, or of what he himself might say that he shouldn't.

"And I'm sure they'll get all the help you can give them," Steven said.

"Absolutely."

"Good." Steven stared at the principal with all the coldness he could muster. "What do you think, Bill, do you think I should sue you over this? I get the impression you haven't been very discreet about things. I could probably cost you your job, you know, after all the suspicion you've thrown on me without one good reason."

Thompson turned abruptly and left, and for the next few minutes Steven stood next to the drive with his hands in his pockets and watched the entire procession file out of the cemetery; car by car passed him. Few would meet his gaze. Standing calmly, smiling and nodding, he visualized himself leaping at each vehicle, fists shaking in the air, pounding on car hoods and screaming, "I didn't do anything!"

When the last of them passed, he let his smile fade. His shoulders slumped, and he took off his sunglasses and massaged his eyes and the bridge of his nose.

"You didn't do yourself much good here today, buddy."

Steven jumped and spun around to face Jimmy. The coach wore aviator sunglasses, and sweat glistened on his forehead. He carried his jacket, and his yellow tie hung loose and his white shirt clung to his body. Behind him stood Sharon and Melinda Samuels.

"Jimmy, you scared the hell out of me," Steven said. "I thought everybody was gone."

"What were you trying to accomplish here?"

"Nothing but coming to Lisa's funeral. I didn't expect to see Gail."

"Did you two get anything sorted out over there?"

Steven shrugged and turned to Jimmy's wife. "Hi, Sharon. How you doing?"

"I'm fine, Stevo. You know Melinda?"

"Sure, one of Thompson's accomplices." Melinda was of medium height, with chin-length blond hair. Steven figured her age to be about forty. He decided that she was peering at him with the unfocused gaze of someone who had intentionally left her glasses home. "Hello," he said cautiously. Though he recalled her being the most nearly sympathetic of the three at the school, he didn't entirely trust memory. She may simply have been a rattler between two cobras, the least poisonous of three snakes.

"Good morning." Her tone was guarded, but not unfriendly. "How are you?"

"Not very well, as you probably know better than anyone else."

She eyed him calmly, then said, "Steven, it wasn't my idea to bring you into the school for that meeting. I said from the beginning that Lisa had some real problems and a history of telling stories that never quite panned out. We should have been more cautious."

"But you weren't," he said. "And now the story's all over town, you've shot my reputation to hell, and most of the people here today were looking at me like I'm the reincarnation of Ted Bundy."

She flushed and looked at Jimmy, who shifted impatiently. "Where's your car?" he said to Steven. "I've got to get out of this heat."

"I walked," Steven replied.

"Come on, then, I'll give you a lift."

"Four of us won't fit in your pickup. I'll walk home."

"Melinda drove," Sharon said quickly. "She and I are going to lunch now, anyway."

Steven looked at each of them, then over to Lisa's grave, where a work crew was moving aside the banks of flowers and beginning to disassemble the green and white canopy. "Fine. Let's go."

The four of them crunched up the clamshell driveway toward the cemetery's exit, he and Van Dusen following the two women. Outside the gate, they parted—Sharon and Melinda to the right, where a red Honda was parked on the grass, Steven and Jimmy to Van Dusen's blue Ford.

"You should have been nicer to her," Van Dusen said. "She wanted to meet you again."

"Maybe she should have stood up to Thompson better a few weeks ago," Steven said, though he knew there was probably no way she could have done any more.

They'd reached the pickup. Van Dusen started it and turned the air-conditioning on before answering. From the high seat of the pickup, Steven could see back over the brick wall and into St. Peter's Cemetery. Already the canopy was down, the flowers were banked to one side, and a backhoe crept up to Lisa's grave. "I wonder why he buried her here. All Saints in Rehoboth would have been closer."

Van Dusen shrugged. "I guess he figures he won't live in Rehoboth much longer."

Steven watched the backhoe for a moment as it reached for the first scoop of earth, and he wished the gravediggers were still required to use shovels, that this final note of Lisa's life didn't seem quite so industrial. His vision swam, and he looked at Jimmy. "Where else would he be living? Have you heard something?"

"Just guessing. Surprised you showed up today."

"Why wouldn't I?"

"Rumors are flying. People are pretty upset."

"I figured." Steven's voice was cold and flat with anger. "Who's spreading them?"

"You probably don't need the details."

Jimmy was right—Steven's imagination could fill in the scenes.

"You actually did pretty good today," Jimmy said. "I'd be a maniac if I ever saw Sharon with another man like that."

Steven thought again of Lisa as he'd last seen her, sprawled on the fiberglass deck of a sportfisherman's boat, and only then of Gail with her arm locked in Jacob's, and then of the gleaming white sailboard as he'd first spotted it in his garage, and he knew he'd have to stay with this until he made it right. "They deserve each other," Steven said. "You know Jacob did all this, don't you?"

"I believe you," Jimmy said. "But nobody else does."

"Why? What have I done or said that makes you believe me?"

Jimmy always got twitchy when explanations were demanded of him, probably because he was too accustomed to issuing unquestioned orders to high school basketball players. He watched the workers around Lisa's grave while he mumbled, "I don't know. I just know you."

"Is that all you know?" Steven said. "You know anything else that I don't?"

"Come on," Van Dusen said roughly, "I explained why I didn't tell you about Gail."

"You thought I already knew. What else do you think I might already know?"

"I think you already know what a goddamned shark Jacob Wood is." Van Dusen's voice held enough sharp bitterness to surprise Steven.

"You think he did it?"

"I think he does whatever he needs to do. He and his cronies have already managed to grab everything they've wanted. You've seen that firsthand, now." Van Dusen considered him for a moment. "Maybe you'd better leave this to the cops, you know?"

"They're as convinced as everybody else that I'm guilty."

"Well, as long as you're not, there's no problem, right?"

Steven wished he could believe that. "Not with this much going against me."

Van Dusen took a deep breath and opened the six-pack cooler that sat between them. "You need to give yourself a break with this shit," he said. "Have a beer."

Steven shook his head. "Too much to do. You mind dropping me off now?"

Van Dusen twisted open a bottle of Moosehead, and put the truck in gear. "Sounds to me like you ought to get some rest instead of finding more to do."

The canal paralleled Pilottown Road; the truck was parked heading east, toward Lewes and Steven's house, and Roosevelt Inlet was behind them. For a moment Steven focused on the steady line of powerboats heading up toward them. "Maybe I'll take the boat out," he said. "Just go out in the middle of the bay."

"We've been talking about fishing all summer," Van Dusen said. "Come on back with me; we can take my boat."

Steven shook his head. "Not today," he said. "I need some time to myself."

"Tomorrow, then. Come on over in the morning."

"I'm working at the Lamplighter tonight," Steven said. "I won't be up early."

"Doesn't matter. Come over about ten-thirty or so. We'll have a brunch ready, then take the boat out for a few hours. No kids."

"Sure," Steven said, but his attention had shifted down Pilottown Road. A cluster of cars was parked on both sides of the road in front of his house, and as they drew closer he could see they were all police cars, some unmarked, some marked state police cruisers, two Town of Lewes cars.

"Now what the hell?" Van Dusen said.

"I don't know," Steven sighed. He'd spent a hot and dusty hour before the funeral returning his garage to a staged shambles, and now prayed silently that he'd found every last piece of sailboard hardware. "This guy Hackett just won't leave me alone."

Van Dusen parked behind a dark blue LTD with state police plates. Cops were all over Steven's yard, standing on the porches of both houses. Hackett stood in the center of the yard, talking to two uniformed state troopers, then turned to stare at the pickup.

"You sure they don't have any reason to be after you?" Van Dusen asked.

"None that I know of," Steven said; after a moment, he added, "But who knows how I'm being set up now?"

"You want me to wait? Anybody I can call?"

"No, go ahead." Steven preferred to deal with them by himself. "Maybe I'll see you tomorrow. If I can."

"Call me," Jimmy said. "If you need anything at all."

"Maybe help making bail," Steven said. Jimmy didn't crack a smile, and Steven took a deep breath and climbed out of the pickup and walked toward Hackett.

The detective reached into his back pocket, then extended a folded sheet of paper. "Search warrant," he said, and his face and voice were cold enough to make all their earlier conversations seem nearly amiable.

"What are you looking for?" Steven said. "Maybe I can help."

"What do you think we might be looking for?"

"I don't have a clue." He was so tired that all of this seemed surreal, and he had no patience for Hackett's habit of deflecting every question straight back at him. "If you want to tell me, I could probably save you time."

Hackett considered him for a moment. "Just stay out of the way, Mr. Blake. Let us do our job."

"Fine." Steven shrugged, then without looking at the warrant folded it yet again, and stuffed it into his back pocket and began to walk toward his house.

"Mr. Blake," Hackett called after him. "I'll ask you once more to keep out of our way."

Steven turned back. "Where would you like me?"

Hackett's lips began to move with the answer he wanted to give, but he stopped himself and pointed tiredly at a lawn chair resting in the grassy shade in front of the cottage. "Just wait there."

Steven settled where directed. Without any orders that he could see, one of the uniformed state troopers hovered casually nearby, studiously not looking at him.

He counted at least twenty cops—plainclothed and uniformed, state and town. They thumped in and out of the cottage, passing him without a word. One bald Lewes cop emerged from the hatchway to the crawlspace under his house, brushing away cobwebs and swearing. A line of four others paced the lawn with slow treads, eyes intent on the grass. Across Pilottown Road, another group scanned the grass leading down to his dock. Steven looked everywhere but to his right, at the gap between the back of his house and his garage, until he could resist it no longer.

The nearest garage door was flung wide and propped back. Storm windows leaned against the back of his house, and he heard the clatter of other junk being moved out.

He could hear his own pulse pounding, felt the sweat rolling down his spine. Across the street, a scuba diver threw his fins up onto Steven's dock, climbed the ladder, and shook his head at the two cops waiting.

He wondered yet again who'd done this to him, who'd tipped off Hackett and timed the call so exquisitely that everyone who'd cared enough about Lisa to attend her funeral had driven past this gang of cops searching his house. If rumors had flown earlier, now gossip would have him arrested, convicted, and sentenced by nightfall.

A cop emerged from one of the state cruisers parked at the front of the lawn, and beckoned Hackett. Well out of Steven's hearing, the detective conferred briefly with the trooper. Several others drifted over to join Hackett, with frequent glances back at Steven, and after a couple of minutes of discussion, most of them got into their cars and left. Hackett strode grimly across the lawn.

"How'd you get the board down to Rehoboth Bay?"

"What are you talking about, please?" Steven looked up from his lawn chair. Hackett stood before him, the house's shadow line cutting across his chest, his face in the full sun. He was sweating heavily.

"You're going to tell me about it now, or you're going to tell me about it later," he said. "Be better if it happened now."

"I can't tell you what I don't know about. What board are you talking about, and what's it have to do with me?"

Hackett studied him. "I almost can't decide whether or not you're lying. We'll find out, though."

He left, and in another couple of minutes all of the others had followed. Still Steven sat in the lawn chair, not trusting his shaking legs yet. What he could see of the place was a shambles, and he was in no hurry to tour the damage, anyway.

Relieved though he was that he'd passed muster here, he prayed that he hadn't forgotten anything—scuff marks, greasy handprints, bootprints—that could link the ditched sailboard to him. And for what felt like the thousandth time in his life, he rued his own pig-headed independence. He'd only gotten himself in deeper, and should have trusted Hackett, or even his own lawyer. They could have been ready, knowing that whoever reported the sailboard was the person who put it there.

No chance now, though. Hackett's mind was closed for good, and saving himself would be an act for the toughest audience he'd ever faced. If his improvisation fell flat this time, he'd face worse than stony faces. But still he felt some satisfaction in knowing that he'd thwarted someone's plans for him, forcing another move, and every action he forced from Lisa's killer must increase his or her risk of exposure.

Like any good soloist practicing a tune, he sat, eyes closed, and replayed and reworked each scene and image and remembered line of speech from the past few days—Thompson's unexpected appearance and summons, the inquisition in his office, the conflict and uncertainty in Gail's eyes, Lisa lax in the bottom of a stranger's boat, the pair of sailboards closing in on him as he swam, the unexpected grief in Jacob's face this morning, and, for the briefest instant before veering away, the fading light and cold calm he'd found under the Delaware Bay. The notes that persisted, the ones he found himself playing again and again, spelled out Melinda Samuels, because at least the possibility of his innocence had occurred to her without his planting it; from there might grow the theme that would reveal the truth.

Jimmy might be some help, but Steven couldn't get past the idea that the coach had known about Gail and Jacob for months without revealing it. And Jimmy and Steven were known to be friends; few would view him as objective.

Melinda had access to files, the administration's ear, a seat at the discussions of Steven's professional fate, and seemed to be the only person in a position to help him who might really do so. At least she'd bothered speaking to him at the cemetery, and she'd been more civil than Thompson, at least until Steven had jumped down her throat.

First step would be to mend that bridge, and he pushed up from the lawn chair and went inside to call Jimmy.

14

Sunday morning was abuzz with power mowers as every able-bodied homeowner seized the brief hour after the heavy dew dried and before the day's heat built to its full, thunderous weight. Steven had only been to Jimmy's new house twice before, and couldn't quite remember which streets to take, so he cruised slowly through the winding development of raised ranches until he spotted the Ford pickup. Then the coach himself flew around the corner of his house atop a green and yellow riding mower, wearing a red DeVries High baseball cap backwards. He looked like a teenager. Steven eased the Jeep into the curb behind Melinda's Honda.

Van Dusen killed the mower in the middle of the front yard, took off his hat, and used the blade edge of his palm to squeegee the sweat from his face. "How you doing today? Cops been back?"

"No, I'm fine," Steven said shortly. He was resolute, determined now to fight back, and he looked pointedly at Melinda's car. "Is she here?"

"Around back. You gonna tell me yet why it was so important for me to get her here? You sure changed your mind fast."

"I told you on the phone. I need all the help I can get with this thing."

The coach perched on the stilled mower like an overgrown kid on a tricycle, all protruding knees and elbows. There was something perpetually adolescent about Jimmy, as there seemed to be about most athletes who'd been successful at a young age. Now his face, flushed with the morning heat, wrinkled in troubled scrutiny. "You ever find out what the hell all those cops were looking for?"

Steven shook his head—he didn't trust anyone enough to give the sailboard away. "None." He raised the sack he was carrying. "You want a cold one?"

Van Dusen reached like a drowning man stretching for a lifevest just out of reach, then downed half a beer in one gulp. "Who's the main cop there, one that was talking to you?"

"Hackett. State police detective."

"Guy looks like he's got it in for you."

"Afraid he does," Steven said. "Until I can convince him otherwise."

"That could be a lot of convincing, from the look of him."

Steven nodded toward the back corner of Van Dusen's house, where Melinda Samuels presumably waited in the shade. "She could help. If she will."

"Go to it. I'll be done in a couple minutes." Jimmy pushed the starter button on his mini John Deere, and the motor roared to life. He tossed his empty beer can at Steven, popped the clutch, and whipped away, leaving two black stripes across the scorched sod.

Van Dusen's backyard sloped down to a muddy tidal stream; this subdivision was so newly wrenched from the edge of the salt marsh that the scarred stream looked more like a drainage ditch than anything natural.

Three spindly saplings dotted the backyard—a sycamore, a sweet gum, and a silver maple—and parked just below the deck was a screened cube with a green canvas roof.

"Hey, Stevo," Sharon called, "get your butt in here before the horseflies eat you up."

Steven opened the flimsy screen door, stepped inside, and quickly shut it. The small screen house quivered. He nodded at Melinda, who sat facing Sharon. She nodded coolly in return. Her eyes were icy, more piercingly blue than Steven remembered, and it took him a moment to realize she was wearing tinted contacts.

The table was laden with the kind of pastries Steven had given up years ago—Danish, doughnuts, sticky buns, all white flour and sugar and fat—braced on one end by a sweating, round glass pitcher half filled with Bloody Mary mix, and at the other by a ceramic bowl of fresh fruit, the latter as out of place as crystal at a crab feast. Sharon, at least twice the width of Jimmy, was clearly the chief beneficiary of years of these brunches. She was a year or two younger than her husband, but looked ten years older. Steven leaned down and kissed her cheek.

"Let me guess," he said. "You're on your second."

"How'd you know that?"

"Your coach voice. Very reliable sign."

"Go to hell," she said good-naturedly. "Or at least pour one for yourself."

For a moment Steven wavered, undecided between the safe seat next to Sharon or the frosty one next to Melinda, then sat next to the psychologist. "The fruit has to be your contribution," he said to Melinda.

"And what's yours?"

Feeling slightly foolish, Steven lifted a six-pack from the sack he'd brought.

"Charming," she said. "For breakfast?"

"For Jimmy. His metabolism's young enough to take it." He glanced around him, then said to Sharon, "Where are the kids?"

"At their grandmother's, thank God. You don't know how glad I'll be when this summer's over."

"Me, too," Steven said, though for far different reasons.

"It's not just the kids," she said, "but it's the bugs, too. Between the horseflies and the gnats and the mosquitoes we can never sit out here, outside of this screen house. Everything comes out of that swamp and lands in our backyard."

"It's not that bad." Jimmy spoke from outside the door. "Just certain hours of the day." He let himself in.

"We never had that kind of problem at the old house," she said.

"Sure we did," Van Dusen said.

"Like hell," Sharon retorted, and she turned to Steven for confirmation. "You tell him. You still live there."

"You were just as close to the marshes over there," Steven said, though he had no wish to be drawn into the middle of the dispute. He turned to Melinda to try to steer a new conversational course, but Sharon rolled on.

"I really miss that old place," she said. "It was so much easier to get to the stores and the beaches, and the boat was right there across the street."

"It's got to be better here for the kids," Steven said. He'd heard the complaints before, but since Jimmy had stood by him the last few weeks, he felt obliged to try to help him out. "Pilottown Road's gotten busy as hell since the university came in."

"That's twenty years ago," she said. "And it's still a dead-end road. Here I have to worry all the time about the kids falling into the ditch at the end of the yard, and if they won't be able to climb back up because the mud's so slippery and there's nothing growing there."

Van Dusen sighed, stooped, and opened a cooler next to the door. He rummaged to make room in the ice. "You want to put those in here?"

Steven handed over the sack. Van Dusen popped a fresh beer and laid the others to chill. Cautiously Steven glanced at Melinda; her eyebrows lifted minutely, and she gave a tiny shrug.

"I still don't understand why the hell we had to move all the way over here." Sharon wouldn't let the issue go. "Jimmy just had to have this place, though. Even his own brothers won't talk to him since he sold his dad's house. Did you know that?"

"Sharon, do us a favor and shut the hell up," Jimmy said. "Steven's got more to think about than the bugs in your backyard."

Sharon banged her glass down, stood, and stalked out. She

slammed the door behind her, and the screen house trembled so fiercely that Steven feared momentarily for the safety of them all. Van Dusen sighed in exasperation, and glanced at Steven, then at his wife's receding back. "Better go make peace," he said after a moment. "Sorry about this."

He left more gently than Sharon had, bounded up the deck stairs, and went inside. Steven wondered whether the entire set-to had been staged to give him time with Melinda.

He cleared his throat. Melinda sat at the other end of the bench, sipping a grapefruit juice, waiting. "Well, they do this," he said. "Don't take it seriously."

"I know," she said. "I've known them both for years."

"You only came to Lewes last year, didn't you?"

"Sharon was my sister's roommate at college. I got to be friends with her then, and hung in there despite him."

"He's not so bad," Steven said, figuring his reservations were best kept to himself until he knew his audience better. "He was a hell of an athlete not so long ago. And he's stood by me in this mess."

She shrugged. "Jimmy said you wanted to talk to me."

"I owe you an apology," he said. "I was upset. No excuse for being so rude."

"No big deal," she said. "I said something stupid and you bit my head off. Fair enough."

"And we're not even married."

She didn't crack a hint of a smile. "What were all those police cars doing at your house yesterday?"

"I don't have any idea," Steven said. "They tore my place apart, then left all of a sudden."

"Did they find anything?"

"Nothing that didn't belong there. I don't know what's going on or why they showed up that way, but somebody's launched some kind of campaign against me."

She studied him skeptically. "Who? Why?"

Voices rose inside the Van Dusen house, and Steven decided the argument either hadn't been staged, or that it had kick-started a genuine battle. Melinda ignored the noise, convincing him that she really *had* known the Van Dusens a long time.

"Lisa's father's trying to pull something on me," he said. "And probably my wife, Gail. About to become ex."

"The one at the funeral yesterday."

"Only one I've got," Steven said. "Look, you know I didn't do this, don't you? Any of it."

"I don't know anything," she said. "I'm fairly sure you didn't drown the girl. Maybe not so sure you didn't sleep with her, but I'll give you the benefit if you say you didn't."

"Thanks. Funny to get more from a stranger than I got from my own wife."

"Not such a stranger. I've read your file at the school. Asked a lot of people about you. Even came and heard you play one night."

"When? Why'd you do all that?" Steven said sharply, more than a little annoyed at once again being inspected and evaluated without his knowledge. One downside of performing publicly was that people always knew where to find you, but weren't necessarily watching you for the reasons you wanted to be watched.

She shrugged. "Curious, I guess. This business sounded pretty suspicious from the beginning, especially after I heard about the history."

"And what'd you find out? Average guy, mediocre sax player, half-assed teacher, wife runs around on him so he chases after young students, old car, no money in the bank, no real ambition."

"You left out 'feels sorry for himself.' "

"Feels goddamned sorry for himself," Steven went on. "Drinks too much. Gets accused of sleeping with his best student, threatened with losing his job, going to jail, et cetera, so naturally takes the easy way out and drowns the girl."

"She had fresh water in her lungs," Melinda said. "Did you know that?"

Steven shook his head, slow to understand. "How could she? I saw them pull her from Rehoboth Bay."

"It's in this morning's paper. Fresh water."

"So she was drowned somewhere else, then dumped in the bay."

"Looks like it. They found her sailboard yesterday, too, washed up on the shore."

He nodded, as though the discovery of the sailboard were perfectly natural and of absolutely no concern. "Anything else?"

"Here's the article."

The newspaper she extended held a lurid color photo of two grim-faced Coast Guardsmen unloading Lisa's sailboard from their launch. Steven skimmed the piece quickly, but there was nothing further in the article he didn't already know. Hackett was quoted as saying the investigation was proceeding vigorously, but that no definite suspects had emerged yet. He laid the paper on the picnic table. "The poor kid deserved a lot better," he said.

"Yes." Melinda gazed at him thoughtfully for several seconds beyond his comfort level, then said, "Maybe you deserve better, too."

"You could help me," he said.

Her blue eyes narrowed. "How?"

Steven hesitated, shaping his words. "It would help if I could clear myself of sleeping with her."

She looked at him hard, refusal waiting on her lips, forcing him to ask.

"Who were the kids who backed up Lisa's story?"

"You know I can't tell you that."

"*Won't* tell me. *Could,* but won't."

"Can't. No way, no how."

"You know, I've faced all these accusations and all this innuendo and it's about to do me in, and I still haven't had a chance to talk to the people doing the accusing."

For a moment she seemed to waver, but said, "I can't. Even if I didn't have so many questions, I couldn't."

"If I could just find out why they were willing to back up Lisa . . ."

She stood, cutting off his request. "It sounds to me like Sharon and Jimmy have either made up or killed each other. Should we check?"

"They'll be out." Steven sat tight. "What are your questions? Maybe it'd help if I answered those."

"Oh, you've already started to." She left the screen house, crossed the lawn to the deck, and Steven watched her for a moment before following. She wore jeans and an oversized T-shirt. Her head was bowed, in thought perhaps, and her hair swept forward and left the pale nape of her neck exposed, and she suddenly seemed quite vulnerable.

Inside, Jimmy and Sharon sat calmly at their kitchen table, she drinking coffee, he a large orange juice. Van Dusen eyed Melinda curiously, then glanced at Steven. "You ready to go fishing?" he said.

"I don't know." Steven was reluctant to get on a boat with Jimmy and Sharon in their present moods—someone was likely to go overboard, and he didn't have the stomach yet for going in after them. He felt, too, that other avenues would probably be more productive than spending more time with Melinda. "It's getting hot," he said. "There's other things I should do."

"No choice," Van Dusen said. "We finally got you here."

In minutes he'd swept the four of them into their cars, and in his pickup led the procession to the marina on Wilson Creek. His Grady-White was already gassed and ready to go, and in minutes more they were making their way across the southern edge of Rehoboth Bay.

Steven rode in the very stern, lost in the motor's roar, and gazed northward across the bay. They passed near where he'd seen Lisa pulled from the water, then turned due south, headed down into Indian River Bay. Sharon and Melinda both disappeared belowdecks, and soon reappeared in bathing suits. Sharon's had a little skirt attached, and she reminded Steven of the hippo ballerinas in an old Disney movie. Melinda, in a bright orange one-piece cut low on her cleavage, sat next to Steven. She was pleasantly round, soft, less scrupulously maintained than Gail. It made her seem less guarded. Steven looked north again. Rehoboth Bay disappeared as they rounded a low, marshy island and headed for the inlet.

Melinda touched his shoulder lightly, and when he turned she was leaning closely enough that his nose brushed against her hair; the scent of her shampoo was wonderfully alien. He leaned back for enough distance to focus on her.

"I've got a question now," she shouted above the boat's roar. "How come it's taken you so long to split up with your wife?"

He shouted back, "What makes you think it's taken a long time?"

"Sharon and Jimmy said you two have been splitting up for the whole four years you've been married."

Steven looked at Van Dusen, who was focused on navigating them out to open water, then at Sharon. Seated across the boat, she smiled vaguely. Her lips moved, but Steven couldn't hear a word she said.

"Guess I was the last one to find out," he said to Melinda.

They'd entered the chaotic waters of Indian River Inlet, where both Rehoboth and Indian River bays came together and drained into the Atlantic; this outrush of water fought the incoming tide, creating a couple hundred yards of ropy swells and standing waves that tossed and pounded the Grady-White like a kid's Boogie board in the surf. Steven held tightly to the railing, and leaned over to shout into Melinda's ear again.

"I was fishing on the north jetty one day when three guys in a nineteen-foot Boston Whaler like mine tried to come out here. They would've been fine if they'd picked a wave and ridden it out. You go too slow through here in a boat that size, you'll get swamped from behind, but these guys couldn't wait and they tried to power through. Just can't do it in a boat that small—they came down the face of one wave and buried the bow in the back of the next one. Then they started taking on water, and the wave they'd just tried to pass caught up with them. Lifted the stern and flipped the boat end over end."

"Did they drown?"

He shook his head. "Two swam over to the jetty, and we helped them up. The other guy stayed with the boat until the Coast Guard got out. They're right inside the inlet, so it was quick, and you can't sink a Whaler anyway with all the flotation they've got built in. Those bozos were lucky they all had life jackets on."

"I hope you're not trying to scare me," she shouted. "I grew up spending half my summers on boats."

He shook his head. "I'm trying to explain something. Sometimes you've just got to pick your wave and commit to riding it—go too slow and you'll get hit from behind, get impatient and try to go too fast and you'll go down even faster."

She eyed him skeptically. "So we should all surf through life? Wait around and time it right and then hang on for the ride?"

"No," he snapped. "I'm trying to tell you things take their own time."

"Oh," she shouted back. "I thought you were still making excuses."

Steven leaned back away from her and wondered why he'd bothered telling the story. Van Dusen powered the Grady smoothly out the inlet and into open water, then turned north. Behind them stretched the wall of high rises that started at Fenwick Island and ran all the way down through Ocean City, miles to the south. Ahead, the flat coastline was broken only by the cluster of houses and shops and low hotels at Rehoboth Beach, by a dozen widely spaced, long-abandoned watchtowers, slit-windowed, concrete cylinders built during World War II to house the submarine watchers, and by the Great Dune at Cape Henlopen State Park, where two huge and decaying gun emplacements anchored the hill. They headed up the coast to Hen and Chickens Shoal, just off the cape, where Van Dusen had reports of bluefish.

Seas were running three or four feet, and the Grady pounded and rolled through the long swells. Van Dusen opened the boat up to full throttle, making conversation impossible, and Steven tipped his face up to catch the sun. Eyes closed behind his sunglasses, he smiled into the heat and salt spray, free and untouchable for the moment.

When he next glanced around, they'd drawn even with the packed beach and boardwalk at Rehoboth. They were traveling a half to three-fourths of a mile offshore, and above them labored a small, white, single-engined plane towing a banner for happy hour at one of the crab shacks on Highway One.

Melinda's eyes were screwed tight, her lips compressed into a thin, drooping line, and she clenched the edge of the seat cushion with desperate fists. Her face was white. Sharon now stood next to Jimmy, the two of them intent on the water ahead, and Steven leaned forward, thinking to alert them to Melinda's distress. But he stopped and glanced back at her. From bitter experience he knew that slowing the boat wouldn't help; calm water or dry land were the only cure, and since neither was in immediate reach there was no point in embarrassing her. And he was curious as to how well she'd tough it out.

The wait was short. They'd cleared Rehoboth and were running off the state park, nearing the fishing grounds, when her eyes suddenly flew open and she spun for the railing and leaned far over and lost brunch. The boat pitched, and from where he sat Steven wrapped both arms around her waist to keep her aboard. Clutching the railing with both hands, she braced her hip against his shoulder and retched into the sea again. For a moment Steven felt the heat of her body through the thin bathing suit, and then she shifted away, pulled from his grip, and turned back into her seat. The roar of the motor dropped, the boat settled back off plane, and Sharon was suddenly at Melinda's other side, towel in one hand and a sympathetic arm around the smaller woman's shoulders. Neither of them looked at Steven as he joined Van Dusen at the helm.

Jimmy grinned surreptitiously.

"She's chumming too soon," he shouted. "We're not there yet."

They made slow headway up the coast now, the boat rolling rather than pounding through the waves.

"What do you think?" Steven said. "Think we better stay out?"

Van Dusen shrugged, intent on the waves ahead. "I don't care," he said. "Get me a beer out of the big cooler, would you?"

Steven stepped below, where Jimmy kept a cooler the size of a small bathtub. At least a case and a half of beer sloshed around in the half-melted ice, and a puddle of cold water surrounded the cooler, numbing Steven's bare feet. He twisted the cap off one bottle of light beer, dropped the cap into the ice, and flipped the hinged lid down.

Van Dusen took the beer with a guilty glance back at Sharon, but she was too busy comforting Melinda to pay him any attention.

"Should've gotten yourself one," Van Dusen said. "Make me look bad."

"Headache," Steven lied. Lack of sleep was the real reason—even one beer would put him under at this point. He checked over his shoulder on Melinda; she offered a wan smile.

"We'd best not stay out," he said into Van Dusen's ear. "Why don't you go on up around the cape, go back down the canal?"

"Long way around," Van Dusen commented, but he made no move to head about.

"Smoother ride," Steven said. "You mind?"

"I don't care," Van Dusen said. "It's your trip. You ask her yet?"

"Ask her what?"

"About Lisa. Who the kids were that backed her up."

Surprised yet again by the coach's unexpected acumen, Steven wondered anew why Jimmy hadn't told him earlier about Gail and Jacob. He had to admit that he probably would have behaved exactly as Jimmy had if the situation had been reversed, though. "I asked," he said. "She can't tell me."

"Work on it," Jimmy replied. "Tell Sharon I need her up here for a minute."

"If she can't, she can't," Steven replied. "I'm not going to lean on her, especially when she's sick."

Both men glanced astern, where Melinda leaned out over the railing again, supported this time by Sharon.

"Better go help hold her," Jimmy said. He eased the throttle down until the boat was barely moving. "I don't want 'em both overboard. Wouldn't know who to pick up first."

Steven sat next to Melinda again, not touching her, but ready to grab her if she lost her balance. After a moment she sat again, holding a towel to her mouth. She shook her head, then lowered the towel. "I'm sorry," she said. "That's never happened before."

Steven resisted the urge to ask her about all those boats she'd grown up on. "We're heading around the cape for calmer water," he said. "Be just a few minutes."

"I don't want to ruin the fishing," she said.

"Jimmy doesn't care, as long as he gets to run his boat out here and drink beer," Steven said. "I don't care if I go fishing, either. Hardly ever do."

She patted his bare thigh. "Thanks."

"For what?" Steven looked at her in surprise.

"Keeping me on board. I don't swim very well."

Steven shrugged uncomfortably, conscious of her light touch on his leg, remembering the heat of her round hip against his shoulder. "You should have a life jacket on, then. Feel any better now?"

"Some," she said.

"Relax," he said. "He'll take it easy. Won't be too long."

She smiled uncertainly, then leaned back and closed her eyes, arms crossed around her breasts, hands clutching her stomach as if she could take hold of it and calm it. Jimmy powered up and brought the Grady around the cape without much more pitching and tossing, though when Steven glanced at Melinda again her concentration was tight. Once they'd rounded into Delaware Bay and motored behind the two big stone breakwaters sheltering Lewes and on into Breakwater Harbor, the water was suddenly as calm and smooth as a pool of oil. Jimmy opened the throttle gradually until the boat came up on plane. They knifed across the edge of Delaware Bay, parallel to the Lewes town beach and not far from where Steven had been run down by Todd Wood's sailboard.

In minutes they entered Roosevelt Inlet. Jimmy turned hard to port to head back down to Rehoboth Bay. The big motor barely loped along as they glided down the narrow canal, Van Dusen religiously holding to the No Wake speed limit, and Melinda's expression gradually turned sunny with relief. They paralleled Pilottown Road now, though, and as they neared Steven's place his own dark worries began to close in again.

"This is nice," she said. "Pretty."

"This is where I live." Steven pointed at his dock, fifty feet ahead.

"Want to stop?" Van Dusen shouted back at him. Steven shook his head. He'd face it all soon enough.

Melinda studied the waving phragmites and saw grass on the canal bank. "It looks a lot different from here."

"Trust me. That's my boat."

She considered it silently. After they'd slid past, she asked, "What's she like? She's very beautiful."

"Just a standard Whaler," Steven said, deliberately misunderstanding. "Nothing fancy."

Melinda shot him a sardonic glance. "You know who I mean."

He shrugged. "Tell you the truth, I don't know anymore. She grew up on the Main Line, and even if she won't touch her family's money, I guess she still thinks she's entitled to do anything she wants. How come?"

In lieu of answer she cast an amused glance at Jimmy and Sharon, who stood side by side at the boat's controls, Sharon with her arm draped companionably across Jimmy's wide butt. "What's with those two? You ask them to leave us alone?"

"No," Steven said. "That's their own doing."

"You planned all this out with them, didn't you? Had them ask me, got them to stage that ridiculous argument and leave us alone so you could try to pump me for information."

"Those two argue as a way of life. Don't blame that one on me."

"But you intended to get me out here where I couldn't get away so you could keep asking me questions," she persisted.

"Is that what I've done?"

"I know it's what you planned, and you probably would have if I hadn't screwed things up for you by getting sick."

"If that's what you thought, why'd you come today?"

"Because that was only one of the things I thought."

"What are the others?"

She peered at him quite intently and said, "I think you're getting into a lot of trouble when I don't think you did anything, and I want to know why."

"So do I," he said.

"Maybe I'm just guilty, too. I felt like part of a lynch mob at the school when Thompson brought you in."

"But that's your job," he said. "You've got to do that the same way you've got to protect those other kids, I guess."

She nodded, then took a deep breath and said, "Jay Bird and Jennifer Moore, you mean."

They were passing Fisherman's Wharf, where Steven had spent the afternoon drinking with Jimmy while Gail moved out, and Steven watched the docked fishing boats slide past them, then repeated, "Jay and Jennie?"

Melinda nodded.

"How come? What did they say?"

She shook her head firmly. "That's all I can tell you. And if you tell anyone I told you, I'll be looking for a new job, too."

"Don't worry," he said. "Thank you."

"Thanks for what?" Sharon Van Dusen said. She stood squarely in front of them, and there was something nearly coy in her voice. She'd never liked Gail. "You two telling secrets back here?"

Melinda stood. "What have you been doing up there with Jimmy?" she said. "Will he let me drive the boat? It's pretty calm here."

She strode up to join Van Dusen at the controls; Sharon lifted a questioning eyebrow. "Fast recovery," she said.

Steven only shrugged in return, and she joined the other two.

Salt marsh bordered both sides of the canal, blocking any breeze, and the August sun beat down on them. Steven shut his eyes and breathed in the same rich, biting stink of mud and rotting vegetation and salt that had surrounded him two nights before on his trip through here with Lisa's sailboard. He had two more pieces of this puzzle now, but couldn't see how they fit together.

Jennie Moore had graduated with Lisa—small, dark-haired, as well-behaved as Lisa had been wild, first-chair trumpet—and was off to the university this fall. Steven couldn't recall the two girls being especially close. In fact, there had been more than a touch of rivalry between the two.

Lisa in her junior year, though, had been one of Jay Bird's main persecutors, poking such persistent and spiteful fun at him that Steven had had to call her to account several times. He still believed she'd been the one to fill Jay's trombone slide with liquid dish detergent before the spring band concert, or at least the instigator.

He couldn't imagine how or why either of those kids had been brought to lie about him, though he pondered this question all the way back across Rehoboth Bay. Melinda held the helm, finally docking the boat with a deftness aimed to atone for her seasickness.

Jimmy and Sharon bustled around the slip, shutting down and securing the Grady, so practiced in their routines that there was little for Steven and Melinda to do but stay out of the way. They stood nearly shoulder to shoulder on the dock.

"Don't worry about telling me about Jay and Jennie," Steven said.

Melinda looked at him innocently. "Who?"

Impulsively he put an arm around her shoulder and hugged her, and for a moment she seemed to let him, then leaned away.

"So are you single or what?" Steven said.

"Define 'or what.' "

"Involved. You seeing anybody?"

She shrugged. "Not seriously."

"How about dinner?"

"What's that supposed to be, my reward?"

"Touchy, aren't you?"

"Sorry. It's a long story."

"I'd like to hear it."

She hesitated, then said, "Not tonight. I'm tired and sunburned and I need a shower."

"Tomorrow, then?"

"Got to teach my last summer class at Del Tech."

"Tuesday," he said.

At last she smiled and, dipping her head, gave in. "Nothing fancy," she said. "And I'll pay my own way."

"I invited you."

"I'm afraid you'll need all your money very soon, Steven."

He let this pass. "You know Lazy Susan's, out on Highway One?"

"No, but I can find it."

He gave her directions, which she wrote down in a small notebook pulled from her beach bag. Jimmy and Sharon clambered up onto the dock as she put the notebook away.

They made their noisy good-byes, Sharon halfheartedly griping about picking up the kids until Jimmy grabbed her, both hands on her ass, and smashed her to his chest in a bear hug that muffled her words to silence.

"Come on," he said. "Let's go home. We'll get the kids later."

Melinda, tired and clearly anxious to be off, followed them back to the cars.

After they'd pulled away, Steven looked around the marina parking lot. He was reluctant to return home yet. In the last hour on Van Dusen's boat, out of reach by telephone, secure from Hackett or Gail or any other surprise visitors, he'd been able to nearly relax for the first time in days. Who knew what new surprises awaited him back in Lewes, though—after the sailboard in his garage, little would surprise him. He wandered idly around the docks inspecting boats, then went to the marina office for a cold soda. In the boatyard behind the office were half a dozen boats in cradles, all bearing "For Sale" signs.

Third in line was a fiberglass sailboat. This he circled several times, and then returned to the office to get the keys.

The boat was a twenty-seven-foot O'Day, seven years old and fully equipped for cruising. Steven clambered aboard and let himself belowdecks, where he poked around for a few minutes. Then he settled in the cockpit, and tried to imagine the mast stepped, sails rigged, the boat afloat, and himself in control. He'd sail to the Caribbean, something he'd fantasized about for years, hop from island to island, month to month, learn to play with a steel drum band, play the island music.

"What do you think?" The boatyard owner stood on the ladder Steven had used to clamber aboard, head just above the stern. He was a heavyset blond guy in his mid-forties. "Belongs to a dentist up in Wilmington. I don't think he took it out more than two or three times a summer the whole time he kept it here."

"Nice," Steven said. "Out of my budget, though."

"I don't know," the guy said. "This dentist is getting divorced. He's pretty desperate."

"I know the feeling."

"Got a boat now?"

"Nineteen-foot Whaler," Steven said.

"Nice boat. You sailed much?"

"Whaler's the first powerboat I've owned," Steven said. "Always had sailboats before that. Nothing this big, though."

"She's a beauty. Easy sailer, too. Take you anywhere."

"That's what I was thinking," Steven said. He stood. "I don't want to waste your time, though."

The man remained in place on the ladder, blocking Steven's way down. "What kind of shape's your Whaler in? Pretty good?"

"I've taken good care of it," Steven replied. "It's docked in Lewes now."

"Bring it down. Let me take a look. Maybe we can work a deal for you."

Steven surveyed the sailboat wistfully. "Maybe I will," he said. "Maybe I just will."

15

On the off chance he could catch Jay Bird at practice, Steven checked the high school on the way home. Randy Wise had granted the kids a Sunday afternoon off, though, and Steven headed home to plot his next step. The names and the fact Melinda had given them were the first bright stars of hope, the first signs that he might be able to save himself.

He threw open all the windows and started the attic fan, and within minutes a hot breeze filled the curtains, billowing them into the house. In the five days since Lisa had drowned, Steven had probably slept no more than twelve hours, and he wandered fitfully through his house, too keyed up and restless to sleep, but too tired to concentrate on any one thing. Patches followed him room to room, keeping an eye on him.

For too long he'd been passive and waiting, he saw, even willfully blind—you see what you want to see, and he'd refused to see Gail leaving him until she was gone.

He put on a Coltrane CD, the classic quartet playing ballads; Coltrane had played as sweetly and lyrically as he could in this session, but still couldn't repress the edge of intense anger and anguish that broke through now and then, hoarsening his tone, cantering between two changes in a melody. There was no need for headphones with Gail gone, and Steven cranked the volume up.

Twice the phone rang, but he ignored it. The ballads soon bored him in his restless mood, and he rummaged through his collection, which was still disorganized from the break-in and yesterday's police search. He found and put on some of Coltrane's later stuff, the long, incantatory, ecstatic, and anguished solos of the years immediately before his death, the ones most difficult in their spiritual rhapsody.

Music filled the house like white water rushing past, unpredictable, startling, gone, and Steven found himself thinking about Lester's big band project. For the first time he realized what made him uneasy about the effort: the codification of spontaneity. How much could really remain of a living thing after you'd named all its points? Once you reduced it to predictable repetition, could mystery remain? It was the mystery of unpredictability, the sense of players venturing out into unmapped, uncharted, netless territory that made him love the music so fiercely.

Pity he couldn't have felt the same about his marriage, he thought. But somehow when he wasn't watching it had passed automatically from the early, heady unpredictability of improvisation to habit, and he'd never pushed beyond that level to find its true heart. Or his own.

He forced himself to recall Gail as she'd looked yesterday, arm in arm with iron Jacob Wood, tall, packaged, impermeable, and then tried to picture himself standing next to her in Jacob's place, and couldn't. The heat of anger rose in his stomach, and he unbuttoned his shirt and laid both palms on his abdomen. It was slick with sweat.

He'd never much cared what people in Lewes and Rehoboth thought of him—the kids changed every school year, families seemed more transient each year as the real estate churned, and he did his job and played his music and lived his life as well as he could and figured that the only judgment he cared about came from Lester and Marian and the few dedicated souls who came out to the Lamplighter weekend after weekend to hear him play.

But he'd never been so publicly humiliated, either, and it was the memory of the hostile faces surrounding him at the cemetery and of the cops picking through all his belongings that spurred him to the only step he could think of taking.

He had the names, a starting point: Jay Bird and Jennifer Moore. He could build from there, clear himself, show he'd never touched Lisa, that it had all been lies from the start. That wouldn't get him back to where he'd been before all this started, but the longer he paced through his small house, familiar objects around him, familiar music soothing him, familiar, devoted pet fastened on his every move, the more he realized he wanted to breathe new air, to taste something new.

He turned off the music, and in a moment had Lester Jones on the line.

"About this audition," he began after minimal greetings. "Wednesday night, right?"

"Seven o'clock," Lester replied. "You know where the building is."

"You think this is fair? You already lined up people."

"Survival of the hippest," Lester said. "Nobody's been promised a seat yet. Not even you, old buddy."

"I'll be there," Steven said. "Do me one favor though, and invite one more trumpet player."

Lester hesitated. "That's gonna make six, Steven, and we're only going to use two."

"This girl probably won't make it, anyway," Steven replied. "Thing is, I need a chance to talk to her."

"You want to tell me why?"

"She's one of the kids who backed up Lisa Wood's story," Steven replied.

Lester was silent.

"If you've got a problem with this, say so," Steven said.

"No, no," Lester said, too quickly to mean it. "We said we'd help you, and we will. Just thinking how to do this."

"I'll give you her name and number." Steven didn't like taking advantage of the friendship, but he steeled himself and did it, anyway. "You call her and tell her you heard about her from Jack King up at the U of D and want her to come try out."

"She at the university now?"

"Starting this fall."

"Doesn't seem fair to call the kid in when she doesn't have a shot."

"The audition will be good experience for her," Steven said. "Get her there early, like six-fifteen or so, okay? Maybe you and Marian could be there, too?"

Lester sighed, obviously unhappy with this intrusion on his project, but willing to go along. "Give me the number," he said. "I'll try it, and if she's going to show I'll let you know."

"Thanks," Steven said. "I owe you. What are the tunes for Wednesday, anyway?"

"Now that wouldn't be fair, would it?"

"All right," Steven said. "We'll make this an old-time Kansas City cutting session, right?"

"How you holding up?" Lester said. "Girl's father or the cops been back?"

"Good enough," Steven said. "Getting the names of these two kids helps, even if it's a kick in the ass to find out two more have turned on me."

"Who's the other one?"

"Trombone player named Jeff Bird. Senior this year, band president."

"What's going on? You never have trouble with your kids like this, not since you been teaching."

"I'm trying to figure it," Steven said. "That's why I need you to get this girl there for me. I'll try Jeff at band practice tomorrow."

"Watch yourself," Lester said. "Don't need any more trouble."

"No," Steven said. "I've already got more than I can handle."

He gave Lester Jennifer Moore's home number, and half an hour later the bass player called him back.

"Made me feel like a shit," he said, "but she'll be there."

"It's sneaky," Steven said. "Blame me if anything comes up."

"Shut up," Lester said. "I'll take responsibility for anything I do. Kid was just so excited."

"She'll live," Steven replied. "Who knows? Maybe she'll be the best goddamned swing trumpeter you've ever heard."

Lester chuckled derisively. "Mm-hmm. Eighteen-year-old white girl from Rehoboth Beach is gonna be one badass horn player, I'll bet."

"Remember who taught her," Steven said.

"Glad to see all your troubles keeping you humble."

SWEAT STREAMED DOWN the sides of Steven's face, coursed down his spine, trickled down through his chest hair. His khaki fisherman's cap, jammed down tight, was drenched, and his sunglasses were streaked. He clenched the top pipe of the chainlink fence that circled the football field, deep-breathing to bring his pulse back down.

At the far end of the field, half the marching band stumbled through their routine; the sections were so thin that the *Star Wars* battle theme sounded more like a dirge. In front of the band, walking backward as they marched up the field, Randy Wise bellowed through Steven's bullhorn.

When Steven couldn't stand it any longer, he vaulted the low fence and strode upfield. The kids in the front rank spotted him and stopped dead, causing those behind to pile into them. Wise, vice principal and Steven's former basketball buddy, walked another few backward paces, still shouting, then glanced over his shoulder to see what the kids were watching.

Surprise froze him for a bare second. Then he spun and stalked toward Steven, as though determined to protect the kids from him. The band immediately followed behind him, though.

Still forty yards away, Wise raised the bullhorn as he walked, and ordered, "Get off of school property immediately, Blake, or we'll have you arrested."

Steven kept walking, and as he drew closer shouted, "Are you out of your goddamned mind? Not even the army makes people drill on afternoons like this."

"What in the hell are you doing here?" Wise stopped five yards away, and within seconds the entire band gathered in a semicircle behind him, and once again Steven remembered the group that had gathered around him as he lay on his back on Lewes Beach puking into the sand, all of them curious and apprehensive. Now Jay Bird stood in the middle of the group. Steven glanced at him, but didn't let his gaze linger. Heat shimmered up from the turf, and for a few seconds there was a complete, pregnant silence. Wise looked around him as if just noticing the encircling band. "You kids go back up to the end zone."

None of them moved, and Steven felt a hint of relief—maybe he hadn't lost them completely.

"Are you crazy?" he said to Wise. "You can't work the band in weather like this. Where's everybody else?"

"You've been barred from school property, Blake." Wise glanced around behind him again, and settled on one of the sousaphone players. "Anderson, go call the police."

The kid wouldn't move. Wise tried several more names in quick succession, and with each failure his face turned a darker shade of red.

"Lighten up," Steven said. "I'll leave in a minute. I just need to talk to the kids."

"You've done enough damage around this school," Wise said. "I'm going to tell you once more to leave the property, Blake, after which I will not hesitate to force you to leave."

Ignoring him, Steven spoke directly to the waiting band. "I wanted to talk to all of you face to face," he began, "because I know how rumors get started and how fast they move."

Wise stalked up to him, chest out, eyes blazing. "Get the fuck out of here," he said, low and tight, "before I kick your goddamned ass all the way off the field."

Five inches taller, Steven looked down and said, loudly enough for the kids to hear him, "You've been ordering kids around for too long, Randy. Let me talk to them."

"Yeah," one of the senior girls called out, "let him talk to us, Mr. Wise." Other kids chimed in, and Wise looked back and forth from them to Steven, then capitulated for the moment with a sigh and a shrug.

"Fine," he said. "Talk. The cops'll know where to find you."

Steven looked slowly around at the circle of waiting faces, taking a moment to clear his anger. They stared at him, a few sullen and suspicious, but most openly, even greedily, curious.

"I'd be pretty suspicious in your position," he began. "Probably you've heard by now that I've been accused of some pretty outrageous shit, and God knows what stories you've heard. I just wanted to tell you personally that it's all bullshit. I've worked with some of you now for three years, since you were freshmen. Is there any one of you who's ever seen me do anything improper with any other student?"

Silence hung for a moment, none of them wanting to be first to speak, until a few heads shook. Then one brave soul in the back of the group said, "No, Mr. Blake," and a chorus of denials joined her.

"Have I ever said or suggested anything out of line to any of you?"

A briefer silence hung, broken this time by a low comment from one of the drummers that provoked a wave of nervous laughter from those nearest.

"What's that?" Steven said.

"I said you told us to practice more," the drummer called out, and the entire band laughed this time, and with that he felt he had them back.

"Before all this happened, did any of you ever hear anything or see anything that might have meant I had any involvement with Lisa?" He let his gaze linger on Jay Bird, who shook his head with the others, but wouldn't meet Steven's eyes in return.

"Come on, Blake." Randy Wise shifted impatiently. "This isn't proving anything. These are just kids, and you're manipulating them."

"Apparently some of these kids backed up the stories and accusations about me," Steven said. "I'd just like to hear those things firsthand so I can respond and clear things up here."

"That's it." Wise crowded close to him. "No more." Over his shoulder, he barked, "Anderson, Bird, Roberts, Strahosky, one of you go call the police immediately, or I'll suspend the entire band."

"School hasn't started yet," one of the kids called out, and a nervous titter passed over the group. Nevertheless, Steven saw a couple of the kids start for the school building.

Gangly Jay Bird suddenly stepped forward. "Wait a minute," he said. His voice broke into a high squeak. Everyone, including Wise, froze for a moment. "I'm the one who said the stuff," he blurted, "and I never thought you'd get in such big trouble, Mr. Blake. It wasn't true."

An immediate babble of questions rose from the band, and Steven closed his eyes, fighting back tears of relief and the urge to strangle the kid; thirty students and the vice principal had heard the words, and they couldn't disappear now. He took a deep breath, settling his voice. Wise had stepped back; eyes narrowed warily, he waited for Steven's next move. He was clearly calculating the best way to cover his own ass.

"Why'd you say it?" Steven quietly asked Jay.

The skinny trombonist licked his lips, and looked from Steven to the vice principal and back. "Um, could I please talk to you and Mr. Wise alone?"

Steven and Randy exchanged a glance, until Wise reluctantly nodded. Steven turned back to Jay.

"That's fine. Let's just make sure everybody here understands, though. Are you saying you never really saw or heard or knew about me doing anything with Lisa that I shouldn't have?"

Jay nodded. "Yes. I mean, that's what I'm saying."

"Okay," Steven said. He raised his voice to shout, "The rest of you go on home. It's too hot to practice. Tell your parents what you heard." He glanced at Wise. "Okay?"

Wise raised the bullhorn. "Band dismissed," he said. "Clear out of here. Practice again tomorrow at one."

"Can't you reschedule your tennis?" Steven asked quietly. "You're going to end up with some sick kids in this heat."

"Look," Wise said. "I don't want this job. I never wanted it, and I don't know what I'm doing. If we can figure out the truth here, you can have it back pretty goddamned quick. Meanwhile I'm going to run it the way I have to, and if that means they sweat a little bit, then so be it."

Steven eyed the vice principal for a long moment. "How'd I work with you for so long without seeing what an asshole you are, Randy?"

Half the kids still lingered nearby, and the guffaws that rose at this question made Wise look around sharply. "Go home," he barked. "Get the hell out of here. Practice tomorrow morning at nine."

Steven suppressed a grin. "Jay," he called out, "come on over here. Let's hear the story."

The trombonist hung back like a seven-year-old called on the carpet; gone was all the cockiness he'd showed a few weeks before when he'd watched the band from the bleachers with Steven.

"You're all right," Steven said. "You told the truth—I'm not pissed."

"Right," Jay said with a defiant wisp of his normal sarcasm. He walked closer anyway.

Randy Wise started in, "You've made a hell of a lot of trouble if you've lied about all this, Bird."

"Back off," Steven said, then: "Well, Jay? You going to fill us in?"

The kid's face was scarlet, and he looked like he'd rather be trying to direct the band again in front of a packed stadium. "I don't know," he said. "She just asked me to do it."

Steven sighed. "So you just naturally said, of course, Lisa, I'll trash Mr. Blake and ruin his life for you? Come on, Jay."

Bird sniffed nervously and rubbed his nose, and Steven wondered absently if the kid had a dope problem; unlikely, but not impossible, and he filed the thought. "She was in big trouble, Mr. Blake. I saw the bruises where her father beat her up."

"Did she tell you her father hit her?" Wise said.

Jay nodded, but his gaze didn't waver from Steven. "He's a pretty crazy dude, I guess, and nobody could fuck with him because he's so rich. She said he was making her set you up."

"How'd she convince you?" Steven asked. "She sleep with you, Jay?"

Jay shook his head, then looked down at the ground and said resolutely, "I'm not saying anything about that, Mr. Blake."

The stubborn set of his voice was convincing.

"You heard enough?" Steven asked Randy.

The vice principal nodded. "Let's go call his parents."

TUESDAY AFTERNOON STEVEN sorted through the two dozen charts Marian had sent, trying to figure which tunes Lester would use for auditions, and dug through his record collection, matching recordings to the transcriptions.

He settled on "Cotton Tail" as a logical first choice, especially if Lester was trying to cut saxes; Ben Webster's tenor solo was the heart of the song, and it could sort the players from the brayers pretty quickly. Slop couldn't hide in the section work, either, tight as it was.

He had this song on compact disk rerelease, which made it even easier to practice. Centering his music stand out in front of his speakers, he cranked the volume as loud as he could stand it, and punched the track number on the CD remote. The Duke Ellington Orchestra blasted out so loudly it could have been staged in the kitchen, and Patches beelined up the stairs; she'd hide under the bed until the music stopped.

The first couple of times through the song, Steven only listened, following along on the chart, tapping the track number again each time the song ended. Then he began to finger his tenor along with the CD, still so intent on every nuance of Webster's phrasing and intonation that he didn't want to muddy it with his own sound.

Over and over he did this, teaching his hands, setting the patterns in physical memory, on and on and on before he blew a single note. Then he began to blow along, softly at first, ever louder, until finally he played at full volume with the stereo. He closed the chart, set up stereo microphones at either side of the room, punched Record, and started the CD once again. He was playing from memory now.

He rewound the tape, listened to it, rewound it, recorded himself with the CD again, listened, recorded. He stopped. Sitting on the couch where he could reach the tape deck controls, he listened to the tape once more, himself playing along with Ellington and the band, Ben Webster's shadow; then he listened immediately to the CD, and then the tape again, and finally he allowed himself a small smile of satisfaction.

He checked his watch, and found the hour he'd intended to spend had stretched nearly to three. He was exhausted, spent. Cleansed. For him this intense practice and discipline and forced repetition was meditation, a path to perfect calmness, but it was a way he'd found too rarely the past few years. His music had drawn Gail to him, but then in her attempts to build him up and convince him to move back to the city to play full time while she supported him, she'd co-opted it somehow. For himself he'd found that only the playing could be shared, not the making of the music.

He stretched, called the dog to begin the hour-long process of coaxing her downstairs again.

A pounding came at the front door. Expecting one of the neighbors with a noise complaint, he flung the door wide and surprised Hackett in the act of knocking again.

Still blissed-out and loose from the music, Steven said, "Hi. What do you want?"

"Mr. Blake," Hackett said, peering past him into the living room. "Can I come in? Need to talk to you."

"Sure." Steven stood aside to let the cop enter; now that Jay Bird had spoken up, his worry level had gone down considerably. Hackett seemed a bit less threatening. "You been out there long?"

"Few minutes," Hackett said. "Heard the music and figured you wouldn't hear me knock any earlier."

"Probably not." He waited.

" 'Cotton Tail' is a great song. Always was."

"Here, listen." Steven punched the Play button, and the Duke Ellington Orchestra with Ben Webster and Steven Blake on tenor filled the room. Hackett winced at the volume, but otherwise his expression didn't change until the song was done.

"You got him," Hackett said. He shook his head and permitted himself a small smile. "Don't know how you do that, over and over. How long you been playing?"

"Since I was eight," Steven said. "What do you need today, anyway?"

"Ah, I talked to Randy Wise and the Bird boy." He glanced around; aside from the spot where Steven had just been resting, the couch and chair were both covered with sheet music. Steven cleared the chair, and they both sat.

"So they cleared things up," Steven said.

"Maybe," Hackett replied. "Still need to talk to the other student who was supporting Lisa. There's a lot to sort out yet."

"Am I still under some kind of suspicion?" Steven said.

"Should you be?" Hackett's gaze was clinical, beady, and Steven suddenly felt like the hare who's just felt the hawk's shadow.

"No," he said quietly. "Someone's going to a terrible amount of trouble over me, though. Look at last Saturday—there was no reason for you to show up here with all those people and tear my place apart. I still don't have everything put away again."

"I'm not sure there wasn't any reason," Hackett said. "Maybe we just didn't get here soon enough."

Steven's gaze didn't waver. "I don't know what you're talking about."

"Figured not. You think Wood's got it in for you?"

"Who else? He's holding a long-term grudge and wants my property. Looks like his ex-wife has gone back to him, but I don't think that's going to calm him down."

"Nobody else has seen those plans you were talking about, Mr. Blake. And I assume your wife is staying with him out of her own free will."

"Ah," Steven said. "So she's staying with him?"

"Assumed you knew that."

"No," Steven said. "I haven't talked to her." He glanced around the room, struggling to mask the mix of emotions that Hackett's words brought. "You want some coffee? Iced tea?"

"No, thanks." Hackett's tone was a touch less official tough-guy. "You want to get yourself something, though, go ahead."

"No. You still haven't told me why you're really here today. I assume you didn't stop by just to hear me play the saxophone."

Hackett sighed and glanced around the living room. "I'm just trying to figure out who drowned Lisa Wood," he said. "And I'm still trying to figure you out, Mr. Blake. I have a pretty good idea that the girl's sailboard was in your garage the night before we came, and I pretty much have it worked out how you carted it down to Rehoboth Bay in the middle of the night. Seems like a couple of hands on the party boats at Fisherman's Wharf saw your Whaler go by about two or three in the morning. If I'd been doing my job right, I would've had a car up here watching, I guess.

"Point is, I'm a bit puzzled, because I don't think you could've drowned that kid, not from anything I've found out about you. Of course, I've been surprised before. But if you didn't have anything to do with it, why wouldn't you just call me when that sailboard appeared back there? Unless you know who did drown the girl, and you're trying to protect that person, even if she's trying to set you up for it."

Hackett's words took a long minute to sink in. Slowly Steven said, "You think Gail drowned her."

"No, no, no." Hackett held up both hands. "I'm just speculating out loud, here, Mr. Blake, maybe hoping you'll let me know if I get warm."

"I can't see it," Steven said. "Pissed off at her as I am, I can't say she'd do that."

"Nah," Hackett grunted. "Nice theory, though—wife thinks you've been messing around with her ex-stepdaughter, gets rid of the girl, and sets you up for it at the same time—gets even all around. Who knows, maybe she even had a grudge against the kid for something earlier. You know how stepmothers and stepdaughters are."

Steven stared at the cop for a moment, outraged, but nagged by a tiny black kernel of doubt. "No," he repeated. "One thing I'm sure about is that Gail doesn't care enough about me to go to that much trouble."

"Well." Hackett stood. "It was an idea. I'll keep digging around. You think of anything that might help me, call me. You're looking a little better now that the Bird kid has talked to us, but we're still watching you. If you did it, we'll find out."

"I didn't," Steven said. "Trust me."

"I'm afraid I've heard that one, Mr. Blake," Hackett said. "I'd hate for you to be one more in a long line of disappointments."

Steven waited for him to finish and leave.

"One more idea has occurred to me," Hackett said. "You're a smart man, Mr. Blake, and I've wondered what would happen if you were smart enough and pissed off enough to try to set up Jacob Wood by making it look like he was getting after you. You follow me?"

"Not remotely," Steven said. "Try again."

"Look, what if you really knew about Wood and your wife all along, and you got it on with his daughter just to get even. Then Wood found out about that, and he turned it around to get back at you, aimed to get you fired, force you out of town. And then, to cover yourself and to really hurt Wood and get him into deep shit, you killed the girl so she couldn't talk anymore, got to the Bird kid and intimidated him into changing his story, and set everything up to make it look like Wood was trying to frame you for it."

Dumbstruck, Steven could only stare at the detective for a moment. "I think you've been watching too many Columbo movies," he said. "I'm not anywhere near that smart. Or that dumb."

"I don't watch television," Hackett said. "I'll be in touch."

After the cop was gone, Steven spent half an hour in the shower trying to wash away the sense of sleaze Hackett's theories had left behind. The water drummed hot down his spine, and by the time he emerged, limp and wrinkled, he was singing the opening bars of "Cotton Tail" again.

"Doo do-do-do dooo doo," he sang at Patches, whose head had emerged from beneath the bed. Her tail thumped the floor in response. "Got a date, Patcho," he said, trying the words out. They seemed wrong, but it was quarter to seven by his clock radio, so he dressed quickly, fed the dog, and drove out to Highway One, then south to Lazy Susan's.

Melinda wasn't there yet, so he staked out a table, ordered a beer, and settled in to wait. Susan's was the latest version of a Delmarva crab shack: wooden picnic tables covered with a fresh sheet of brown paper for each meal, crabs and shrimp served hot and spicy in the shell, plastic tubs of potato salad and coleslaw, lots of beer and cheap wine, and not much else.

The place was owned and run by a heavyset, long-haired guy with a handlebar mustache who looked a lot like David Crosby in the late sixties. He presided from a bar at the back of the room, flanked on either side by a wall-mounted TV. Every time Steven had eaten here, the sets had been tuned either to MTV or to the same home-mixed video of Roy Orbison, Bruce Springsteen, Crystal Gayle, and the Judds in concert. Tonight the home-brewed tape played, for which Steven thanked him.

Posters from every major beer manufacturer adorned the pine-paneled walls; Steven was doing a count on bikinis versus horses versus mountain streams when Melinda slid into the seat opposite him. Her sunburn from Sunday was still bright.

"Hi," she said. "Great atmosphere."

"Hi," he replied. "You feeling better than you did Sunday?"

"Yup. Starved now."

"You ever been here?"

She shook her head, looking around at the posters, then at the TVs.

"Ever eaten crabs?"

"Sure."

He ordered a dozen number ones and half a pound of shrimp, and a glass of the house burgundy for Melinda.

"Thanks for coming," he said.

"Thanks for asking me. How come you keep looking around? Nervous?"

"I suppose I'm not used to being out to dinner with anyone."

"Anyone but your wife, you mean."

Steven shrugged. "I guess."

"You'll get used to it."

"I already am," he said. "Anyway, thanks for the names the other day."

"Now you're going to make *me* start looking over my shoulder."

"I talked to Jay Bird yesterday. He confessed in front of half the band, so you're protected."

She sipped her wine, leaving a thin red mustache on her upper lip. "I'm not really worried. I heard all about it." She licked the wine away.

"Randy call you?"

She nodded. "I met with Jay today, too."

"Why did he do it? He wouldn't tell us yesterday."

"I'm not sure. I suspect the girl slept with him once, though, and had his head so turned around he'd do anything."

Steven imagined himself at seventeen faced with Lisa Wood, a year older than he, looking the way she did, behaving the way she did. He figured the siren call of hormones probably could have led him into the other side of the same fiasco. "As long as he's changed his story, I don't want the school going after him. Can you take care of that?"

"I'll try. Thompson's ranting a lot about looking bad."

"He'll look worse by the time I'm finished with him," Steven said. He took a sip of his beer. "Where you from, anyway?"

"Near West Chester. West of Philadelphia."

"Wyeth country. Longwood Gardens. All those mushroom houses."

"Not the mushroom houses so much anymore. The Japanese and Koreans put them out of business."

"You go to West Chester State? Good music school there."

"No," she said. "Bard College. Columbia for grad school."

The food arrived, the crabs a steaming orange tangle of legs and claws atop a plastic cafeteria tray, the shrimp in a small, brown plastic bucket. Melinda looked quickly from the crabs to Steven and back, then seemed to wait for him to start, and he realized she had no idea how to attack them.

"Look." He flipped a crab onto its back. "Take the claws off first, and crack them. Then there's a little bit of meat in the first joint of each of the legs, if you want to work that hard."

She whacked her first crab claw with one of the miniature wooden mallets, smashing it and splattering them both with juice.

"Good," Steven said. "A little enthusiastic, maybe."

She picked away fragments of shell.

"See this strip of shell on the bottom?" he said. "It's like a key; just lift it up and pull it back, then you can lift the top shell off." He demonstrated. "These evil-looking things on top are the lungs, I think. My dad used to call these the devil fingers, and he always claimed they'd make you deathly ill if you ate them. I've never tested the theory, myself."

He finished dismantling the crab, showing her how to pry the flaky white body meat from each cavity, pulling apart the translucent internal shell. "Voilà. Just like life. Eat as you go."

"So I see." She'd gotten as far as peeling the top shell back from her first crab, and now eyed the carcass a bit skeptically. "Devil fingers, you say?"

"Just scrape them off." He watched until she did so. "How come you gave me those kids, anyway?"

She didn't miss a beat. "Seemed like the thing to do. Time to take a chance."

"Thanks."

She shrugged and broke the crab in half. "Turns out you didn't even need me, did you?"

"Yeah, I did. In a big way."

She flashed him a quick smile, but let this pass. "How'd you get to be such good friends with Jimmy Van Dusen? You don't seem such a likely pair."

"I give him a link with his glory days, I suppose. I grew up not far from here, and Jimmy was always the local superstar in just about every sport. He's six or seven years younger than I am, so we didn't go to school together, but when he started teaching at DeVries I mentioned remembering his name from the newspapers, and I guess he sees me as his last loyal fan. I don't know if I'd say we're close."

"He tells me you're his best friend."

Steven was frankly surprised. "He's a nice enough guy. Drinks too much, pretty adolescent most of the time, but basically goodhearted. The kids love him."

Melinda finished her first crab, and swept aside the litter of broken shell with a proud flourish, then started in on another. "What's the deal with their house? Sharon never lets up."

"They'd already moved by the time you came, hadn't they? They used to live a few doors up from me. Jimmy grew up there, and his dad moved there when he was just a kid. Great old house. Jimmy just got it into his head to sell it, and the place was snapped up before anybody in his family could talk him out of it. They're all pissed at him."

"Why'd he do it?"

Steven shrugged. "You know how men get at our age. Decide any change is better than the same old shit."

She licked crab juice from her fingers. "What's that mean?"

"I don't know," Steven said. "Maybe I'm tired of my life."

"You can't say yours hasn't changed," Melinda said. "What do you think about Sharon and Jimmy? They going to make it?"

"I'm not the guy to ask right now," Steven said. "I'd say yes, but don't count much on my judgment. Once upon a time I thought Gail and I would last." These words sounded false to him even as he spoke them; he'd known from the beginning, and from the way they'd begun, that it would never last. He'd just never admitted it.

"I hope you're right about them," Melinda said. "So what do you think happened to Lisa?"

Steven shrugged. "I'm not a cop. Seems like she and her father were pretty stormy, though." Melinda said nothing, and Steven couldn't tell whether she disagreed or was waiting for him to say more. "I take it you know things, but you're not saying?"

"I've met Jacob," she said. "More than once in the past year."

"And what's your professional opinion?"

"Your basic pond scum. Sorry for the technical term."

"Think he did it?"

Now she shrugged. "Like you said, I'm not a cop. I'll swear I never told you this, but I saw him smack her across the face once. In my office."

Steven recalled the scene he'd observed at the Beebe emergency room, when Jacob had zipped up Lisa's wet suit for her, remembered the half-gloating smile on Jacob's face and the fear on the girl's, and the skin along his spine prickled just as it had then. "Have you told the police about this?"

"Not officially."

"What had she done?"

"Can't tell you," she said. "She didn't deserve to get hit, though."

"Who does?"

Deep into dismembering her fourth crab, she didn't answer. "Spices are hot," she said after a minute, and drained her wine. "What do they boil these in?"

"Old Bay seasoning. Lots of cayenne, celery seed, paprika, mustard powder, salt. Boil them in water and vinegar."

Steven signaled for another glass of burgundy for Melinda and another beer for himself. "How do you think he made her lie about me?"

"She was scared to death of him. So's her brother, from what I understand. I know this is really important to you right now, but would you mind if we talked about something else for a little while?"

"No, that's fine." He cast around for a moment. "I wandered

around the boatyard Sunday after you left. Saw a sailboat I liked a lot."

"That's more my speed," she said. "We always had sailboats."

"Where was this?"

"My family has a summer house near Annapolis. What was the boat?"

"Twenty-seven-foot O'Day," Steven said. "Used. Belongs to a dentist in Wilmington who's getting divorced."

"Nice," she said. "We had an O'Day once."

"I'd like to get back to a sailboat. This Whaler I have is the first powerboat I've ever owned."

"Then do it. Why not?"

"Money. Have to see if I still have a job."

"You will," she said. "If the kids change their story, and the police don't suspect you, how could the school keep you out?"

"Leaving aside the police, I'm not sure I want the job anymore."

She reached across and touched the back of his hand. "Don't get so angry that you do yourself harm. It was an honest mistake the school made. They've got to take things like that seriously."

"I know they do. It just came on top of a lot of other things. Burnout. All these troubles with Gail. Just seems like it could be time for me to do something else."

"Like what?"

He told her about Lester and Marian's big band project.

"You should see your face," she said when he'd finished. "Do it."

"Believe me, I hope to. I went to New York after I got out of college, spent four years breaking in, and never got this good a chance."

"What happened?"

"I don't know. My dad died suddenly, and I came back down to help my mom out. Turned out he left the Lewes houses to me, and I just kind of stuck around. Always felt like I gave up, though. It was tough to find a jazz gig back then—everything was funk and fusion and rock and roll."

"Will you sell your house?"

"Not if I have any choice about it," he said immediately. "Depends on how hard Gail fights, I guess."

"What went wrong between the two of you?" she said. "Sharon says you and Gail couldn't be separated the first year you were together."

"I don't know," Steven said. "I'm not even sure how we got together. Gail chased after me pretty hard, and I guess I was flattered, let it go to my head. And to be honest, I guess I got some kind of charge out of the fact that she'd been Jacob's wife, although I'm still not sure why she left him for me."

"Don't be ingenuous. You're fifteen years younger than Jacob, tall and good-looking, you're a musician who puts all of himself into his performances, and money and power don't seem to mean very much to you."

Steven shifted on the hard bench, uncomfortable at the direction of the discussion. "Anyway," he said, "I guess Gail and I just should have had an affair and left it at that. Probably would have been a whole lot less damage all around."

"I just don't understand why you stayed in the marriage for so long after it went bad. If you know someone's having affairs, why do you punish yourself by putting up with it?"

Steven blinked several times at her use of the plural, then asked offhandedly, "Which affairs would those be?"

"Oh, dear," Melinda said. She'd turned scarlet. "Sharon and Jimmy both said you knew."

"Knew what?" Steven asked sharply.

Melinda sighed. "I'm really, really sorry," she said. "One more time I've opened my goddamned big mouth."

For a long moment Steven studied her, then decided to let it pass. Even two weeks before, he probably would have been bouncing off the walls, but now he was so drained and depleted by Gail's betrayal, his accident in the bay, and Lisa's death that it just didn't matter. "Forget it," he said. "There are things I don't need to know any more about."

She opened her mouth, closed it, then said, simply, "Thanks."

"You finished?" He gestured at the three crabs remaining from the dozen. "You can take those home."

They squabbled momentarily over the check until he gave in and agreed to split it. He walked her across the parking lot to her car. It was another sultry night, with silent sheets of heat lightning flickering off in the distance, and clouds of moths and gnats swirling around the sodium vapor floodlights.

"I enjoyed this," he said. "I'd like to see you again."

She stood next to her car and considered him for a moment. "I'd probably like that," she said. "But I need to think about it."

"Why? Did I say something?"

She stood on tiptoe and kissed him square on the mouth. "I like you," she said. "But we're both adults. You've got a lot of troubles right now, Steven, and I'm not sure I'm up to getting into the middle of them. Especially if you're getting ready to leave town."

"Fair enough. How long do you need to think about it?"

She shrugged. "Just give me a while, okay?"

"You'll call me, right?"

"I'll help make sure you get out of the Lisa Wood troubles," she said softly. "Let's see where it goes from there."

"Fine." He reached out tentatively, touched her forearm, then stepped back. "Take care, then."

"Good night." She smiled and turned to unlock her car door, and Steven walked away.

"Hey," she called after him, and he stopped. "Good luck with that audition."

"Thanks," he said. "I think."

All the way home he thought about the questions he should have asked. Melinda had obviously counseled Lisa, or at least met several times with her and Jacob, and she knew more than she was telling about the relationship between the two. Or, for that matter, about Lisa's relationship with anyone else who could have wished her harm.

He could only wish that Melinda had been as reticent about Gail and that she'd let him stay as blind as he'd been for the past four years. This new knowledge did him no good beyond driving home his own willingness to let total infatuation rule out all common sense or wariness.

There should be a way, he thought, to practice scenes and stages of your life before they happened, to figure out the best approach the same way you could work a song into memory, playing it over and over and over until you got it just right before you ever stepped on stage. But even that, he thought ruefully, probably wouldn't have saved him.

16

Fear froze Jennie Moore's nervous smile. The girl was barely five feet tall, and had been quiet and shy all through high school—one of the straighter kids. Steven's most vivid memory of her was the one time he'd given her a solo, in Spring Concert her junior year, and how she'd risen on stage, lifted her trumpet to her lips, and then, despite weeks of flawless rehearsals, stood silently while the band thumped on. He felt almost guilty now for bracing her this unexpectedly.

"Hello, Jennie," he said gently. He leaned back against the practice room door, and for a few seconds the only sound was the rush of the air-conditioning through the vent above.

"Mr. Blake," she whispered, then cleared her throat and said more strongly: "They didn't say you'd be here."

"I talked to Jay Bird yesterday," Steven said.

Her gaze flicked beyond him, out through the glass and into the tiered music room as she looked for rescue. "I don't think I want to stay in here," she said; her voice held only a slight quaver now, but she remained seated on the piano bench, her trumpet cradled in her lap.

"Talk to me," Steven said.

She licked her lips and fluttered the trumpet's valves. "About what?"

"I think you know," Steven replied.

Again she looked beyond him, saw no help, then looked squarely at him again, a touch of defiance in her gaze now. "Will you let me out of here, Mr. Blake, or should I tear my blouse and start screaming?"

Steven stepped smoothly aside, determined to keep his face and voice calm. He opened the practice room door, then leaned against the wall next to it. "Go anytime you want. I'm just trying to figure out what Lisa did to you and Jay to make you lie about me."

"I didn't lie," she said sharply. Now that her way out was clear, she seemed to relax a bit. "I said what I saw."

"What did you think you saw?" Steven asked calmly.

Jennifer's face flushed darkly, and she shook her head.

Steven took a breath. "There will probably be some kind of hearing about this," he said. "Jay's recanted, so that leaves only you."

The girl glared up at him, tears near the surface, but her eyes dancing with anger. "I'll tell you what I saw, Mr. Blake. I came back into the band room one day after school because I'd left a new box of reeds sitting on my stand. I heard a noise from one of the practice rooms, and when I looked in through the door, I saw you and Lisa on the floor. Naked." She glanced around at the dingy, acoustic-tiled walls. "A room just like this one."

Steven felt his cheeks going hot as memory connected. "When did you see this, Jennie?"

"Two years ago."

"Are you sure it was Lisa you saw?"

"I saw *your* face. And Lisa told me it was her."

"After you told her what you saw?"

Jennie showed the first cracks of uncertainty, but she nodded. "She had dark hair."

"So does my wife," Steven said quietly, and he tried not to smile.

"Mr. Blake," Jennifer whined, "on the band room floor?"

Steven was so relieved and embarrassed he laughed out loud. "I'm sorry you saw that," he said. "She told me she locked the door."

The girl shook her head violently and hammered out her next words. "I saw you and Lisa fucking." Her tears welled, and for a moment Steven thought the girl would bolt, but she brushed back her tears with her knuckles and held fast.

Steven's anger and dismay rose; he'd convinced himself this would be as easy as Monday's scene with Jay Bird. "My wife will back me up," he said, though he hoped he didn't have to put that claim to the test.

"I'm not lying," she said. "Why are you doing this to me? Everybody knew she was your favorite. You thought she was the greatest musician you'd ever seen."

"She was the best student I ever taught," Steven said. "But I sure as hell never did what you're saying I did. What did she do to you to make you say this?"

"I'm not making anything up," the girl insisted. "You're just like everybody else—her father and her brother and half the teachers and every other guy in school. You always had extra time for Lisa. Extra lessons, anything she wanted." Jennifer's voice was waspish. "Who knows what you did."

Suddenly Steven felt very tired and worn. "Nothing," he snapped. "Jennie, you're going to go home now, and you're going to tell your parents that you don't really know anything about me and Lisa. And then you're going to call the school tomorrow and tell Mr. Thompson the same thing."

"Why should I?"

Steven's eyes flared wide. His patience was shot. "Because if you don't, I'm going to take you and your entire family to court and I'll own everything your parents have worked for and you can go work at McDonald's for the next twenty years to support them. Understand?"

"What are you going to do if I don't? Drown me, too?"

Steven held himself absolutely motionless—control was a wisp, an apparition of smoke that a strong breath would disperse.

"What did you say?" His voice came out low and cutting.

The girl hesitated, glanced down at the worn, gray industrial carpeting, and sighed, and though none of this really felt like victory, Steven knew he'd won. She looked up. "Okay, Mr. Blake. Maybe I didn't know what I really saw."

Now he needed the restraint of a witness, so over his shoulder, Steven said tautly, "Come in now, please."

Lester stepped into the open doorway, and Jennifer's angry glare flashed back and forth between them. "You never wanted to hear me play," she said to Lester.

"I just did," he said. "And you were so far out of tune I couldn't even guess what song it was. Sounded like a bunch of noise to me."

"It's all right," Steven said, though it wasn't. "She thought she was helping Lisa."

Lester snorted. "You out of your goddamned mind?" He dug into his trousers pocket and came up with a quarter, which he extended to the girl.

"What's that?" Jennifer said suspiciously.

"Were I you, young lady, I would take this quarter and make that telephone call the first thing tomorrow morning. I might be able to persuade Mr. Blake not to pursue any further action here."

She finally stood, ignoring the quarter that Lester still held out to her. "You bet I'll call the school, Mr. Jones, and the police, too. And I'll tell them all about my big mistake, which was coming here tonight. I'll tell them how you both tricked me and tried to trap me in here so you could make me change my story."

She brushed between the two of them. Steven winced as he heard her jam her trumpet into its case; in a quick moment she'd slammed the lid, snapped the clasps, and stalked out of the big music room.

Only then did Steven let out a long breath. "How long were you standing there?"

"Whole time," Lester said. He held his face rigidly solemn, but his jaw shook with suppressed laughter. "The band room floor, man?"

"I know," Steven said. "She missed me."

"Sure," Lester said.

Steven shook his head. "This is ugly. I thought Jennie would be as easy as the other one." He sat on the piano bench and leaned forward, elbows resting on his knees, and sighed deeply. "This sucks," he said. "Spend three years with each of these kids, put up with their moods and tricks and never practicing, put in all the hours after school and weekends, listen to them fumble through the same goddamned songs over and over and over, fight off their parents when they all don't get to solo or make first chair, and they turn around and fuck me first chance they get. And to top it off, I've dragged you into this bullshit now."

He looked up at Lester, who only shrugged and said, "Kid was bluffing, Steven. Sounds to me like this girl had one major thing for her band teacher and got pretty worked up over the other girl he liked better. She'll go home and tell her parents and they'll call their lawyer in the morning and she'll make a meek little retraction and that's all she wrote."

"Yeah, right. Then which one will turn on me?"

"I'll give you ten more seconds to wallow in this shit," Lester said. He stared at the wall clock above Steven's head. "Then I recommend you start to warm up. I got an audition to run."

Steven watched Lester watching the clock and thought about how much he really owed this old teacher of his, until the bass player looked down at him again.

"Finished?"

"Yeah," Steven said. Outside in the main music room half a dozen players already warmed up in a boisterous, contentious swarm of brass and reeds. The electric feel of musicians out to impress each other penetrated even into the dead air of the practice room, but for once it left Steven unmoved.

"Good," Lester said. "We've got some good musicians here tonight, and you're gonna need to blow your ass off, buddy."

He left, and Steven followed slowly. The rehearsal room was nearly identical to the one he'd taught in at DeVries High, and the one where he'd gone to college, and the one where he'd attended high school: a tiered, semicircular room, windowless, lit by hanging fluorescent lights, squares of white acoustic dampers affixed to painted cinderblock walls.

Lester now stood next to the piano with Marian, sorting charts.

Steven's tenor case felt like it weighed a hundred pounds more than normal, and he laid it across a folding chair and flipped the latches. The heavy, familiar smell of crushed velvet liner, cork grease, and leather pads rose around him, and his spirits rustled and stirred for a moment. This was his life, this smell and the liquid chatter of the trumpets and saxes and trombones around him as they worked their way free of all the day's ties and ideas and words and into the immediate joy of sound. The solid, well-oiled click and stop of his horn in his hands felt as natural and automatic as waking. He never remembered how much he missed playing until he began again each time, but today he was cold, and the warm-ups around him began to grate like a chattering flock of grackles.

He blew softly through his tenor, warming the horn and his lip, and surveyed the musicians. It had been years since he'd played with a band this large, though he'd run student groups like it: stage band, dance band, jazz band, big band—whatever it was called from year to year.

None of these players looked like students. Male and female, black and white, they ranged in age from their mid-twenties to the baritone sax player, whom Steven knew to be over seventy.

Twenty or more musicians had gathered by now. Lester Jones stood in the bottommost level of the room, the smallest inner half-circle. Marian's piano also sat on this level, and the two of them were softly tuning up.

On the first tier, next to the piano but up a level, a guitarist cradled a big old Gibson L-5 jazz guitar, a fat, hollow-bodied electric with a full, plummy sound, small amp next to his chair, and waited for Marian and Steven to finish so he could tune. Next to him, across the remainder of the tier, milled a gang of saxophone players, still sorting out stands and music folders. Above this group sat the brasses: trombones and trumpets, a flügelhorn. On the highest level sat Ahmed. Next to him a vibraphonist loosened up, mallets flying.

Steven counted the saxes: two other tenor players already there, one apparently doubling on clarinet, flanked by the old baritone player, who doubled on flute, and by four altos. With him, this made eight, at least two altos and a tenor too many. A wave of tiredness and depression rolled over him, and suddenly the effort of out-playing these other musicians seemed greater than any energy he could muster.

Steven strolled over to where Lester stood with his bass, and said quietly, "Listen, you've got a lot of reeds to cover you tonight. I think I'm going to split."

Lester scanned the bottom tier, where the oversized sax section had now settled behind a solid rank of music stands. "Squeeze in there in the middle. They'll move."

"You don't need me," Steven said. "I've got some things I should probably do."

"You get those charts Marian sent?" Lester said.

"Yeah," Steven said.

"Then just sit the hell down and play your horn when I tell you to. Dig?"

Steven shrugged and joined the section. Once again he glanced through the charts, wishing he'd practiced them all the same way he'd gone through "Cotton Tail." Most of the tunes were vintage Ellington, with a smattering of others: "Take the 'A' Train," "Lush Life," "Body and Soul," "Night Train," "Satin Doll," "Perdido," "Ko-Ko," "Sentimental Lady," and on. Though Steven guessed this balance would shift as more songs were transcribed, he couldn't quibble with any of the choices so far.

Lester cleared his throat, then waited for the last warm-up note to die. "Start with 'C-Jam Blues,'" he said. "Everybody got it?"

Charts rustled quickly.

"Okay, everybody solo to warm up. Just use the head as it's written, and don't worry about the transcribed solos. I'll cue you, and show us what you got," Lester said. "Steven Blake, first break."

Before Steven could even glance over the changes and collect his thoughts, Lester counted the song down. Uncharacteristically rattled, Steven sat through the melody, then missed his cue and jumped into his solo a beat and a half late with a flurry of notes. Lester flicked him a quick, impassive glance, then pointed at the tenor player to Steven's right to take the next chorus. Steven faded out indecisively, then listened with a deepening sense of depression as Debbie, the next player, built a careful, complex solo, and Lester nodded her into another verse. She was a blond woman in her late twenties, but Steven had to look twice to make sure Ben Webster hadn't sneaked back from the grave and started wailing away next to him.

She wrapped up and one of the trumpets and one of the altos soloed before Lester nodded at the other tenor player, a short, slightly built man named Karl who was sitting to Steven's left. If depression had greeted Steven when the first tenor played, then something close to despair gripped him as Karl mockingly played back Steven's own opening notes, then built what should have followed. Lester nodded another verse from him, too, and Steven figured he'd humored Lester enough by staying, and might as well pack up his horn and go home.

Lester circled around the room, signaling each musician to take a verse, and, if he liked what he heard, another one or two after that. Finally the sections came together on the ensemble parts, the eight saxophones a reedy wail, trombones moaning underneath, two trumpets winging slick and flashy as a pair of green-winged teal skimming just above the water's surface.

The band punched out the last verse, and as bad as he felt about his own performance, Steven had to admit that Lester and Marian had assembled a first-rate gang of musicians. Lester cut the last note, and the band sat in a brief, self-congratulatory silence.

"That was awful," Lester said. They all laughed nervously, and he added sternly, "I mean it. Remember, this is dance music, not tunes for a wake. And you goddamned saxophones sound like a freight train meeting a herd of cows in a ten-mile tunnel—listen to somebody besides yourself and try to balance it so those brass players have got some lip left. Hit it again from the top."

He began to count it, then stopped. "Steven," he said curtly, "stand up when you solo this time. You're not cutting."

Embarrassed and angry now, Steven rose well before his solo, nailed the first note dead-on, and flawlessly sight-read the original Ben Webster lead from the chart. He got the nod from Lester for another verse, and added what Ben surely would have played if Ellington had let him go on. He sat down, smug until both the other tenors buried him once again. All he'd done was prod each to a new level. Steven caught Lester grinning slyly, and scowled in return.

Lester called out, "Okay, people. 'Cotton Tail.' "

Now Steven allowed himself a small grin, for this was the song he'd worked for hours the day before, committing it to memory.

"Steven," Lester said, "you just got first solo. Debbie, you take it second time around, and then Karl. Come on, Steven, show us how it *should* be played."

The skinny guy next to Steven snorted in derision and leaned close. "What I hear is that you got other things you could show us."

Eyes narrowed, Steven studied Karl; the guy's thin brown hair was plastered across his scalp, and he flashed a cold grin at Steven.

"Do I know you?" Steven said.

"No, but everybody sure knows about you by now. Surprised they're even having you audition, when I hear you won't be able to tour outside of Smyrna."

Before Steven could come up with a reply, Lester boomed out the count and the band plunged into "Cotton Tail's" flashing lead. Still staring at Karl, Steven didn't even bother joining in, and remembered to stand only at the last half beat before his solo.

He got barely eight bars in, lost the changes, and stopped. Lester's face registered plain astonishment as the rest of the band fell silent, and Steven stood there foolishly studying the sheet music, as if that could tell him where he'd gone astray.

Lester cleared his throat loudly, caught Steven's eyes, nodded and counted it again, a little faster.

This time, Steven made it nearly halfway through before stopping. He kept his head down, eyeing the chart as though it had shifted lines and tricked him. Still Lester said nothing, only paused briefly and counted the song again, slightly faster. Steven fumbled his way all the way through this time, and sat down quickly in relief.

"Again," Lester said, and again came the count.

Steven felt twitchy with anger, ready to blast Karl for his jabs and Lester for forcing him through this humiliation yet again. He punched his way through the solo this time.

"Uh-huh," Lester said when they'd finished. "Sounds like a diesel coming through. Let's do it again, but try to swing a little harder than my car door this time, Mr. Blake."

Again Steven made it through without mishap, although he knew he'd sounded nowhere near as smooth and slick as the other two tenors. Lester finally called a break, and Steven jammed the score for "Cotton Tail" back into his folder, left the music on the stand, and carried his tenor over to the corner. He opened his case, yanked the mouthpiece off, and loosened the thumbscrew that held the neck snug to the body of the horn.

"Thought you were going to eat your reed," Lester said behind him.

"What the hell were you doing?" Steven said without even looking back at Lester. Despite the anger shaking his hands, he laid the tenor gently on its side, and only then did he turn around. The bass player was fifteen years older, loomed four or five inches taller, and suddenly twenty years of mutual respect didn't seem to matter. "Haven't I been through enough lately without you jumping on me, too?"

Lester waved him peremptorily into the nearest practice room, the same one where Steven had tried talking to Jennifer, and closed the door behind them. "You haven't been through anything but a little hard time that you brought on yourself, facts be facts," Lester said. Though his lips turned up in a half-smile, his eyes were cold. "What are you gonna do now? Give up? Go home and feel sorry for yourself?"

"I don't need this bullshit," Steven said. "Why do I need to stand up there and humiliate myself? My playing was the one thing I still had left to feel good about."

"You got the chops," Lester said. "If you care to use them. But that's always been the thing about you, Steven, and I've known it since you first landed in my band when you came to college. You don't really care enough about anything to be much more than good at it. You don't let yourself care, don't ever really let yourself know what you want and don't want, and you never set out to get the one and get rid of the other. You're like most people—just take what comes along, then bitch and piss and moan when it doesn't fit. That Gail came after you the way she did, and you knew better, Steven, but you just let yourself fall into trouble."

The truth stung. "Come on, let me out of here," Steven said. "I'm splitting."

Lester wouldn't budge from the door. "You thought you could just come in tonight and that girl was going to realize what a terrible story she told and make nice and clear you all up and your troubles would be gone. Instead you had to push her some to get it, and you're all fucking bent out of shape. When the hell you going to grow up?"

"What are you, my father?"

"Not hardly. I'm gonna give you a choice now, though. You want to split, go ahead, get the hell out and don't let us see you again. I mean ever, at the Lamplighter or anywhere else. Or get back up there and play like you goddamned mean it for once."

Steven studied his old teacher for a long minute, and it began to dawn on him just what he was risking here.

"Don't do to me what you're bitching about your own kids doing to you," Lester added quietly.

Tight-lipped, Steven nodded once. Stiff with anger, confused, mortified, he could only say, "Let's do it, then."

Moments later, Steven stood in the midst of the sax section, closed his eyes, took a deep breath, and shouted out the count for "Cotton Tail" faster than any band had *ever* played it. They raced through the melody, Karl struggling now, Debbie note for note with Steven. Straight into the solo Steven rolled, and both the other tenor players fell away from his hearing like yesterday's wind.

A tremorous chill ran up his spine; his neck unleashed its tension, and all the small muscles running up around his skull fell free so his head felt like it was expanding. Steven rode the crest of the song, taut and trimmed, right on the edge of losing it, the way he imagined Lisa riding the wind, body and board and sail held in perfect triangular tension, the way she'd looked as she'd raced across the bay toward him.

Athletes call it The Zone, that place where you can count the stitches on every pitch, chart the perfect arc as the football descends to your patient hands, hover above the hoop forever. It's a place where the body takes over, where time slows and stretches so that each movement, no matter how quick in real time, becomes discretely perfect and unhurried. Mistakes not only become impossible, the very concept of mistakes becomes irrelevant. Musicians, too, reach for this place, where the hours of practice suddenly become performance and the mind thinks in pure sound. The path from mind to body through instrument to sweet vibrations in the air becomes so immediate that thought becomes song without mediation. Chords open up, the rhythm stretches out, all the needed notes fit, and every single one is perfect.

This was the trance the best players strove for, and hit from time to time. No one could stand to reach it too often—Charlie Parker and too many others had tried to live there, and paid dearly, for there the song could steal your breath, you could sink beneath all sense of surface, lose the distinction between yourself and the shimmering notes that rose around you. And when the sound inevitably faded because no breath could be sustained forever, the attempt to rise, too late, could lead only to drowning.

But this was also the ultimate extension of what Steven had tried to learn and teach for years, beyond the idea of thinking a note to play a note. Yes, learn the theory, practice scales, memorize the changes and melodies, hammer out the songs over and over, but never forget to think the sound; if you could make of emotion a fat, clear, round, ripe note hanging in the air, the body would give it to you without any effort you knew about. Though earned, it was a gift: uncontrollable, never willfully summoned.

Tonight Steven's pent-up anger, the mounting sorrow of loss and betrayal finally became too much, and knowing better than his own mind what he needed, his body offered this gift, respite, salvation. Chorus after chorus he played, calling in everything he'd heard and learned and sweated over in twenty-five years of musicianship. He kept his eyes closed, not looking to Lester for cues or cuts, taking all the time and sound he needed.

One more, he thought, then another, and finally he built his last chorus to the only possible cascading end and hit the first note of the machine-gun melody again. To his surprise, Debbie was right there with him, as were both the trumpet players and one of the altos. Karl came in weakly a couple of measures late. Steven opened his eyes then, and Lester grinned slyly, winked, and nodded at one of the trumpet players to take it away.

Steven sat down again, satisfied. When they'd finished the song, Karl said grudgingly, "Nice solo."

Debbie leaned across in front of Steven to speak directly to Karl. "I've never heard anybody play tenor like that, and neither have you, asshole."

"Still doesn't mean he can do it all the time."

"I don't know," Steven said. "Why don't you ask Lester to let you pick the next tune?"

Karl grazed him with a flat glance, collected his charts and stuffed them back into his folder. "Later," he said, and left.

Steven gathered his own music and crossed the music room to his tenor case. He took the horn apart and swabbed it out carefully.

Behind him, Lester said softly, "Better get measured for a tux." Steven turned around, and the bass player grinned devilishly. "Best woodshed a bit on those chops, too. Thought Karl had you there for a while."

"Not a chance in hell."

"I'll let him know not to come back," Lester said.

Steven felt not the slightest regret. "Where do we go from here? Got any gigs lined up yet?"

"Long way before this gang turns into a band," Lester said. "All that's set right now is the ballroom at the Hotel Dupont for Christmas Eve and New Year's Eve, and we've got two weeks on one of those Caribbean jazz cruises in February. Maybe the New Orleans festival, end of April. Some big do the Smithsonian's running on the Mall in D.C. in May. And I got somebody in New York working on Newport and Montreux and some other stuff."

"Jesus Christ." Steven was stunned. "This is for real."

"No shit," Lester snorted. "That's what I tried to tell you. We got some heavy backing behind this thing."

Steven looked down at his tenor, gleaming in the plush of its case, and felt the relief deep in his soul. "Hey," he said to Lester. "Thanks."

He was still grinning as he drove home, the only car on the dark highway. There were miles of empty farmland to cross before he reached home, and the flat, dark, lonely fields stretched away on either side. For the first time, Steven realized he was free—free of planning new marching band routines for each week's game, free of botched solos that distressed him more than the kids responsible, free of weekly lessons with the children of chicken farmers who had as much feeling for their instruments as a hen had for a tennis racket.

And, working up to this one slowly, tentatively, he wondered, free of Gail, too? He rummaged his thoughts as though checking for a familiar loose tooth with his tongue, and got the expected vicious jolt, for he'd snagged on the sharp memory Jennifer had stirred, when she'd seen him and Gail in the band room. It was nothing but high-octane lust that had kept the two of them going those first two years.

Now she'd stolen away his trust in his own perceptions, his ability to discern truth, for if he'd been so mistaken about her, anything and everything was suspect.

Steven sighed heavily, suddenly tired to the bone. He was entering the town of Lewes now, driving down the deserted weeknight streets. The music's glow faded as the town closed in around him. He clung to the last of the high, though, clutched the last notes of the evening all the way down to his own driveway.

For there, gleaming in its regular spot, as he'd known it would be one day sooner or later, sat Gail's red BMW.

17

Gail waited in the center of the cottage living room, hands on her slim hips in a pose of defiant outrage that she must have struck the second she heard his car. Steven stopped just inside the doorway. This was the first he'd seen of her since Lisa's funeral, and despite the still vivid image he carried of her emerging from the limousine and locking her arm in Jacob's, his illusions of easy freedom were blasted away. Before any of this, he'd sometimes imagined his response if he discovered she'd been unfaithful, and had always found it easy to conjure steely rage, cold condemnation, the immediate denial of love, as though a switch could be thrown and passion wiped clean. Reality was a good deal messier and more confusing. For a long moment, he met her full-force glare with a look equal parts anger and sorrow, tinged with the memory of recent desire.

"What in the hell have you done with my Limoges?" she snapped in a voice so imperious that things were suddenly less complicated.

Steven kept his own tone as neutral as possible. "In the garage. I had to clean the place up to rent it out."

"How much did you break?"

He refused to let her crack his facade, and he held her with the longest, coldest stare he could muster. "What are you doing here? Jacob turn you out?"

"No." She glanced around the cottage; after hours of Steven's labor, it was as impersonal as one of the crackerbox summer motels down at Dewey Beach, and probably less cheerful. The place had been closed up for days, and the dead, overheated air was rank with the smell of dried seawater and ammonia detergent. "Who's renting it?" Now her voice was as intentionally and artificially calm as his.

"Nobody yet." He had a flash fantasy of her asking to move back into the cottage, then of himself refusing her. "Why?"

"Just curious," she said indifferently. "Did you pack up everything?"

"Pretty much." Steven couldn't hold back the question any longer, and asked, "Why'd you show up at Lisa's funeral with him?"

"He wanted me to."

"And you went along, knowing half the town would be there?"

She shrugged, but wouldn't meet his eyes. "Sooner or later I had to make a choice."

"It's too bad you're not as smart as you think you are, because you made the wrong one. It doesn't happen like we did more than once, you know."

Tight-faced, she looked away from him for a moment, then back. "Maybe it does. Show me where my things are now." Steven heard the faintest crack in her voice.

"If we've got to split, we've got to," he said, "but you're not going to convince me we never had a real marriage, and you're not going to convince me now that you're somebody you're not."

"You don't have any idea who I am," she said, and the crack in her voice broke, exposing a raw edge of anger. "You've been too busy chasing teenagers into bed."

"I knew you'd try to turn this all around to me."

She nodded. "You started it."

"I didn't sleep with the girl, Gail. Or drown her."

"I know you didn't drown her," Gail snapped.

"How?" Steven said immediately. "What do you know?"

"I don't know anything about it. I just know you."

"Stop saying that. It was Jacob, wasn't it? How the hell can you stay with him?"

For a moment she was silent. "What makes you think I am?"

Several different replies struggled for voice, but the question that came out was blunt: "Did he drown Lisa?"

"No," she said, but her gaze wavered slightly. "He couldn't have."

"Come on, Gail. Look at everything else he did to her."

"The girl was a problem from the time she was small. She was at him constantly—I saw enough of that for myself, and I understand she got much wilder after her mother died. Jacob's done enough wrong in his life, that's for certain, but he'd never drown his own daughter."

Her belief in her own words was so firm that Steven paused, recalling the ravages of unexpected grief obvious in Jacob's face at the funeral, and for a moment he entertained the uneasy notion that she might be correct. He'd focused so exclusively on Jacob that the idea of another being responsible for Lisa's drowning left him feeling unmoored. Slowly he said, "If you think neither Jacob nor I did it, then who did?"

"I have no idea," she said immediately. "Nor do the police, though they haven't ruled out you or him or even Todd."

"Do you know everything the police know?"

"No," she said. "I don't know yet what they were doing here last Saturday."

She was clearly fishing, and for a moment Steven wished he could confide in her the way he'd once thought he could, that he could turn her sharp mind to the puzzle of Lisa's sailboard in his garage. "They didn't find whatever they wanted, but if any of your stuff's broken, don't blame me."

She sighed. "Don't make this uglier than it already is, Steven."

"I'm not the one who came in here with an attitude, Gail. For the past few years, I've been doing my job and playing my music, not sleeping with half the state. For my idle curiosity, though, who were the others? Other than Jacob?"

Gail's lips compressed into a thin scar across her face. "Why do you think there were others?"

"Come on. It's over. Mainly I want to know what kind of risk I'm at for diseases."

"There weren't enough to matter."

Steven's gut clenched. "You're right, I suppose—none of them matter after the first one. But humor me. Two? Three? Twenty?"

She strode forward as though trying to walk right through him. "Move, Steven. I'm out of here."

He stared at the strange woman opposite him, for the moment at least trying to see her objectively: beautiful, sharp-planed features ten years younger than her real age, lips so full they might have been the model for all the collagen-injected actresses filling the magazines, body taut and tanned in her sleeveless blouse and baggy shorts. She suddenly seemed all dangerous edge, and he remembered a time when he and Jimmy Van Dusen had been fishing on a party boat and three drunks had boated a four-foot shark before anyone else realized they were doing it. Five seconds out of the water, the shark was suddenly all thrashing muscle and gnashing teeth, and the back of that boat became a very small world—nearly as small as his living room felt now.

"Come on," he said, and turned away. "Get your things and get out of here."

She followed him out to the garage, where he dug through the tangled aftermath of the police search until he found her china, then three other cartons of books and clothes she wanted. He tossed them all into the back of her BMW, scraping them ruthlessly across the leather seats. He slammed the door and dusted his hands.

"You're rid of me now," she said. "Keep the house. Have somebody draw up whatever agreement you want; send it to my office and they'll forward it. As soon as I get it, I'll sign it."

"That's big of you," Steven said. "Where are you going to be?"

"Gone." She stood next to the closed front door of her car, dark-haired, dark-eyed, dark-tanned in the dim light. Steven watched her with a mounting sense of confusion and turmoil. Despite his anger and the depth of his hurt, part of him wanted to deny her betrayal, brush it aside. All at the same moment he wanted to hold her tenderly and crush her and fling her away. Lester had told him earlier that very evening that he never bothered to want or not want anything; *then* Steven had thought the assessment might be true, but now, in this instant, he both wanted and not wanted passionately: he wanted Gail back, still, but as much, or more, he wanted her gone, wanted not to want her, wanted never to have desired her, known her, wanted her vanished, even, he admitted, dead, so he might mourn her cleanly.

This was the silence that led down to their final parting, and it was all Steven could do to break it. His stomach churned and fists clenched, but he kept his voice low and calm as he asked despite himself, "What happened to us?"

Gail sighed, patience gone, and enunciated each of her next words as clearly and separately as the taps of a gem-cutter's hammer cleaving a diamond: "We just wore out waiting for you to move."

"No. Not before you did all this."

She gave him a long stare, liquid in the darkness, then said more softly, "It was good, Steven, for those few months before you gave up and settled back into the same half-assed life you were living before I met you."

"I thought it was a good life."

"There's the problem."

"But why this way?" Steven said. "We could have done this like adults. You've torn down everything on your way out."

She shook her head. "You don't know how far from the truth you are."

"Then tell me."

"I've got another job," she said. "With a firm in Philadelphia."

"And Jacob?"

"He's my last favor to you. That's all it's ever been."

Steven snorted. "Any more favors like that will probably kill me."

"I started it all by leaving him the way I did. He was just going to take that out on you until he beat you down completely, Steven."

Steven could only shake his head. "And what about all that time before the funeral? You were seeing him all along, Gail."

"No," she said. "Not all along."

"I don't know whether my biggest question is how or why. Why'd you bother staying with me?"

"Because I really wanted to," she said. "You have to believe that. I just couldn't . . . I told you at the cemetery that it was like being in orbit—as long as I stayed this close to Jacob, I never seemed to be able to get completely away from him. There's just some kind of thing between the two of us that I'm not going to try to explain to you, Steven, because I can't understand it myself. I hate the man, but I keep going back. I tried and tried to get you to go away from here with me."

Steven had real trouble believing anything would have been different if he'd moved with her. He heaved a deep breath, then said, almost gently, "You'll hear from DeFlavis, Gail."

She nodded; the split final, she almost seemed to lean toward a last touch. He steeled himself.

"Take care," she said at last, and shifted away. "Watch out for Jacob. He blames you for Lisa."

He waited for more, but with this grudging warning she'd obviously spent the last scrap of feeling she held for him. "So that's it?" he said.

"Life goes on," she said, but the toughness was only in her words, not in the tone of her voice.

"For some of us," he said. "Lisa's not that lucky."

In a voice suddenly so hard it turned the August night chill, Gail said, "We earn our own endings, Steven. She got what she deserved."

Steven suppressed a surprised shiver. "How the hell can you say something like that about an eighteen-year-old girl? She was your own stepdaughter, for God's sake."

"Do you think you were the only one she slept with, Steven? Do you think this was the only home she wrecked?"

After a stony moment as he considered the implications behind her words, he said, "I hope you get whatever it is you've earned, Gail, but I expect you won't. Get out of here."

Swiftly she climbed into her car, then started the engine, backed out and drove away in one long, fluid motion. Brake lights flared as she tapped the pedal at the stop sign; then she rolled through, turned right onto Pilottown Road, and sped away. For one swift, shaky moment, the light of the corner streetlamp swam in Steven's eyes. He felt a hole in his center, as though something vital had just been ripped out of him—no, nothing vital—more as if a tumor, roots tentacled deep into his gut, had been torn free and now there was a brief, silent pause when the patient had equal chance to expire or survive.

He took a deep breath, then retrieved the tenor from his car. They'd left the lights on in the cottage, so he crossed the lawn and locked the place up again, and returned to the sanctuary of his own house.

Patches had obviously spotted Gail or heard her voice, for she bolted between Steven's legs the instant the door opened, leapt from the porch to the ground, and circled back to the garage at full speed.

Steven waited in the kitchen doorway while the dog raced completely around his house, then back to the cottage, where she lunged up the porch steps and stood outside the locked door, wagging wildly. Steven whistled. Patches looked back across the yard at him, eyes eerily reflecting red.

"Come on," Steven called. "Time for dinner."

Even this failed, and he crossed the yard once again, unlocked the cottage, and let the dog inside. She ranged excitedly from room to room, sniffing, slowing, until she finally returned to Steven, stood and looked up at him and wagged tentatively.

"She's gone, baby," Steven said, trying out the words. "Gone away for good this time." His voice sounded strange, tight and thin and half an octave too high, and he knelt next to the dog and buried his face in the fur of her neck. She stood patiently while he held her and breathed in her clean dog smell and tried to hold back the possibility Gail's parting words had raised. "She got what she deserved," his wife had said about Lisa, in tones so cold that they alone could have killed. And what other homes had the girl supposedly wrecked—Gail and Jacob's? So much he thought he'd known about Gail had proven false that he could believe nearly anything of her, except revenge on her own stepdaughter.

He waited another moment, hoping his pain and confusion would pass, taking his suspicions with them. He dug for some last scrap of faith in her, worked uselessly to convince himself Gail knew no more about Lisa's death than she'd told him. The dog stirred, gently reminding him of her existence, and finally he sat back on his heels and ruffled the fur between her ears. She swiped at his face with her tongue.

"That's right, free at last," he said, though he couldn't recall ever feeling less free.

Patches padded back across the yard with him, sat in the middle of the kitchen watching and wagging as usual while he fixed her dinner of kibble and canned chicken parts. He set the bowl down next to the porch door. She sniffed at her food, then walked away and curled up under the table. Chin on her paws, she stared morosely up at Steven.

"You, too?" He opened the refrigerator door, thinking the dog might eat if he choked something down as an example, but he closed the refrigerator without even looking inside, turned off the overhead light, and sat at the table. Patches moved her chin to rest on his left foot.

Steven took the wall phone from its hook and, without having to look up her number, dialed Melinda. Her telephone rang on and on, and he sat listening to the ring long past the time he should have hung up, not even thinking about Melinda or the call anymore. When her sleep-thick voice finally answered, he was so startled that he couldn't think what to say for a moment.

"It's Steven Blake," he blurted.

Silence, then: "Do you know what time it is?"

"No," he said.

"Neither do I. What do you want?"

"I'm sorry," Steven said. "I couldn't tolerate sitting here by myself."

She sighed. "How was the audition?"

"Fine," he said, though it seemed so long ago he couldn't remember. "I've just had the final round with Gail."

"Who won?"

"Nobody."

A long silence, then: "I'm sorry for you."

"Look," Steven said tentatively, "I know you need time to think it over, but I really need to see you again."

"I think I'd like that," she said. "Can you call me sometime tomorrow when I'm awake?"

"I really need to talk to you."

"So talk. I'm listening."

Steven took a deep breath, then said very quickly, "I know this is a lot to ask, but I'm going to go out of my mind if I have to sit around this house right now. Something came up, something Gail said, and I really need to talk it out. Can I see you?"

"When, right now?"

"Yes."

Now came the longest silence yet, and Steven feared he'd lost her completely. Finally she asked, "Are you stable, Steven? Do you feel like you want to harm yourself?"

"God, no," Steven said. "But I think Gail might have drowned Lisa. Or at least knows who did."

She drew a sharp breath. "Did she tell you that?"

"I've just got an evil feeling from something she said."

"Do you know the doughnut shop on Highway One? Near Midway? Give me thirty minutes."

18

She took forty-five. Steven sat at the end of the counter farthest from the door, drinking his third cup of black coffee. It was after one-thirty; two customers sat at the other end of the counter, near the cash register, regulars from the way they chatted up the waitress. A lone cook clattered pans in the back room. He felt a little foolish as the near panic of loneliness that had prompted him to call Melinda ebbed into the sheer normalcy of the place.

The smell of old doughnuts and stale cooking fat permeated the air. The aroma seemed familiar, but as he glanced around at the garish pink and tan Formica, at the scratched stainless steel coffee machine and the dirty white tile floor where it was worn through to the concrete slab, at all the cheap bright surfaces harsh under fluorescent lights, Steven couldn't recall the last time he'd been here. After a moment blind memory traced the odor back to DeFlavis's office in the renovated bakery a couple of miles down the highway.

He imagined DeFlavis facing off against the steely Gail he'd seen tonight, and decided it was probably just as well she didn't intend to contest anything.

Melinda bustled in, wearing a lavender sweatsuit, pink running shoes, and the bleary-eyed look of a woman recently woken from the deepest cycles of sleep. She looked defenseless, sincere, endearing, and as she approached, Steven realized that he felt absolutely none of the electricity he'd always felt with Gail, of which he'd even felt a faint buzz when he'd first seen her this evening. It remained to be seen whether that missing jolt was a real loss, or whether it was even permanent.

"Hi." She perched on the stool next to him. "Been here long?"

"No." The waitress drifted down toward them, coffeepot in hand, and he waited until she'd poured for them both. "Thanks. Sorry to call you out like this."

"It's fine, really. I've come here a few times in the middle of the night, mostly when kids have called with one tragedy or another." Her voice was so falsely bright that Steven wondered just how haggard he really looked. Without being too obvious, he strained to glimpse his own reflection in the window, but was too far away to make out the smudged details.

"You're not required to take the job that far."

"Yes, I am." She blew across her coffee to cool it, sipped, looked up at him with the cup still held near her lips. "Tell me," she said.

"I need to ask you something first about your conversations with Lisa." She started to speak, but Steven kept on. "I know you can't violate confidentiality, but I have to know this. Did Lisa come between Gail and Jacob somehow?"

"Why are you asking this?" Melinda said sharply.

"One of Gail's last shots was that we earn our own endings."

He waited. Melinda blinked, processed, said, "Usually we do. What's your point?"

"She said it in reference to Lisa."

"Gail said Lisa deserved to drown?"

Steven nodded.

"And that was it?"

"No." His coffee cup shook in his hand, and he lowered it to the counter. "She asked if I thought ours was the only home that Lisa had wrecked."

"There wasn't really much there to wreck, was there?"

"You're dancing all around my question."

Melinda looked at him coolly. "Do you really suspect, based on those comments, that Gail killed Lisa?" Melinda asked. "I mean, come on, Steven. It's pretty harsh, but . . ."

From the take-out counter at the other end of the shop, a state trooper glared hard at him. Steven thought it was the same cop who'd guarded him the day Hackett and his crew searched the house, but he hadn't looked at the guy closely enough that day to remember him. Chances were it was—this was a tiny town in a tiny state, and there weren't many troopers around. After a moment the cop left with his coffee, and as Steven watched him back out to his cruiser he understood how absolutely his life had changed. A month ago he wouldn't have given or warranted a second glance in the same situation—no, a month ago he would have been home at this hour of the morning, probably dreaming he still had a life.

The cop sat in his car, still watching Steven through the big plate glass windows, and talked on his radio.

Only then did Steven realize Melinda had been watching him the whole time.

"You're staring," he said, irritated.

"I see a lot of fear in your face, Steven." Her voice was clinical.

"They're so busy trying to prove what they already believe about me that they'll ignore the truth."

"So tell them about Gail. If you really believe she knows anything."

"You don't think so."

"I didn't talk to her tonight."

A long, pained silence hung between them. Finally Melinda said, "You still love her, don't you?"

"Absolutely not," Steven said. "Credit me with *some* pride."

"I'm not saying you don't hate her," Melinda said. "You probably should right now. But there's still something else under there."

Steven was silent, unable to look at her. "I read a little story in the paper last year," he said. "Came off the wires, no byline, just a couple of paragraphs. It said that a Japanese fisherman who'd been missing for two years had come to his senses standing chest-deep in the Pacific, just off the village on Hokkaido where he'd lived. Everyone thought he'd drowned. He had no idea how he'd gotten there or where he'd been—the two years had just disappeared. That's how I feel. Like I've just come back from being drowned, like I've been away for a long, long time without even knowing I was gone, and everything's so different that the place I thought I knew is less familiar than someplace I've never even been."

Melinda fiddled impatiently with the tray of blue and pink and white sweetener packets in front of her. "Did you really believe that story, Steven? You don't think the guy just spent a couple of wild years in Tokyo, then came back in the middle of the night and made that up to cover himself?"

"The point's not whether the story's true," Steven said sharply.

"No," she agreed. "The question is what happens next for that fisherman. Does he pick up and make his life over again, or does that story of his two-year disappearance become the story of the rest of his life?"

Steven glared at her, then relented. "You're not going to let me wallow at all, are you?"

"Wallow on your own time," she said. "Not on mine at this hour of the morning." Melinda let the silence hang for a minute or two, then finally shrugged and made the move to safer ground. "How was your audition?"

"So long ago I can't remember."

"Tell me about it. What did you play? What happened?"

Steven hesitated, then said gently, "I wish I could shed her that quickly, you know. But even if I said I could, you wouldn't believe me."

Something flared behind her eyes, whether anger or pain he couldn't tell, as it was quickly quelled. "Thanks," she said. "Tell me about the audition, please."

Over the next thirty minutes Melinda asked more questions

about music and the mechanics and emotions of playing and the process of improvising than Gail had in all his years with her. Finally Steven told her, "I talked to Jennifer Moore tonight."

Melinda nodded, unsurprised. "Where did you see her?"

"I had Lester invite her to the audition."

"Did it do any good?"

Steven shook his head. "She's sticking to it."

Melinda sighed. "I suppose if I hadn't expected you to talk to the kids, I never would have given you their names."

"But you're pissed off at me now."

"It's been a long night." She brushed her hair back from her forehead. "I'd better go home and try to sleep for a couple of hours."

Steven glanced past her, out the window. The sky was beginning to lighten. "Me, too. I've got a lot to do today."

As they sat motionless, gathering their energy to go, Jimmy Van Dusen's blue Ford pickup rolled through the parking lot and pulled up just on the other side of the glass from them. Van Dusen waved as he got out.

"Shit," Melinda said.

"What the hell's he doing here?"

Melinda wouldn't meet his eye. "I called him before I came out," she said. "Things have been so crazy lately, I just didn't know . . ."

"You didn't know if I was the reason for all the craziness," Steven finished for her. "What did you think I was going to do? Feed you to my dog?"

"Steven," she said, and made a move to touch his hand, but Jimmy was upon them.

"What a surprise," he boomed. "Two of my favorite people. I'm just on my way out to Henlopen to meet my brother for some surf-fishing, and who do I spot?"

"Cut the shit," Steven said. "She told me."

"I didn't ask him to come out here," Melinda said defensively. "I just wanted to check and make sure you were . . ."

"Safe," Steven said.

"Come on," Jimmy said. He sat next to Melinda and put his arm around her. "You can't blame her, buddy."

Steven looked from Melinda to Jimmy, then back. "Is this another situation I should have known about? Am I the last fool one more time?"

"You have got to be joking!" Melinda was scarlet, and her voice held such disgust that Steven flinched for Jimmy, but Van Dusen pulled Melinda close in a bear hug.

"Admit it," Jimmy said. "You're consumed with lust for the coach."

But Steven could see Jimmy was watching him closely, gauging his response, as if there really was something illicit between them masked by his clownishness.

"Let her go," Steven said. "I just needed somebody to talk to, Jimmy. Gail pulled out tonight."

"Good," Van Dusen said. "She leave town?"

"Philadelphia."

"Back to mom and pop, huh? Thought she wasn't going to join the family firm."

"Made her point, I guess. She practiced on her own here for years."

"The woman's a right bitch," Jimmy said. "She say anything before she left? What happened with her and Wood?"

"I don't know or care," Steven said. "Why?"

Van Dusen shrugged, and looked around for the waitress. Melinda squirmed free of his arm.

"I've got to get some sleep," she said.

"I really am going fishing," Van Dusen said. "Come sleep on the beach."

"I'm going home, too," Steven said. He stood and stretched. "You think that's okay, Jimmy? You trust me not to drown this woman?"

"Hey, don't come after me." Van Dusen held up both hands; he wouldn't look Steven in the eye. "She's smart to be careful. Melinda doesn't know you the way I do, friend."

"Maybe. Thanks for clearing me, I guess."

"I didn't lie too much."

"I'll call you. We still haven't gone fishing."

"Anytime."

Melinda had nearly reached the door, and Steven hustled to catch up with her.

"I don't blame you," he said. "I must have sounded crazy when I called."

"You did," she said.

They walked out into the parking lot. Steven's legs felt curiously light, and his bladder was near bursting from coffee. Melinda's Honda stood three spaces down from his wagon, and he walked down to her car with her. They stopped.

"We seem to spend a lot of time standing in parking lots," Steven said.

"Three times," she replied. "Marina, Lazy Susan's, Dunkin' Donuts. What time is it?"

"I forgot my watch. Why?"

"I don't know." She was looking over his shoulder, and Steven turned to see what she was watching. A town police car had pulled into the slot nearest the doughnut shop door, and a skinny blond cop got out.

"He doesn't look old enough to carry that gun," Melinda said.

"Tommy Langtree," Steven said. "One of my students a while back. Drummer."

Langtree headed toward them.

"I promise I didn't call this one," Melinda said quietly.

"Tommy," Steven called. "Find out who trashed my house yet?"

"We're still checking on that, Mr. Blake." The young cop hid behind his brusqueness, a kid afraid of being taken lightly.

"You know Melinda Samuels? Psychologist at DeVries these days," Steven said.

"Morning." The cop nodded without really looking at her, and said to Steven, "Can I talk to you for a minute, Mr. Blake?"

"Is this official?"

Langtree glanced at Melinda, then back. "Semi."

"It's okay," Steven said. "Melinda's a friend."

"I don't know what the deal is with you and Mrs. Blake these days," the cop said, "but if you're talking to her, will you tell her to slow the hell down? I clocked her doing eighty-seven in that red Beamer of hers a couple of hours ago."

Steven didn't bother correcting the cop on Gail's name. "You sure it was her?"

"I ran the plate," Tommy said. "Was a woman driving. Moncure, right?"

"Should've written her a ticket," Steven said. "That's probably the last chance you had."

Tommy shrugged. "Next time. Truth is, there wasn't any traffic, and if I had a car like that I'd probably blow it out once in a while, too."

"I probably won't see her again," Steven said. "She moved back to Philadelphia last night."

"Well." The cop was suddenly awkward. He glanced at Melinda again, clearly having something else to say.

"Tommy," Steven prodded, "what's up?"

"What the hell," he said, "she can hear this. I just want you to know I don't think you had anything to do with Lisa, Mr. Blake. You've always been real straight, and you were probably the guy who had the most to do with me finishing school."

Though he recalled no special relationship with Tommy, or even any particularly meaningful discussions, Steven was touched. He reached out to pat the kid's shoulder, then realized how inappropriate the gesture seemed toward a uniformed cop, and lowered his hand.

"Thanks, Tommy. That helps me out more than you could know."

"*I* think it's Todd," he blurted. "He's always been the kind of guy who'd cut the fins and tail off a fish and throw it back in the water just to watch it try to swim."

"Have you shared this with the state police?" Melinda asked; her manner was gentle with the young cop.

Tommy seemed to remember her presence for the first time. "Yes, ma'am, I have. Detective Hackett says he's investigating it, but I don't think he takes me very seriously."

Thinking that Tommy wasn't quite as dumb as he looked, Steven exchanged glances with Melinda, who didn't seem to know how to reply. He said, "Thanks, Tommy. We'll see you later, right?"

Langtree seized the exit line and hustled for the doughnut shop.

Melinda eyed Steven, then said sardonically, "Small town."

"Small town," Steven agreed. "What do you think about Todd?"

"I don't know." She rubbed her eyes with the heels of her hands. "I just don't know. If that kid's a sample of the police they've got on it, I suppose we'll never know."

"Tommy's a nice kid," Steven said. "Hackett's a pit bull."

"I guess. What do you think about this small town? Think you'll stay in it after the divorce and everything?" Her tone was determinedly casual—the terrain had shifted between them, possibilities seemed closed before they'd been explored. A new distance had opened.

He kept his own tone as light. "Probably, off and on. I'll travel for a while with this big band, see where the music goes."

"Pretty uncertain life."

"My life seemed too certain for a long time when it never really was."

She took this in with a small nod, then asked, "Tell me one thing, honestly—did you ever sleep with Lisa?"

Steven felt like he'd been sucker-punched. "If you had doubts, why the hell have you helped me?"

"That's not an answer."

"Of course I never slept with her, or made love with her, or anything else with her. Why?"

She stared unflinchingly at him. "I knew so much about Lisa. That girl had slept with more men by eighteen than I have at forty."

Steven wondered if this was an indirect answer to his earlier question about Lisa and Gail and Jacob, but couldn't tell for sure. "I wasn't one of them," he said stiffly.

They stood in place for an awkward moment.

"Thanks for helping," he said. "I'm sorry to call you so late at night." He leaned down to kiss her, and she flinched away.

"Cut it out," she said tiredly. "Don't say you'll call me, and I won't say I'll call you. We'll just leave it."

Steven's smile felt false and dumb, as though his lips were novocained. This was his second parting in a single evening, and though he had nothing invested in this one, it didn't seem much easier. In fact, the two seemed to blend together into a single, depressing failure.

"I hope Gail didn't do anything to Lisa," she said. "For your sake."

"She didn't," Steven said. "I'm going to believe that for the time being."

"I'm sorry I called Jimmy. I'm usually not that timid."

"Why'd you call him, of all people?"

"He knows you."

"You trust me now?"

Her gaze was reserved. "I don't know. Who do you trust, Steven?"

"Myself," he said automatically, and closed his mouth.

19

The sky had lightened enough that he didn't need his headlights. Steven's stomach and mouth were sour from too little sleep, and his hands were caffeine-jittery on the wheel. Between Highway One and Lewes, he cut off onto a side road that took him in a sweeping circle to the southeast, where he met the canal and turned left toward town. A row of locust trees lined the road, and he pulled off onto the shoulder and stumbled down the bank to piss six or eight cups of doughnut shop coffee into the dark waters.

A heavy mist lay on the canal, and Steven stood for a moment and watched a great blue heron that stood on the opposite bank and watched him. After a moment of this mutual contemplation, the heron gave a croak like a cartoon pterodactyl and unfolded into clumsy flight. Still Steven stood in place, more exhausted than he remembered feeling in years. So jumbled and confusing were the events of the past twelve hours—the conversation with Jennie Moore, the audition, Gail's departure, Melinda, then Jimmy, then Tommy Langtree at the doughnut shop—that he could scarcely tell what he thought anymore.

One fact stood out like a hummock rising above the salt marsh—Lisa Wood was dead, intentionally drowned—and around this swirled the currents of conjecture and rumor and accusation and betrayal that had brought Steven down.

He turned away, struggled back up the slippery bank, and drove home. Patches leapt wildly, as though she'd feared both Steven and Gail had abandoned her, and after he got her calmed and fed, Steven turned off his telephone ringer and slept.

It was late afternoon when he woke, gray and mistily raining. His answering machine held one message, from Lester, letting him know about the next few practices and an open rehearsal to be held at the Lamplighter in a couple of weeks. Steven called Hackett.

"Mr. Blake, what can I do for you?" The detective's voice held the brusqueness Tommy Langtree had only mimicked.

"I just wanted an update," Steven said. "Am I cleared or what?"

"We're still investigating all the possibilities," Hackett replied. "Why? You planning on skipping town?"

"I want to know who you're looking at," Steven said. "Have you taken a close look at Todd Wood?"

Hackett paused. "Is this a tip, Mr. Blake?"

"I don't know any more now than I did earlier. I told you he came after me twice, though—once in the bay, and once at Lisa's car the day she was found."

"Yeah, you told me that. And I told you that we're still investigating all the possibilities. You have any new ones to give us?"

"No," Steven said. "I just want to know who killed her."

"You think I don't?" Hackett's voice was so dark with hostility that Steven was almost tempted to apologize for his call. "You find out who did it, you call me," Hackett snapped. "Otherwise, don't."

Restless with energy after this conversation, Steven tried to practice, but lacked the patience. Finally he put on a swimsuit, sweatpants, and sweatshirt, bundled Patches into the car, and headed for the state park.

Stopped at the traffic light next to the drawbridge, they were passed by Melinda, who was heading back toward Steven's house. She waved wildly, as though to flag him down, but the light changed just then and Steven pretended not to have seen her.

The entrance booth at the park was empty, and Steven swept past without slowing—on a late, gray afternoon near summer's end, the entire park would be nearly deserted. Cape Henlopen was a rough triangle of loblolly pines, sand dunes, and salt marsh, thirty-four hundred acres bounded by water on all three sides: to the east, the Atlantic; to the north, Delaware Bay; and along the inland leg, the canal. It had been an army base, built during World War II to protect the mouth of Delaware Bay, and he wended his way over the cracked, dune-swept roads, past the decaying wooden barracks and crumbling concrete bunkers and gun emplacements.

He parked his car at the small lot just beyond the Maritime Exchange tower, a squat concrete cylinder bristling with radar and radio antennae, where the ship pilots watched for tankers and containerships heading up the lanes to Wilmington and Philadelphia. His was the only car there.

He followed the path down through the dunes to the beach on the bay side, then turned right and ambled slowly up the peninsula. Here the cape became a narrow sandspit separating the bay and the Atlantic, like a bottom lip sticking up. The tide was out. Sandpipers, plovers, and terns paced and prodded the glistening sand flat, and Patches, cooped up for days now, skimmed across the flats like one more low-flying seabird.

A mile over toward Lewes, the Cape May ferry set out for the seventy-minute journey across the bay to New Jersey. Steven squinted out to the hazy horizon, where a containership toiled down the bay, outbound, and he wished he were aboard it, no matter where it headed.

This was his first trip to the beach since he'd nearly drowned a few weeks before, and that memory led him to test his ribs, clenching the muscles, then prodding with his fingertips. He found only the faintest memory of pain. More vivid were his memories of settling, drifting so easily to the bottom of the bay. He wondered about Lisa, whether her drowning had been the tempting peace he'd discovered, whether she'd even known she was drowning. Fresh water had been found in her lungs, he remembered, and bruises on her shoulders, but he didn't know whether she'd been conscious, whether she'd knowingly struggled for breath while being forcibly held down.

He walked slowly, stopping to contemplate the drying husk of a horseshoe crab, then the sandy carcass of a small shark cast aside by a fisherman, until he rounded the point to the Atlantic side. The long, broad beach stretched due south, horizontal expanse broken only by a few isolated surf fishermen. The sand was deeply rutted by their big-tired four-by-fours.

Inland, behind the protecting dunes, stretched a line of long-abandoned observation towers, perfect concrete cylinders with slit windows where observers once searched for U-boats and directed the Fort Miles batteries.

The sky was flat gray, the sea dark green shading into gray at the horizon. The scene looked more like November than the end of August, and was as melancholy as his mood. Steven stopped at the surf line, glanced left, then right. The nearest fisherman was three-fourths of a mile south. Steven stripped off his sweatshirt and pants and flung them up to dry sand, then kicked his sandals up to follow. Patches came bounding up at this, and Steven ordered her to stay; she hated the water, so there was little chance of her following him in.

Clad only in his black nylon racing suit, Steven waded into the surf. The waves were running three or four feet, and the first to splash up his legs was painful, tightening his skin into goose bumps, shriveling his scrotum, and he plunged in all at once. It felt like diving into fire. He struck out, swimming strongly straight away from the beach. His muscles stretched and complained, then heated up, loosened. Three hundred yards offshore, he stopped and rolled onto his back. The bottom sloped steeply here, and seventy or eighty feet of water now lay beneath him. He floated on its skin, staring up at the sky and feeling the black depth below and the pitifully small sac of air in his chest that kept him afloat.

He wondered if he could will himself to sink now. If he expelled every last breath of air from his lungs, would his mind let his body drift down? He tried it, felt his body settle deeper into the water until a wave washed across his face and up his nose, and he surfaced, coughing and sputtering.

He bobbed upright, treading water, and coughed and blew some more to clear his head, then once again expelled all his air, and this time dove straight down, eyes wide open, and swam as hard and fast as he could move. The water quickly chilled, and his movements slowed, until each downward stroke became a separate, struggling effort, like pulling himself down a ladder to the ocean's floor. His lungs ached. Finally he stopped, felt the currents tugging, tossing him. His chest and throat and nostrils twitched, reflexively trying to draw breath, but he held the seawater back. His vision turned red, then white with the pain and effort, and suddenly he kicked for the surface, pulled with every last fiber of muscle and will, afraid now that he'd gone too deep and held off too long. His mouth flew open and he felt the cold seawater shoving deep into his chest, then a moment later he flew through the water's surface, coughing and shouting and gulping in sweet air.

For long minutes he floated on his back once again, resting now on the ocean's breast, gathering breath and his remaining scraps of energy. His heat seeped away.

Just this side of hypothermia, he turned and began a slow crawl for shore. The current had carried him back up the point, toward the mouth of the bay, but no closer in, and it took all his weary body could muster to make it back to the beach. Finally his feet touched bottom and he waded through the surf, stumbled near shore, and crawled the last stretch through spent waves, up onto dry sand, where he collapsed onto his stomach. Though the Atlantic stayed permanently icy, the beach clung to a full summer's sun, and the stored heat fed his body.

He lay this way for long minutes, listening to the crash of the surf as the tide turned in again, feeling the vibration of the waves through the sand, the sea spray on the soles of his feet and the backs of his legs.

"Are you breathing?" someone said.

He rolled onto his back and looked up at Melinda. After a second she sat down next to him, drawing her knees up to her chest. She was barefoot, but wore long white slacks and a sweatshirt. Patches stood next to her, tongue lolling, and inspected Steven as though he were something the waves had offered up to her.

"I didn't know if you were coming back or not," Melinda said.

"I found out what I had to find out."

She nodded, not asking. "I don't swim."

Steven sat up. "What are you doing here?"

"I followed you," she said. "I was on my way to your house when I saw you driving up Pilottown Road."

"I would have called you," Steven said.

"I needed to talk to you again," she said. "After last night. I was pretty abrupt with you."

"Best thing for me," Steven said. "Sorry I woke you up."

They stared out at the ocean. It was near dusk now, and the horizon far to the east was dark. Three ships stood off the cape, lights flickering across the water, and a little to his left the lighthouse beam from the outer breakwater winked past. The breeze stirred, cold against his chest, and he drew his knees up. Patches sat next to him, leaning against his hip.

"I've got to get my clothes," he said. "Thanks for the apology."

She extended his sweatshirt and pants, folded into a neat bundle atop his sandals. "I'm not apologizing. Sometimes things happen that are so far outside what you thought was really possible that it's really tough to recalibrate yourself and know how to act."

Quickly Steven dressed, awkward as she watched. "Are you talking about me or you?"

She stood and brushed the sand from her butt. Wordlessly they trudged up the beach, back through the dunes to the parking lot. Her car waited next to his.

"I've worked out some things I think you should know about."

Tired now, Steven looked at her for a moment, then shook his head. He'd had enough. "Do me a favor," he said. "Call Hackett at the state police if you've got any ideas about any of this."

"I already have," she said. "You'd better hear it, too."

Steven unlocked his car. "Come on, then, let's get out of the wind."

Shivering now, he started the engine and turned the heat on low. The parking lot sat atop a dune, a hundred yards seaward from the pilot tower. Spread before them in a twinkling arc around Breakwater Harbor was the entire town of Lewes: closest to the park, a new development of big houses and condos where the menhaden processing plant used to be, then the ferry docks, then the town beach and its strip of low cottages, and at the far end the green and red channel lights marking Roosevelt Inlet. Nearer and to their right was the lighthouse marking the inner breakwater, and farther out and to the south stood the outer light. Both beams flicked past now, pulsing like two slow, unsynchronized metronomes. Even with the windows rolled up and the engine running, Steven could hear the mournful moan of the foghorn.

"What's the story?" he said.

"I've been thinking about all of this for days, and rereading the files on Lisa and Todd. There's a lot in there. Things I probably should have told you before."

"Like what?"

She took a deep breath. "I wasn't sure until we talked to that young Lewes policeman this morning, but I think it's Todd, too."

"Why didn't you say anything?"

"Because I didn't want to let anybody know I'd revealed those files to Hackett. What kid would ever trust me again?"

"You're sure about this?"

"He's one messed-up kid," Melinda said.

"Messed-up is one thing," Steven said. "What do you know?"

"This is all from confidential files," she said. "I shouldn't have given the information to Hackett without a court order, and I shouldn't be telling you."

"So what's prompted your change of heart?"

"I'm worried about you." Her eyes glittered earnestly in the fading light, and a new chill ran up Steven's spine.

"Why?"

"I believe Todd killed Lisa to get at Jacob. He wanted to hurt him, and figured he could do it in a couple of different ways. I think he meant to set Lisa's death up to look like Jacob had drowned her, but then you got in the middle and everyone blamed you, so he's right where he was, except his sister's dead. I think he'll probably come after you next and make it look like Jacob has done it out of revenge."

Steven gazed out across the bay for several shocked moments, recalling the day Todd had run him down so deliberately in the waters in front of them. Then he peered at Melinda. "Todd already tried for me," he said. "But this sounds a little farfetched."

"Lisa's dead," she replied. "Do you have a better explanation?"

"Jacob's the most logical choice."

Melinda shook her head. "Why would he do it? He's got nothing to gain and too much to risk."

"But why would Todd do all of this? He doesn't seem capable of it."

"Todd's a highly intelligent kid," Melinda said. "And he's been royally screwed over by his father, both figuratively and literally. I've been over his school records, his medical records, everything. I've dug into things that I'm not even supposed to see. His records show a long history of abuse—bruises, breaks, a torn rectum. It makes me sick. Did you know he was in the house the night his mother died?"

"No," Steven said slowly. He was still hung up on the litany of injuries, and, even worse, on the knowledge that Gail must have known about all of this. He didn't see how she couldn't have; though the kids had never lived with her and Jacob, they'd visited several times a year. "Why the hell hasn't anything been done?"

"Somehow Jacob has kept everything quiet. Todd woke up and got out of the house, but his mother was trapped. Todd and Lisa both believed that Jacob arranged the fire, because their mother had told him she'd discovered what Jacob had been doing to them; she'd already confronted him and was preparing to go to the police in South Carolina, where they were living. Todd thinks he was supposed to die, too. On the physical abuse, some of it got chalked up to sports injuries, and Todd claimed that he'd been persecuted here at the high school his senior year because he was new—he said a couple of boys on the football team caught him in the shower and turned the lights off and raped him. He wouldn't press charges, and his father backed him up on it so loudly the police dropped the whole thing."

All of this was so far beyond Steven's depth that he felt more lost than he had earlier, three hundred yards offshore. "What am I supposed to do with this?"

"Protect yourself," Melinda said. "Hackett knows all of it, and he's supposedly tying up the details now. In the meantime, please take care of yourself, Steven."

"I saw Todd the day they found Lisa—the kid was absolutely shocked."

"The boy lies more than he tells the truth," Melinda said gently. "He needs real psychiatric help. He needs to be hospitalized."

"Don't you have some kind of professional obligation to make sure he gets that? Now?"

"I've done what I can by telling Hackett, and I'm sure he'll act soon," Melinda said. "I don't want you disappearing in the meantime."

Again Steven tried to process Melinda's theory, but he still couldn't make it work. "I don't understand why Todd would drown his own sister to get at his father," Steven said.

"He hated her," Melinda said. "Both their files are full of that."

"But why?"

"A lot of mixed-up reasons. It looks like Jacob abused Todd sexually up until Lisa was about twelve, when he turned to her. Todd had a lot of very confused feelings about that—felt like his sister had taken his father away in some way, felt like she was offering herself to protect him, that she was able to take care of Todd in a way he'd never been able to take care of himself. Probably he felt guilty for not being able to protect Lisa from her father. And I'm sure that ultimately he felt like Jacob had come to hate him and love Lisa. The other factor, too, was Gail—despite the fact that Todd really hadn't seen that much of her, he'd developed quite an attachment to her. I think he probably hoped she'd be an ally, and when she split from Jacob, Todd was devastated. He focused a lot of his anger around that on Lisa and on you."

"So Jacob Wood has had sex with both his son and his daughter?"

"It's not about sex," Melinda said brusquely. "It's child rape, and it's about power and domination."

"If people have known enough about this to think up theories and write reports and keep files, then why the hell hasn't anything ever been done?"

"It's a crime," Melinda said. "But it can be very tough to bring charges in cases like this, especially when the children won't agree to testify, when the other parent is gone, and when the parent has the kind of position in the community that Jacob Wood has. No one wants to believe this kind of thing happens, especially in families like that one. And in this case, the family kept switching doctors. It's taken me a lot of lies and favors to get the pieces I've found—files were scattered, and a few people were suspicious, but the caseload is so heavy that nobody ever really set out to collect everything and look at it all together. There are just too many pressing cases every day to go after one where nobody's actively complaining."

"Do you think Gail knew?"

Melinda was silent for a long moment, then said, "I don't know. The kids never lived with her."

Steven watched as two ferries crossed paths about a mile out on the bay; by the time the inbound boat docked and began to discharge its load, he knew what he had to do next.

"I need to talk to Jacob."

"No," Melinda said immediately. "You're smarter than that, Steven."

"You know it's the only thing to be done."

"No," she repeated. "You won't accomplish anything but getting in the way of the police."

"Then what do we do?" Steven said. "Tell me. I'll do it if it'll work."

"We wait for the police to clear it up."

"You've talked to Hackett. Do they have a scrap of physical evidence that ties Todd in?"

"Not that I know of, but how would I?"

"That's because there isn't any," Steven said. "First they tried to nail me—now it's going to be the kid. You know as well as I do that if Jacob Wood could do what you've told me about to his kids, then he could do anything. And for whatever unknown reason, the police seem to be absolutely unwilling to go after him."

"Possibly," she said. "That's for Hackett to figure out, though, Steven. I think you're letting your feelings about Jacob and Gail get into this."

"Of course I am," Steven said. "But that doesn't mean I'm not right. You want to come with me? Bear witness?"

Melinda met his gaze for a moment, eyes reflecting the flicker of the lighthouse beams, warning, warning. Then she shook her head. "This was a mistake. I should've just left this with the police, and the hell with warning you. All you're going to do is get yourself into deeper trouble, you idiot."

"I don't think that's possible at this point," Steven said.

"Please go home. You're smarter than this, Steven."

"No, I'm finally smart enough to take care of myself," he said. "If you're not going to come with me, go to Hackett now, tell him where I'm headed, and tell him to come if he wants to pick up the pieces."

"Fine." She opened the door and stepped out, then slammed the door hard. She circled around to Steven's side, and he lowered his window. "Don't do this," she said.

Steven smiled, glad she couldn't see the coldness in his eyes. "Don't worry," he said. "I just need to make something happen."

20

Redlined in third gear, the Jeep's engine screamed like a powerboat running ahead of a storm. Steven wove from lane to lane, coursing the crowded highway like a video game, beating red lights, tucking into gaps in the traffic that he usually wouldn't dare.

He was drained from his bout with the sea, too exhausted to restrain himself—the tumult of past weeks had all come into focus in the rage he felt for Jacob Wood now. Dried salt itched on his skin, the sand in his clothes seemed to rasp every pore raw, and he ran on straight, high-octane adrenaline.

Melinda's suspicions had convinced him more of Jacob's guilt than Todd's. A father capable of such betrayal could do any evil. And whatever Melinda's fears, Steven had no intention of being the next to drown.

In the months after Gail had first pursued him, Steven had driven many times past the house she shared with Jacob, trying in every way imaginable to gain some insight into who she really was and where she was coming from. Now he drove from memory directly to Wood's white, twenty-room colonial near Silver Lake. A twelve-foot arborvitae hedge, precisely barbered, shielded the house from the street. Steven coasted to the curb. Without a moment to reconsider what he was about to do or to try to plan what he'd say, before he could give himself the slightest excuse to turn around and drive home, he leapt from his car.

He paused inside the narrow gap in the hedge. From every window spilled golden swaths of light, washing out into the tall loblollies, the pin oaks, and the sweet gums, across the broad-leaved magnolias and shining hollies and feathery yews.

A weather front was sweeping through, clearing away the overcast and leaving only tatters of high, ragged clouds that whipped across the moon. The night air had a chill edge to it, as if it bore the first, much too early, hints of autumn.

Within the house Steven could see no motion, and this calm smugness, this placid, undisturbed, wealthy mask of solidity and untouchable position only stirred new anger.

The doorbell sounded a single, faint chime deep within the house. Steven heard nothing more—no approaching footsteps, no movement at all, until the heavy door swung in and Jacob Wood faced him. Dressed in khakis and a light pink oxford-cloth shirt, Wood still looked tired and hollow-eyed, but composed. It took a moment for recognition to light his eyes; when it did, he smiled coldly. "Come to gloat, Steven? I already know she's gone, I'm afraid. Neither of us has won, have we?"

He stepped back and swung the door closed without waiting for an answer. Steven leapt before he thought, catching the last few inches of opening, and shoved his way inside.

Jacob backed up five or six feet and stopped, wary and poised. Steven's breath came fast, his pulse drummed a good one-fifty beat in his ears, and his hands shook with anger. He shoved them into his pockets.

"We need to talk," he said.

"You're the last person I'm interested in talking to," Wood said.

"You're about to become very interested in me," Steven said. "I've figured out what happened to Lisa, Jacob."

The look Jacob cast on him was scornful and disbelieving. "What the hell are you talking about?"

From a room to their immediate left, a television set blasted a football game. Steven glanced quickly in, saw the room was empty.

"Let's go in there." He motioned with his head. "I need some facts from you."

Wood shrugged, then turned and preceded Steven in. The room was precisely what Steven would have expected Jacob Wood to present as a library—brass-tooled fireplace flanked by two green leather-upholstered wing chairs, an antique globe on a stand in one corner, floor-to-ceiling-shelved ranks of books obviously selected more for the color of their bindings than their content. To the right of the doorway was an antique walnut desk nearly as broad as Steven's Jeep; its gleaming top was clean of all but a telephone, one green-shaded lamp, and a pristine blotter.

The one jarring note in the room was a wide-screen color television that took up an entire corner next to the fireplace. A camera zoomed in close on the play, and the screen was a frenzy of orange and white uniforms on one side, blue and white on the other; the volume was quite high, and Steven, adrenaline pumping, fought back the impulse to hurl anything—his shoe, a book, himself—through the four-foot TV in order both to silence the noise and to shatter the order of the room.

As though reading Steven's thoughts, Wood picked up a remote and killed the picture. "What do you want?"

Revenge, Steven thought, plain and simple, for all that had been done by this man to him, to Gail, to Lisa and Todd. "I want to tell you about a theory a friend of mine has," he said. "I don't think I believe it, but I want to try it out on you."

"What friend?" Wood said impatiently.

"Not important. My friend has an idea that it's not you or me who did this. My friend thinks it's pretty likely that your boy Todd's responsible."

"Ridiculous," Wood snapped.

"That's what I said. My friend has this crazy idea that Todd's getting even with you for all the years you abused him. And for the fact that you killed his mother."

"His mother died in an accidental fire, and the boy's never been abused one minute in his life," Wood said. "Why the hell would he kill his own sister to get at me?"

"To make you suffer. And he hated her, anyway."

"This is that goddamned school psychologist making this up, isn't it?" Wood said. "That woman's paid to believe any lie those kids manufacture."

"There's truth to most of it," Steven said. "Medical records for both kids that point to abuse. I don't know how you managed to get away with it for so long, Jacob, but it's caught up with you now."

"This is ludicrous." Wood glared at him for a moment. "You've got about ten seconds to turn around and get out of my house before I call the police."

"My friend has this idea that you're in danger, too," Steven said. "She thinks Todd will go for the direct approach next. I wish I could believe that, because I'd surely stand back and let him have at you. But I think it's Todd who's next. Or maybe you've got me in mind?"

"Theories are easy to come up with," Wood said. "You want to hear my favorite? You took advantage of problems Gail and I were having, and caught her in a vulnerable stage. Then when she came to her senses and started coming back to me, you blamed me rather than yourself, so you went after my daughter as some warped way of getting back at me. When you got caught, you got rid of her. And now that Gail has left you for good, I suppose you think you're here to get rid of me."

"But you don't really believe that," Steven said. "Or you wouldn't have been standing here talking to me all this time."

Wood laughed shortly. His eyes burned into Steven. "You're right, Mr. Blake. Regardless of what you believe, I had nothing to do with Lisa drowning. Nor did you. Trust me when I say I know who did, and that he will be taken care of."

Steven shook his head. "No, I've figured that part out, too—I'm willing to bet that you've got an expensive private hospital lined up for Todd, where they'll store him away for a year or two, after which you'll quietly relocate him somewhere far away."

Wood's laugh rang sharp and bitter. "Todd? Come on, Mr. Blake—do you really think you were the only teacher at the high school who screwed around with Lisa?"

Steven hesitated, remembering he'd asked Lisa almost the same question the day she'd visited his house with the plans. Jacob's suggestion was unexpected, but not unbelievable. "Who was it?"

"He's the one who set this whole thing in motion," Wood said. "I'd guess he saw what was happening to you and decided to protect himself. Now get the hell out of here."

"You don't understand, Jacob—I know what you've pulled on your kids, I know what you've been up to in Lewes. Do you think Gail kept all your secrets? You know how sharp she is—you figure out what she knows."

Wood was unshaken. He took a step toward his desk. "Do I really need to call the police?"

"Go ahead," Steven said. "I'd like us to have a discussion with them together."

"So you can make more wild accusations about me and my children? I'll have your ass in court so fast you won't know what hit you, Blake."

"Good thinking, Dad. Let's see what the court says when I talk to them." Todd's voice, young and hard from the open doorway, startled them both. Wood paled visibly, and Steven's gaze snapped right, to where Todd stood in a gray baseball uniform. He held a glove and a black cap in one hand and an aluminum baseball bat in the other.

"What the hell are you doing in that getup?" Jacob said. "I thought the season was over."

"Play-offs," Todd replied automatically. "What happens if the one kid you've got left finally tells the truth about you?"

"Calm down," Wood said sharply, "and get the hell out of here. Mr. Blake and I are having a private discussion. I'll deal with you later."

Gambling that Todd had heard only the last of Jacob's words, Steven said quickly, "Your father was just telling me it's pretty likely that you were the one who drowned Lisa."

The effect was more than Steven had expected, as Todd strode into the room, face flushed, eyes glued on Jacob. "You're not going to do this," he said thickly. "You're not going to twist things around again and blame me just to save your own ass. Mom's gone and Lisa's gone, but I'm not going."

Jacob lifted his right hand, palm out, as though ordering a dog to stay. "Todd, calm down," he commanded. "Nobody's trying to blame you for anything."

Todd stopped, but Jacob continued backing away, edging around the corner of his desk.

"Dad, get away from that fucking alarm," Todd said, and he half raised the baseball bat.

Jacob froze. "Todd," he said quietly. "Take it easy. There's no problem here. I'd just been telling Blake that you *weren't* responsible for anything, and he's trying to set you against me."

"Shut up," Todd screamed. "It's not Blake's fault, either. It's you and the way you treat everybody like a goddamned piece of meat. You always think you can screw everybody and then throw them away when they get in your way."

Steven cleared his throat. He stood six or eight feet from the boy's left shoulder. "Todd, let the police take care of this," he said. "Nobody really believes you did anything."

"Shut up," Todd said without looking at Steven. His voice seemed calmer. "This is between my father and me."

"What are you going to do?" Jacob said, contempt clear in his voice. "Stand here and shout at me all night?"

"No," Todd said flatly. "I'm going to mess you up, Dad."

Jacob Wood's gaze was locked on his son, and for the first time, Steven saw the faintest glimmer of doubt in the man's eyes.

"Todd," Jacob said, slowly and carefully, "we both know it wasn't you and it wasn't me, don't we? We know who it was. Think! Remember?"

"Stop it," Todd screamed.

Wood glanced at Steven, a hint of panic in his expression, and in that instant Steven probably could have stepped forward and tried to stop Todd's swing. But he waited, and the bat rose, then slashed out in a gleaming flash of aluminum, one blow left, one blow right. Wood raised his arms to protect himself, but the sound of metal against flesh and bone was as distinct and sickening as the sound of clenched hands trying to pound a heartbeat back into a waterlogged, lifeless rib cage. Wood crumpled without a groan. Todd stood over him, bat poised for another blow.

Now Steven stepped quickly forward, reaching for the bat. "Don't do it," he said. "Let the police have him."

Todd spun around. The bat rose and shone in the air, hesitated. His eyes were wild. "Leave me alone," he said. "I didn't do it."

"I know," Steven said. "I know you didn't." He pointed down at Jacob. "Let's call an ambulance, now, before your troubles get worse."

Steven waited another long, breathless moment, until Todd's eyes cleared and he slowly lowered the bat and looked in horror at his father, then back at Steven.

"He deserved it," he said, but his tone was tentative, even beseeching. "He deserved it, Mr. Blake."

"Yes," Steven said. "He deserved it, Todd."

21

Over the next several days, the case occupied the front pages of both local newspapers and the Wilmington paper. From all accounts, Hackett took Todd's attack on his father as the last piece of the puzzle, and though the boy had not yet been charged with his sister's murder, arrest seemed imminent. Jacob Wood remained unconscious, but was expected to live.

Despite Todd's two attacks on him, Steven still thought the boy innocent. His anguish had been real the day Lisa's body was found.

His calls to Hackett went unanswered, and Steven was both bemused and irritated by the speed with which he'd moved from being the subject of endless inspection and suspicion to being as invisible as a homeless man on the Rehoboth boardwalk on the Fourth of July.

Melinda and Jimmy Van Dusen each left multiple messages, but Steven needed solitude to work out what had happened with Gail. The harder he worked, the more he found himself wishing that if a victim had been necessary in all this, that if someone had to be sacrificed to bring Jacob Wood down, it had been Gail rather than Lisa. He could almost have mourned her then, or at least moved cleanly on.

Instead he woke and slept with the image of Gail prospering on in Philadelphia, building a new life. None of the newspaper stories mentioned her name, as if she'd played no role, or possibly never even existed outside Steven's nightmares.

Two statements lived with Steven, though he'd taken both as weak attempts at self-justification when he'd heard them: Jacob's reference to Lisa and another teacher, and Gail's parting claim that her last time with Jacob had been her final favor to Steven. The two claims were connected, like snatches of a melody heard at a distance without the intervening phrases, but he still couldn't fill in the missing notes.

A week after Todd's attack on his father, Jacob Wood regained consciousness. Though his jaw was wired together and he was unable to speak, his doctors suspected a considerable impairment of his mental faculties and probably a loss of memory.

The idea that truth could die with Jacob Wood's missing memory tipped Steven over the edge of hesitation. Knowing the telephone would never be enough, he made the three-hour drive to enemy territory—Gail's family home in Bryn Mawr—unannounced, on a weeknight. He knew she'd either be camped out there short-term while she lined up her own living space, or that someone there could be convinced to direct him to her.

The house was a formidable stone mansion set a hundred yards behind an iron fence. The driveway gates were open, but Steven parked on the street to avoid giving Gail warning of his approach. He followed the matched row of boxwoods up to the front door.

Gail's mother answered the door, a tall, bony, fish-lipped woman who merely looked Steven up and down disapprovingly, then said, "Wait here."

With the quiet, solid whisper of money, the door closed in Steven's face. It would be locked if he tried it. He waited. Sharp pains of anger and humiliation lanced his stomach, and he breathed deeply to calm himself.

Gail opened the door, and he could see by her face that she was still trying to decide how to play this. She stood in the doorway, poised to retreat should his hostility prove dangerous.

"Steven," she said cautiously. "What are you doing here?"

For a moment he simply looked at her, dark-haired and chiseled, tanned and moneyed—he looked for whatever had once drawn him to her, and saw nothing. He wanted to turn away and go back where he belonged, but held on for the answers. "I don't know," he said. "You heard about your . . ." He hesitated, ready with a hundred different names for Jacob, then decided there was little percentage in setting Gail off if he truly wanted information from her, and he continued, "About Jacob?"

She nodded.

"I notice you haven't rushed down to his bedside."

"I told you that was through."

"I must have forgotten your truthful habits. Sorry."

She said flatly, "Did you have a reason for coming here, Steven?"

Matching her deadpan tone, he said, "I want to know what happened to Lisa."

"It seems to me the police have that figured out."

"You don't really believe Todd did it."

"I play no part in this whole thing," Gail said. "And I *will* keep it that way, Steven."

He looked at the hard determination of her face, and believed her.

"Will you give me a couple of answers?"

"Depends."

"When you left Lewes, you claimed Jacob Wood was your last favor to me. What did that mean?"

She studied him. "I wondered why you didn't push me on that."

"I'm pushing."

"Why should I tell you anything now, Steven?"

He looked around, at the solid stone house with its gleaming windows and manicured shrubs, and couldn't think of a single reason that might move her.

"I don't know," he said. "Leave me something, Gail."

"Why? You'll just assume I'm trying to make myself look better than I really am."

"No. You're no better than I think you are."

This provoked an ironic half-smile. "So you'll hate me outright no matter what I do?"

Steven shrugged. This was going nowhere, and he was almost ready to give up and head back to Lewes. "Sure. For a while, at least."

Gail seemed to make a decision, and she stepped forward onto the porch, and pulled the house door closed behind her so no one could hear them.

"Don't repeat this to anyone, because I'll deny it, and I covered my tracks so well you don't have a chance of proving it. I got into the network of holding companies Jacob was using to buy up all the properties on Pilottown Road, and screwed up all the deeds and surveys so badly it'll take a team of lawyers ten years to straighten them out. And they're going to run afoul of coastal zoning when they do, even if Jacob's ever capable of doing anything again. From what I hear, he'll be lucky to feed himself again."

He was almost there, had almost made the connection he'd been trying to avoid for days. "And do you know anything about any other teachers who might have been involved with Lisa?"

"Not for certain. But I know what you're asking."

"How?"

"Who else lived on Pilottown Road, Steven, and sold his property unexpectedly?"

"But he sold to an Italian family from South Philadelphia . . ."

Gail waited for him to make the connection, then, voice thick with the exaggerated patience he hated so much, filled in, "The holding company rents it to them, Steven."

"Jimmy?" he said. "You're sure about this?"

She nodded. "Think about it. You'll fill in the pieces."

He stood on the front step, saddened and suddenly very wearied by this confirmation of his suspicions. "I'm afraid I already have."

Gail stepped back into the house, and turned off the interior hall light; standing on the lit porch, he could hardly see her.

"Steven," she said, "don't come here again."

"Wait," he said. "Tell me, you knew about Jacob and Lisa, didn't you? It was why you left him."

"Yes," she admitted.

"Then why'd you go back? How could you? Why didn't you tell someone about all of it?"

She seemed about to withdraw completely into the house, then stopped. Her voice was bitter. "Who could I tell without dragging myself down, too, Steven, or risking Jacob taking it out even more on me? I thought the kids were almost grown and they'd get away from him and go on with their lives. But after Jacob's first wife died and those kids ended up at his house, I had to try to make him change."

Steven stared at her for a moment, reluctant to believe she still couldn't see her own culpability, that she could somehow have twisted Lisa's plight around into a means for justifying her own obsession with Jacob. "How exactly did you try, Gail?"

"I did," she said again, but the strained undertone in her voice told him she really hadn't convinced herself of this. Not yet, at least.

Knowing the satisfaction was small but all he was likely to get with her, he said, "You'll never outlive this, you know. And even if you think you have, I'll always know."

The door swung quietly shut; its glossy black surface was almost perfect enough to reflect his face. He'd probably never see her again, he knew, and he felt as unexpectedly spent as a breaking wave, as empty as the falling finish of a flawed solo.

He walked quietly down the driveway, the moonlight fragmenting down through the trees to light his way. Back at his car, he pulled his tenor case from the back and assembled his horn by the light of a streetlamp, like a hit man assembling a high-powered rifle. Then he walked half up the drive, set his feet wide apart, and blew at the front of the stone house; he flowed from one fragment of song to another as erratically as Lisa had on his Steinway, and he could hear his waves of notes splashing up against the walls and windows, frothing over the slate roof, as he tried to wash her away.

22

"Are we ready?" Marian, seated at the piano, gazed regally up at the band; they were crammed onto the Lamplighter's tiny stage, and her expression dared any one of them to cough, speak, or rattle his charts in a flurry of lost pages. Steven, sitting in the front row, fluttered his tenor keys. His fingers felt as though they were wrapped in splints: stiff and hopelessly unmusical.

"Play the song," Lester rumbled from his station back by the drummer, and he counted the beat down.

"Night Train" had been a slow freight the last time Steven made practice, but tonight it was a flash streamliner smoking an all-night run from Chicago to New Orleans. The track lay smooth, the firebox was red hot, and the band was pulling out of the station without him. The lift Steven had felt outside Gail's house had proved short-lived; battered by the betrayals and losses of the last month, borne down by his suspicion of Jimmy's role in Lisa's drowning, he'd done little but sleep for the past week.

For the first time he could remember, the music seemed as silly and meaningless as a soap jingle or a sitcom theme song. It was at total cross-purposes to the busyness of his mind, a distraction from all he had to think about and accomplish this evening. A hundred and fifty friends and relatives of the band jammed the Lamplighter, more than Steven had ever imagined in this smoky room, and by midway through "Night Train" the dance floor was packed.

He played mechanically from memory, without even glancing at the chart, and he felt like a pretender. All his notes were right, his timing was exactly on, but any one of his students could have played just as capably. Lisa could have played far better.

Between a gap in the dancers he spotted Jimmy, Sharon, and Melinda at a table near the center rear of the room, all three of them watching him, Jimmy grinning as though he had a right to enjoy himself. Steven closed his eyes and hoped yet again that Gail's intimations had been one last dig directed at him, her attempt to sabotage any friendships she thought Steven had. But he knew it wasn't, that she'd given him at least one bit of truth.

He was sick of them all, saddened and disgusted by the tawdry self-interest that governed the human race, himself too much included. He heard the voice of his own sax amongst the reedy chant of the section; he was slightly sharp, and his tenor grated thin on his ear. It sounded, he realized, almost self-pitying, and he adjusted his mouthpiece on the cork as he played until the horn came into tune.

Harder to adjust his mind, but he forced himself to imagine Lisa, the true victim, the point where all the greed and lust and betrayal and panic had intersected. He envisioned her as he'd seen her at his house, drawn immediately to his piano, three-quarter profile bent over the keyboard, rhapsody of escape fleeting across her face as she'd played whatever wisps of melody floated down through her hands, and he wondered what voice she might have grown into given the chance.

On the band rolled, through "Ko-Ko," "C-Jam Blues," "Cotton Tail," "Perdido," each song a new leg between stations, the group loose and sloppy and eager. Steven drifted into the music, felt it lifting him gently, and he imagined that Lisa was there listening, that this was the eulogy he hadn't been able to give her earlier; and then he imagined that she was in the band, playing, that her sound was a part of the music that now existed in the room as a presence of its own, a combination more than the notes of the individual players and the concentration of the listeners, a thing more real than the cloud of cigarette smoke that dimmed the lights.

Steven listened more intently than ever to all those voices weaving around him, and he looked out at the faces around the room, and he realized they were all spellbound by a rare, precious harmony. And because it was necessary to find some proof of value in the human spirit, because it was essential to demonstrate to himself that many voices could really, voluntarily become one, he pushed them all out of mind—Gail, Jacob, Jimmy, even Lisa—and threw himself into the music and blew his sax as sweet and hard as he'd ever played.

He felt himself playing above himself, beyond the zone of infallible performance he'd hit at the audition—then he'd been blowing strictly to prove skill, to secure his place, to vanquish. That ego was irrelevant to this real harmony, this raising up of common voice, this testament to the sweet, elegant songs that Duke Ellington himself had raised despite depravity and discord, despite the heritage of racism, despite oppression and Depression and a world crumbling into war.

They played and played as though breath and lip and hand were tireless, on beyond the first-set list without a break, Marian swaying on her piano bench, eyes closed, barely pausing between tunes as if they all had every note of every chart committed to memory, on through the entire second-set list, as though this music were the only spark of fire in a dark world and only their absolute, unbreaking concentration and submission and celebration could keep it lit. By the time Marian let her hands fall to her lap and bowed her head, they might have been playing two hours or half a lifetime. The room was dead silent as the last of that presence, that unity of spirit, hovered over it, then slowly faded like a dream interrupted an instant before its meaning became clear.

Steven bowed his own head and sat for an instant, tenor in his lap, hands limp, mind empty and quiet. In raising his voice with those others, he'd worked his way back to the real reason he'd become a musician, back before all the demands of pride and career were layered on top. And he'd touched something deep inside himself—a tension had been released, and tears rose to his eyes. From the audience rose a tentative patter of applause, as though they were all afraid to dispel the last notes that hung in their minds; then the sound rose, and Steven heard the musicians around him shifting music, speaking softly to one another, setting their instruments down.

He set the tenor in its stage stand, swapped compliments with the players on either side, then stood and stretched. Both hands in the small of his back, he rolled his head back and cracked the bones in his neck, easing the tension where the neck strap cut.

"You sounded great, Steven."

He looked down from the stage. A hundred miles away, Melinda smiled up.

"Thanks," he said. "They still here?"

"They've already bought you a drink. You want to explain this to me?"

"When I'm sure, you won't need me to. Just watch Jimmy."

He crossed the dance floor a couple of reluctant steps behind her, his euphoria already fading. They were still three tables away when Jimmy, already a couple of drinks down and as raucous as one of the kids he coached, yelled, "All right, Steven! Outfuckingstanding."

Steven sat at the one empty space, directly across the table from Jimmy, where a double Scotch on the rocks awaited him. "Thanks for coming." He stared at Jimmy for a moment, remembering all the times Van Dusen had encouraged him to give in to Lisa's accusations and Thompson's pressure and leave town, and how he'd thought at the time that Jimmy had nothing but Steven's interests in mind.

"Where the hell have you been?" Jimmy said. "We've been calling you every day."

"I've had a lot to sort out." Steven took a healthy belt of Scotch to calm the tremor in his voice.

Sharon leaned across the table to be heard. "The only way we knew about tonight was Melinda, you big jerk." Her face was flushed, and she took another sip from a tall mixed drink. It didn't look to be her first, either.

"The band is phenomenal." Melinda's voice was so artificially bright that Jimmy's gaze snagged momentarily on her, and when he shifted back to Steven, there was a new wariness in his eyes. He wasn't as drunk as he'd been acting.

Steven shrugged. "We've all played these songs for years."

That killed conversation for a long minute, and Steven looked back up at the stage, and wished he'd been able to keep on playing for the rest of night without a break. He turned back to Jimmy, who met his eyes for a long, uncomfortable moment, and Steven tried to detect fear or guilt or shame, anything that might finally confirm his suspicions. He still didn't want it to be Jimmy, though, and all he could see was the coach's usual mask of self-satisfied good cheer. He didn't trust his instincts enough to confront him head-on, so he took a deep breath and said, "I drove up to Philadelphia to see Gail last week."

Jimmy was suddenly alert; Steven was aware of both women watching him, but he concentrated only on Van Dusen, who said, "You feeling extra masochistic, or did you go up there to blow her away?"

"We had some final business to settle," Steven said. "I had some questions for her about this whole business with Jacob and Lisa."

"I'm sure she was tickled to see you." Jimmy laughed roughly at his own humor, then took a gulp of beer, looking quickly over his glass at Sharon, then Melinda, then back at Steven.

"Actually she had some pretty fascinating answers," Steven replied. "She doesn't think Jacob *or* Todd drowned Lisa."

"Of course she's going to cover for Jacob," Jimmy said. "Is she still accusing you?"

"No, she thinks it was someone else entirely."

"Come on," Van Dusen said, "Jacob Wood is guilty, and I hope they hang that son of a bitch."

"The police haven't even sorted it out yet," Steven said.

"They will. Wood got away with some awful shit for too many years, but he won't skate on this one. And the cops can take their time building their case, because he's sure not going anywhere, is he?"

Jimmy laughed so harshly that Steven felt his own heart go cold at the sudden memory of Todd's aluminum bat flashing down, the sickening, dull ping as it struck bone, and the shame of his own frozen, half-intentional hesitation. "They don't know for sure it was him. Todd's in pretty tough shape, and might have done anything. Or maybe Gail's right, and it was somebody that none of us have even thought of."

Van Dusen shook his head, and said stubbornly, "Jacob Wood is slime. I don't know why you're so goddamned intent on defending him."

"I'm not." Jacob had spoken with such cold assurance when he told Steven he knew who'd drowned Lisa, and that the person would be punished for it, but Jacob wasn't in any shape to follow through on that promise. Steven wondered whether Jacob had set anything in motion to fulfill his plans for Jimmy, but decided it didn't matter. He said, "Whoever really drowned Lisa *will* pay for it, Jimmy, whether it was Jacob or somebody else."

Van Dusen returned his stare for a moment, then broke away, and Steven knew he had him. "You know," Steven said, "now that I'm past the first shock, I'm actually almost grateful to Gail. A lot of men our age go through all kinds of upheaval to change their lives—just up and buy a new boat or a sports car or a new house for no apparent reason. Or they'll do what I was accused of doing, and screw around with teenagers. Now I can skip all that stuff, right, Jimmy?"

"Not all of us have to go through it," Jimmy said. He was curt now.

"Seems like some of us do."

"Are you telling us you really did screw around with that girl, Steven?" His voice and face had hardened, and he leaned back in his chair and stared at Steven as though challenging him to push on.

"I wasn't talking about myself," Steven said. "I guess I've always been real curious what made you sell your place in Lewes so suddenly, Jimmy."

Sharon looked sharply at Steven, then laid a hand on her husband's forearm before he could reply. "Calm down, Van Dusen. You're being an asshole." She turned back to Steven, and in that brief second, he saw that she knew, and that Jimmy didn't know yet that she'd figured it out. Steven's one lingering reservation had been around the damage he was going to do to Sharon and the kids, but that evaporated now. Jimmy had done the damage himself. Sharon's gaze seemed to plead with him for a moment, then skidded away when she saw it was no use.

"Melinda called us three times to come here tonight," she said. "What's going on with you guys, anyway? Are you an item or what?"

Jimmy laughed explosively, seeming to draw in half the room's air in his relief. "Sharon," he said, "shut the hell up. Talk about *me* being an asshole."

Steven glanced at Melinda—her expression was pinched and pale, her eyes scared. Clearly she'd followed Steven's thoughts, and had reached the same conclusions, and now couldn't tear her gaze from Jimmy. She wasn't going to answer Sharon, so he said, "Melinda and I are just good friends."

Sharon giggled, out of nerves and tipsiness, and pushed on with her clumsy change of subject. "At least you're better friends now than that night when Prince Valiant here had to go rushing out so late to save her from you."

"For Christ's sake," Jimmy said, "when the hell will you learn not to drink, Sharon?"

Steven glanced from Jimmy to his wife and back, wondering whether this routine had been rehearsed as they'd probably rehearsed their fight the day he met Melinda at their house. "I really wondered why you stopped in that night," he said to Jimmy. "Just want to check my rabies tag, or were you curious about what I'd found out?"

"I told Melinda on the phone you were the safest guy I knew," Jimmy said. "Come on, don't make a big deal out of this, buddy. You can't blame her for getting scared."

"I don't," Steven said. "But I'm not the one she should be scared of, am I?"

"Who do you think she should be afraid of?" Van Dusen said.

"I wish I knew for sure," Steven said, though as he looked at Jimmy he did know, without doubt now. The only question was how he followed through on the knowledge. Behind him he heard with some relief one of the trumpet players softly tuning to Marian's piano, then one of the alto saxes joining in. "I hate to cut this short," he said, "but it's time to go back to work."

Immediately Jimmy said, "Glad to see you again." His tone thoroughly contradicted him. "Don't be such a goddamned recluse, okay?"

"Sure." Steven stood, glanced at Melinda. "See you around."

To Sharon, he said a curt good night. He turned then to Jimmy, and caught a glint of quickly masked speculation, and he saw the calculations of panic working in Jimmy's face.

He leaned down so only Jimmy could hear him clearly. "You see why I haven't talked to anybody in a while?" he said. "I'm still pretty worked up about Lisa, and I hope the bastard that drowned that girl has the sense to turn himself in before somebody else does it. Or decides to come after him."

Jimmy didn't blink. "What makes you think it was a man?" he said. "Maybe Gail did it."

"She didn't."

"They'll have their case against Wood tied up real soon," Jimmy said. "Once they've sorted out all the wild theories people are coming up with."

Steven didn't know whether he'd expected Van Dusen to crumble and confess when confronted, or attack in return, but he knew he hadn't expected this imperviousness. He felt his own anger rising, but fought it back under control, forced himself to smile and shrug and spread his hands and say in a completely new and transparently light voice, "Hey, I've just been by myself too much. Too much time to brood since Gail left."

Van Dusen's expression was wary. "Well, it's your own fault for sitting around the goddamned house by yourself."

"I guess," Steven said. Most of the band had collected on the stage again, and the room was quieting. "Listen, give me a call," he said. "I need somebody to talk all this shit over with."

"Sure," Jimmy said, falsely hearty again. "Why don't we go fishing? We've been talking about it all summer."

"Yeah, great," Steven said, "maybe next weekend." He had no intention of getting onto a boat with Jimmy Van Dusen at this point, but he could use the time to figure out his next step and to let Jimmy stew. "Come on over and get me, and we can run out Roosevelt from my place."

"I'll check the tides and call you," Jimmy said.

With that Steven returned to the stage. He was spent, and so was the rest of the band after the peak of the previous set. They floundered through, hitting all the notes as mechanically as a gang of wind-up monkeys beating on metal drums.

Once again the planet had shifted beneath him, and he'd fallen through a surface that just a month before had seemed perfectly stable. He realized that he'd spent most of his life as a hopeless innocent, a fool who saw only his own good nature and goodwill reflected in all those around him. His trust and naïveté had been a frail vessel bearing him up above an ocean of sharks, a place ruled by the brutal indifference of sheer self-interest, where accusations could be manufactured at a whim and believed without proof or witness other than a boy led by his hormones and a girl whose jealousy tinged her vision. It was a world where a wife became a knife to the heart. Betrayal circled. There was no solid ground.

23

Steven stood at the very top row of the still-paintless bleachers, leaning back against the pipe railing. It was a hot Saturday afternoon in mid-September, and the second game of the season was tied six-all at halftime. The stands were half full, and though he'd been cleared of all charges, the taint of accusation remained—no one sat within a twenty-foot radius of him. He felt radioactive, or contagious, but he also thought it likely that these students and parents realized how he felt about all of them at the moment. He'd like to imagine that some felt shame at the speed with which they'd turned on him a month ago, but at heart he recognized the folly of that illusion.

From the end zone, the DeVries High Marching Band strutted up the field, knees pumping, ranks a little ragged, blasting an arrangement of Paul Simon's "Graceland" that Steven had never given them. Three days before Labor Day, the school had hired a young woman two years out of the West Chester State music program to fill Steven's job, and she was clearly out to mark the band with her own style.

He wished her nothing but luck, though he'd never met her and probably wouldn't try to. The last month was a wall between himself and all that had come before, and it was difficult to imagine himself married to Gail, teaching these kids. Though he could recall in perfect detail the days and weeks of that life, they were like a story he'd read, and were certainly the memories of a man more innocent than he could ever imagine himself being again.

One rank of five forgot the drill and turned squarely into another, and Steven smiled. A month ago that move would have knotted his stomach in embarrassment for the kids.

His smile faded as Melinda Samuels trudged up the bleachers toward him. She wore sunglasses that seemed to cover half her face.

She stood next to him and watched the end of the routine until the band straggled off through the opposite end zone to feeble applause. "Kind of sloppy," she said.

"They'll get it," Steven said. "It's pretty astonishing they came up with a new routine so fast."

"I've been wondering how you were."

Steven shrugged. "I've been busy."

"You decided not to take your job back."

"I waited until Thompson had to ask me," he said curtly.

"You don't give any quarter, do you?"

"Sorry." Steven relented just a little. "I just don't feel very sociable these days."

She nodded, then asked with forced casualness, "You're not really going fishing with Jimmy today, are you?"

"Yeah," Steven said. "Why?"

"Because he called me last night and invited me to go, too."

Steven looked directly at her for the first time, feeling the raw rush of fear and adrenaline in his stomach. "Why *did* you call him that night? You two have something going?"

"No. I panicked after you called." Her regret and embarrassment were so clear and immediate that any last, lingering doubts Steven had held about her and Van Dusen faded.

"What did you tell him then?"

"That you'd found out something about who drowned Lisa."

"Ah," Steven said sadly. As he'd suspected, Jimmy had been worried for his own hide, not Melinda's, and he'd come to find out whether Steven had discovered him yet.

"Do you still think Jacob didn't do it?"

"I know he didn't," Steven said.

"You know he claims not to remember anything at all, don't you? Maybe he did it," she said.

"What do you think? You saw how Jimmy acted at the Lamplighter last week."

She shook her head. "Why would Jimmy have done something like this? I've known him for years."

"Then you know how much he loved that house in Lewes, and how suddenly he sold it. I've given this a lot of thought," Steven said. "I think Jimmy screwed around with Lisa and got caught by her father. I'm sure Jacob had already cooked up that scheme to get to me because of Gail, so he took the chance to blackmail Jimmy into selling off the house, and that played right into his plans. But when Jimmy saw what was happening to me at the school and heard that Lisa was trying to help me get out of it, he panicked; he was afraid Lisa was going to name him, and he was going to lose his family and his job and everything else after he'd already given up his house."

"I don't want to believe this," she said, but her face said she already did.

"You knew about Jimmy and Lisa, didn't you?"

She shook her head quickly. "Suspected it, but didn't have anything to prove it. Lisa never told me the teacher's name."

"You'd better believe it all," he said. "Don't get on that boat."

Face pale, she nodded. A wave of applause rose around them as the teams returned for the second half, but neither of them turned to watch the field fill.

"You'd never make it to my dock," Steven said. "Either that, or both of us would go out with him and not come back."

She took off her sunglasses then, and peered intently at him. Two vertical furrows creased her brow. "If you really think Jimmy's guilty, tell the police."

"I already talked to Hackett," Steven said. "He's not paying much attention because he thinks he's got Wood nailed."

"I'll talk to him," she said. "He'll believe it if you and I both do."

"Didn't you already go to him a while back with a pretty thorough case against Todd?"

Melinda thought for a minute. "If you think Gail knows something about all this, why don't you tell Hackett to talk to her?"

"From what I've told you, would you trust Gail to tell the truth to anyone if it involved any risk to her?"

"So what are you going to do, Steven? If Jimmy really did it, there's nothing you can do but convince the police."

"I want to look him in the face when I tell him what I know, and I want to *know* that he's guilty. Do you understand that?"

She shook her head. "I think it's pretty stupid for you to confront somebody that crazy and desperate."

"What else can I do?"

"You can at least have some help." Her face was grim. "Last time I let you go charging off, Todd Wood caved his father's head in, and could have done yours. I'll be at your house by three-thirty."

Steven started to say no, but stopped. He could use a witness, and probably some kind of backup. "Talk to Hackett first. Maybe he'll save us the trouble."

HE RESTED IN a wicker peacock chair on his front porch, straining to pick out the pitch of Van Dusen's boat motor from all the other traffic tooling up and down the canal. He'd finally trimmed the hydrangeas so he could see out over them, and the porch seemed unnaturally bright.

Melinda pulled up in front of the house in her Honda, and he waved her to park it in back, where Jimmy wouldn't spot it. In a minute she joined him, and sat in the matching chair to his left.

Steven waited.

"Hackett's looking into it," she said. "He didn't seem very interested, though."

Steven nodded, unsurprised. "Where is he?"

She shrugged. "Not coming. He said we should just stay away from Jimmy if we really think he did something."

"Too late," Steven said as he watched Van Dusen's Grady-White slip into view. Van Dusen eased the big sportfisher gently up to Steven's dock as if he had all the time and none of the worries of the world.

Steven took a deep breath, and picked up the new plastic rod case that lay at his feet. His mouth was dry, and his lips stuck to his teeth as he tried to plaster on a grin.

"Steven," Melinda said, "what are you going to do? You're not going out with him?"

"I'm not setting foot on that boat," he said. "The best help you can give me is to watch from here, and call Hackett if it looks like I need it. Jimmy's not going to say anything if you're there watching."

By the time he crossed Pilottown Road, Van Dusen had already cut his engine and stood on the dock, making his lines fast.

"Yo," Steven called out. "Let me give you a hand."

Van Dusen turned, and glanced around behind Steven, making sure he was alone; Steven hoped the cropped hydrangeas hid Melinda well enough. "Ready to catch some fish, then?" Jimmy's voice was tight and high with nerves.

"Ready to catch something." Steven raised the rod case.

"New rod?" Van Dusen said. "Let me see it."

This was the question Steven had wanted, and he knelt on the dock. Van Dusen squatted opposite him.

The rod case was a plastic tube about five inches in diameter and four feet long, with a handle at the middle, designed for transporting disassembled surf and deep-sea rods. At either end was a plastic cap that fit over the tube and was held in place by a hinge and a buckled strap. Steven fumbled a moment with one of these straps, then pulled the cap free. Watching Van Dusen's face carefully, he tipped the case up and spilled out another tube—this one a cardboard mailer, mustard-colored, with stainless steel end caps.

Van Dusen's blink rate shot up, and his gaze flickered between Steven's face and the cardboard shipping tube. "What's that?"

"A set of plans, Jimmy. Ever seen these?" Steven kept his voice low and reasonable, playing out his bluff. It had taken him three days of searching local stationery shops before he'd found a tube identical to the one Lisa had left him, and it held nothing now but blank rolled sheets from a flip chart.

Jimmy shook his head. "What plans are those?"

"I think you've seen them," Steven said. "You seem nervous."

"Let me see." Jimmy held out his hand.

"You've already seen them," Steven repeated. "They cover most of Pilottown Road, remember?"

"The ones you talked about," Jimmy said. "The ones Lisa brought you."

Steven waited, neither confirming nor denying.

"How'd you get those back?" Van Dusen said. "I thought they'd been stolen."

"Why would you think that?" Steven said. "I never told you that."

Recognizing his mistake, Van Dusen shook his head, then quickly stood. Steven stood to face him, the shipping tube clutched as tightly as a baseball bat in both hands. "Did you take the other set of these from my house, Jimmy?"

"Come on," Van Dusen said. "Why the hell would I steal anything from you?"

"You know Jacob's been cooperating with the cops."

"How much can he cooperate? His jaw's wired shut, he's got both arms in casts, and his memory's shot."

"Memory doesn't let you go that easily, Jimmy, especially about something like this."

Van Dusen shrugged, and looked nervously back at his boat. "Look, you want to go fishing, or did you just want me to come over here so you could insult me? I understand you're pretty bent out of shape by all this, but this is the second time you've come on like I've done something wrong. I've been the best friend you've had through all of this shit."

"I know you want me to think that," Steven said. "But Jacob's doing a hell of a lot of nodding, and Todd's filling in some pieces. What we've worked out is that before he started on me, he worked on you. Only you really slept with the girl, and you were a pretty easy mark to blackmail."

This was all bluff; Hackett wouldn't let Steven near Jacob, but Jimmy wouldn't know that.

"Why the hell would Jacob ever admit to a crime nobody's ever accused him of?" Van Dusen said. "He never blackmailed me."

"He's pretty worried about being convicted of crimes he never committed," Steven said. "Like drowning his own daughter."

Van Dusen stood transfixed, seeming to waver, and Steven said quietly, "I'm sure Hackett will help you out if you go in on your own."

"Bullshit. I saw how much that asshole helped you."

"Come on, Jimmy." Steven unveiled his last bluff. "Gail tracked the sale of your house back to Wood. I've got copies of everything."

Steven traced Van Dusen's thoughts by the workings of his face: bluster slowly fading as his cheeks turned pale, then fear filling his eyes, a quick glance toward his boat that gave away his first impulse to flee, and, finally, his head bowing slightly and shoulders slumping in the first hints of despair and resignation. It was like watching him die, and at the last instant, Steven was seized with the urge to clap his hand over Jimmy's mouth, to shout him back into silence before he could condemn himself.

"I didn't plan to drown her," Jimmy said dully, and it was done. Steven said nothing, and Jimmy went on, "I saw her out on Rehoboth Bay that day, though, and knew she was screwing up Jacob's plan to get you out of here, giving you the plans and all. She was going to blow the whole thing open." He halted, and looked beseechingly at Steven. "You understand? I would have moved out to that fucking ranch house for nothing! Once things came out I would have been in the same kind of shit *you* were when they thought you'd screwed around with her. I would've lost my job, Sharon would have taken the kids, I would've gone to jail . . ." He shook his head.

"So you saw Lisa out windsurfing and you stopped and got her to come aboard your boat?"

"Yeah. I told her I was helping you, and we loaded her board in so I could bring her to meet you."

Steven closed his eyes, not wanting to watch the next of Van Dusen's memories cross his face. "How'd you do it?"

"In my big cooler," Van Dusen said. "I'd been out fishing, and it was full of melted ice."

Steven opened his eyes again to fend off the vision these words conjured. "Then what?"

"Then I went out again and came in after dark and dropped her in the bay."

Steven imagined Jimmy cruising aimlessly offshore, killing time until dark, Lisa's cold body tucked below, and although he could picture the scene, he couldn't conceive what could have been going through Jimmy's mind, either then or since. "Why didn't you just dump her out at sea?"

Van Dusen shrugged. "I wanted it to look like an accident—just get her out of the way. If she'd disappeared completely, they would have looked harder at everything."

"But they found fresh water in her lungs, and then you decided to set me up for it by dumping her sailboard in my garage."

Van Dusen looked away uneasily and shrugged. "Jacob would have done something else to you, anyway. How'd you get rid of it?"

"Shut up," Steven said.

"My whole life was going to turn to shit."

"It did that the minute you slept with that little girl," Steven snapped. "You should have saved everyone a lot of grief right then and jumped off your boat about twenty miles offshore. What was she when you started with her, fifteen, sixteen?"

"Spare me the self-righteous bullshit," Van Dusen said. "You know the way she was always hanging out—the girl would practically come right into the locker room after her brother and his friends. What do you want me to do?"

"I don't want anything," Steven said. "You deal with it now."

"The cops have got Jacob and Todd for this—they're not going to arrest me." Jimmy's voice held a last, desperate note of defiance. "Come on, I panicked, I fucked up. But you know as well as I do that Jacob was the main cause of it all, and he deserves everything he gets. Hell, you're even to blame for coming between Gail and Jacob and getting him started. Let them have Jacob for it and I'll do whatever the hell you tell me to. You want me to quit teaching? Leave Sharon? Shit, I'll give away everything I own."

Quietly Steven said, "Jimmy, let's go call the police."

Van Dusen's eyes closed, and he swayed enough that Steven half expected him to collapse. Steven turned back toward his house, finished with this business. Let Hackett sort it out.

"Please, Steven, give me a break."

Jimmy stood near the end of Steven's dock, shoulders sloping, head bowed, big hands curled unnaturally on his thighs. Steven stalked toward him, gut twisting, and he stopped a bare eighteen inches from Van Dusen. This was the ultimate betrayal—he'd told Jimmy about Lisa trying to help him, confided in the guy, trusted him. He hated Van Dusen enough to kill him, he realized, and this discovery about himself scared him more than anything.

He said into Van Dusen's face, "What kind of break do you want? You want to be able to just walk away from this, Jimmy?"

Van Dusen wouldn't meet his eyes. "What good's it going to do to ruin Sharon's life now, too? What about my kids?"

"*I'm* not ruining their lives, Jimmy. They'll cope."

"With me in jail for the next twenty years? How?"

"People do."

Van Dusen seemed to have come back to life—his face was flushed, his whole body quivering with tension, and he seemed ready either to charge Steven or to bolt. Steven half wished Van Dusen would attack him so he could find release in fighting back.

Instead, Jimmy looked around at the dock, back at his boat, out at the canal. "I'm not going to do it," he said. He backed away from

Steven, then crossed the dock in two long steps and began to descend the dock ladder.

"It's not going to do you any good to run away," Steven said, but he didn't move.

Van Dusen stopped halfway down the ladder, head just above the level of the dock. "I know." He seemed to search for words, then shrugged. "I never meant to do all this. You were right when you said I should have jumped off my boat a long time ago."

"Jimmy, come on," Steven said. He glanced back over at his house, waved to signal Melinda to call Hackett.

Van Dusen was watching him, calm again. "I'm going to have an accident. At least they'll get the insurance."

"Come on, Jimmy, get back up on the dock," Steven said impatiently. "You're not about to sacrifice yourself for Sharon or anybody else."

"This is what you're doing to me, anyway—at least witness this, okay? So Sharon doesn't have any trouble?"

Van Dusen's head dropped from sight as he continued down the ladder. Steven walked across the dock, still not entirely convinced this was anything more than histrionics. Jimmy was waist deep, and as Steven watched, he released from the ladder and plunged backward into the water. For a few seconds he floated on his back, watching Steven; then he began a thrashing backstroke away from the dock and his boat, so clumsy in the water that Steven realized he'd never seen him swim in all their time together.

Jimmy stopped in the middle of the canal, thirty feet away, bobbing like a sea lion, then noisily emptied his lungs and dove.

Steven remained quite calm as he scanned the water's surface, still not believing Jimmy would drown himself, but quite prepared to watch him do so. He waited for some sign of Van Dusen. The currents could be strong here, and it was difficult to know just how far he'd traveled.

Finally Jimmy struggled to the water's surface, just a few yards from where he'd first gone down; Steven glanced back to his house again, and Melinda stepped out onto the front steps and waved and nodded.

Now Van Dusen swam clumsily back toward his boat, making little headway against the current. The canal was ten or twelve feet deep at this point, its banks steep and slickly muddy, and Steven knew there was no way Van Dusen was coming out unaided. He watched, remembering Lisa as he'd seen her at his house, bent over his piano keyboard, then Lisa again as she'd been stretched lifeless on the deck of that boat in Rehoboth Bay.

"Steven, help me," Van Dusen called. "Get me out of here."

Still Steven watched as Jimmy's head slipped again beneath the surface and he came up spouting, coughing, and choking. Steven pictured Lisa's terror when she realized Van Dusen had betrayed her. Jimmy called out again, weakly, then disappeared once more.

As much as Steven steeled himself, as much as he hated Jimmy, he finally couldn't stand by and watch the man drown, and this was nearly his undoing. He slipped off his shoes and dove from his dock in a long, flat arc. Swiftly and cleanly he swam toward the spot where Jimmy last went down, then past it. He dove beneath the surface, eyes open, but the water was too murky for him to see much. He groped around, surfaced for breath, and spotted Van Dusen sputtering ten feet away. He swam to him, grabbed Jimmy's shirt, and just at that moment Van Dusen smiled at him.

"I knew you'd come in," he said, and like a steel spring his arms locked Steven in.

Steven struggled. They drifted slowly down through the murk. Tons of water pressed them down, ready to fill Steven's mouth, his head, his lungs, ready to suck the heat from him the second he gave in. With a surge born of fear, he pushed desperately against Van Dusen's arms, but couldn't budge them.

All time slowed. Steven's chest strained to draw in air, even water, but he forced himself to wait, each second an hour, each pounding heartbeat one more cry for breath. Desperately he hoped that Jimmy found some scrap of survival instinct that would lead him upward, or that his own summer of swimming and years as a woodwind player would grant him some extra measure of breath. Survival lay in his ability to control his body, to outlast Jimmy's breath, to outwait his pulse.

His own red heartbeat pounded in his vision, and he wished he could at least see Jimmy's face so he could gauge his determination. They were settling, tugged along by the rush of the incoming tide through the narrow canal, and Steven recalled the first time he'd lain underwater so passively, after Todd Wood hit him and he rested, dazed and giving himself to the current, and the calmly blinding understanding he'd reached then: *Drowning is not struggle, but surrender; body's heat ebbs, and death's grip warms.*

He pushed against Jimmy's grip once more, felt the slightest give, and struggled harder. Suddenly he was free, and felt Van Dusen's hands make the weakest fluttering moves, as though Jimmy would make some final effort to save himself. Before thought could stop action, Steven circled one arm around Jimmy's chest and kicked for the surface. He felt Jimmy choking with spasms of indrawn water, shaking free of his grip, and suddenly he was gone.

Steven swam for the surface, climbing as swiftly as his own bubbles, until he rose for the third time that summer. He gasped his lungs full again, the air as sweet as the first breath he'd ever drawn.

Blood sang in his ears, the cross-rhythms of pulse and ragged breath shook his body, and Steven scanned the water around him, willing Jimmy to surface, but already knowing that he wouldn't be found until he fetched up against someone's dock or mooring chain, or snagged on one of the bridges farther down the canal. Given time, current, and accident enough, he could even travel all the way down the canal to Rehoboth Bay, down to where he'd left Lisa, but somehow Steven couldn't find any idea of justice in this.

Melinda shouted at him from the dock, and Steven waved to let her know he was all right, then floated on his back and began a slow, even backstroke up the canal. As he swam, he stared up into the blue September sky, and pictured himself from outside himself, balanced between these two layers—air above, water beneath, gravity hugging him back to the center, and only the music of his own breath keeping him afloat. Life was a tenuous, unpredictable song, sustained not by a good ear or perfect pitch or a matchless set of pipes, but by the simple grace of luck and the need to hear what came next.